Four Crows

~

Dream Maker

Book One

Andrea Peters

Many of life's circumstances are created by three basic choices: the disciplines you choose to keep, the people you choose to be with; and, the laws you choose to obey.

Charles Millhuff

Chapter 1

Day Ten.

2005. Peace Arch Memorial park. Blaine, Washington.
USA – Canada border.

"Do you see them?"

"What? Those four over there?"

"Yeah."

"And?"

"And what?" He walked through the grass ignoring his friend.

"They look terrible," his friend said.

"So what? They all look strange. I mean, look at their eyes and their noses—the way they walk. And what's with the clothing, anyway? It's winter, for God's sake." He stopped to pick up something off the grass.

"Well, I say we go over and see if they have anything we want." His friend took two steps and then hopped up on a short cement post where he adroitly balanced himself.

"Go ahead. No one is stopping you." He walked off to his friend's left in the opposite direction.

"Fine," he said. "Hey Gracie, you want to come?" He looked over to the female standing off to his left. She was using a stick to torment a beetle that was stuck at the base of a tree.

"Where?" she asked.

"Over there. Check out those four people. There's something different about them," he said.

"Sure, why not." She dropped the stick, walked over to him, and they proceeded toward the four people that were sitting on the bench.

The grass had been warmed by the sunlight and it tickled their toes as they got closer.

"I don't think that's a very good idea." They both stopped and looked over at their other friend. She had been methodically dismantling a small bush. A pile of leaves had gathered at her feet.

"You're too cautious Kimmy. Live a little. Come on," he said, as he yanked his head in he direction they were going.

Four Crows

Kimmy hopped over behind them.

"OK. You go first." The three of them headed west to the edge of the park where the bench and the four strangers were.

The sun cast a long shadow in front of them and Gracie dashed out and pirouetted in front of the group.

"Look! Lawn art!" She struck a ridiculous pose that her shadow only exacerbated.

"God, Gracie, you're so...left headed," Kimmy said.

"Left head, right in the mind," Gracie replied.

"Uhhh. Did we forget something? Oh! Shoot. They're getting up!" The male replied.

"Want to follow them?" Gracie said.

"And do what, mug them?" Kimmy asked. "Let's just go back and do something else."

"Yea. I doubt they have any food anyway," the male said.

Gracie stopped to pick up something on the ground.

"The ..m...alwa..mmm..ys..erms," Gracie said.

"Gracie, we can't understand a word you've said."

"I said..." Gracie stopped and looked at both of them with her brilliant ebony eyes and shiny black beak.

"... There are always worms."

Chapter 2

Several weeks prior.

"How much?" Mr. Pandit asked.

"Twenty million," Mr. Baldwin spoke into the Satellite phone without hesitation, "and that is a deal."

"It's larceny is what it is. For that kind of money I could hire a professional crew and permanently solve the problem," Mr. Pandit replied.

"Yes, you could. But why use a sledgehammer when all you need is a velvet glove? You came to me for my subtlety. If you want something else I suggest we stop wasting both of our time. I'll wait for your call." Mr. Baldwin hit the end button and put the handset down on his side table while he stared out over the rippling blue water, his feet slightly buried in the warm talcum sand.

The phone rang a minute later and Mr. Baldwin smiled, then took a sip of guava juice before reaching for it.

"I have a proposal," Mr. Pandit sounded reticent, but Mr. Baldwin could picture his darkly tanned face seething with resentment.

"I'm listening," Mr. Baldwin said.

"I'll give you ten percent of the deal, IF you succeed. That will be worth much more than twenty million if we go public."

"And what are your expectations?" Mr. Baldwin asked, as he reached for his hat. The sun had just peeked out from behind a large cloud and it made him squint.

"Just stop him. I need twelve months, then I don't care," Mr. Pandit said. "Actually, I do have one request. Use Americans. I think it will maximize the effect."

Mr. Baldwin pondered the offer for a moment as a young couple walked by, oblivious to the world. Yes, typical Americans, he thought.

"Fine," he finally said.

"We have an agreement then?" Mr. Pandit asked.

"I want two million up front to handle expenses. You can deduct it from the back end," Mr. Baldwin added with a smile. He could almost hear Mr. Pandit's aggravation, and he loved it.

"Done. That's it. I'll have it delivered as usual. I assume you will be using four people?" Mr. Pandit asked.

"Don't I always?" Mr. Baldwin replied and hung up the phone again. He stood up from the lounge chair and walked back into his house where he paused at a large black cage.

"Hello my pretties, and how are you this bright and beautiful morning?" he said, as he passed by running his fingers along the fine steel bars. The creatures stared at him silently.

"I think, soon, you shall all have names. Fate will make sure of it." Mr. Baldwin walked past the large enclosure toward his office where he logged onto the Internet and deliberately wrote then submitted, advertisements in four North American newspapers. He assigned the billing information to The DreamMaker and notified them that they would be receiving payment by mail.

When he finished placing the ads he walked over to the large teak bookshelf that sat opposite his desk and pulled out his favorite book. His custom printed copy had gold gilded pages and the front cover was embossed with four crows dancing around a circle. Mr. Baldwin ran his fingers lightly over the birds, tracing the ridges of the embossing, then put it back on the shelf and left the room.

It was a good afternoon for a swim.

:

Ralph read the announcement in the Memphis Sunday paper with great interest.

Dream Maker

Interviews for a new TV reality show are taking place at the Memphis Cook Convention Center Monday morning at 9:00 a.m. The show's directors are looking for people that are willing to go on an unknown adventure for one week. In exchange, the winners will have their dreams fulfilled.

Ralph tore out the ad, folded it, and put it in his pocket.

"Ralph, can I have the Real Estate ads when you're done?" Melanie, his wife, asked from the kitchen.

"Sure, honey." Ralph sorted through the paper and set aside the section. He didn't bother looking through it.

"Hi, Dad! Want to play some basketball?" His youngest son Devin walked in, already covered in sweat. He was ten and didn't look like either of his parents. He was carrying his well-worn basketball.

Ralph looked up at his son as he walked over. He tried to hide the newspaper section before his son could see it.

"Cool! Are we going to buy a house? And then I can have a dog?" Devin dropped the ball, which rolled off and hit a lamp, making it sway.

Ralph opened his mouth to reply and was interrupted.

"A dog!" Somehow Jerry, his youngest son, appeared out of nowhere and jumped up and grabbed his father around the neck.

"Jerry! Come on…" Ralph extracted his eight-year-old son's arms from their grasp and looked at his earnest face.

"I want a golden retriever!" Jerry said.

A loud scream pierced the air and all three of them plugged their ears as Lynn arrived. She was seven and was barely dressed in anything.

"A dog?!" she asked breathlessly. Her bare feet churned on the carpet like she had to use the bathroom.

Ralph sat there and looked at his three children. Their trust and belief in him melted his heart.

"Soon, children. Very soon." Ralph kissed Lynn on the cheek and patted Jerry and Devin on the head as he got up and went to the kitchen. He could hear the children chanting 'Dog', 'Dog' as they headed out the door to play.

Ralph sat down at the kitchen table, the real estate section in his hand. His bare feet stuck to the linoleum floor as he watched his wife put a casserole in the oven.

She turned around with the oven mitt still on her left hand.

"What are you looking at?" She smiled and took off the mitt.

"You," he asked.

"Is something wrong?" she asked, as she contorted to look at her back.

"No. Everything's fine. You're perfect," he said.

Melanie walked over and sat on her husband's lap and put her arms around his neck. She could still smell the fresh cut grass from that morning.

"What were the children so excited about?" she asked.

"Oh, the usual," he said, and smiled. He turned his face up toward her and she kissed him, and got up on her feet.

"Dinner in thirty minutes," she said, and rushed out of the room as the dryer bell sounded.

Ralph got up and looked out the kitchen window. The children were playing 'Dog'. Lynn had on a pretend leash and her two brothers where walking her around the yard as she crawled over the lawn. He could see cut grass gathering on her torn shorts.

:

The next morning Ralph went to in work early at 6:00 a.m. He grabbed his green produce apron from the locker, hanging it over his neck as he checked himself in the mirror. His mustache was a little disheveled, and he smoothed it out by licking two fingers and patting it down before he adjusted the Assistant Manager badge. After he was satisfied, he then took his cart, filled it with vegetables, and headed onto the floor. He needed to get the produce displayed early.

Dave, the produce manager, arrived promptly at eight and found Ralph in the stock room.

"What's up, Ralph?" he asked.

"Oh? You mean the stocking?" Ralph asked. "I really need a few hours off today, Dave. I was hoping to get my morning work done early. It's something personal that I really need to take care of." Ralph looked down at the floor.

"Sure. I don't see why not. Can you come back later and do a restock?" Dave asked.

Ralph looked up at him and smiled.

"Yes! Absolutely," Ralph said. Dave left him alone and Ralph added a few more yellow onions to his cart and wheeled back out to the floor.

:

At eight thirty he clocked out and walked to the parking lot. His 1986 Ford Taurus had a large dent on the driver's door from a shopping cart accident some years ago. He opened the door, put down a paper towel over Lynn's sticky mishap from the last weekend, and sat down.

He arrived at the Cook Center a few minutes to nine, parked the car, and pulled out the ad as he walked around to the West entrance where he found a line.

He showed the paper to the last person in line, a middle aged woman carrying a cat.

"Excuse me. Are you waiting for this?" he asked.

She peered over her bifocal glasses that were attached to her neck by small black ropes.

"Yes." The woman turned her back toward him and he assumed his place.

Just after 11:00 a.m. a wiry man with dungarees and a baseball cap invited him into a room. There was a long folding table with three chairs on the far side and one on his side.

"Sit there," the wiry man said. "They'll be back from lunch in a few minutes.

Ralph took a seat in the plastic chair and looked around the room. It was bare, except for a few posters of concerts and beer advertisements. On the table in front of him there were three yellow legal sized pads with scribbling on them. It looked like a list of names and contact information. On the side of each name there was a number from one to ten. Ralph heard some noise behind him and turned around. There were sounds coming from outside the metal double doors. It sounded like someone was upset, probably from waiting too long in line. He saw a water fountain and got up to take a drink. When he turned back around, two people were seated at the table and were looking at him. He jumped, and grabbed his chest.

"Sorry, Mr... Mr. Gabriel?" A thirty something Caucasian woman, with black hair and a nose ring, looked down at her pad, then back at him.

"Please have a seat." She pointed to his chair, and he walked over and sat down, his legs together.

"What is your dream, Mr. Gabriel?" Her partner, a man about fifty with gray hair and a two piece business suit, spoke to him.

11

Ralph put his hands on the table and took a big breath. Neither of the interviewers smiled.

"I want a house," Ralph looked up at them to see disappointment, anger, anything, but their eyes revealed nothing.

"A house is expensive, Mr. Gabriel. What are you willing to do for it?" The woman spoke.

Ralph thought about the question for a moment.

"Anything," Ralph said, then paused, "within reason, of course."

The comment brought a smile to the man, and he said: "Of course, within reason. Tell me, Mr. Gabriel. Why do you want a house?"

Ralph had anticipated the question.

"Because my wife and three children deserve one. We live in a modular home in a park, and my two boys and daughter share a room. We want a place to call our own."

Ralph looked at the man again and saw a hint of something.

"Besides. They really want a dog and our landlord won't allow it," he added.

"What do you do for work, Mr. Gabriel?" the man asked.

"I'm an assistant produce manager at a local grocery. It pays just fine to put food on the table but there is no way we can afford a home."

"And does your wife work?" The man put down his pad and Ralph looked at it. He didn't see any number written beside his name.

"Uhh... no. I don't want her to. She is happy as a mother, and is very good at it." Ralph's eyes softened when he spoke about Melanie.

"Besides, if she worked, who would care for the children?" Ralph said.

"Do you have any allergies or medical problems?" the woman asked.

"I'm allergic to cats, if that counts... oh, and mold, I guess. No medical problems."

"How old are you?"

"Twenty-eight"

"Do you speak any other languages, Mr. Gabriel? Even a little?"

"No."

"Where have you traveled outside of the United States?"

"I've never left the East Coast," Ralph said.

"Do you have other family, Mr. Gabriel: father, mother, brothers and sisters?" the woman asked.

"My mother is here in Memphis but my Father is dead, and my only brother is god knows where," Ralph said. He hadn't thought of Tony in a long time.

The man got up, and offered his hand.

"Thank you for coming, Mr. Gabriel. We will let you know if you are a candidate for our program within the month."

Ralph grabbed his hand and was taken aback at the man's firm grip.

"Uhhh… can you tell me if a house is a possibility?" Ralph asked.

"Certainly. The program is called Dream Maker. What is more American than a home?" the man said.

Ralph headed out the door, and could hear the man and woman talking behind him. He desperately wanted to know what they had ranked him.

Chapter 3

Sarah had just finished her 10:00 a.m. psych class and took a break in the school courtyard. Someone had left the Toronto Star newspaper, and she flipped through the pages while sipping on her bottle of water.

"Hey Sarah! How's it going?" Sarah looked up at her friend.

"Hi Brenda. Fine. I can't believe the year is almost over," Sarah said.

"Year? Not just the year, the whole shebang! We graduate next month! I can't believe I'll have to find a job…" Brenda's voice drifted off as she sat down.

"Yeah, unless I can find a way to pay the tuition for Law school," Sarah said.

"Aren't you sick of school? Why not take some time off? Maybe it'll help you loosen up a bit. When was the last time you had a date, anyway?" Brenda asked.

Sarah smiled and grabbed her arm.

"Brenda, sister, not every woman lives for a man. I plan on keeping my goals clearly in mind, and men only mess that up," Sarah said.

"Whatever, Sarah. I plan on having everything… maybe I'll win the lottery this week: twenty-one million!" Brenda flung her head back and extended her arms skyward.

"Waste of a good Loony, Brenda. I have no time for those kinds of fantasies. What I is need a lot of money for tuition, and I don't have enough to even buy a car," Sarah said.

"How about dreams, Sarah? You know those things you have as a kid. 'I want to go to Paris, speak to a monk in Tibet, climb mount Everest, sing on Broadway?'"

"I have goals. No time for dreams – they're too hard to control," Sarah said. It wasn't quite true, but it was all she would admit to.

Brenda ignored her. She had turned the newspaper toward her and was flipping pages. She stopped at one and picked up the sheet.

"Here's your answer, and it sounds like an adventure." Brenda handed her the page.

Dream Maker

Looking for a few University students. Interviews for a new TV reality show are taking place at the Crowne Plaza, Toronto Centre, Wednesday morning at 9:00 a.m. The show's directors are looking for people that are willing to go on an unknown adventure for one week. In exchange, the winners will have their dreams fulfilled. US citizens preferred.

Sarah looked up at Brenda. "No way. Why would they want me?" she asked.

"Beside the fact that you're stupid and have a boring personality, I have no idea!" Brenda said. "Come on girl. You're beautiful, young and smart. Of course they would want you."

Sarah looked at her with disapproval.

"Yeah, Yeah, I know: Judge me for my brains and accomplishments not my looks. Whatever. What have you got to lose?" Brenda ripped out the ad and handed it to her.

"Got to go meet up with Sam. I'm skipping the rest of the day. Ta ta!" Brenda got up and left Sarah alone. She read the ad again and put it on the bench. A gust of wind picked it up and carried it off across the forum.

Wednesday at 9:00 a.m... Why not?

:

Crowne Plaza was full of businessmen and women milling around. The buffet breakfast was on its last legs, and Sarah watched the wait staff as they removed the empty dishes. She was almost tempted to have something to eat, but it was already past nine and she could hear her mother's voice ringing in her head about the ill affects of buffet food.

The reader board said that the meeting room was on the second floor. Sarah took the stairs and walked up the carpet with her hand gliding along the wood banister. At the top, she paused to look around and saw a line of people extending from the far room. Sarah joined the line. Several people carried the ad with them and there was much discussion about what it was all about.

Every interviewee that went in never came out. Sarah figured they must be exiting through another door and it made her wonder why.

At a little past noon, Sarah was starving and about to give up. No one had been taken into the room in over half an hour. The couple in front of her yelled something at the closed doors and then walked off – right before the door opened and a young blonde woman dressed in a pair of jeans and shirt came out.

"Name?" she asked.

"Sarah Connell."

"Age?"

"21"

"Occupation?"

"Student."

"Address and contact information?"

Sarah gave it to her.

"OK, come with me." The girl opened the door and allowed Sarah to pass. It was a large room with only a single table located in the far corner. There were three seats at the table facing her but only two people, a woman about thirty with a nose ring, and a fifty-ish man with gray hair.

Sarah looked at both of them, and they held her gaze until she looked away. She was self-conscious as she walked beside the girl, but pretended not to be.

The woman spoke first.

"Sit down, please."

Sarah sat in the wood chair facing the man and woman. The assistant handed her the paper with Sarah's information on it. Sarah looked at the woman and wondered if it really hurt to have your nose pierced.

"What is your dream, Ms. Connell?" the woman asked.

"I want to be an attorney. I've just finished my BA and would like to continue in Law, but I don't have the money...oh... and I need a car," Sarah said.

"What about your parents?" the woman asked.

"They have helped as much as they can, but I need to do this on my own. Besides I *want* to do it on my own."

"Then why are you here?" the woman asked.

"Because, in a way, I'd be earning it. From the ad I don't figure this is a gift."

"No. Quite." The man spoke up and smiled at her.

"What are you willing to give up for your dream?" the man asked.

"My goal? You mean like eat live termites, or jump in a vat of pig intestines? I'm not interested in that." Sarah spoke directly to the man.

"Hmmm. So what kind of things would you expect to do for this money?" the man asked.

"Well, the ad said an adventure. So, if I could use my physical or mental skills and accomplish the goal, I think I would be well suited. Once I put my mind to something, I do it."

"Are you involved with anyone?" the woman asked.

"You mean romantically?" Sarah asked. The woman nodded.

"No. No one."

"Why not?" the woman asked.

Sarah hesitated and thought about the question.

"Too messy," she finally said.

The woman and man looked at each other.

"Do you speak any other languages?" the woman asked.

"A little French," Sarah replied

"Have you traveled?"

"North America and once into Mexico, but that's all," Sarah said.

"Allergies? Medical problems?"

"None that I'm aware of."

"Citizenship?"

"US. From Buffalo."

"What is your weakest attribute?" the man asked. Sarah was surprised by the question.

"Weakest... I suppose I'm not great at math." Sarah tried to avoid the question.

"Let me re-phrase. If you are good at achieving goals, what are you bad at?"

Sarah struggled with the answer. She mentally pushed aside all the things she thought were too self-condemning, then answered.

"I suppose I'm a bit of a perfectionist, and that drives some of my friends crazy."

The man stopped and made a note on his pad, then looked up at her.

"Ms. Connelly. We will let you know this month if you meet our requirements. Thank you for coming in."

Sarah remained sitting.

"Umm. Can I ask what kind of show this is? I mean, will I get more information if you select me?"

"The program is simple. If you are selected you will be required to meet a test. As you said – complete a goal. If you do, you will obtain your dream. If not, you will still have had an adventure."

"What about television and book rights?" Sarah asked.

The man smiled.

"They're all ours. Thank you for coming, Ms. Connelly."

The assistant reappeared beside her and escorted her to the side exit. Sarah could hear the man and woman talking as she left.

Chapter 4

Kristen took a step back from her easel and looked at the abstract painting. Her smock was covered in bright red and blue paint, with smudges of various other pastels. The canvas looked very similar. She rinsed her brush in the acetone and set it on the shelf. Sting was playing in the background and she started singing along with *Sacred Love.*

She smiled as she removed her smock and lay it over the chair beside her workstation. A book, *Power vs. Force: The Hidden Determinants of Human Behavior,* was open on the stool beside her, the pages splattered irreverently with splotches of red. Kristen took a paper towel and tried to wipe them away, but only succeeded in making them run. They looked like miniature comets shooting across the page. She put the napkin in the book to mark the page and moved over to the kitchen table where she took a gulp from a lukewarm cup of coffee. She immediately pulled it away and frowned, then walked over to the sink and poured it out, but some of it splattered onto the floor.

Beethoven, her cat, came over and tried it, but gave up after the first drop. Kristen bent over to wipe up the rest. Beethoven's food and milk dish sat on top of yesterday's newspaper, that Kristen had failed to read – again, and she pulled it over to sop off the remaining spots of coffee. She stood back up and pressed the newspaper onto the liquid with her tennis shoe.

"There, Beethoven, it's all cleaned up," she said, as she looked at her calico and petted the cat's chin with the top of her shoe.

"Go do something useful, like catch a mouse or take a nap... have a great dream...whatever," Kristen said, starting to turn and walk away, but the word 'dream' triggered something in her peripheral vision. She glanced back to the open page of the newspaper, which lay on the floor, and saw the ad.

:

Dream Maker

She bent over and read it.

> *Interviews for a new TV reality show are taking place at the Thunderbird Inn, Portland , Friday morning at 9:00 a.m.. The show's directors are looking for people that are willing to go on an unknown adventure for one week. In exchange, the winners will have their dreams fulfilled.*

A loud knock disturbed her and Kristen walked over to the front door.

"Kristen? You in there?" It was Andrew. He was yelling through her loft entrance.

"One second, Andrew." Kristen stopped to look at the mirror. She was a mess, and there was little she could do in that short of time. She managed to tie her brown hair back into a ponytail with a rubber band on the way to the door.

Andrew stood there in a black turtleneck, black pants and shoes. His leather coat was wrapped over his arm.

"Hello, beautiful," he said, and bent over to peck her cheek.

"Hello, Andrew." She blushed a little and closed the door behind him. He looked around at the loft. It always looked the same: disorganized.

"What are you doing in town?" she asked.

"Business. I have a deal going down in a month or so. Just sorting out some details. Are you busy?" he asked. He was always polite.

"No. I just took a break to grab a bite to eat. Want something?" She walked over to the refrigerator and opened the door. He came up behind her pulled the ponytail aside and kissed her on the nape. If he could have seen her from the front he would have watched her eyes close as soon as she felt his breath on her neck.

"Want to have some fun?" he asked. Kristen spun around and looked at him. He had a wicked smile on his tanned face.

"What?!" She gazed up at him and gave him a look of disapproval, but didn't move.

"This." He pulled a newspaper ad.

"That's strange. I just read that." She pointed to the floor behind him and he turned to look at it. "It's under Beethoven's food."

"Ah. Kismet!" he asked, and turned back toward her.

"You said you needed an adventure. What's your dream?" he asked, as he pulled her to him.

She loved the warmth. "You know what it is: Life. Life is a series of experiences, a list of moments, and I want to have as many as possible," she said.

"Well then. It sounds like this could be fun. An unknown adventure. But I think you should make up another material dream, just in case. Ask for some money or something. They are interviewing Saturday in Seattle, so I'll go to that one. You go on Friday here," he said.

"Do you think we should tell them?" she asked.

"Nah. Why reveal more than you have to?"

Kristen pulled out some lunch meat, cheese and condiments from the fridge and put them on the table, along with some French bread, utensils and some water, then sat down. Andrew took the seat opposite her and they both worked on creating a sandwich.

"So..." Kristen stopped and looked at him. He could see a question coming in her vivid blue eyes.

"Yes?" He took a bite of some cheese.

"What is your dream?" she asked.

He paused and considered it.

"Success," he said, after swallowing his bite.

"But what kind of success?" she asked.

"You know. I want people to remember me... Build something... Make a fortune... Become Sir Richard Branson," he said.

"Who?" she asked.

"The owner of Virgin – you know: Virgin Records, Virgin Airlines..." he said.

"But what has he done for the world?" she asked. It was a frequent conversation.

"He gave us the best selection of CD's anywhere...and great business class seats to Europe!" he said.

"Andrew...."

"Yes, I know, we must be aware of giving back. And I plan to, Just as soon as I have everything I want." He saw her look of disapproval and added: "OK, just as soon as I have *some* of the things that I want." The look didn't change. "Alright then, I will go out and give a homeless person ten bucks today. Happy?" She finally smiled.

"You realize you are too ambitious. I think it comes from the lack of praise that your mother didn't give you," she said, as she took a bite.

"Kristen – are you trying to get in my head again?" he asked. Her psychology book was upside down on the table, and he picked it up and read the title.

"Dang," he said, as he looked at her and they both laughed.

"Did you fly down yourself?" she asked.

"Yes. I'm at PDX," he said. "I leave later today. So you want to take a walk or something? I realize the rose garden doesn't have many roses this time of year, but it has a nice view. We can pick up something to eat on the way," he said.

"Sure why not," she said. Andrew got up and picked up his coat off of the seat.

"Just give me a minute to freshen up," Kristen said, heading toward her bedroom. Andrew sat back down and folded his coat on the table.

Thirty minutes later they headed out the door got in his rented Jaguar and drove off to Washington Park.

Chapter 5

The Thunderbird Inn at the Quay was packed. Kristen got out of her Toyota Prius, grabbed her small purse, and walked into the main lobby. She saw a row of meeting rooms and walked down the hallway until she noticed a reader board that said. *'Dream Maker Interviews. 9:00 a.m.'* It was eight and only a few people had gathered. She took her place at the end of the line and the young man in front of her turned around.

"Hi, I'm Matt." He held his hand out and she reluctantly took it. It was clammy.

"Kristen," she said, and looked off to her left as she wondered how to wipe her hand off without being too obvious. He didn't turn around.

"You know anything about this Dream Maker?" he asked.

"No. Just what I saw in the ad." She was tempted to leave and come back but the line was growing rapidly.

"Someone told me it's a mix of Survivor and Fear Factor. You into eating spider milkshakes?" he asked, and smiled. He had a tongue ring.

"Not really," she said, hoping he was wrong.

"Just wondering." The young man turned back around and Kristen let out a slow breath.

At precisely nine, the door opened and a young girl came out and invited the first person in. She returned a few minutes later and started taking down information on everyone in line.

Someone behind Kristen had a coffee and she thought it smelled wonderful.

"Name?" the assistant asked her.

"Kristen Conrad."

"Age?"

"29"

"Married?"

"Divorced."

"Address?"

Kristen gave the information to her.

"You're tall." The woman said and proceeded down the line.

Forty minutes later she was invited into a large meeting room. Directly in front of her was a long folding table with three chairs behind it. A thirty-year-old woman with a nose ring and a fifty-ish man in a business suit stared at her as she walked up.

"Please sit down." The woman gestured. Kristen folded her khaki skirt under her and took the only seat facing the table. She was aware of her bare legs as they touched each other.

"You're divorced?" the man asked. He was looking at the questionnaire.

Kristen thought it was a weird question to start with.

"Yes. Is that important?" she asked.

"Could be." The man wrote something down and looked at her.

"What do you do for work?" the woman asked her. Sarah wondered if it was hard to blow your nose with a ring in it.

"I'm an artist," Kristen said.

"And you make a living at that?" the woman asked.

"I guess. I also paint murals and do some photography to pay the bills."

"Do you speak any other languages?" she asked.

"Yo hablo un poquito español," Kristen said.

"Have you traveled much?"

"A little. Europe – specifically Italy, France, and I've been to Hawaii, Mexico and Canada," Kristen said.

"Are you in a relationship?" The man asked.

Kristen hesitated. She actually didn't know the answer to the question.

"No," she said. The man looked at her.

"Are you sure?" he asked.

"Yes. I mean, no. I'm not in a relationship," she said. He paused then wrote down something.

"Can you be gone for ten days or so?" The woman asked.

Kristen was happy to get the information.

"Sure. With a little notice," she said.

"Do you have any allergies?" The woman asked.

"Penicillin, and I have prescription lenses for driving," Kristen said.

"What is your vision?" the man perked up and asked.

"Twenty-ninety and twenty-hundred." Kristen pointed to her left, then her right eye. She was wearing contacts.

"And what is your dream?" The man asked.

"I want to get a degree at the Pont Aven school of Contemporary art, in France," Kristen said.

"What are you willing to do for your dream?" The man asked.

"I'm not sure what you mean…" Kristen looked at him.

"What sacrifices are you willing to make to fulfill your dream of going to school in France?"

"I'm willing to… I guess I'm willing to do whatever is necessary…within reason of course," she said.

"And what would you consider unreasonable?" The man asked.

"Obviously things like murder, sex… but I guess I'm not quite sure how to answer that." Kristen didn't want to give them a reason to disqualify her.

"Alright, Ms. Conrad. We will let you know this month if you have been selected. Good day." The man started talking to the woman. Kristen took the hint and got up and left through the side door. She needed to get something to eat.

:

Andrew arrived at the Double Tree Sea-Tac right before 9:00 a.m.. There was quite a line and he put a fifty-dollar bill into his palm, then walked up to a young man near the front of the line.

"Hey, John, sorry I'm late. Thanks for coming early to save me a place." Andrew said it loud enough for the people behind him to hear. The man gave him a look and started to say something as Andrew pressed the money into his hand. The man looked down and closed his fist.

"No problem. What are friends for?" the man said. Andrew thought the man's performance was a bit forced, but he slipped in front of the guy and no one complained.

A young, reasonably attractive woman opened the door at precisely nine and started interviewing the people. Andrew gave her his best smile. She ignored him.

"Name?"

"Andrew Lee."

The woman looked at him.

"Nationality?"

"Eurasian."

25

"What?" The woman asked.

"Eur – Asian. That means part European and part Asian," Andrew said.

"Oh," she said. Andrew noticed the spelling wasn't even close.

"Age."

"Thirty-five."

"Address and phone."

Andrew gave her the information.

"It'll be a few minutes." The woman said as she moved on to the next person.

Andrew was invited in to a room with a folding table with three chairs facing him but there was only one person, a middle aged man with gray hair occupying the seats.

"Have a seat, please," the man said.

Andrew flipped the seat around so the back was facing the man and sat down with his legs straddling the chair.

"What do you do for a living, Mr. Lee?"

"I own a wholesale food company – mostly import, Eastern-Western Imports," Andrew said.

The man looked at him and stopped writing. It appeared that he recognized the name.

"And you own this company?" The man asked.

"Yes," Andrew said, "Actually it's a corporation, so more correctly, I am the sole shareholder. Yes, I own the company."

"It is a fairly large company?" The man asked.

"We did about ten million last year," Andrew said.

"I'm sorry, Mr. Lee, but I don't understand why you are here."

"Because I saw the ad," Andrew said.

"And what do you want, Mr. Lee. What is your dream that you think we can help you with?"

Andrew expected the question.

"I want my fifteen minutes of fame. Maybe more if the cameras like me," Andrew gave the man a big smile but it was not reciprocated.

"And that is important to you?" The man asked.

"I've always wanted to be famous. Doesn't everyone?" Andrew asked.

"Perhaps," the man said. "What are you willing to do to achieve your dream?"

"Anything. Within reason of course," Andrew said.

"And what would be unreasonable to you?" The man asked.

"I don't know. Killing someone, I suppose, but that isn't going to happen, so... other than that, I guess we will have to see when I'm given the chance."

"Are you married, Mr. Lee?"

"No."

"Are you involved with anyone?"

"No," Andrew said. He had anticipated that question as well.

"Do you speak any other languages?"

"No," Andrew lied. He did speak a little Mandarin, as well as a rudimentary knowledge of a couple of other languages.

"Have you traveled outside of the continental US? If so, where?"

Andrew thought for a minute, then said: "Hawaii, Canada, Australia, Mexico, Western Europe." Again, this was only a partial truth. He had been to several other lands and countries.

"Do you have any allergies or medical conditions?"

"Let's see... Nope. None."

"Can you take at least ten days off if required for this adventure?"

"Not a problem if I'm given some notice. I do have a big deal coming down next month that I need to be present for."

"What day?"

"December 14th," Andrew said. It was actually the 16th but he wanted a cushion."

"What is most important to you?" the man asked.

"Success," Andrew said.

"Mr. Lee, we will contact you this month if you fit our profile. Have a good day." The man stood up and offered his hand. Andrew took it and was surprised at the firmness.

"Thanks," he asked, and left through the side door where the assistant stood.

Chapter 6

Monday, November 14th, 2005.

The Chicago offices of Dream Maker sent out five 'Next Day Delivery' envelopes. Each one contained an invitation and airline tickets addressed to Ralph Gabriel, Kirsten Conrad, Sarah Connell, Andrew Lee, and Matt Garrison. The next morning each of the participants received the envelope before the 8:00 a.m. deadline and opened it.

Dear Entrant,

Through a long and tedious search, you have been selected to participate in the Dream Maker Adventure series. Enclosed you will find an itinerary for your trip to the Cayman Islands, which is scheduled in a little over two weeks time (Friday, December 2, 2005). This should give you adequate notice to make your preparations. You are invited to bring a single carry-on bag, not to exceed twenty pounds. Absolutely no recording devices are permitted, neither are cell phones, pagers or laptops. If you do not currently have one, it is strongly recommended that you obtain a current U.S. Passport (there is an expedited service available). Should you miss the flight to the Cayman's we will assume you have withdrawn from the adventure.

Welcome to the adventure of your life. We look forward to meeting you at the airport on Grand Cayman.

The Dream Maker team

The first thing that Andrew noticed was the absence of a lot of paperwork. All that he found was the invitation, a round trip airline ticket departing December 2nd returning December 13, 2005, and an ID tag that he assumed was for his luggage. Andrew put down the paperwork on his work desk and immediately made several phone calls. He needed to make some arrangements.

When Sarah received the envelope after school, she thought it was a gift package from her dad. He would surprise her once in awhile with something like this. She opened it up and saw the airline ticket, then read the letter. Her first call was to her friend, Jessica.

"Hey, Jessie! It's Sarah."

"Hi, Sarah, what's up?" Jessica said.

"Do you still have your PayPal account?" she asked.

"Of course," Jessica said, "I use it for Ebay – just like you. Why?"

"I have a favor to ask…" Sarah said.

:

Ralph had just come home from work and Melanie was not at the door to greet him. She sat at the kitchen table with the three children.

"Dad's home!" Devin shouted, and Jerry and Lynn surrounded him and impeded his walking.

"Children! Go outside and play. I need to speak to your father, " Melanie said.

Ralph's spirits dropped and he looked at her. She was holding a next day air envelope.

"Go ahead, kids. Listen to your mom. I'll come out in a minute." He padded Devin's head and ruffled Lynn's hair. They all took off to the back yard.

Ralph went over to the kitchen table and sat down. The seat was still warm from Jerry.

"What is this?" Melanie pushed a letter and airline ticket across the table toward him.

Ralph picked it up and read it. He wanted to smile and jump up to celebrate, but the look on Melanie's face tempered him.

"Uh…I didn't think they'd take me," he asked.

"Take you where? What for?" Melanie asked.

"It's a game show; Reality show or something. If you make it through an adventure they grant you a dream." Ralph looked at her.

"What kind of adventure? Is it dangerous? Are you going to do something that would…." She stopped.

"No! Nothing like that. I'm sure it's probably something like the Amazing Race or Survivor TV show. I'm not exactly sure, but it's only a week long or so." Ralph was not getting the reaction he had hoped for, and added: "they said they would buy us a house..."

"What good is a house if something happens to you?" She looked worried.

"Nothing will happen to me. Maybe they just want me to eat some grubs or something. I'd be willing to do that for a house. The kids really want a dog, and you know the Muller's won't let us have one here." He referred to their landlords.

"And I promise," he put his hand to his heart, "I would never do anything to hurt you or the kids."

"This says you have to leave on December 2nd. Will work give you the time off?" she asked.

"I don't know, but I think so. Maybe you could go stay with your mom and dad. They always love to have the kids."

"We'll see. I need to get dinner ready." Melanie got up and turned on the stove. The action made Ralph feel like he was eight years old and his mother was mad at him for writing on her favorite wallpaper. There was nothing he could do about it so he got up and went to play with the children.

:

Kristen almost missed the envelope altogether. It had been shoved under her door, and Beethoven decided that it was something to be played with. He had pushed it around until it was half under the sofa and she didn't find it for almost a full day. When she had read it, she made a call.

"Well?" she asked.

"Well what?" Andrew asked.

"Do you have anything to tell me?"

"I suppose so... what would you like to hear?" Andrew said.

"I got it!" she said.

Andrew paused for a second.

"I did too," he asked.

"You turkey! Why didn't you tell me? When did you get it? Are you going?"

"Whoa! Slow down. Number one: I didn't tell you because I was waiting to see if you got in. Number two: I got it yesterday. Number three: of course!"

Kristen screamed then stopped suddenly. "Any idea what is going to happen?"

"None whatsoever," Andrew said.

"What are you going to pack?" she asked

"I have no idea. That's in over two weeks. The end of the world could come before then," he said.

"So, where are you anyway?" she asked.

"Seattle," he said.

"Oh," she replied.

"Sorry. I would have called you if I was in Portland," he said.

"No big deal. I'm busy anyway. See ya." Kristen hung up the phone and waited only a second before jumping around the loft, screaming with excitement. After a few moments it occurred to her that her neighbors may think she was being murdered or something, and she ceased her screams, instead churning her feet on the floor in silence like she was madly peddling a bicycle till she was exhausted. She then collapsed on the sofa with the airline ticket still grasped in her hand.

Chapter 7

December 2, 2005 Grand Cayman Island.

The passengers arrived at Owen Roberts International Airport a little after sundown. It was 6:30 p.m. local time and the passengers were very warm. It was still over eighty degrees Fahrenheit.

As they waited in line for immigration, Andrew looked around and noticed Kristen standing in the next line. They barely acknowledged each other, but he could tell she was excited. He tried to see if anyone else had a luggage tag like him and Kristen. Behind him there was a possible match, however the man kept fidgeting and Andrew couldn't quite see it clearly enough. He wondered how many contestants were there.

"Passport?" The Immigration officer had his hand out. Andrew handed it to him with his the photo side up.

"What is the purpose of your visit?" said the officer.

"Fun. Recreation, I guess," Andrew said. He should have had a better answer prepared.

"How long will you stay?" the agent asked.

"I'm not quite sure. A week or so," Andrew said.

"All right." The agent stamped a page and handed him back the passport.

"Next please!" Andrew took that as the signal to move on.

Most of the passengers stopped at baggage claim to pick up their checked luggage, but a few passed through to Customs, and were waived through. On the other side, people headed off to the rental car booths or ground transportation. A man stood off to Andrew's right with a sign that had five names on it. 'Andrew Lee' was listed second from the top right, below a Sarah Connell. Andrew wondered why she was listed first. A young woman stood by the man with a single bag at her feet adorned by the unique luggage tag. He walked up to both of them, and Kristen joined him.

"Hi. I'm Andrew Lee." He introduced himself to the man, whom he assumed was the driver. The man was dressed in a pair of worn shorts, wide brimmed beach hat and a casual buttoned shirt.

"OK. Wait here. We've got three more passengers." The man failed to smile.

"I'm Kristen Conrad." Kristen walked up and intentionally leaned against Andrew's arm as she talked to the driver. He smiled and stepped away.

"Fine. Please stay here. We need two more people."

"I'm Sarah Connell." Sarah was quite a bit shorter than Kristen or Andrew, and she held out her hand to Kristen first.

"I'm Kristen...oh, you already heard that didn't you?"

"I'm Andrew Lee." Andrew took her hand. It was small and soft, but he noticed that she had a few calluses on her fingers. She was probably a student. He shook Kristen's hand next, smiling as if they had just met. Sarah looked at both of them quizzically, and it made Andrew wonder how long he and Kristen could keep up the pretense until the others realized that they knew each other, but he pacified himself with the knowledge that no one had said it was prohibited to know another contestant.

They all turned to look at the sound of approaching footsteps. A twenty something male walked up. He was Caucasian, and a couple of inches shorter than Andrew. His belly protruded just a little, and was held in check by a wide brown belt. He looked disheveled and somewhat flustered.

"Hi, I'm Ralph. Ralph Gabriel." Andrew grabbed his hand first. It was a weak handshake and he released it quickly.

"I'm Kristen... and this is Sarah. I guess we're waiting for one more person." At Kristen's comment the driver just nodded.

They all watched the line of people as they cleared Customs. One by one the people cleared. Sarah evaluated each person as they interacted with the agent. She was happy that some of the people did not walk their way. At the very end of the line a young man was having trouble with the handle on his bag, which had broken off. He stumbled over to the group, cradling it in his arms. Kristen remembered him from the line up at the interview in Portland. When he opened his mouth, she saw that he still had his tongue ring too, and then, as he got closer, she realized that he didn't smell very good either. She found herself holding her breath, waiting for the air to stop moving.

"I'm Matt." He held his hand out to the group but no one took it. Finally Sarah grabbed it and pumped it once then let go.

"I'm Sarah. This is..."

"Kristen." Kristen grabbed her bag so she wouldn't be offered the hand.

"I'm Andrew." Andrew had both his hands wrapped under his leather coat.

"I'm Ralph." Ralph looked exhausted.

"Let's go." The driver interrupted the exchange and they all followed him out into the night.

They approached a large square van unlike anything they had seen in North America. All of them waited until Matt boarded first, taking a seat in the rear, and then they all took various other open spots while opening as many windows as possible. They drove along a road with sand on both sides for about thirty minutes, until the Ocean appeared on the left. Several of the buildings had perimeter lights illuminating the grounds, and they could see what appeared to be intense turquoise-blue water, and white sand. Many other houses and buildings adorned the waterfront, and people of all races milled around in bathing attire. An exotic smell permeated the van as they passed by street vendors barbecuing meat.

"What is that smell?" Kristen finally asked the question they were all wondering.

"Jerk." The driver said.

"What?" she asked

"Jerk. Native seasoning. Very good," he said.

They all wanted to ask him to stop, but he seemed to be on a scheduled mission, so they left him alone.

After about two miles, the driver pulled up to a gate and pressed the intercom button. The gate slowly opened to a circle drive and they were driven around the fountain in the center, stopping in front of the colonial double doors. The house was a two-story stucco home painted in either peach or pink. It was difficult to tell because of the dim light.

After all the passengers disembarked with their single bag, the driver opened the front door and signaled for them to go in. The foyer floor was covered in pink marble, with veins running through it, and it felt slick on their soles as the five contestants entered the room. There was an ornate chandelier hanging from the second floor. A crescent staircase, complete with a wide barrister, framed the small room.

"Come in!" The man that each of them had seen from the interview stood in front of them. He was wearing a two-piece beige suit, and Kristen noticed he wore glasses this time. He waved them down a couple of steps into what appeared to be the living room. White leather sofa's framed a large 'U' around the mantle, above which hung a large impressionist painting. Kristen immediately went up to it and inspected the work. It was a picture of three women walking in a garden. The picture was typical impressionist, everything was a bit of a blur, but in this picture one face jumped out at you, a lithe, young brunette wearing a pair of cream pants and a lace top. "Ze-Ju Guan," she whispered. "A Red Chinese impressionist from San Francisco. His work is exquisite."

Kristen could hear the other contestants behind her taking seats on the leather couches, and she turned to face the room. Andrew was to her left, along with Sarah. Ralph, who had hardly said a word the entire trip, sat on the right, along with Matt, though a wide gap separated the two men. She watched an older man walk into the room from the back of the house. He stopped at the top of the stairs and she smiled at him. The group noticed her reaction and they turned to see who it was. The man was impeccably dressed in a casual suit, with a worn, but still handsome, face and intense blue eyes.

"Hello, Ladies and Gentleman. Welcome to the Cayman Islands. My name is Mr. Henry Baldwin." Mr. Baldwin stepped down into the living room and made his way over to where Kristen stood. It made her uncomfortable and she walked past him to the top of the 'U', sitting in the only chair available.

"You five have been selected to participate in the adventure of a lifetime. This adventure will take between seven and ten days. In the next twenty four hours you will have an opportunity to get to know one another, ask a few questions – but not too many, and prepare for your journey." Mr. Baldwin paused for a moment and looked at each of them.

"All of you have told us your dream. We agree to grant you that dream if you successfully complete your adventure. This is to be done within the timeframe, and by using only the assets, that we grant you. Oh. And one very important item: from this point forward you are a team. You succeed as a team, or you fail as a team."

"What do you mean? Do we all have to complete?" Andrew asked.

"Exactly," the group grumbled and Mr. Baldwin put up his hand to stop them.

"This is not just a personal journey. This is also a test to see how well you operate with people of different personalities, desires, ways of thinking, and perspectives."

"Starting when?" Sarah said.

"Starting right now," Mr. Baldwin said. "There is one exception, but we will not get into that at this time."

"Who is in charge?" Andrew asked.

"Anyone, no one, it doesn't matter to us," Mr. Baldwin said.

"Where is the TV crew?" Matt asked.

"Be patient, Mr. Garrison, you will see them in due time."

Mr. Baldwin held up his hand as several others asked questions.

"Hold on. Let me finish, and then you may ask questions, but I may chose not answer all of them." He smiled.

"Your adventure will require that you accomplish certain tasks that you will be given. Failure to complete any of the tasks, or the final goal, will mean forfeiture of *everyone's* dream. Cheating will mean forfeiture of everyone's dream. There are also consequences for cheating or violating rules. Some of these consequences can be quite severe."

Sarah narrowed her eyes and spoke up.

"What do you mean severe?" she asked.

"Exactly what it sounds like, it may include corporal punishment," Mr. Baldwin said.

The contestants all looked at each other.

"I'm not really into that. I mean, no one said anything about getting physically abused," Andrew said.

"Remember – if you follow the instructions, and don't cheat, it really doesn't matter. Do you cheat, Mr. Lee?"

"No. Of course not," Andrew said, "I just don't like the idea of someone being able to touch me for something I may or may not be guilty of."

"Mr. Lee… everyone, no one has forced you to come here. You may leave if you wish. Robert will take you to the airport if you wish to do so. Just remember if you leave – you all fail." They finally knew the drivers name was Robert. Mr. Baldwin paused, but no one made a move.

"Good. Then why don't you get to know one another and I'll be back momentarily." He left the room as did Robert. The contestants were finally alone.

"I don't like the sound of this." Ralph spoke, and everyone looked at him. "What?" he asked.

"You speak! That's cool. I thought, for awhile there, they gave us a mute," Matt said, as he played with his tongue ring.

"Am I the only one hungry?" Kristen said, as she looked around the room. There was a tray with crackers and cheese on it in the corner, and she brought it over and ate a piece of Swiss.

"Are you sure it's OK?" Sarah asked.

Kristen's eyes got big, and she grabbed her throat and fell to the ground, throwing herself into mock convulsions.

"Great. We have a comedienne as well," Andrew said. Kristen got up and smiled at him.

"I'm serious. We don't know anything about these people. What if they are lunatics or something?" Sarah said.

"I agree. Something feels weird. I'm about ready to head out of here," Ralph said.

"What's your hurry... Ralph, right?" Andrew asked. Ralph nodded.

"It's not like we are stranded in some African jungle or anything. We can walk out the door anytime we want. Remember, the guy said we are all in this together from this point on. If you leave, we go home as well. And I'm not ready to go home, at least not until we find out what this is all about," Andrew said.

"Listen. Let's get some more information from this guy, then we can discuss this as a group. I mean, Andrew is right, we are not in some third world country. If things get weird, we can all walk out of here," Sarah said.

"At least the Swiss cheese is good," Kristen said, as she put another piece in her mouth. Matt bent forward and took some crackers, and they all dug in.

"So, Sarah, where are you from?" Andrew asked.

"Toronto, but born in Buffalo, New York, " she said. "How about you?"

"Seattle."

"And what do you do there?" she asked.

"I'm in the import-export business, mostly food stuff," Andrew said.

"Anything I would recognize?" she asked.

"Maybe, if you go into the oriental section, there is probably some stuff from my company," Andrew said.

"Sarah, what do you do in Toronto?" Kristen interrupted the conversation.

"I'm just finishing my BA. I want to go on to law school," Sarah said.

"And that's your dream? I mean for this adventure," Kristen asked.

"Yes. And a car," Sarah said.

"Hmm, so why not a scholarship?" Kristen asked.

"I've tried. It's been a little more difficult than I anticipated," Sarah said.

"And the parents?" Andrew asked.

"I want to do this on my own," Sarah said.

"What do you do, Kristen?" Sarah was relieved to turn the conversation.

"I'm an artist,"

"What kind of art?" Sarah asked.

"Abstract, mostly. I like impressionism as well."

"Did you go to school?" Sarah asked.

"No. Well, yes, but not for art. I took three years of psych, then got distracted and never finished," Kristen said.

"And how do you make a living?" Matt chimed in.

"I actually make a living off my art." Kristen wasn't willing to divulge any more information on that front, and changed the subject.

"Ralph, where are you from?" she asked. Ralph looked like a Raccoon caught in the headlights.

"Umm. I Ummm. Tennessee," he finally said, "Memphis."

"Elvis! Cool!" Kristen said. "Ever been to Graceland?"

"Uh. No. Never have. I like country," Ralph said.

"And what do you do for work?" Sarah tried to save him.

"I work in a grocery store," Ralph said. They all waited in vain for him to explain further.

"And, Ralph, what is your dream?" Sarah asked.

Ralph looked up at Sarah with a determination that surprised her.

"I want a house for my family," he said.

"You have children, Ralph?" she asked. Ralph pulled out his wallet and handed her a picture.

"Three children, two boys and a girl," Ralph said. Sarah looked at the picture. It was obviously a family that liked each other. She handed the picture on to Kristen.

"Beautiful children," Sarah said. She had often stated that but this time she meant it.

"Uh huh," Kristen agreed, and handed the picture to Andrew. He handed it back to Sarah since Matt didn't show any inclination to look at it.

"What kind of house, Ralph?" Kristen asked.

"Four bedrooms, one for each of the kids, and a dog," he said.

"The dog comes with the house or the house is a dog?" Andrew asked, and smiled. Kristen elbowed him.

"Ouch. That hurt," he said to her.

"Never mind him, Ralph. I think that is a great dream," Kristen said.

"So what about you, Matt?" No one really wanted to know, but it seemed the polite thing to ask. They were all thankful that he finished chewing his cracker before answering.

"A million bucks!" he said.

"And what do you want a million dollars for, Matt?" Andrew asked.

"I'm gonna build my own skateboard park," Matt said.

"Now that sounds like a worthwhile life goal!" Andrew said, giving Matt a big smile. They all dropped the subject.

"How about you, Andrew, what is your dream?" Sarah asked.

"I just wanted to see if I could get on the show!" Andrew said.

"And that's all?" Sarah asked.

"Well, I wouldn't mind being famous for a day or so. You know, screaming fans, lots of beautiful women..." Andrew stopped himself and looked at Kristen. She smiled.

"And you, Kristen. What is your dream?" Andrew asked. He realized he had never inquired as to what she had told the Dream Maker.

"I want to go to school in Paris," she said, with a smile. He looked surprised.

"I've always wanted to. It would only be a year or two. But studying in Paris…." Kristen gazed off in the distance.

"But you don't speak French…do you?" Andrew asked. He was unsure of the answer, and it surprised him.

"No, I don't, but I can always learn!" she said, as she got up and walked over to the mirror to straighten out her hair.

:

"She is the artist," the fifty-year-old man said.

"Ms…. Ms. Conrad. Yes. She is going to be exciting to watch— completely spontaneous," Mr. Baldwin said. They looked at the group from the other side of the mirror.

"And Andrew? Mr. Lee?"

"He will try to be the leader. But it will be interesting to see if Sarah allows him to be. Notice how she is always observing. She never speaks without thinking first." Mr. Baldwin pointed to the pretty blonde.

"What about Matt?"

"He's superfluous. Won't even make it a day," Mr. Baldwin said.

"And Ralph?"

"He is the dark horse. He seems like he is timid but, when he speaks about his family, look at his eyes. He will fight for them. Mark my words."

"Then we shall have to test that."

"Yes indeed," Mr. Baldwin, said.

Chapter 8

"Dinner is served!" Mr. Baldwin reentered the room.

"Finally!" Andrew said, as the whole group got up and followed Mr. Baldwin.

The dinning room was on the waterside of the home and had been set for eight people. The five contestants sat down along with Mr. Baldwin, but the other two seats remained open. Andrew sat next to Kristen with Sarah on her right, then Ralph and Matt. Mr. Baldwin sat at the head of the table with the ocean to his left. A light turned on outside the window and the group could see the white sand and the edge of the crashing surf.

"Welcome!" Mr. Baldwin held up a glass of wine and they all picked up their respective chalices. "Cheers!" he said, and took a drink of the Zinfandel. All the contestants except Andrew and Sarah willingly went along. The two of them barely pressed the liquid to their lips. Andrew looked at her as they did it.

Mr. Baldwin took a spoon and rang an empty glass. In a few moments two waiters came out with individual plates of food and set it on the table. Each plate had a lobster on it along with drawn butter and polenta. The waiters walked around the table tying a white bib on each diner.

"Awesome!" Matt said, as he received his bib. He already had his hands on his meal when a waiter started handing out lemon scented steaming towels to each of them. Mr. Baldwin took his, wiped off his hands, and put the soiled cloth back on the serving tray. Matt hesitated for a second, then kept on eating.

"So, ladies and gentlemen, you have had a chance to get to know one another a little. Do you have any further questions?" he asked.

"You mentioned that there were some exceptions to the all for one and one for all rule," Sarah said.

"Yes. Mostly those have to do with unfortunate incidents. If a person becomes incapacitated due to circumstances beyond the control of the group we will consider waiving the… as you say 'all for one and one for all' clause."

"What are we allowed to take with us?" Ralph asked.

"We will let you know when we get closer," Mr. Baldwin answered.

"Will be asked to do anything illegal?" Sarah asked.

"Very good question, Ms. Connell. The answer is perhaps. As in life there may be gray areas, and you will have to decide as individuals and as a group what to do."

"Is there a chance for physical harm?" Ralph asked.

"Yes. There is also a chance to be physically harmed when crossing the street."

"But that's not what I meant. Will we be put in harm's way?" Ralph asked.

"Some of the journey will involve danger. You were asked during your entrance interview if there was anything you wouldn't do for your dream…" Mr. Baldwin squinted a moment, "I believe you said 'within reason'. Well, Mr. Gabriel, I guess we will have to find out what that means to you."

"Are we going to have to eat rats and worms and things?" Matt asked.

"Mr. Garrison, that is entirely possible, but again it will be up to you. You will not be forced to do that."

"What exactly is the adventure?" Kristen spoke up between bites of lobster.

"Now it wouldn't be an adventure if I told you, would it Ms. Conrad?" Mr. Baldwin smiled.

"Will we be given a plan, or it will just be a goal?" Sarah asked.

"You will be given both. There will be tasks to perform as well as an ultimate goal," Mr. Baldwin said.

"Can I tell my family where I'll be?" Ralph asked.

"No. In fact, if any one of you makes contact with anyone, friend or family member, from this point forward you may all forfeit your dream. So I strongly encourage you all – if you know that someone here has a communication device you should tell me immediately." He looked at each of them before continuing.

"Who is sponsoring this… adventure?" Andrew asked.

"A private benefactor. He wishes to remain anonymous," Mr. Baldwin said.

"How do we know you will keep your end of the bargain? After we go through this, do as you say and succeed, what assurance do we have you won't renege or vanish?" Sarah asked.

"Good question, Ms. Connelly. We have placed the sum of five million dollars U.S. in an account with all of your names on it. The account is at the Cayman Island National Bank. The account can only be accessed by all five of you at the same time – but only until December 15th. You must complete the adventure by that date. If you do not do so, the funds return to the benefactor. Keep in mind that this is only a guarantee. It is not meant to be actual payment for your dreams should you succeed. Each of you has asked for different things. Mr. Lee's request was not monetary, however the money is there as an assurance. You may verify the funds and the account instructions in the morning should you wish to do so."

"How do you know we won't just walk in there tomorrow and take the money?" Matt asked.

"Yes, Mr. Garrison, I realize that is a temptation but several of your fellow contestants were selected because of their moral fiber. I don't think that you could get all four of them to agree to do so, but you are welcome to try if you want." Mr. Baldwin smiled.

It sounded good to Matt.

"What about the TV crew?" Andrew asked.

"Ah. You do not give up, do you, Mr. Lee? Exactly how we will monitor your progress will be revealed to you when necessary."

Andrew looked like he was going to protest and Mr. Baldwin stood up.

"Ladies and Gentlemen, this has been a long day for all of us. I am going to head to bed. Feel free to eat as much as you want. In the morning you will all receive a medical exam, then you will be given your final instructions." Mr. Baldwin pushed back his chair and walked off toward the living room. They waited until they could hear his footsteps ascend the stairs.

"Let's blow this joint tomorrow. You heard the man. All we have to do is –" Matt stopped when a waiter entered the room and filled up the water glasses. When he departed Matt continued. "All we have to do is all go to the bank and take the cash." He looked around the table, but no one spoke.

"Anyone want to give us a good reason why we shouldn't?" he asked.

"Other than they know all our names and addresses, and we would be stealing. Not really," Andrew said.

"Oh," Matt said. He looked as if it was a new thought to him.

"Fine," he added, as he picked through his plate.

"Matt, do you understand the concept of stealing?" Sarah asked him.

"Of course." Matt scowled at her. "But these people are loony. I don't see the real problem, other than you all are afraid..." his voice drifted off.

"Anyone up for a walk?" Andrew asked.

"Not me," Ralph said. "I'm going to hit the sack. Any idea where the bedrooms are?"

A waiter appeared again and answered him: "Up the main staircase. Each room has a name on it." He pointed back to the foyer.

"Me too," Kristen said. "It's been a long day." She yawned and stretched as she pushed away from the table.

Her and Ralph got up from the table and left. Matt stayed a while longer to suck on the lobster tail, then he left without saying a word.

"What do you think about this?" Sarah asked Andrew when they were alone. She motioned with her hand.

"I'm not sure. It's a bit... unexpected," Andrew said.

"I don't have the best feeling about it," Sarah said.

"You want to go for that walk?" Andrew said. She hesitated for a moment, and looked at the table as if contemplating the potential consequences.

"It's only a walk – not a marriage proposal." Andrew grinned.

"Sure, why not," Sarah said.

There was a set of French doors that opened up to a deck from the living room. Andrew opened it for Sarah and followed her out. There was a cool breeze running parallel to the beach, and it caught the door and slammed it against the house. Sarah jumped and Andrew quickly grabbed it by the edge and softly closed it.

"Sorry about that," he said.

Sarah ignored the comment and stared at the dark water. He walked up to her side and they moved to the edge of the deck where Andrew kicked off his shoes.

"Good idea," she said, as she sat on the deck and removed hers as well.

The sand still radiated the heat from the sun and the wind danced around their heads like spinning tops. They walked toward the edge of the water where the texture under their feet became firm, then they headed south along the beach. The moon appeared from behind a cloud and illuminated the path in front of them, painting the beach like a stroke from a wide paintbrush. Neither spoke for a long time.

"Why are you here, Andrew?" Sarah asked.

"What do you mean?" he said.

"I mean, why are you really here?" she asked.

He though about it for a minute. "To feel alive," he finally said.

She stopped and walked toward the water letting it touch her feet. Her back was to him and he walked up behind her without touching.

"And why are you here?" Andrew asked. He was unsure if she heard him and was about to repeat himself.

"To…" she stopped. "I don't know," she said.

Andrew could tell that wasn't the truth, but didn't pursue it.

"You know what?" he asked, and Sarah turned around. "I like to pick up a stone from every place I've been and bring it home. I have a whole collection of them. Help me find one." Andrew bent over and picked up a small marbled black and white rock and tossed it in the water. They both walked along, picking up stones until he finally found one he liked and put it in his pocket. Sarah picked up a small piece of driftwood and played with it until it fell from her hands. She looked at it for a moment and Andrew bent over to pick it up. He placed it in his palm and presented it to her. She looked up at him for a second, then removed it with two fingers, just barely grazing his hand.

"Could we go back now?" she asked.

"Sure. It's getting late anyway," he said.

"It's a beautiful night," she said.

They walked back in silence to the house. Neither of them felt the need to say anything.

Chapter 9

A loud bell announced the morning, and Sarah got up from her bed wearing her sleeping shorts to look out the window. Her room faced the ocean, and she opened the door and stepped out onto her balcony.

"Good morning!" The voice surprised her, and she turned to her left to find Andrew standing there.

"Morning," she said with a smile, then looked back at the crashing waves.

"Did you sleep well?" he asked.

"Yes. Not too badly, how about you?" she asked.

"OK. I never sleep very well. My mind just never stops." Andrew looked out at a group of four young men walking by the house.

"Isn't that Matt?" he asked. Sarah followed his finger.

"I think so," she said. Matt was saying something to one of the guys who gave him what looked like a couple of cigarettes, then he headed toward the deck doors.

"Did I just see what I think I did?" she said.

"Yup," Andrew said. "We have a real winner with us. Well – this is a reality show, right? Maybe he is just into another kind of reality!" He laughed.

Sarah smiled at him and went back into her room.

"I'll see you downstairs, " she said, before she disappeared.

:

Breakfast was fresh fruit and pastries. By the time that Sarah made it downstairs, the other four were already there.

"Good morning!" Kristen said to her.

"Hi, Kristen," Sarah answered and took her seat facing the ocean.

"Isn't this incredible," Kristen said, as she followed her gaze.

"Amazing," Sarah answered.

"So, Matt, I saw you made some new friends this morning," Andrew said.

Matt had just smeared a croissant with strawberry jam and put it up to his mouth. He pulled it away, looked at Andrew, then the others.

"Yeah. Ran into some guys on my jog this morning." He opened his mouth to take a bite and everyone could see his tongue ring.

"Hmmm. Sure," Andrew said, as he looked at Sarah. She was scooping some fruit on her plate.

"Anyone see Mr. Baldwin?" Andrew asked.

"Nope," Kristen said.

"How did you sleep, Ralph?" she asked.

Ralph looked up a little surprised. He had just put a piece of melon in his mouth.

"Fine. Thanks," he said, by moving the melon over to his left cheek. He chewed a few times and swallowed. "I'll be happier today when we get more information."

"Hello, everyone!" Mr. Baldwin appeared wearing Bahama shorts and a matching shirt. He had sandals on his feet.

"I trust everyone had a restful night?" He sat down amidst the murmurs and took a cheese pastry from the serving tray.

"So, what is happening this morning?" Ralph said. He looked noticeably more uneasy after Mr. Baldwin joined them at the table.

"Each of you will undergo a medical exam by our doctor," Mr. Baldwin looked at his watch. "He will be here in about thirty minutes. He'll do the men first, and then the women. In the meantime, you may go out to the beach or deck. Just remain close. You will require an inoculation, so you may feel a bit tired afterwards. It would probably be a good idea to lay down for an hour or so."

"Innocu...what?" Matt asked. "Is that like a drug test?"

Sarah and Andrew looked at each other and smiled.

"No, Matt, it is a vaccination. " Kristen paused to see if he understood the synonym, but only received the same nonplussed look. "It helps to protect you against things like Malaria..." Matt still look dumfounded and she gave up.

"Why would we need an inoculation?" Sarah asked.

"Just in case, Ms. Connelly. Better safe than sick," Mr. Baldwin said, right before he took a bite of cantaloupe.

The doctor arrived a few minutes late and Andrew was the first one called. The nearly fifteen minute examination took place in a study off of the living room.

"What is that exactly?" Andrew asked, upon seeing the syringe.

"You are going to receive vaccinations against, typhoid, hepatitis A, polio…oh, and since you haven't had a tetanus shot in over eight years – one of those as well. I also recommend you carry insect repellent, as Dengue fever and malaria are a danger."

"Where are we going?" The question noticeably shook up the doctor.

"Uh. Oh. You know what, I'm sure Mr. Baldwin will let you know the details. I'm just performing what he has asked to be done." The doctor took the syringe in his hand and Ralph looked away. He felt the shark prick, and then the cotton swab.

"That's it. You may feel pretty tired so taking a nap for a bit would be recommended."

Andrew came out of the study feeling a little bit dizzy, and he headed immediately up the stairs to his room. Before he fell over, he slipped a small card and envelope from his pocket into his underwear. He recalled an old proverb 'The truly wise are rarely surprised'.

"Hey, Andrew! What happened?" he heard Ralphs's voice call out, but was concentrating hard on each step up the staircase and didn't answer him.

"Next! Mr. Gabriel." The doctor appeared and had a chart in from of him. Andrew, Kristen and Sarah were in the living room.

Ralph got up with a concerned look on his face and stopped to whisper something to Kristen. She watched as he walked by, then went back to her magazine.

After his exam, Ralph also slowly headed up to his room. The inoculations had made him much more tired than he had expected, even though he had seen Andrew's reaction.

Sarah was called next, because Matt was missing, and was even more nervous after observing Ralph and Andrew.

"Just one second. I have to use the bathroom," Sarah ran upstairs to her room and looked around. She dug through her suitcase until she found a small plastic card and discretely inserted it into her bra, then took a small package of pills and put them in her waistband and headed back downstairs. After watching last year's Survivor show, she was not going to be caught totally unprepared.

Within seconds after receiving her last shot, Sarah felt herself getting dizzy. The last thing she heard was the doctor's voice.

"I need some help in here!"

When she awoke the room was pitch dark. Sarah didn't move. There was something definitely different about her room. She could no longer hear the waves crashing on the shore or smell the fresh, crisp ocean air. The room was humid and warm, and her bed was lumpy. It occurred to her that she could be just dreaming, and she carried the thought for quite a while before being confident that she was indeed awake. The musing triggered her mind to remember her dreams. She recalled voices of men, and being carried somewhere, the sounds of an airplane. Something about being lost in a jungle and there had been wild animals. Andrew was there. She thought it strange that he was in her dream. She was in trouble, but no one would help her. It was all she could remember, and she drew her mind back into the present. The last thing that was definitely real was the shot she had received from the doctor. Then the feeling of dizziness, which would logically mean that she had fallen asleep, but for how long? She silently moved her legs against one another and felt some small stubble. At least a day, maybe two, she determined. What was she wearing? She could feel the socks on her feet and her shoes, her pants, her blouse and bra. Her hair was touching her face and her hands were at her sides. She moved her fingers to touch the bedding. It was coarse, and felt ragged.

Sarah strained to see some kind of light. The darkness was heavy, like a cloak, and she blinked her eyes several times to see if she had lost her sense of sight. She couldn't tell. A sound barely broke the silence. Something, or someone, was sliding over the floor underneath the bed. She couldn't tell how far away the sound was but it was definitely moving toward her. She braced herself for some kind of contact, but the sound stopped and she willed her fear away. Her mind needed to be in control, not her emotions.

A voice broke through the stillness and it made her heart jump, which physically hurt her, but it also allayed the fear that she was alone.

"Hello?" it was Andrew's voice.

"Andrew?" Sarah asked, softly.

"Are you OK?" Andrew asked.

"I think so. I haven't really moved yet," she replied.

"Me neither," he said.

"Any idea where we are at?" she asked.

"Only a guess. The doctor slipped up in giving me the shots. Sounds like we were inoculated for tropical jungle types of illnesses," Andrew said.

"Oh. That doesn't sound too promising…" Sarah's voice drifted off.

"My bet is either Africa or South East Asia. He specifically mentioned Dengue fever," Andrew said.

"Is anyone else here?" Sarah asked.

Andrew paused, "I don't know."

"Do you know what that is on the floor?" she asked.

"Only a guess, and it's not something I'd really like to deal with," he said.

She didn't either.

"Any idea how long we've been here?" she asked.

"I think a day or so. My beard is only stubble," he said. The comment brought an unseen smile to her face.

"I agree," she said.

"How long have you been awake?" he asked.

"I just woke up." It was Ralph.

"Don't move, Ralph," Andrew said.

Ralph was silent.

"Did you hear me, Ralph?" Andrew said.

"Uh…yes. We're not at the house anymore are we?" he asked.

"No. Kansas is long gone, Ralph. There is also something on the floor. Don't move," Andrew said.

"Is anyone else awake?" Andrew increased the volume in his voice, and they all froze as they heard the sliding sound again.

"Yes," Kristen replied, as softly as she could. "Where are we?"

"We don't know, Kristen," Sarah whispered back.

"Matt?" Sarah asked.

"Matt?" The next time was a little louder.

"Huh?" They all heard his voice.

"Wake up, Matt." Andrew said.

"Huh…what's happening?" Matt said. They all heard him move in his bed like he was trying to sit up.

50

"DON'T MOVE!" Andrew hissed.

"Huh? Why not? Where are we?" Matt said. They heard his feet hit the floor.

"What the!...Where are – Damn! There's something on the floor!" His voice shook in a vibrato and they could all hear him jump back on the bed.

"Well, get off of it then!" Andrew was obviously ticked. "We told you not to move!"

No one spoke as several creatures moved across the floor. They all listened until the movement stopped.

"What was the floor made of, Matt?" Andrew asked.

"Huh?"

"Matt! Pay attention!" Andrew hissed again.

"What is the floor made of?"

"Oh. Dirt, sand, something like that" he said.

"Can anyone feel an outside wall?" Andrew asked.

"Yes," Kristen said, "it feels like sawn timber. It's splintered, and rough."

"Can anyone see anything?" Sarah asked.

No one spoke.

"Does anyone have any idea where we are?" Kristen asked.

There was silence for a moment.

"Not really. I think in a jungle somewhere," Andrew said.

"I'm getting a bad feeling about this whole thing," Ralph said.

"You're not the only one, bro'. Told you we should have taken the money and ran," Matt said.

"That's great hindsight, but what do we do…" Ralph said.

"Any one have something on their wrist?" Sarah asked.

"A watch…no, I don't know what it is, but it's not my watch," Andrew said.

"Everyone?" Sarah asked.

"Yes."

"Which wrist?" She asked.

"Right," they all said.

"Anyone left handed?" she asked.

"Me," Kristen said.

"Do you wear a watch on your left or right hand?" Sarah asked.

"I don't wear a watch…" Kristen said.

"There are some buttons on mine. Should I press them?" Matt asked.

"NO!" everyone replied.

"We don't know what it is. Don't do anything until it's daylight and we can see what we are dealing with," Andrew said.

"Fine," Matt said. They could all hear the irritation in his voice.

"Hey. I have my GPS," Matt said, "they didn't find it. Cool."

"What?" Sarah asked.

"I bought a small GPS unit and put it in my cigarette pack. They didn't find it."

"Matt – that's a violation of the rules…" Kristen said.

"Does anyone really give a flying rat's ass about the rules? I mean, come on – we don't even know where we are…" Matt said.

No one answered him.

"Let's just all wait until morning and we have a better idea of what we are dealing with," Andrew said.

Sarah tried to close her eyes and rest. She knew she would need it but sleep never came, and morning arrived several hours later. Someone was snoring.

Chapter 10

They all stayed motionless until it became light enough to see around the room.

"Someone please tell me that whatever was on the floor is gone," Kristen said.

Ralph rolled over and looked underneath the cots, which were about eighteen inches off the floor.

"Snakes," he said, and pointed under Matt's bunk. Matt was still snoring.

Kristen didn't move. She lay on her back, frozen.

Andrew bent over to look.

"Any idea what kind?" he asked.

"No. Never seen them before – but by their markings I would say they are probably dangerous. At the least, they could bite."

"How big are they?" Sarah asked. She tried to control her voice but they could all hear the slight quiver.

"About four to five feet," Ralph said. He was the only one that didn't sound overly concerned.

"Oh, God," Kristen said.

"No. God has nothing to do with it," Sarah said, "we however, need to figure out how to get out of here." She had command of her voice back.

Andrew looked around the room. The cots were separated by a few feet of space between them, and formed a cross with Matt's cot in the middle. The only door to the room was near Kristen. They could just walk across the cots without ever touching the floor.

"Ralph, will they attack if we leave them be?" he asked.

"Doubt it. We have copperheads and rattler's back home. If you just give them space they don't want to have anything to do with you," he said.

"Who wants to wake up Matt?" Sarah asked.

"You mean without him freaking out and getting bit?" Andrew asked.

"That would be the kind thing – yes," she said.

"Fine. I think it's better if a woman's voice did it. Kristen?" he asked.

Kristen turned toward Matt.

"Matt!" She waited a moment and looked around for something to throw at him. She finally pulled a splinter off of a piece of wood and threw it. It hit him in the face.

"Huh?" Matt rubbed his right palm against his cheek.

"Wake up!" Kristen said.

"Huh? Oh. What's…." Matt sat up in his cot, his eyes wide open as he looked at Kristen.

"Don't move, Matt," she said. He froze in place.

"Listen carefully. There are two snakes under your bed," she said. He looked down without moving his head "You need to calmly stand up on your cot and hop over to one of the other beds. Got it?" she asked.

"Uh huh," he said, as he stood up. He had to bend over so as not to hit his head. Ralph motioned for him to come his way, and Matt took a quick look towards the floor before jumping over. Ralph steadied him and they both sat down and looked back under Matt's cot. The snakes were awake but had not yet moved. One of them looked directly at Matt and Ralph and the other uncoiled and slithered in the opposite direction.

"I hate snakes!" Matt said.

"OK. Now that we are all awake – let's get out of here," Andrew said, as he stepped over to Kristen's bunk and tried the door. It swung away from him, but what he saw didn't make him feel any better. On top of that, the thing on his arm started beeping.

Andrew stepped out of the room followed by Matt, Kristen, Sarah and then Ralph. Ralph made sure the door was shut behind them, and they all looked around. They were outside, in a small clearing. What looked from the inside like a single room was actually a stand-alone hut with metal siding. The clearing extended about fifty feet on all four sides of the structure. There were several other small buildings scattered about the property, and a single wooden bench.

The beeping on Andrews's wrist drew his attention and he examined the bracelet. It was made of some kind of black metal with a display on the front running along the band. He looked at the back to see if he could find a means of removing it, but didn't see anything that looked like a locking mechanism. The other four contestants examined theirs as well, however Andrew's was the only one that was beeping, so they gathered around him. The display scrolled down in a continuous loop. It simply read:

"Go to the bench and read the letter."

Andrew looked around the clearing and saw a bench about twenty feet away, next to what appeared to be an outhouse of some kind. On the bench they found a piece of plastic held down by a large stone. It was a letter addressed to the five of them. They all gathered around to read it.

Friends,

Your adventure has begun. As you can see, you are in a remote location somewhere in the world. Your goal is to complete certain tasks, which will be delivered to you by your wristbands, or by personal messenger. You are not allowed to remove these bands, as they are there for communication as well as your safety. Removing of any of the bands will result in serious adverse consequences. You are not allowed to have, or use, any electronic devices. If you are caught using any such devices you will be penalized. The ultimate goal is to make your way back to Grand Cayman no later than December fourteenth, while successfully completing every task given to you. It is now December 4, 2004. Remember, you are a group. Any failure by an individual is a failure of the group.

Your first task is to figure out what country you are presently in. We advise that you head west until you arrive at the first river (not stream). Follow the river south until you reach the first village. In the village, you will find a man with a bamboo hat who sells fruit. Your second task is to change his life so that he is viewed as someone different than he was before.

Welcome to day one.

Andrew finished reading the note and looked at the group. He immediately noticed that Ralph was about ten feet away putting a short stick in the sand. The stick made a shadow from the sun and

Ralph marked the tip of it with a pebble, then walked back to the group.

The heat was already nearly unbearable, and the humidity was soaking all of their shirts. Matt took his off and everyone could see that he had nipple rings as well. It made Kristen wince.

"It's so beautiful here," Kristen said, "look at the foliage!"

"We'll, that's not what I would have said, but I guess it is," Andrew said.

"It looks like a big problem to me," Sarah said. "Has it occurred to anyone that we don't have any of our gear? No clothing, no tools, for that matter – no food or water."

"That would appear to be the case," Ralph said.

Kristen walked over to where the jungle began and picked something off of a tree. It looked like a brown string bean on steroids. She peeled back the skin and tasted it.

"Are you nuts?" Matt said, "it might be poisonous."

"Nope. It's called tamarind," Kristen said. She pulled the fruit husk apart further, and took another bite. "Sweet," she stopped for a moment and looked at the group. Her eyes were wide.

"What? Are you OK?" Sarah asked, as she took a step forward.

"Yes. Yes, I'm fine," Kristen said.

"So, how do you know what that is?" Sarah asked.

"I have a Filipino friend who gave it to me once, " Kristen said.

"Oh! So are we in the Philippines?" Sarah asked. Everyone started to get excited.

"No. I'm not sure. This stuff grows all over Southeast Asia as well…" Kristen said.

"Still, we now have a better idea where we are. Nice job Kristen," Andrew said.

"And we have at least *some* food," Ralph said, as he walked over to join her. He picked one off the tree and tasted it. "Not too bad."

"I remember someone saying something about sour in the South and sweet in the North… I wish I could remember what that meant…" Kristen took one more bite of the fruit and tossed the remnants on the ground. "See. Paradise!" she said. No one replied to her.

"And what about water?" Matt said, as he looked around. "Anyone have any? I'm *famished* and thirsty."

"Might want to stop partaking of that righteous weed while we are out here," Ralph said to Matt. Andrew and Sarah looked at each other. Ralph was surprising them.

"God. I feel like I've just walked on to Survivor Thailand. Only I don't see the television crews," Matt said. "What's with that anyway?" He wasn't speaking to anyone in particular, so everyone ignored him, except Kristen.

"Actually, Matt. This may *be* Thailand," she said. Her comment made everyone look at him, and he smiled, holding out his arms.

"What? You guys just think I'm some stoner? I got skills! You'll see." Matt walked around like a rooster for a moment until Andrew changed the subject.

"What was that about, Ralph?" Andrew asked, pointing to the stick.

"Old Boy Scout trick. It will tell us which hemisphere we are in, and which way is east and west," Ralph replied.

"Forget that," Matt said, as he pulled out a very small electronic device. "I'll tell you where we are." He pushed a button and waited.

"Matt, put that away! We are prohibited from using that thing and, after all we've been through, I'm not going to let you blow this on day one," Andrew said.

"Take a walk, then. I'm finding out where we are," Matt replied. The group looked at each other and Andrew opened his mouth to speak when a large crack sounded. Everyone looked around to see where it came from.

Ralph had dropped to the ground.

"Gun shot," he said, "Oh my God." Ralph pointed to Matt who was still standing with the miniature GPS in his hand but there was something wrong with his face. It was frozen as if in shock. A bit of blood appeared at the corner of his mouth, and Matt tried to say something before he fell forward to his knees, then flat on his face. The sound of his head hitting the ground was like dropping a bowling ball on wood.

Kristen screamed at the sight of the back of his head. It was torn apart like someone had taken a machete to it.

"Get down!" Ralph screamed. Everyone hit the ground and lay prone. They looked to Ralph for direction.

"We need to get cover," he said, as he got up and ran into the nearest part of the jungle. The rest of the group followed him till he stopped, about fifteen feet into the bush. It was so dense they could hardly see anything. Sarah was churning her feet in case there were snakes.

"What the hell was that about?" Andrew said.

Kristen had her hand over her mouth, her eyes filled with fear.

"They killed him," Ralph said.

"*Who* killed him?" Andrew asked.

Just then his bracelet started beeping, and the four of them again found themselves staring at his wrist. It was the second time in five minutes.

Chapter 11

"Are you going to read it?" Sarah asked. Andrew had his hand over it to mute the beeping. He turned it over to her.

"We are very sorry for the loss of Matt. Unfortunately, we failed to mention...." Sarah had to wait until the display scrolled, "the woods are full of bandits and smugglers. You must be careful." She waited longer, but nothing appeared.

"That's it?" Ralph asked.

"Why would they kill Matt? And if it wasn't them, how the hell do they already know?" Sarah asked no one in particular. She had stopped moving her feet.

"Look, Obviously these things are some kind of locator," Andrew pointed to his wrist. "They must have cameras here, or maybe these things are also cameras... who knows. Actually..." Andrew tried to fit a finger between the bracelet and the backside of his wrist, "they may be a medical monitor of some kind. If they had monitors, they would know that Matt's heart stopped. Whatever the case, we have to leave here. The question is, do we follow the directions, or bag this whole thing and just try and get gone?"

"Buut – they can–n-n't *kill* people," Kristen's eyes were filled with tears, and she looked at Andrew. He opened his arms and wrapped her up, holding her.

"It's OK, Kristen. Maybe it was just a coincidence. We're going to be OK. I promise you." He pulled back, and wiped a tear from her cheek with his thumb. "Take some deep breaths," he synchronized his breathing with hers, then turned back toward the group.

"So, what's it going to be?" he said.

"I say we forget this whole thing and just leave," Ralph said.

"To where? How?" Sarah asked. She could finally feel her heart start to slow down.

"I don't know...wait..." Ralph made his way slowly back to the clearing then returned.

"That is west," he pointed to deeper inside the jungle, "that is east," he pointed to where they had come from. "We are in the Northern Hemisphere. It's not a lot of information, but we can at least pick a direction and go while we have daylight," he said.

"Do we really have a choice?" Andrew said. "We have to follow the directions, at least until we get to civilization. We're sitting ducks out here."

"They could be lying…" Sarah said.

"Yes. But that would make this a really short adventure and I assume they want us to live, at least for a while. What good is dead entertainment?" Andrew said.

"Then again, these people… who knows what gets them off," Ralph said.

"Well, unless anyone has a better idea, I say we head west," Andrew said.

Sarah and Ralph both agreed. They all looked at Kristen, who was still in shock. Andrew put his arm around her.

"OK, what are our assets?" he asked.

"At least we all have long pants and shoes with socks. We need to stuff our pants legs into the socks for some kind of protection against insects," Ralph said. Andrew and Sarah bent over and did as he instructed. When he was done Andrew helped Kristen who stood motionless.

"How do we tell what direction is west from in here?" Sarah asked.

They all looked around and realized they could tell it was daylight but nothing else. The canopy seemed to go up about twenty feet.

"Hang here. I'll be back," Andrew said, and started climbing a tree whose trunk went up past the canopy.

"Ralph, how do you know we are in the Northern Hemisphere?" Sarah asked.

"The shadow moves clockwise in the North, counter clockwise in the South," he said.

"Oh," Sarah replied, "where did you learn all this?"

"Boy Scouts. I almost made it to an Eagle Scout. I don't remember much but I have a feeling I'm going to wish I had studied harder," he said.

Kristen looked at him.

"Water?" she asked. Sarah thought it was a strange question. However, with the amount of perspiration coming off of her body, she realized she was quite parched as well. Ralph looked around and saw a cluster of bamboo.

"OK. Let's see if my scout master was right." He went over to an older cracked bamboo and gently peeled back the paper. "Here." He waived them both to come over and he bent the stalk over. "Open your mouth," he said.

Kristen obediently tilted her head sideways and he poured out a clear liquid into her mouth. He did the same thing for Sarah.

"Hey. Not bad. It's water," she said, then found another stalk and repeated it on her own.

Ralph did it a couple of more times for Kristen, then twice for himself.

"I'm glad we have you, Ralph," Sarah said. For the first time, she meant it.

They heard Andrew hop down from the tree, and he walked over.

"What's with all the bamboo?" he asked.

"Show him," Sarah said. Ralph repeated the task.

"Fantastic," Andrew said, "we have water and food." He wiped his mouth off, then pointed.

"So, that way is west. There is a mountain in that direction. We'll have to check if we are on course during the hike," he said.

"Now. What are our assets?" Andrew asked.

"Our clothing is at least protective. We should keep it on no matter how hot we get. I imagine we will get exposed to many kinds of potential infections. Let's hope those shots were real. Andrew, you have a belt and so do I." Andrew looked down toward his stomach as Ralph spoke.

"We could really use a knife of some kind and a way to make fire. I don't suppose anyone has that?" he asked.

"I bet Matt had a lighter or at least some matches," Sarah said, but no one moved.

"I'll check, "Andrew said. "I hope whoever was out there is long gone." He wandered back to the clearing.

"Please be careful, " Kristen said. He turned back and kissed her on her cheek, then walked off as quietly as he could.

"Do you know each other?" Sarah asked Kristen.

"Uh… kind of. We're… friends," Kristen said.

"Oh. Did they know that?" Sarah asked.

"No. Well, at least I didn't tell them," she answered.

"Sorry. I didn't mean to pry, it's just…"

Hurried panting and footsteps from the direction of the clearing interrupted her.

"Got it," Andrew reappeared with a lighter.

"Good. We're going to need that. Especially tonight if we're still stuck out here," Ralph said.

"I don't suppose you..." Ralph said. Andrew looked at him and shook his head.

"No way I was going to touch that thing," he said. They both turned to look at the girls and Sarah put her hand inside her shirt and withdrew something that looked like a thick credit card. She showed it to the three.

"It has a knife and some other tools. My friend gave it to me before I came. She had just watched a reality show where they stranded a bunch of contestants without notice. Boy, am I glad she's a TV holic," Sarah said.

Ralph took it from her and withdrew the knife. It was as sharp as a razor blade. "Well, look, we could be in a lot worse shape. All in all we have a good chance."

Everyone wanted to ask 'at what', but no one did.

"Should we do something about... you know... him," Sarah jerked her head back towards Matt.

"We should at least bury him, don't you think?" Kristen said, but she was shaking as the words stumbled out.

"Look. There is nothing we can do for him and the longer the time we spend hanging around here the more likely it is whoever did that will come looking for us," Andrew said.

"I agree. Kristen, we need to go, " Sarah said. Kristen just nodded her head.

"This way." Ralph took the lead and turned sideways as he started through the jungle. The group followed.

After about thirty minutes they stopped at a cropping of bamboo and drank water. Andrew climbed another tree.

"Are we going to live?" Kristen asked.

"Sure honey, we're going to live, but we all need to keep our heads cool. Can you do that?" Sarah was just a bit patronizing but Kristen didn't notice it. She nodded in consent.

"Ralph, you didn't say if you had anything with you." Sarah said.

"I wasn't as prepared as you, Sarah. I only have this," he pulled out a picture from his shirt pocket and handed it to her. It was of his family.

"That might be just as important to keep us focused, Ralph," she said, as she looked around.

"Kristen, do you think that is edible? I'm getting really hungry." The question seemed to help focus Kristen's mind and she looked around slowly.

"That. Over there," she pointed to a tree with a small pale appendage.

"What is it?" Sarah asked.

"It's a cashew tree," Kristen said. I saw one in an art class once. The whole thing is edible," she walked over to it, plucked off the nut and ate it. "Needs some salt, but it's good!" she said. Sarah walked over and did likewise.

Kristen pulled off a fruity looking thing and took a bite.

"I've never tasted this before, but it's not bad. Cashew fruit," she handed it to Sarah who smelled it and took a tentative bite. She frowned a little but tried it again.

"It's edible," Sarah said.

Andrew reappeared.

"How come every time I leave someone finds food or water?" he asked. They all laughed. It felt good to break the tension.

"It's a cashew tree," Sarah said.

Andrew walked over and suddenly slapped his neck. It made the girls jump.

"Am I the only one getting eaten alive?" Andrew asked, as he pulled his hand away and flicked off the mosquito.

"They must like to eat oriental, " Sarah said, then added: "Sorry. Bad joke."

Andrew ate a couple of nuts and took the fruit Kristen offered.

"So we are a little off course," he pointed about twenty degrees south of the route they had been taking. "That way," he said. This time he led. The girls followed and Ralph took up the rear.

"Perhaps we should stop more often and check the route so we don't get too far off course?" Sarah asked, as they walked.

"Only if you want to climb the next tree." Andrew turned toward her and grinned. She didn't verbally respond, but he could tell she didn't think it was too funny.

"I need a bathroom," Kristen's comment stopped the group's progress. She looked sheepish.

"Well, I don't know what to tell you. This whole place is one big outhouse. Pick a spot," Ralph said.

"Uh. I don't suppose anyone has any tissue?" Kristen asked.

They all looked at each other.

"Nope. Lot's of leaves though. Don't pick anything red. It could be poisonous. Stick with the broad leaf green things. They're likely safe," Ralph said.

"OK," Kristen said, "Um… Sarah? Could you come with me?" she asked.

"Sure, Kristen," she said. "We'll be right back," Sarah said, as she followed Kristen a little way off.

That left Ralph and Andrew waiting in silence. They could hear strange sounds emanating from all around them in the woods, sounds they hadn't heard because of their own noises. They both found it unsettling. There were obviously animals around them but they hadn't seen any of them, which made them nervous. It definitely felt as if something was following them.

Chapter 12

"Do you have any children?" Ralph asked. He much preferred the familiar sounds of talking to that of the jungle.

"No," Andrew said.

"Why not?" Ralph said.

Andrew found it a little strange that another man wouldn't know the reason. "I guess I just had other things I wanted to do right now," he said, then reflected, "and I guess the right woman hasn't presented herself."

"What about Kristen?" Ralph asked.

"I like her. She's a great friend, but children? No. I don't think so," Andrew said. He actually had not thought of her in that context until now. It helped him clear up some things.

"Why all the interest?" Andrew asked.

"I don't know, just curious. I love my kids," Ralph said.

They could hear the girls making their way back and they waited for them to appear.

Andrew wanted to make a remark but decided the moment wasn't appropriate. He started walking again, and Sarah followed him. He could hear Kristen and Ralph talking behind him as they moved.

The walk through the jungle was slow and painful. By mid morning they all had small scratches, bruises and bites. They finally came upon a rudimentary trail that headed in the general direction they wanted, and it provided some relief. Ralph had taken the lead and was beating the brush to notify any local residents of their proximity. Although they were not in the direct sunlight, the canopy created a cover that was smothering. The air was hot and thick. It felt just like a sauna.

As they crawled under a fallen tree, Kristen stood back up and grabbed the trunk.

"I'm really dizzy," she said.

Ralph yelled out to Andrew and Sarah, whom he could hear but no longer see. They returned in a few moments.

"I think we should take a rest," he said.

Andrew looked reflexively at his wristband to check the time, but it was blank.

"How long do you figure we've been going?" He asked.

"I don't know, about three hours or so," Ralph said. He had found some bamboo and was helping Kristen get a drink.

"Sarah, would you mind gathering some of the cashew fruit or what about some of that?" he pointed to a yellow green globe that looked like a porcupine.

Kristen looked up. "Jackfruit, I've eaten that before."

"Wow, Kristen, you never cease to surprise me," Andrew said, as he walked over to the tree and carefully removed one of the prickly orbs. He carried it back over to them.

"Can I borrow your knife, Sarah?" She had already removed it from it's sheath and handed it to him. The insides of the fruit looked like large chestnut seeds. It had a pungent smell, but tasted a bit like pineapple and banana.

"Not bad," Andrew said. He gave some to Kristen and then handed the open fruit to Sarah. She peeled off a seed and bit into it.

"So, any ideas as to what we should do if we have to camp out here," Andrew asked.

The question caused Kristen to look up at him, then around at the surroundings. There was absolutely no way to have any protection from animals if they were stuck there overnight.

Sarah looked up at a large tree.

"We could always climb a tree," she said.

"I hate to point this out, but look over there," Ralph used his forefinger and pointed up at the canopy.

"What? I don't see anything." Kristen tried in vain to follow his finger from where she sat but finally gave up and aligned herself with his arm.

"Oh!..No! We can't do that," she said. A green snake with a black head moved slowly from a branch. She started to tremble.

"I agree. I've had enough of those things for a lifetime," Andrew said, as he walked over to Kristen and took her hand. "Let's just keep going until we find a better place." He started walking again, and Kristen stayed with him.

Ralph took up the rear position and hung back just slightly. Something was bothering him. It was almost as if there was an echo to each step that he made. He stopped suddenly and spun around and slowly looked at the forest behind him. He could hear Andrew's voice but concentrated on the surrounding sounds. The density of the jungle only allowed him about a fifteen-foot radius in which to look, and he saw nothing. He turned around and touched the pocket with his family's picture in it, then jogged to catch up with the group. Whatever it was, he was sure that he didn't want to be in the jungle when night came.

They went on until they were nearly exhausted. It wasn't just the physical walking but the heat became unbearable. It felt as if they were breathing fire into their lungs. Kristen sat down and started to cry. It was too hot to touch her, so Sarah stood by and waited. Andrew walked up to Ralph and motioned for them to move off out of earshot.

"Any ideas? I don't think she's going to make it much farther," Andrew said.

"I can see that. I just don't really want to spend the night here." Ralph looked around his eyes were wide with intensity. Andrew couldn't tell if it was the exhaustion or something else.

"Is there something you haven't told me?" Andrew asked.

Ralph looked at him and unconsciously touched his family's picture again. Andrew had noticed him doing it often during the day. It was like Catholics and their crosses.

"I think something is following us," Ralph said. "I tried to catch a glimpse of it several times… I swear that something is there."

Andrew looked at him. He, too, had the feeling but he didn't want to add to the panic.

"Should we make some weapons? If we stop now we waste time that could potentially take us to somewhere more protected. If we don't and get caught in the dark here…." Andrew looked worried as well.

"Mel was right. I shouldn't have come," Ralph said, speaking to the jungle.

"Ralph!" Andrew's voice turned him around. "Look, you've been a lifesaver so far. We need you to keep it together. Give us some ideas." Andrew saw the fear in Ralph's eyes dissipate a little.

"I suppose we should at least make a couple of spears. There are plenty of branches around. They can be sharpened on a stone… like that one," he pointed to a ragged stone a few feet away. Andrew picked out two four-foot branches, about an inch in diameter, and handed them to Ralph. "Here, sharpen these two. I'm going to have a talk with the girls."

Andrew walked back to where they were. Kristen was still sitting on the log but had stopped crying. Sarah stood beside her.

"You OK?" Andrew asked. Kristen looked up at him. Her eyes were red. He wasn't sure if it was due to the crying or the constant stuff that had been hitting them in the face.

"Yes, I guess I'm really not cut out for this…" she said.

"None of us want to be here, Kristen. I certainly don't. I can't even figure out what we are doing. This whole thing doesn't seem like any reality show at all. I feel like I've been dropped into a combination of the story of Nimrod and the Island of Dr. Moreau. I don't know what to think... then there is the whole thing about Matt..." Sarah said. She stopped at Andrew's prompting.

"Kristen. We really need to try and make it a little farther. Do you think you can go a bit more?" Andrew asked.

Kristen looked up from her seat with sad eyes. Her skin was covered in red blotches and her hair was a complete mess. Andrew refrained from making a comment and held out his hand. She grabbed it and got up to her feet slowly.

"OK," she said, "any idea of how much daylight is left?" It was a question that they all had thought but no one wanted to ask it out loud. The jungle was already starting to lose it's light.

Ralph appeared with the two spears and handed one to Andrew. Sarah looked at both of them but said nothing. She picked out her own branch and started removing the twigs.

"The good news is – I think I hear running water. That way," he pointed in the direction they had been walking. "Let's go," he took off at a fast pace, and Sarah and Kristen followed him. Andrew took up the rear. Within a few yards he knew what Ralph meant. It felt like something was watching them. Andrew grabbed his spear with both hands and walked loudly behind the girls.

About fifty yards later Ralph stopped and held up his hand. Kristen immediately grabbed Sarah's arm and Andrew turned around to check behind them.

"Listen," Ralph said. They all strained to eliminate all extraneous sounds and concentrate on a faint rushing sound.

"Water," Ralph said, "it can't be too far away." He took off once again and this time the group eagerly followed him.

Within another hundred yards they broke out onto a muddy beach. A wide river lay in front of them. It was murky and carried lots of flotsam, but Kristen was so hot she didn't care. She waded into it and cupped the liquid over her body. The sun was going down behind them, reflecting a burnt orange on the opposite bank.

"Um. Kristen. We don't know how safe the water is. There could be..." Ralph started saying. Kristen was waist deep and turned to look at him. Her smile turned to a frown.

"I mean, I'm sure it's fine but there could be piranha's or..." it was all she needed hear and she barreled out of the water. Ralph dropped the subject and they all stood by the bank and used their hands to provide some refreshment.

"Don't drink it," Ralph said. They had already figured that out.

"Now what? Shouldn't we make some kind of shelter?" Sarah asked.

"We need to build a fire and some kind of protection," Ralph said.

"You and Kristen gather as much dried wood as you can and pile it here, include some twigs and dried moss if you can find some," Ralph said.

"I'll start working on something larger for a shelter of some kind," Andrew said. "Sarah, after you're done with the firewood, see if you can find some food."

Within thirty minutes they had made a makeshift lean-to with the back of the hut to the jungle and the fire pit in front of them. Andrew had gathered some large leaves and laid them down on the bank for mats. Ralph worked on getting the fire started with Matt's lighter. Sarah had found enough cashew and jack fruit to hold them over, although she was worried about the diuretic effect of too much fruit. Still, they didn't really have much choice.

By the time the fire was going it was pitch dark outside. The back of the lean-to made them feel a little safer, but none of them deceived themselves into thinking they would sleep well.

"I think we should take turns keeping watch," Ralph said, as he looked at Andrew. They sat a few feet away from each other and the light from the flames danced on his face.

"I agree. I'll take the first watch. You want the next?" Andrew asked.

"Sure," Ralph said, but Sarah interrupted him.

"I'll take it," she said. Andrew looked at her and saw no hesitation. She hid her fear well, he thought.

"Ok. I'll take the third, wake me up," Ralph said.

"What should I do if I see or hear something?" Sarah asked. Andrew and Ralph looked at each other.

"Uhh. I guess wake us up," Ralph said, as he ate a couple of cashews and stoked the fire.

"It's really important that the fire is kept alive," he paused and considered if he should explain it further, but Kristen had already lain down on the leaves and it looked like she was sleeping. He figured Sarah and Andrew could deduce the reasons for themselves. Ralph took a position behind Kristen and lay on his side facing her back. Sarah worked on cutting a jackfruit open and gave half of it to Andrew.

"Are you doing OK?" he asked, as he bit into a fleshy seed.

"Yea. I'm OK. Not what I expected, but I'm OK," she said.

"You ever lose control?" he asked. Sarah looked at him. Her blue eyes looked brown in the firelight.

"No," she said.

"Must be kind of hard."

"Not really. You just have to tell yourself to not go there."

"Have you always dealt with life that way?" he asked.

"Yes. It's the only way I know how."

"And you? How do you choose to deal with... this?" she looked around them. He could hear the river lapping at the bank and Andrew gazed toward the darkness.

"Just think it through. I've learned that most of the time either the best alternative presents itself or you only have one option and you take it. This is one of those times. No use thinking about what you would prefer to happen. I mean, I'd much rather be in a Four Seasons than eating tree grubs..."

"Hmmm..." Sarah lay down on her side, facing him, and looked up at his face as he added wood to the fire. He had a kind face, but she had no doubt that he also had a rock solid will. She couldn't decide if that was a good thing or bad.

:

Andrew watched her fall asleep. He was surprised at how quickly they were all unconscious and snoring, and he smiled to himself. The physical and emotional exertions might even provide him a needed rest but, for right now, his senses were acutely aware of his surroundings. Every few minutes he heard something larger than a rodent move in the forest behind him, there were all sorts of muted noises and chirping from the woods and, once in awhile, something in the river would cause a splash. Strangely enough, the small sounds were actually comforting.

Andrew reviewed what had happened that day… Where they had woken up, the wristbands, Matt's death, which he was convinced was not coincidental. He knew that this was not something scripted by TV executives. He was absolutely sure that it was some sick game, however he couldn't figure out what Mr. Baldwin and his compatriots wanted of them. Sooner or later the group would be faced with the decision of whether to continue being marionettes or go their own way. Would Mr. Baldwin kill them all if they did that? It scared him that he didn't know the answer.

He looked at the group in front of him. Ralph had been full of surprises, all in all, good ones. He wondered, though, if push came to shove, whether Ralph would be a team player or look after his own skin. Unlike the rest of them, Ralph had a family and it was obvious that they were the most important things in his life. Then there was Kristen. He really liked her. He loved her temperament, her creativity her laughter. But he had to admit she didn't do all that well under pressure, though without her they would have been a lot hungrier that day. He was not sure she had the mental control to make it through much more, and that concerned him. Sarah's comment about children earlier had made him look at Kristen in a whole other light. He had no doubt she would be a fabulous, but haphazard and disorganized, mother and he had to admit that was not a life that sat well with him.

Sarah was another story. He had never met a woman like her. She was independent, ambitious, intelligent, but at the same time detached from her feelings. For some reason she felt like she had to be in control of herself or she would fail. She wanted to be thought of as an equal, a partner, and she was driven by an objective, though he wasn't sure if that objective included the group or not. He wondered where that personality had developed from.

71

His thoughts consumed him for an unknown period of time until something shook him from his mental journey. He looked around at the darkness and had a hard time putting his finger on what had changed, but something was definitely different. He looked at Ralph and considered waking him up, but decided against it. Suddenly the noises of the jungle came back to life as if someone had turned on a sound machine and it occurred to him what had happened. For a moment everything had gone silent. It sent a shiver up his spine. He could only imagine what would cause that.

Chapter 13

Andrew attempted to occupy his mind by picking out unique sounds and trying to figure out what kind of creature could be making them, but after a couple of hours his attempts only resulted in him getting even more tired. When he couldn't last any longer, he lightly touched Sarah on her shoulder and she opened her eyes. He knew they were intense blue but in the shadow light they almost looked black.

"I'm sorry, but I can't last any longer," Andrew said. Sarah sat up and rubbed her eyes.

"How long was I out?" she asked quietly.

"I think a couple of hours but I'm not sure," Andrew said.

"Go ahead and lie down. I'll be OK, " she said. Andrew thought there was almost sadness in her voice.

"Are you sure?" he asked, though he knew that he had no choice.

"Yes, I'll be fine."

Andrew looked at her eyes for a moment and she didn't turn away. He felt as if she was reaching out to him to tell him something, but couldn't find the words. It was an unusual feeling for him.

"I do need to tell you something… but don't be too alarmed, it's probably nothing serious. I think there is a large animal nearby. If the forest suddenly becomes quiet, wake me or Ralph up," he said.

She didn't even flinch when he said it but he could see her mind working.

"OK," she finally said.

Andrew lay down and looked up at her. She put a couple of logs on the fire and sat with her legs crossed. Her spear was next to her right hand. Andrew closed his eyes and, despite all his misgivings, fell asleep.

Sarah watched him until his breathing became deep and regular, then looked at the rest of the group. Of the three she was most disturbed by Andrew, not because of anything he had done, but because of the feelings that he elicited in her, feelings she was not accustomed to. They made her uncomfortable and, at the same time, she liked feeling them. In the past such feelings would have never even been allowed to surface. She would have controlled their appearance by simply willing them away. This time, for whatever reason, she was not fully able to do so. That disturbed her more than the situation they were in. And it was quite a situation. She had started off the 'adventure' viewing it as a large goal with a series of smaller challenges. It was a way she was used to approaching obstacles. It worked for her. Her personal goal was clear in her mind, however she now found herself wondering if the goal was even obtainable and, if it weren't, it would mean she would fail... and she *couldn't* fail. She couldn't allow that. It just wasn't an option.

Ralph and Kristen were good people. They had provided needed support and information, and she was sure they would continue to do so, but she and Andrew were the key. She didn't know whether she could learn to trust Andrew completely, like she trusted herself, but she had already determined that she would not be able to do that with Ralph and Kristen.

:

Sarah's attention was drawn back to the surroundings by a splash that she heard in the water a few feet away, and then another. Soon it sounded like dozens of animals were running into the river but she couldn't see any of them. It was then that the jungle became completely silent.

She grabbed her stake with her hand and sat perfectly still. Andrew was still breathing heavily on her left, as were Ralph and Kristen on her right. She added more fuel to the fire and it increased in brightness, which enabled her to see a little farther but, other than the riverbank, she saw nothing. Even the water had become silent. Sarah used the stake to push her up to a bent over position and peered over the back of the lean to. It was so dark that she couldn't even see the trees that were no more than ten feet off. She looked down at Andrew but decided not to wake him just yet. She needed to figure out what was going on.

The shadow crossed no more than three feet away. It was large and moved with deliberate slowness. Sarah clenched the stake with both hands and pointed it in the direction of the animal, but it was already gone. She used her foot to touch Andrew and she watched him immediately open his eyes. Without moving he looked up at her and she nodded. Andrew picked up his stake and then grabbed a branch from the fire and stood up. Their shoulders were touching and he whispered in her ear.

"Did you see something?" he asked. She nodded. He looked at her hands on the stake. They were strangling the piece of wood.

"Where?"

"Right here, about three feet away. Something very large, it didn't act scared at all," her voice quivered and belied her stance.

Andrew took the branch and used the ember on the end of it in order to light up the riverbank on the other side of the lean to. There were a series of very large prints in the ground. Andrew and Sarah looked at each other.

"Some kind of large cat," Andrew said. "I think we should wake up Ralph." Sarah bent over and tapped him with her stake. He didn't respond and she did it again.

"What?!" Ralph said, and flipped over to his back, his hands shielding his eyes.

"Quiet!" Andrew whispered.

Sarah bent over and put her hands on his chest.

"We need your help," she said. Ralph's eyes got wide as he realized where he was and he quickly got to his feet. Andrew pointed out the prints.

"They look like cougar prints, only much larger," Ralph whispered and looked at Andrew, obviously concerned. "Could be a lion or tiger. I've heard about tigers in Southeast Asia that hunt humans." As soon as he said it he turned to look at Sarah.

"I've already figured out we are in some deep shit," Sarah said. "What do we do?"

Andrew looked at her quizzically. It was the first time he had seen a break in her emotional armor.

"I don't know. All cats are supposed to be scared of fire but I have no idea."

They all froze as a rumble rolled over the water. It was like a menacing purr. Sarah turned around to face it and suddenly the sound occurred again, only this time behind them toward the jungle. Andrew faced the new threat. Ralph took a burning branch from the fire and threw it on the ground about five feet away. The outline of a very large cat appeared momentarily and then disappeared into the distance.

"What's going on?" Kristen said, way too loud.

"Shssh!" Ralph said.

"Wha —" Sarah bent over and covered her mouth. "Quiet Kristen, we have company."

Kristen looked frantic and she twisted herself around to face whatever Ralph was looking at. There was nothing Sarah could do to help her, so she took her place with her back to Andrew's. Everyone stood perfectly still. A couple of frogs started croaking in the distance and the reassuring sound allowed the four of them to gather their thoughts and take a breath. Andrew turned toward Ralph and opened his mouth to say something when a piercing roar broke through the air and all of them hit the ground. Kristen pulled her legs into her chest and was mumbling something. Sarah and Andrew were on their knees looking at the direction of the sound. Ralph pulled another branch from the fire and threw it out in front of Sarah. It landed on the beach, casting a flickering light far enough so they could see the edge of the jungle. They all saw the movement and realized, too late, that the two glowing spots just beyond the growth line were eyes.

The tiger moved as if on air and hurled itself at Andrew, who stepped in front of Sarah at the last second. His stake caught the cat slightly askew and Sarah heard it snap as the cat fell on top of Andrew. His breath was expunged from his lungs from the weight of the beast. At the instant that Andrew's back hit the ground, Ralph jumped over the sitting Kristen and tried to take aim with his stake, but everything was a blur of man and fur.

Andrew was screaming and Sarah was trying to beat the cat with her stake. Ralph lunged at the big cat and felt the tip of the stake find something soft. There was a loud howl and the tiger paused long enough to look at Ralph. Andrew's shoulders were pinned by the animal's front paws and he had his head turned away from its mouth, his arms pressed like bars into its neck. The moment seemed frozen in time as the tiger bared his fangs at Ralph and gurgled a warning growl. Sarah took the opportunity and turned her stake on the cat, using all of her five foot four frame to thrust it at the side of the tiger. Instantly the beast howled and faced its new attacker.

Andrew was yelling something at them, but no one could understand what he was saying, and Sarah found herself petrified by fear. Her stake was still in her hands, the end bloodied by the puncture, but the cat was obviously just angrier, and was hissing and spitting at Sarah who stood just a few feet away. Ralph grabbed another branch from the fire and thrust the burning end into the cat's face. The tiger hit it with a paw but Ralph held on and pressed it further.

Finally it turned around and fled into the jungle.

Ralph and Sarah bent over Andrew. He was covered in mud and blood but they couldn't tell how seriously he was hurt.

Sarah cupped her hands around his face and looked at him. His eyes were vacant and for that moment she couldn't read anything in them, then the life seemed to return like a curtain being opened. He looked back at her.

"Are you OK?" Ralph said. It sounded so stupid as the words rolled off his lips.

They could see Andrew mentally check himself and then he looked back at Sarah, who still had her hands on him.

"I think so," he said. He moved his hands and felt the top of his legs and his chest.

"Does everything look like it's still here?" Andrew asked.

Ralph looked him over.

"Yes," he said, "can you move?"

Andrew put his hands to his side and pushed himself to a sitting position, he moved his neck around and looked at his torso.

"Any blood?" he asked.

"Yours? I can't really tell, " Sarah replied, "Perhaps you should rinse off with some water," she moved out of the way and Andrew got on his knees, then tried without success to stand up. He stayed there on his knees until Sarah came over and put her hand on his back.

"My legs are too weak," Andrew said.

Kristen had stopped crying and managed to crawl over to him.

"I'm sorry, Andrew. I'm so sorry. I just…" Kristen looked at the ground and Andrew sat back down and grabbed her arm.

"Don't worry, Kristen. I'm fine," he said.

"Let's hope it doesn't come back…" Andrew tried again to get to his feet and Sarah helped him walk to the water and wade in. After what had just happened, Piranha's didn't seem like the threat they had been a few hours earlier. Andrew washed himself off and returned to the fire where Ralph had remained, his stake in one hand and a glowing brand in the other.

"Thank you," Andrew said. Ralph looked at him and nodded. His face was hard, unemotional.

Kristen sat beside him and inspected his face, chest and arms. Incredibly, other than a few mildly deep scratches, he was unhurt.

None of them slept the rest of the night, and when dawn broke they headed down river.

After about an hour of walking a wristband starting beeping. They all gathered around Sarah and read the message.

> *"Good job. You have made it to the Wang river. Nice handling of that problem. Welcome to day two. A reward awaits you in the village. Go to the house of Nan."*

The group understood the hints about where they were. It just didn't seem to really matter anymore.

"Dammit! I don't want to follow these directions. I don't want to play this damn game! We were almost killed last night, and this idiot thinks we are going to comply with his instructions?" Ralph said.

It was obvious that they all felt the same way. But they were also acutely aware of the last time someone disobeyed the message. It had been less than twenty four hours ago.

No one responded and they continued walking. Andrew and Sarah led with Ralph and Kristen following.

Sarah caught up to Andrew and walked beside him on the riverbank.

"What went through your mind last night?" she asked.

"I thought I was going to die," Andrew said. "I realized how many more things I wanted to do."

"Like what?" she asked. Her voice was soft and she spoke toward the ground.

"Like fall in love and maybe have children, write a book, climb a mountain...." His voice drifted off.

"Did you think about your business?" she asked. He looked at her for a second.

"No. Never occurred to me," the question and his answer made him think.

"What about you?" Andrew asked.

"When the tiger turned to me, all I could think about was that I had so many things left that I needed to do."

"You *needed* or *wanted?*" Andrew asked. Sarah stopped walking for a second and looked at the river.

"Needed," she said. Andrew had stopped beside her. "I'm not sure if I see them as different," she said.

"A need is like having to eat something. A want is eating what brings you pleasure. A need is working as a janitor to pay your rent. A want is doing what you love to do," he said.

Kristen and Ralph were about twenty feet away, and Sarah started walking again. She found the conversation difficult enough to have with one person, let alone three.

"What do you love to do? What are your passions?" Andrew asked.

Sarah was silent for a while. "I guess I'm not sure. I thought they were to go to law school, become an attorney. I also have goals to master—my violin and my French," she paused long enough for Andrew to wonder if she was finished, and he opened his mouth, but she finally continued. "I want to be happy. I guess everyone wants that. I want to experience love, but I'm not sure I believe it exists in the state that we would be led to believe."

"Fair enough," Andrew said. He wanted to press further but didn't think it was the proper time.

"I have another thought about death and that whole experience," he said.

"Uh huh," Sarah looked at him.

"When the cat had me pinned, and I could feel its breath on my face, it occurred to me I wanted to be remembered for more than this," he waived his hand around. "I want to do something that will be worth...something."

"Like?" Sarah asked.

"Like... William Randolph Hearst, Henry Ford..." he said.

"But all those men were just rich..." she paused for a moment. "I guess that's not entirely true. They also changed the way people thought," Andrew continued the idea, "and they were philanthropists... OK, how about, Albert Einstein, Mother Theresa."

"So you want to change the world through science? Compassion? I'm sorry, but you don't seem the type," she looked at him and smiled.

"I just mean I want to do *something* with my life," he said, a bit defensively.

"I understand. I don't know if my goals reach that high," she said.

"Perhaps they should," he said.

"Perhaps."

:

Ralph and Kristen followed them at a measured distance.

"I'm sorry I froze last night. I always hated those scenes in the movies when the person can't run or scream, or anything. I guessed I wanted to believe that I would never react that way. I now know differently," she said.

"Don't spend too much time thinking about it. It's done and over," Ralph said.

"But we could have been killed, and I just sat there like a blithering idiot."

"Let me tell you a story: A man was riding a bicycle between cars and traffic in downtown Memphis. He had to be going about twenty miles per hour. I was standing on the curb as he passed, and I noticed that a taxi had just pulled over and a person was about to open the door right in front of him. My brain wanted to scream 'STOP!' or something, but all that came out was 'bad thing!' Remarkably the bicyclist actually heard what I had said and gave me the strangest look as he passed by. Unfortunately, and just as I feared, the cab passenger opened the door and the poor guy hit it full on and sailed over the window onto the pavement."

"Was he OK?" Kristen asked.

"Amazingly – yes," he got up and walked back to his bicycle, which was in a lot worse condition than he was. The point is that sometimes the brain freezes up and we just can't react like we think we should. I tell my kids this all the time. We are human and have limitations. Facing death is an extreme condition. Hopefully, one we don't face often."

"So what did you think about when it was happening?" she asked.

"You know, I didn't think a whole lot when it was happening, but afterwards I realized that I really wanted to be with my family. I think, in my mind, I was fighting for them," he said.

"In reality, I think you were. If something had happened to you it would be terrible for your family," Kristen said.

"Exactly," Ralph replied. "It also made me realize that there are a lot more important things than having a house. I guess that idea occurred to me a little late."

"Epiphany," Kristen said.

"What?" Ralph looked at her.

"Epiphany: Revelation, inspiration," she said. Ralph didn't answer.

"What would you do if you were home right now?" she asked.

Ralph smiled. "I would go into the kitchen and grab Melanie from behind and sit her on my lap."

"That's sweet."

"Then I would take the three kids out to the park and let them play with the dogs. They love dogs..." his voice drifted off.

"You love your wife?" she asked.

"Of course," he said, "what do you mean?"

"I was married. Thought I was in love with him. He turned out to be a real trip," Kristen said, "he always made fun of my ambitions, my art and music, and he told me it was a waste of time. I don't think it's a waste of time to do something you love."

"How long did it take you to realize he was the wrong man?" he asked. He thought about his wife and wondered if she had similar doubts.

"About seven years too long," she answered, "of course now I realize that he was just having self-esteem problems of his own. He was afraid if I succeeded I would have viewed him as less of a man."

"So you don't think a man is measured by his success?"

"Depends on what the definition of success is. I don't think it has anything to do with fame or fortune. It is the impact you have on other people's lives," she said.

"So that is why you paint? In order to impact peoples lives?"

"Yes. I love to have my work elicit emotions. Make them *feel* something. These artificial ecstasies that the world says will satisfy us really don't."

Sarah and Andrew had stopped in front of them and Kristen slowed her gait down.

"You believe in God?" Ralph asked.

"Yes. But not like the religions teach. I don't think God gives a flying rat's ass about money or huge cathedrals, and he certainly

81

doesn't give his smile of approval to terrorists who live by creating fear in other people."

"Like the situation we find ourselves in right now," Ralph said.

"Exactly," she said, "so do you believe in God?"

"I have to say I wasn't sure until the birth of my first son. Now I have no doubt," he said. She could hear the emotion in his voice.

"Devin," she said. He smiled in response.

"So you don't think much of people like Andrew?" she asked.

He looked at her. "No. That's not true. Andrew seems like a good guy." Ralph wondered how close their friendship really was. "He just has different priorities than me."

"I know. Me too. They say opposites attract," she said. Ralph didn't feel the need to comment on it.

∶

The group stopped for a break about mid day. The sun was burning hot, and they tried their best to use the shade of the foliage to get some rest. They all gathered some food and water and sat down on fallen trees or rocks to eat. The Wang River had gotten progressively wider and faster moving.

"Anyone have the foggiest idea how far to go?" Kristen asked.

No one replied.

"Guess not," she said, as she took a bite from a cashew fruit, "a hot bath would sure be nice…"

"Amen," Ralph said.

The comment made Sarah think about how she looked. She wasn't overly concerned with her personal appearance, however, as she observed her three companions, she could only imagine what a fright she must look like.

"And a *cold* glass of water," Andrew said.

"Well, this is a depressing conversation. Anyone think about a way out of this mess?" Sarah asked, to resounding silence.

"OK, then. Shall we carry on?" Andrew asked, as he got up. By the looks of the sun it was about mid-day. He broke off a large leaf and used it to shade his head. The others watched him and did the same thing.

After another hour or so the Wang River dumped into a much larger body of running water. The group followed it south for several miles. As they walked, they were starting to see evidence of humans, primitive roads and broken down carts and wagons littered the landscape, and the forest thinned out significantly. They followed a slow bend in the river and saw a small powerboat heading upstream with two boys in it. They looked to be around ten years old.

"What do you think? Vietnam? Indonesia?" Ralph asked Kristen.

"I think Thailand," she said.

"I agree," Andrew said.

"I don't suppose anyone speaks Thai?" Sarah asked. They all looked at Kristen, then Andrew.

"Nope," Kristen answered.

"Not really. I know how to say hello," Andrew said.

Around two hundred yards ahead a group of men surrounded a small boat. Andrew approached them with the three others following apprehensively. No one appeared to have any weapons, and when they were almost within speaking range a boy tugged on an older man's arm and pointed to them. They all turned around and stared at the strangers. They were a skinny bunch of men, darkly tanned by the sun, and they all wore open sandals, with worn shorts and no shirts.

"Hi! Does anyone speak English?" Andrew asked. His question caused a lot of halting gibberish, but no reply.

"Suh- by- dee- crap," Andrew smiled and waived. The men's faces lit up and they bowed.

"OK. I think we are in Thailand," Andrew commented without looking back at the others behind him.

One of the men came up and started talking to him and Andrew put up his hands and looked sheepish.

"Sorry. I do not speak….English…Americano…" he wasn't sure if that was a Thai word or Spanish. He feared it was Spanish.

"American!" A teenage boy appeared and came up to Andrew.

"Yes. Do you speak English?" Andrew asked.

"A little!" the boy said, "my name Sook," he said.

"Can you tell us where your village is?" Andrew asked. The boy looked lost.

"Home," Sarah said, "Ask him where his house is. Maybe he has a telephone."

"Home there," the boy pointed and started walking. Ralph looked at Andrew, and shrugged his shoulders.

The group followed him. It felt a little comforting just being around other people — at least people without guns.

"More American," the boy said.

"What?" Andrew asked. The boy stopped and thought for a moment. He pointed to all of them and showed them four fingers. "More American," he said, as he added one finger to make it five.

Sarah interrupted. "You mean there is another American. Like us?" she asked. The boy nodded but she couldn't tell if he understood or not. She pointed to him and then off to the distance.

"You take us to American!" she said, and clasped her hands and bowed.

Andrew walked up beside her and whispered in her ear. "That's Japanese. I don't think Thai do that," he said.

She looked up at him and shrugged her shoulders. "Oh well, at least he'll think I was polite," she said.

"Actually, I think Thai etiquette is that a woman's head should never be above a man's," Kristen said, "uh…or that could be Laotian, I don't remember."

"That's going to easier for me than you," Sarah said.

Kristen smiled, "Yeah. Well who cares anyway, we're dumb Americans."

They followed the boy for several hundred yards until they came to an old hut. There was a man sleeping outside. He was definitely a Caucasian.

"American!" the boy said, as he pointed. His job finished, he took off back toward where he had come from.

Ralph walked up to the man and touched him on the shoulder.

"Hey," he said.

The man rolled over to his back and sat up. He was blonde with wispy hair and blue eyes. Andrew thought he looked like a commercial for surfboards.

"Whoa! Hey! What's up?" the man asked. "You guys look like crap."

Andrew walked over and grabbed the man's right wrist. It had a black band on it.

"I have no idea what that is. Found it when I woke up here this morning," the man said.

"How did you get here?" Andrew asked.

"I have no idea. One minute I'm in Grand Cayman, the next thing I know I wake up here with nothing but the clothes on my back." The story sounded familiar to all of them, and they felt kind of sorry for the guy.

"I'm John. John Matthews," he held his tanned hand out to Andrew.

"What happened to you guys? Honestly, you look like you've been through hell," he asked.

"You could say that," Sarah said.

At the sound of the beeping, everyone except John looked at his wrist. Andrew re-grabbed it and, as usual, the group gathered around to read the message.

"Say hello to Mr. Matthews. The same rules apply. Your reward awaits as well as your second task."

Chapter 14

"What the heck does that all mean?" John said. The four looked at each other, and Andrew spoke up.

"You mean, you don't know the rules, or why you are here?" Andrew asked.

"Nope. Ignorant as a Jew in Catholic school," John said. Andrew found that hard to believe.

"We'll explain later. For now we need to find the nearest village," he paused and looked at John, "I don't suppose you know where that is?"

"Sure. Right down the river about a mile. Found it this morning while I was wondering what to do after I found this note," he dug in his pocket and pulled out a piece of paper wrapped in plastic. Andrew took it and read it to the others.

"Wait here. Company arrives today."

"I thought I was waiting for the TV crew or something," John said.

"No TV crews here," Ralph said.

"Do you know what happened to the guy you replaced?" Sarah asked. They all wanted to know.

"Not really. Should I?"

"He was killed the first day," Sarah said. She observed him to see his reaction. Unfortunately his shock seemed real.

"Do I want to know how?"

"Gun shot to the back of the head," Ralph said, as he pointed to his own.

"Man. I didn't sign on for this. Maybe I'll just bag it. It's not worth dying for," John said.

"What isn't?" Sarah asked.

"I just wanted to spend a couple of years climbing. I was told that was doable if I did this adventure thing. But it's kind of hard to climb if you're dead."

"No doubt about that," Andrew said. This guy seemed a little too unreal. He wasn't sure if it was the blonde hair, the whole 'surfer' look or the fact that he just appeared out of no where. He could just as easily be a spy as a replacement for Matt. Still, Andrew decided to play along. No point in showing his hand now.

"You take us to the village and I'll fill you in on the rules," Andrew said.

Andrew introduced him to the others and started walking.

It took about twenty minutes to reach the edge of the town. Andrew and John led the group, and Sarah, Kristen and Ralph observed them.

"So, do you think he's for real?" Sarah asked.

"I have no idea, but I would have much preferred we didn't have him at this point. For all we know, he may work for Baldwin," Ralph said. "I know that's what Andrew is thinking."

"So, what do we do? If we were going to try and get help, it's certainly going to be a lot harder with him around – even if we trusted him, which I do not think any of us do," Sarah said.

"It probably is a moot point anyway, these things obviously record where we are at, our vital signs and, for all we know, what we are talking about," Kristen said, as her fingers grasped the black band. The last comment was a new thought to Ralph.

"Look. It's a chance we have to take. Besides they didn't say we couldn't talk about abandoning the journey, we haven't done anything to violate their precious rules," Sarah said. She threw up her hands. "This is so aggravating. We are so… so trapped. And I hate feeling manipulated!"

They stopped speaking at the sight of a village about two hundred yards ahead. There were horses and carts, wagons, and even an old truck. People were milling around living their lives. As they approached, a few of them looked at them but just as quickly turned away. Sarah wasn't sure if it was because of the color of their skin or how disheveled they appeared. Andrew was still in the lead, along with John. Sarah could see him stopping to talk to people, but most of them just waived him off. Finally, another young man responded to his question and pointed across the unpaved street and down from where they were. Andrew waited until they all caught up, and pointed to a home with a table outside the door. A worn down man with a bamboo hat sat behind a pile of fruit, some of which they recognized.

"That must be the man," Andrew said.

"What man? Why do we care?" John said. Andrew ignored him.

An equally shabby woman came out and started chewing him out. As she spoke they could see that her teeth were almost black. It reminded Ralph that the dentist back home told him Devin was going to need braces. The poor guy was obviously hen pecked, because he just cowered as the woman pointed inside the house and screamed at him. Passersby actually moved into the middle of the road to avoid her wrath. After about a minute of berating, the woman ran back inside the home and returned a few seconds later with a small-emaciated child. They didn't know if the tot was dead or alive until they heard a faint, plaintive cry.

"No wonder she's upset," Kristen said.

"But why blame the poor guy?" John asked.

"Maybe she wants to take the child to a hospital or something, and they don't have the money," Kristen said.

"Let's go," Andrew stopped the conversation. "We will need to handle that obstacle later. For now we need to find food and shelter for the night. Do we want to see what this 'reward' supposedly is?" He faced the group.

"No. Absolutely not, it just gives them more power over us. We look like rats ringing the bell for morphine," Sarah said.

"Well, I think we should at least see what it is… I mean, maybe it's something that could help us get out of this god forsaken place." Kristen wiped her forehead with the back of her hand. They could tell that she was near exhaustion.

"I don't like it either but we should probably find out what it is. It's probably just some Gatorade, or something stupid like that," Ralph said.

"I'd go for that, man. We need those electrolytes," John said, to no one's surprise.

"Sounds like a vote is in order. All in favor?" Andrew asked. Kristen, Ralph and John raised their hands.

"I guess we go," Andrew said. Sarah looked unhappy, but didn't say anything. As they walked down the street Andrew asked everyone that passed: "Nan? House of Nan?" But no one would stop and talk to him.

"Lot of good having an Asian person with us," John said, and smiled at Sarah. She didn't respond.

A draft of air passed them by as they walked across a threshold. Someone was cooking and it made all of their stomachs grumble. Whatever it was, it smelled delicious.

"I don't suppose you have any Thai money?" Andrew asked John.

"Sorry man. I got nothing. I don't even have a change of underwear." It was news none of them wanted to think about.

Andrew stopped another man and repeated his request. The man paused, pointing down the street further but Andrew shrugged his shoulders. Sarah walked up to him. Fortunately, she thought, she was just slightly shorter than the guy. She clasped her hands together and looked at him with her blue eyes.

"Please. House of Nan?" she asked. Andrew thought to himself that not even a monk could have passed by that pleading.

The man shook his head and motioned for them to follow. About a hundred feet further he pointed to the nicest building they had yet seen in the small village.

"Hong Nan," he said, then left.

"Nice way to use them baby blues....uhh...Sarah right?" John said. "Damn. It would have worked on me too."

The group walked to the home and stood outside.

"Let's not all go in at once... just in case," Andrew said. "Besides we could use some things." He dug inside his pants and pulled out a small envelope, from which he withdrew a hundred-dollar bill.

"Where the heck..." Ralph started saying.

"Listen. I don't think it's going to help us much but Sarah, would you take it and try and buy some decent food, and maybe some clothes," he gave her the bill. "Who knows, maybe you'll find someone who will exchange it.

"Ralph, you want to go with her? I'll go with Kristen in here and check it out. Let's meet by the man with the fruit stand in about thirty minutes. If something happens to any of us...well, I guess you'll have to decide what to do," Andrew said.

"And me?" John asked. Everyone turned and looked at him. "Man. I can just stay here; that's fine with me," he had his hands in the air as if to surrender.

"Good. Do that," Andrew said. He tried not to sound as irritated as he was.

Sarah took the money and put it in her pocket. She was pleased that Andrew trusted her with the task. She also wondered what else he had in that envelope. The group separated and Andrew waited for them to be a distance away before knocking on the painted door.

A woman in a simple, but clean, dress and no shoes greeted them.

"Hello? Do you speak English?" Andrew asked. She just smiled at him and waved them in.

"Do you know who we are?" Andrew tried again. The woman didn't say a word but started walking off down a hallway. Andrew and Kristen looked at each other. Their shoes were filthy but Andrew was not about to remove them in case he needed to run.

"I guess we follow her," he said. They were escorted down a passage, and then up a flight of stairs. The home seemed unoccupied. It had the feel of a motel, except it didn't look like one, at least none that they had seen before. There were several rooms on the upper floor that the woman passed by until she stopped and opened a door. Andrew and Kristen looked inside. It was a small, clean room with two beds in it. The woman walked in front of them and proceeded to the opposite side of the hallway where she opened another door. It was identical. She continued down a little further and showed them a small bathroom, complete with an old bathtub, then a final room with one bed. They tried desperately to hide their exultation but Kristen was grinning from ear to ear. Andrew tempered his own excitement by reminding himself that it could all be an elaborate trap. However, he noted happily that the doors were quite flimsy and there appeared to be several ways out of the home.

He walked over to one of the open windows and looked out. There was a small faux porch under the window that connected to the roof structure – it would be no problem to escape if they had to.

"Thank you," Andrew turned toward the woman, but she had disappeared. They checked the hallway but she was gone.

"Now what?" Kristen asked.

"We'll, I suppose if you want to take a bath I can stand guard," he said. She looked delighted, but suddenly her smile fell.

"I don't have anything to change into," she said.

Andrew walked over to the only dresser in the room and opened the drawers. There were several sets of clothing in them.

"Looks like someone was expecting us," he said, as he withdrew the clothes and laid them on the bed. Kristen was nearly jumping for joy and he had to smile.

"Go ahead. I'll wait," he said.

She grabbed a native blouse and pair of loose fitting pants and ran off to the bathroom. In a few minutes Andrew could hear the water start running and Kristen's familiar alto singing. He sat on the floor so he would not soil the bed and thought about what this strange turn of events could mean.

:

Sarah was more than frustrated. Ralph and her had approached nearly everyone that sold food, and none of them even so much as looked at the US currency. Even her best try at pleading was to no avail.

"So, now what?" Ralph asked her. They had paused at the very end of town and looked back down the street.

"I have no idea. I don't have anything to trade, I don't speak the language and no one will take this perfectly good money." She held the hundred-dollar bill in her hand and waived it around. There was absolutely no risk of anyone mugging them. "And I'm starving. I'm so sweaty and dirty I can't even stand myself..."

"Well, look, let's split up and walk down the other side. We've come this far. Maybe we'll at least find someone who speaks English who can tell us where a bank is, or something," Ralph said.

"Fine," Sarah said, and took off at a fast pace. She needed to complete this task. It had been entrusted to her and whatever it took she wanted to do her job. She passed several more food vendors, found a small store, and went in. Another old woman sat in a hand made chair and looked at her.

"Hello," Sarah removed her hair from her face and gave her the best smile she could. "You take this?" She gave the woman the bill. There was no point in asking if she spoke English. The woman surprised her by taking the money and turning it over in her hands as if inspecting a piece of fruit. Sarah felt herself getting excited and quickly motioned to her mouth in the international language meaning 'food'. The woman grinned at her with a mouthful of black and rotting teeth and shook her head, then gave Sarah back the hundred. It was devastating. Sarah took back the money and walked out the door. For the first time in her life she considered taking some the cans of food off of the shelves and making a run for it, but reminded herself that she was the only blond woman in town. It would be really hard to hide.

The only place left was the man wearing the bamboo hat selling fruit. It was the last thing she wanted to eat but she couldn't go back empty handed, so she approached him with the same spiel. She realized, up close, that he wasn't that old. His skin looked like folds off a Shar-Pei, and they actually moved when he shook his head 'no'. She must have looked very disappointed because the man handed her a large Jack fruit and signaled for her to take it. Sarah stood there a moment with the large prickly globe in her hands and contemplated what to do. She finally smiled and bowed, then walked away. As she left, she could hear the cry of the child coming from the recesses of the home.

Ralph met up with her a few minutes later outside the house of Nan. He was empty-handed and looked at the fruit that Sarah was carrying.

"Don't ask," she said. He didn't.

John showed up eating something that looked like a tortilla wrapped around some kind of meat. It smelled heavenly and Sarah was more than miffed.

"I thought you two were supposed to get some grub?" he asked.

"We couldn't find anyone that would take the money," Ralph said, as he looked at Sarah.

"That's ridiculous, here, give it to me," John extended his hand, "I'll take care of it."

Sarah still held the bill in her right hand and couldn't decide what to do.

"What? You don't trust me? We're in the middle of Asia – where am I going to go?" John said. That wasn't the point, but Sarah couldn't get herself to say what she thought so she gave him the money and he took off. She was thankful that Ralph didn't say a word, she felt bad enough as it was.

"So, you think we should knock?" Ralph asked.

"Why not," Sarah put down the Jack fruit on the porch and wiped off her hands, then rubbed them together. They had little marks from holding onto the heavy orb. Ralph knocked loudly on the door. A few seconds later they heard footsteps and it flew open.

Kristen stood before obviously bathed and in clean clothes.

Andrea Peters

"They have a bath! And clothes, and beds! I'm in heaven! Come on," she said, and took off down the hallway. Ralph and Sarah looked at each other, then followed her.

Upstairs, they found two bedrooms, and Andrew walking out from a room wrapped in nothing but a towel. Sarah averted her eyes quickly and blushed. Andrew ducked into the closest room.

"Sorry! I'll be right out," he said, and shut the door.

"Sarah, look at the rooms! Real beds!" Kristen had opened the adjacent door and was bouncing on the mattress.

"And there are clothes in the dresser..." She pointed to an open drawer. Sarah wasn't sure what to make of all of it. It felt like the Twilight Zone.

Andrew walked out a minute later and said something to Ralph, then walked into their room wearing a loose shirt and shorts. Sarah thought they looked good next to his brown skin.

"Are you sure this is a good idea? After all they have put us through?" Sarah asked.

"You're right, Sarah but the thought of a bath and clean clothes... I never thought I'd be willing to sell my soul for hot water, but what can I say?" Andrew looked a bit sheepish as he shrugged his shoulders.

"Sarah – there's no one here. It's not a trap. Remember the message said it's a reward for making it this far. We should enjoy it!" Kristen said.

"A reward for watching a man get killed? A reward from almost being mauled to death by a tiger? For making us march through malaria infested jungles without so much as a first aid kit? It's like beating your kid half to death and then giving him an ice cream cone to make up for it," Sarah looked at Ralph after the illustration.

"She's right... but since we're here, we might as well clean up and then decide whether to make a stand on principles..." Ralph said, as he picked up some cloths and went into the bathroom.

"Am I the only person who sees what they are doing to us?" Sarah looked at Andrew and Kristen.

"Sarah. You're right, what can we say?" Andrew said. Sarah looked disappointed in him.

"Did you get any food?" Kristen asked. Sarah's face dropped and her voice lost it's edge.

"No. I'm sorry, I just couldn't get anyone to take the money," she said.

"Well we can always go get some more fruit, don't worry about it," Andrew said. At the comment Sarah could feel her emotions start to let loose and she willed them to go away before the tears started.

"I'll be right back," she said, and turned around and left. Andrew and Kristen looked at each other questioningly but they could tell she needed some time alone and let her go.

Ralph joined them in the room a few minutes later. He had to admit it felt good to be clean. The bed felt even better as he lay on it.

"So – where is John?" Kristen asked. Andrew looked surprised.

"God. I totally forgot about him. He's probably waiting downstairs, taking a nap or something."

"Actually, he took the hundred and said he was going to find something to eat," Ralph said. He hoped he came back soon. Some meat would sure soften his conscious for compromising on the accommodations.

Ralph closed his eyes for a moment and fell asleep. Kristen was lying on the bed next to him talking to Andrew, who was leaning against it while sitting on the floor. Within minutes they were all snoring.

:

"Hey!"

"Hey! Wake up!" Andrew heard the voice, but it seemed to be emanating from a fog bank and he couldn't discern who it was.

"Andre. Andrew – whatever your name is – wake up!" Andrew opened his eyes with a start and found he was staring at the waist of a man in shorts. He looked up. It was John.

"Man. You guys were out!" he said.

"What? How long?" Andrew tried to get his mind working.

"I don't know. I've been gone an hour or so. Ran into some guys down by the river cooking fish. They gave me some," he held up a couple of fairly large charred carcasses. They smelled good.

Andrew got up from the floor and shook Kristen and then Ralph. Both of them woke up and rubbed their eyes. Immediately, they smelled the food and looked at what John was holding.

"Food! Let's eat!" John said. They all gathered around, and John put the fish on the top of the dresser. Ralph and Andrew tore off a piece and started eating. Kristen took a moment to say a prayer. It made Ralph feel guilty, and he paused for a moment until she finished.

After a short while Andrew looked at the three of them and stopped chewing.

"Where is Sarah?" he asked. Immediately a look of worry came over Kristen's face and she looked at Ralph. He swallowed and gazed at John.

"Don't look at me, man. Last I saw of her was when she came back here empty handed. I told her I'd take care of it," he said. Andrew knew instantly that, when she had left, she must have gone back out to try again.

"How long has it been? An hour?" he asked.

"Something like that, maybe a couple," John said.

"We need to go look for her," Andrew said, as he got to his feet. Ralph put down what he was eating and went to the bathroom to wash his hands. They all followed.

"Ralph and Kristen, you go south. I'll go north. John, you check the river to the west. Whatever happens we meet back here before dark. Everyone understand?" Andrew asked.

They all nodded and walked downstairs to the street. They could see the sun was going down rapidly. Ralph figured they had less than an hour of sunlight.

"Back here by dark. No matter what," Andrew reminded them and took off at a fast trot. He was more than worried, his heart hurt as well. He didn't even want to think if anything bad had happened to her.

Ralph and Kristen walked all the way to the south of town but there was no sign of Sarah. There were not many people on the streets and the few that were left seemed to be in a hurry to get home. Ralph noted that no one had any kind of light outside their front doors and, if they were caught in the dark, it would be difficult to find their way back.

"Where do you think she would have gone?" Ralph asked.

"To look for food? She had already tried the town, so perhaps she went back to the jungle to gather what she could... that's what I would have done," Kristen said.

Ralph looked at her questioningly.

"Yes. Let's try. We can't just leave her out here," he said, as they walked behind the row of houses about a hundred yards to the forest. There were many trails heading into the jungle, and they picked the widest one to start down. Ten minutes into their walk they heard the sounds of male voices. They were soft, but unmistakable. Ralph cupped his hands around his mouth and shouted.

"Hello!" he paused for a moment, then repeated it. Within seconds they could hear the movement of plants and branches as a group of people approached them. Kristen got closer to Ralph and grabbed his arm. He could feel that she was shivering though it wasn't cold. He, too, was concerned, but forced himself to breathe steadily, and decided to stand perfectly still as the footsteps advanced from in front and behind them. Kristen was anxiously turning both ways to see who it was.

A man with a cigarette appeared first. He was wearing worn camouflage pants and a dirty brown shirt. An automatic rifle hung over his shoulder. Behind him a half dozen other men, all skinny, young and filthy, waited. Kristen could smell them from where they stood. It made her nose itch. Within a minute a dozen men surrounded them and she started visibly shaking. The leader walked up to Ralph and blew smoke in his face. Ralph looked toward the ground at the man's old boots as they stopped in front of Kristen. He watched out of the corner of his eye as the soldier reached up and touched her hair. She immediately shrank back and held onto Ralph's arm even tighter. For a second the thought of trying to grab the man's rifle crossed his mind, but then he remembered his family and it was just as quickly squelched. He didn't know how he would react if they tried to do anything to her.

The man spoke, and Ralph was forced to look at him.

"American. I speak English," he said.

The man grinned at him.

"I speak English," he said, in a very heavy accent.

"We are looking for a friend. A woman," Kristen said. She still held her death grip on Ralph.

"Woman? Ah. Yes. We know woman," the man said something to his soldiers and they started laughing.

"Do you know where she is? Sarah is her name." Ralph was starting to understand this was a futile conversation, but he was just hoping to keep the man engaged until he could think of something better to do.

"Woman? You follow us. We show her." If the man had spoken any worse, Ralph could have feigned that he didn't understand, but the facts were they had no choice. Still, he had to try.

"We will come back later. Tomorrow," Ralph said, as he pointed to the sun, then turned around with Kristen on his arm and took several steps back down the path. The men that were blocking them made no move to get out of the way.

"No. You come," the leader's voice became very serious and Ralph stopped. Several of the soldiers adjusted their grip on their weapons and placed their fingers on the triggers.

Kristen started crying and Ralph put his hand on hers.

"Kristen, please stay calm, we have no choice," he whispered. Her eyes were full of tears but she nodded her head and started walking with him. The men separated into two groups, half in front and half behind them. The only escape route was directly into the jungle and, with night coming, that seemed like a death wish although Ralph acknowledged - so did following these men.

"Who are they?" Kristen asked softly between turns in the path.

"I assume they are rebels or guerillas..." Upon hearing Ralph mention the word, the leader turned around to face them and gave him a nasty look. Ralph pretended he didn't see it and gazed toward the ground. He was thankful that Kristen didn't pursue the topic any further.

Right before it got dark, the soldiers led them off the main path and followed what looked like a game trail into the jungle. Within a hundred yards or so it opened into a small clearing where they saw a least two dozen more men seated around small fires. Most of them were roasting some animals that they had skewered on stakes. There were three green army type tents, and Ralph and Kristen were led over to the largest one. A small Buddha guarded the entrance with a stick of incense, and the man signaled for them to take a seat on the dirt facing the tent. Kristen hesitated just a moment because of her new clean change of clothes, then gave in and sat down.

They waited as the leader had a discussion with several other men, and they could hear some of them get up and move around. A minute later there were footsteps behind them and Ralph couldn't help but turn toward the sound, Kristen followed his lead.

"Sarah," Ralph looked up to find Sarah blindfolded and gagged, her hands tied behind her back. Her face looked bruised and her shirt was worn in several places. Kristen put up her hands to her own face to prevent the gasp from escaping her lips. The leader went to Sarah and removed the gag and then the blindfold. Ralph thought, for the first time since this ordeal had begun, that she looked really scared.

"Are you OK?" he asked.

She nodded her head. "I'm sorry. I've been such a failure," she said.

"Sarah, it's all right. We're all in over our heads." Never more so than now, Ralph thought.

Chapter 15

"Do you know who they are?" Ralph asked. The men had moved away to continue their discussion.

"No. Guerrillas would be my guess," she said.

"How long have you been here?" Kristen asked. Sarah took some deep breaths and closed her eyes for a moment. When she opened them, Ralph could sense that she was back in control of her emotions. He wondered if he looked as scared as he was.

"After I left you guys, I came to the forest to collect some food and, before I knew what was happening, I was surrounded by a bunch of men with guns," Sarah said. Ralph was hoping that Kristen didn't mention that John had returned with fish. Kristen took a step toward Sarah and touched her face.

"Did they hurt you?" Sarah understood the meaning behind the words.

"No. I tried to run and tripped," she pointed to her face, "this was the result."

"What are we going to do?" Kristen looked at Ralph, who stared back at her, mystified. He was sure that Andrew would have something to say, but he didn't.

"I don't really think we have many options here. We can run and likely get shot, or die in the jungle, or wait and see what they do," he said.

"My guess is they want a ransom, but who is going to pay it? My family doesn't have any money…" Sarah's voice drifted off. "I'm really sorry I've gotten you all involved in this. I was just trying to help…"

"There is nothing we can do about it, so let's not even go there," Kristen said.

They all stopped talking as the leader returned. He signaled for them to sit down.

"We want money," he said. His look was dead serious.

"How much money?" Sarah asked.

The man rolled up his eyes and was obviously looking for the right words.

He held up his index finger.

"Millian dollars," though he mispronounced it, the word was clear.

"One million dollars?" Sarah asked.

"Yes. Million dollars."

"That's impossible, we do not have a million dollars. We are poor!" Sarah said. The man either didn't understand or didn't care.

"One million dollars or die," he pointed his rifle at Kristen and she screamed, then covered her mouth with her hand. She moved next to Ralph and he put his arm around her.

The leader put up his index finger again and pointed to all three of them.

"One you - here," he pointed to the ground, then put up two fingers, "Two - go," he said.

Sarah wasn't sure that she understood.

"You want two," Ralph said, and pointed to the girls, "to go," he indicated where he thought town was, "and one to stay," he said.

The man nodded and smiled. His teeth were mostly missing.

"Which one stays here?" Ralph asked, pointing to the three of them.

The man shrugged.

"One here. Two go," he said, as he got up and walked away. Three guards surrounded them, about ten feet away.

Ralph looked at Sarah and Kristen. He knew what the man would do in the movies, but he didn't want to stay here and likely die. As Sarah aptly mentioned, who had a million dollars to pay these men, and who could say if they would let the person go once the ransom had been paid?

Kristen looked terrified, shaking uncontrollably, and Sarah had turned to look at the men. No one said a word.

"How do we decide?" Sarah finally asked.

"I don't know," Ralph avoided her eyes.

"We could draw sticks. Take a vote. We could make them choose," she said.

"I...I can't stay here... I mean I haven't done anything," Kristen said, and looked at Sarah. "I don't mean *you've* done something, I just mean I shouldn't be here..." she finished by looking at the ground.

"Do you feel the same way, Ralph?" Sarah looked at him calmly. Ralph looked up and averted his eyes.

"Well, it seems we have arrived at a decision," Sarah said. Even she was surprised that her voice sounded so calm when, inside, all hell was breaking loose. Her heart has hammering, and her chest felt like someone was sitting on it. She struggled through the numbness to hide the panic she could feel rising. It was a feeling that she had only felt once before, only twenty-four hours ago, facing the tiger.

Neither Ralph nor Kristen said a word. Ralph felt an overwhelming guilt, but he didn't want to lose his family over this, and it was Sarah who had gotten herself into the mess. It seemed only fair. He mentally blocked out the consequences of their decision. Somehow, a miracle would save her. It was the only possible outcome.

Kristen couldn't even think. Her fear had paralyzed her again and all she wanted was to get out of that camp alive, whatever that took. She would think about her decision when she was far, far away from here. She felt no guilt, because she didn't acknowledge that anyone was getting left behind or hurt, her sole focus was pretending that the entire situation didn't exist.

The leader returned. He had a piece of paper in his hand.

"Who go?" he asked.

Sarah pointed to Ralph and Kristen. The man looked surprised but gave the paper to Ralph. Most of it was written in what looked like scribbles, but he could see a number with seven digits - it wasn't in English, but he had no doubt what it said.

Ralph and Sarah got up, their eyes averted from Sarah.

"Two days," the man held up two fingers, then pointed toward town and Ralph. "You come. I find you," he said.

The three soldiers moved toward Sarah. Ralph and Kristen were drawn to look at her. Kristen started gasping for breath and was making retching sounds like she was about to vomit. Sarah looked at both of them with a placid face. It took every bit of control she had.

"Please, tell my parents I love them," she said, as they men escorted her off to a tent. Sarah looked back at them one final time, waiting for an acknowledgment. Ralph tried to smile, but couldn't. He nodded his head instead, and she turned around and allowed the men to guide her into the tent.

"Go!" The leader signaled for Ralph and Kristen to follow a guard. As they walked, Kristen grabbed Ralph's hand. He could feel her body shake with swallowed sobs but neither of them thought about changing their decision. It was done. There was no looking back.

The guard led them out the trail to the main path, handed them an extra flashlight, and pointed to his left before disappearing.

They walked about a hundred yards before Kristen totally lost it, and she turned toward Ralph. He stood still, and held her in his arms until she stopped shaking. A sliver of moon appeared and a small deer walked across their path and looked at them. The sounds and smells of the forest filled the air. Life goes on, Ralph thought. Life must go on.

:

Andrew was sitting on the porch, waiting for them when they finally found the house of Nan. They had gotten lost several times on the way back, and it was quite late. It had started to rain and Ralph and Kristen were soaked.

"Did you find her?" Andrew asked anxiously. He acted unaware of the present weather situation as he blocked their path to the door.

"Yes. Can we come in?" Ralph asked.

"Yes? Oh. Sorry - yeah," Andrew quickly moved out of the way and ushered them inside, where he stopped and again blocked their path. A single light shone in the hallway.

"Why isn't she with you? Has something happened?"

"Something has happened." As Ralph said the words he felt his eyes fill with tears and his throat constrict. He had no idea how to tell Andrew what they had done.

"What happened? Talk to me!" Andrew's voice grew more panicky by the second.

Ralph could only think of one thing to say that wasn't horrific.

"She's alive…" he said.

A small amount of tension left Andrew's face.

"And?!"

"She's been taken hostage," Ralph paused, and Kristen took his arm again. She really didn't want him to tell Andrew everything.

"By whom?" Andrew sagged against the wall and sat on the floor. Ralph stood above him.

"No idea. They found us, too…" Ralph thought about what he had just said, and added, "and they gave us this ransom note." He handed it to Andrew, who looked at it, then up at Ralph.

"How did you get away?" Ralph knew the question was coming but didn't yet have a good answer.

"They let us go... to deliver the note," Ralph realized as he skipped out on the other part of the story that, if by some miracle Sarah lived, Andrew would eventually find out. He wondered how upset he would be with him if that occurred.

"Andrew, there was nothing we could do," Kristen said, she sat down next to him and held his arm. In that brief moment she wondered if Andrew would have been so upset if she had been the one left behind. She dismissed the thought as worthless.

"How much?" Andrew asked, his mind was preparing for the amount and running through the options to get the money.

"A million dollars," Ralph said it, and then almost cowered.

"WHAT?" Andrew said, "how in hell are we supposed to come up with that amount of money?" He paused and looked at Kristen this time.

"Did they say what would happen if we didn't pay?"

Kristen bit her lip and looked down. Ralph could see her tears from where he stood.

"They said they'd kill her," Ralph said. His bottom lip was quivering as well.

Andrew sat on the floor, his face like stone.

"How much time?" he asked.

"Two days," Ralph said, then told him of the meeting arrangements.

"That's impossible," Andrew said, "we don't even know where we are..." he looked off down the darkened hall, then got on his feet. Kristen remained.

"We need to find someone who speaks English, now. Maybe we can get help from..." they all knew what he was thinking, but they also had no doubt that Mr. Baldwin would be of no help, even if they could reach him, which they couldn't.

"Andrew, do you have the money? I mean, if somehow we could get to Bangkok, could you get it?" Kristen had gotten to her feet.

Andrew thought about the question. The answer was 'yes' but it would cost him dearly. He had almost twice that amount ready to make a deal in less than two weeks. His main competitor had finally agreed to sell to him, but the price was steep, and the engagement costly. Andrew had agreed to a million-dollar penalty, should he fail to execute on the buyout. If he paid the ransom, he would not be able to fulfill the purchase and would lose the additional million. It would cripple his business and ruin him personally. Everything he had worked the last eighteen years for would be lost. All of it for a person he had only met a day ago, albeit someone whom he felt a connection to. The question that he had to ask himself was: could he live with himself if he didn't try and save Sarah? Only he would know what he had done. Neither Ralph nor Kristen would ever find out. He could simply walk away from this whole ordeal. Without Sarah they had already failed the adventure, and the entire house of cards would fall down. He could return to his life.

Andrew closed his eyes and stretched his neck. He needed time to think about the consequences.

"There's nothing we can do tonight. Let's try and get some sleep. Who knows, maybe some epiphany will clear things by morning."

Ralph noticed that Andrew had not answered the question, but he was not about to ask him again; not after his own decision earlier that evening. They all headed upstairs to the bedrooms. Andrew took the room to the left and shut the door before Ralph could follow him. Kristen noticed it and held the other door open for Ralph, who went in and sat on the far bed. Kristen headed to the bathroom. She thought that perhaps a hot bath would wash away the grime on the outside, but she knew it wouldn't do anything for the shame that was growing inside her.

She returned awhile later to find Ralph sitting, still, on the bed. He had removed his shoes, but remained clothed in his shorts and shirt. Kristen went over and sat beside him, her hair was still wet and her skin was moist from the steam of the bath. They sat stationary and in silence for a minute, until Ralph traced a bead of water that had started it's way down her bare leg. She put her hand on top of his and held it there, the warmth from his palm calmed her and she reflexively took a deep breath. They both felt the need to be reassured for the devil's decision that they had made. They both needed to feel that there was a benefit to being left alive. Ralph looked at her, and with his other hand he wrapped a lock of hair around her ear. His fingers rested against her scalp and she leaned her face onto his open palm and closed her eyes.

She felt the exhalation of air as he moved closer to her mouth and sensed his lips a moment before they touched hers. She reflexively parted them and gave in to in the intimacy of his kiss. He laid her back on the bed and released her towel, which fell to the covers. His hands found her soft breasts and he caressed them until a soft moan escaped her lips.

In the silence of the still air, they moved slowly and made love until they were satiated. It was something both of them desperately needed.

:

Andrew was consumed by the impossible decision that lay before him. He found his sleep wrested away and replaced by an anxiety that refused to be quenched. As soon as it was daylight, he got up, wrote a note to Ralph, Kristen and John, and left with the ransom letter. The village was just stirring, and this morning he was insistent on finding someone that spoke decent English. He hounded a middle-aged woman until she took him to a shop at the edge of town and pointed inside. Right before he entered, his bracelet started beeping.

> *"Welcome to day three. John is your new addition. The same rules apply. We understand Sarah is separated. Remember, you must all succeed or fail."*

Andrew didn't have time to deal with the impossibly all knowing Mr. Baldwin, so he entered the shop. It was full of dried herbs and small animals. It smelled like a pet shop he had once visited.

"Hello?" he asked. There was no one there.

"Is anyone around?" he walked toward the back of the store and a man that looked around forty walked out.

"Yes?" Andrew smiled reflexively at hearing English from the darkly tanned face.

"You speak English?"

"Yes. How can I help you?" the man had a slightly British accent.

"I'm an American," Andrew immediately realized it was a ridiculous statement. "Sorry... I have a friend in trouble, and I need help." Andrew handed him the ransom note. The man reached down below the counter and put on an old pair of glasses. Andrew could tell by his reaction that it wasn't going to be good news.

"Where was your friend when they were taken?" he asked.

"She was behind the town in the jungle," he said, as he pointed to the south.

"These are very bad men, government rebels, but with no political ideals. With them only money talks. I am surprised they have come this far to the West..." the man stopped and read something again. Andrew was amazed at his perfect command of the language.

"They say no police or they will kill her. In case you are thinking of involving them, be aware that many of the police are corrupt here, the Rebels could be bribing them. The letter says to go to Bangkok and purchase a gold and emerald necklace at this Jeweler," the man took out a pencil and wrote a name and address down in English, then a translation under it in Thai, "it is currently for sale for a little over one million US dollars. You are to return here in two days time and wait for further instructions." The storekeeper returned the letter and his translation.

"I'm very sorry about your friend. These men regularly kidnap for money. If it is paid, they generally keep their word. Of course, there are no guarantees," he said.

"Thank you," Andrew said. He was truly grateful, "how far is Bangkok from here?"

"About a day's journey by road, or three hours by boat. I can ask for a friend to take you there if you want," the man said. Andrew was amazed at the kindness and felt compelled for more information from this stranger.

"May I ask why you speak English, and how come no one told us about you yesterday? We asked everyone for help," Andrew asked.

"I am from Bangkok, but went to school in England. I returned to Thailand and married my wife, who is from this village. Unfortunately, they do not view me as native. I am still an outsider, so it is no surprise they would not mention me."

Andrew had many other questions running around his mind but he reminded himself of the time limitation he was under.

"I would very much appreciate your friend's help. I can pay him..." Andrew said, but the man put up his hand.

"It is no problem. I am happy to help. I have been to the US and was many times was helped by strangers," the man said. Andrew wanted to know what city he had visited but again didn't push his luck.

"Follow me," the man turned and said something in Thai toward the rear of the store. A pretty young woman came out. The man said something to her, and she nodded at him. Andrew said 'thank you', even though he doubted she understood, then followed her husband outside.

"What is your name?" Andrew asked.

"You can call me Lew," he said. "That was my name in England."

"Thank you again, Lew," Andrew said, as he followed him back up the road to the river. They emerged at a small quay and Lew spoke to a young boy with a boat. Andrew noticed it had a twenty HP Yamaha engine. The thing would move fast. The boy listened to Lew and nodded, signaling for Andrew to get in, which he did.

"I told him to take you to Bangkok and wait a day for you there. He said the fishing was bad anyway because it hasn't rained, so it will be no problem," Lew said. "When you return, come see me if you need more help."

Andrew was at a loss for words as the boat took off like a Jet Ski. He waived at Lew, and held on to the sides as the young boy sped away. Amazingly enough, the kindness of this man that he had just met made his personal decision so much easier.

:

Kristen was awakened by the beeping of her bracelet, it took a few minutes for her mind to digest everything that had happened the night before, and she stared at the white ceiling as she tried to decide whether to first look beside her at the bed or the bracelet. She turned to her right and saw Ralph staring at her. His eyes were moist with tears.

"Hello," she said gently, as she watched his reaction. She didn't know what else to say. 'How did you sleep? Did you have good dreams?'

"Hello...I..." he closed his mouth and took his right hand and ran it through his hair, then flipped on to his back.

"I'm sorry," he said. It wasn't the best compliment she had ever had after sleeping with someone, but she tried to understand.

"I'm not sure what you feel, but if you need some time..." she said.

"No," he turned back toward her "I don't know how to explain. I'm not sorry for meeting you, or for even... choosing to be with you last night. I guess I feel guilty. What have I done to my family?"

"Look, Ralph. It was a terrible ordeal yesterday. I needed to feel... loved. I'm sorry you are feeling bad for your family, but what happened is done. Perhaps we should deal with it later when we are both in a place that makes more sense."

The comment seemed to lift Ralph's dark mood and she looked at her bracelet again. It had continued beeping.

"Welcome to day three. John is your new addition. The same rules apply. We understand Sarah is separated. Remember you must all succeed or fail. No one must quit."

Kristen had totally forgotten about John.

"Have you seen John?" she asked

"No. I haven't gotten up. There was someone in the bathroom a while ago. It was probably him."

Kristen got out of bed in her shorts and top, and went over to the dresser. Sarah hadn't taken her clothes and they were still sitting there. She closed the drawer, opening the next one down, and found another set of clothes. It made her wonder if they had brought people here before. It seemed increasingly odd at the foreknowledge that Mr. Baldwin had shown. She took the clothing, leaving Ralph in bed, opened the door to the hallway, and walked out, pausing before Andrew's room. She did want to see him, but not at that moment, so she continued past the bathroom and knocked on the room that she assumed John was in.

"Hello?" she asked.

"Yeah. It's open," John said.

Kristen opened the door and found him sitting on the edge of the bed eating something with noodles. He finished his slurp and signaled for her to come in.

"So, John, who are you?" she asked. He looked at her strange.

"I haven't changed from last night, Sarah," he said. She immediately corrected him, "I'm Kristen."

"Oh yeah, my mistake, Sarah is the blonde." He nodded to himself and took another bite.

"Yeah. The blonde that we were all looking for last night." Kristen was more than a little peeved.

"Oh yeah. That's right! She OK?" He started chewing on his next bite of food.

"No. As a matter of fact, she's not." She waited for his reaction, and was almost surprised that his eyes got wider and he stopped chewing for a moment.

"She was kidnapped by some guerrillas or something. They want a million dollars for her," again, she stopped to watch him. John swallowed, and looked visibly shaken.

"Man. Damn. I don't know what to say. I just figured she was sulking or something. What are we going to do?"

"I have no idea. I'm going to take a shower, then wake up Andrew, then I suggest we talk," she said, as she turned around heading to the bathroom while leaving his door open.

Kristen took a brief shower and put on the new set of clothing, when she checked back in with Ralph, he was still a bit disheveled but he was standing. John was also in the room.

"Anyone talk to Andrew yet?" she asked, as she dried her hair with the towel.

"No," Ralph said. He looked embarrassed, and Kristen hoped he would be able to hide it better, she realized that what had happened the evening before, would need to be dealt with but, at that moment, they needed to consider more pressing matters. She knocked on Andrew's door several times without a reply and looked back at Ralph and John. They both shrugged their shoulders, so she grabbed the knob and opened it. Andrew was nowhere to be seen. His bed looked like someone had laid on top of it but had not removed the covers.

Kristen looked around the barren room and saw a note on the dresser.

Kristen and Ralph,

I'm going to try and find my way to Bangkok. I have to try and save Sarah. If I am successful, I will return in a day or two. Whatever you decide to do, try and leave me a note.

Andrew

Kristen was neither surprised nor happy about the letter. It was like Andrew to try and solve the problem, no matter how difficult, however she had no idea what they were supposed to do. She took the note to Ralph and John, and handed it to them. They both read it, then Ralph threw it on the nearest bed.

"And what are we supposed to do now?" John asked.

"I have no idea..." Ralph said.

"Well, look. I don't think this whole thing is going to work out. I'm just going to take off. I saw a policeman in town this morning, even had a motorcycle. Maybe he'll get me out of here," John looked around at the room, but there was nothing else to do and he walked out the door.

"Hang on a second, John. Look, Kristen got a message this morning. It said that no one must quit..." Ralph said.

"So what? What are they going to do... spank me?" John asked.

"Just fair warning: the last time someone disobeyed the instructions, bad things happened," Ralph shrugged his shoulders. "You can do whatever you want."

"And I'm going to. This is all an elaborate ruse anyway. Waste of my time," John said, and left the room.

"So now what?" Kristen asked.

"I'm half tempted to just follow John. Maybe it's time to go home," Ralph said, waiting for a response from Kristen. She sat on a bed and looked up at him.

"You know, it could have been one of us instead of her." It was an obvious statement, and Ralph really didn't want to think about it any more.

"If she dies..." Kristen looked at the floor.

"She's not going to die. Andrew will take care of that," Ralph said. Kristen thought about Andrew. He was a good friend: loyal, always kind and caring. If Sarah could be saved, she knew that he would find a way to do it. The fact didn't make her feel any less guilty.

"I think we should stay and wait for him. He may need our help when he gets back," she said.

"IF he gets back," Ralph said. He was thinking about how he just wanted to pretend the last three days never happened and go home. Maybe his wife would never need to know what he had done. He sat on the other bed.

"He *will* come back, I know he will," she said. The conviction got his attention.

"So what is it with you two, anyway. Are you together, or not?" he asked.

Kristen let out a sigh and kicked out her feet.

"We kind of were, are, seeing each other. I mean, really, he's everything a girl's supposed to want, but I don't know... he is a bit intense. I like things a little more laid back and romantic..." her voice dropped away and she thought about the question. To be honest with herself, she liked spending time with him. He spoiled her, treated her well, he was funny... but a 'soul mate'? Probably not. The thought would take some self-negotiating to come to term with.

"OK. Well, let's assume he does return. What do we do? And how about food?" Ralph asked. The mention of it made Kristen's stomach rumble, and she stood up and looked around the room.

"Let's find something to trade. There's no one here anyway." She walked out of the room and Ralph followed her downstairs. They opened up all the doors, but everything was too large. Kristen looked up at the ceilings and walls for art or pictures, and saw a small temple with some idols and incense on it. She carried a chair over to it, climbed on it, and pulled out some small artifacts that appeared to be, at the minimum, gold plated. Ralph took them from her as she got down, and they gathered the pieces together.

"Isn't this stealing?" he asked.

"From who? They didn't say we couldn't take anything. Besides, we took the clothes."

"Fine. If we can't trade them, maybe we can pray and ask it for a miracle," Ralph said.

"Very funny. I just hope we don't insult someone by trying to sell... whatever it is," she said.

They walked out the front door to the street. It was busy with people and, once in a while, someone would turn to look at them but, all in all, they were fairly ignored. Ralph looked both ways.

"Do you think he found him?" he asked.

"What? You mean John and the policeman?" she asked.

"Yeah. I mean, if he did find someone, maybe they could help us too."

Kristen took off walking, and Ralph followed until they found what looked like a small grocery. They went in, and the shopkeeper ignored them until Kristen walked up and pointed to the small gold icon in her hand. She attempted to mime that she wanted to trade and the woman took the idol turned it around in her hands, then set it on the counter and reverently bowed to it. The woman pointed to some items and nodded her head. Kristen took that as a yes, and picked up some canned goods, some vegetables, and a can opener. Ralph added some more items that he had found, including a lighter and a small ball of twine, along with a jug of water. He had no idea what any of the food was but, at this point, he didn't really care, as long as it was edible. The woman looked at the small pile of groceries and handed them a previously used rice bag, which they put their groceries in before leaving.

"That was fairly painless. Do you think she ripped us off?" Ralph asked.

"Probably. Or she was afraid of the gods, who knows. At least we have something to eat," Kristen said.

They exited onto the street and a commotion caught Ralph's attention.

"Looks like some excitement in this sleepy town. Let's see what's going on," he said.

Maybe we shouldn't, "Kristen had already experienced more than enough excitement for the next year or so. "It could be dangerous," she said.

"Or it could be the weekly bus bringing tourists and cell phones," he said. She doubted it, but followed him down the street and around a corner where they saw a group of people standing in a circle.

"It's not a bus," Kristen said, but Ralph either ignored her or didn't hear her.

They were both taller than almost everybody else, so they moved up behind the thinnest part of the crowd and looked over their heads. Kristen was not pleased to see the back of a man lying on the ground. He wore a shirt that she definitely recognized. Ralph saw it at the same time, and looked at her, her eyes wide with fear. At that moment, someone in the crowd pointed them out, and the locals parted, forming a path into the center. Kristen felt herself walking toward the prone body of John but, at the same time, hearing the voice inside her head yell 'don't!' Ralph bent over the body and pulled it over.

Kristen gasped as she saw John, pale, and looking up toward the sky with a blank stare. His face was swollen and bruised, his clothes ripped. There was blood on his hands and torso. It looked like he had put up quite a fight, but ultimately failed.

Almost immediately, Ralph and Kristen both heard the beeping. They looked at one another and backed away from the body. There was nothing they could do for him anyway. Once they were clear of the crowd, Ralph grabbed her arm and pulled her into an alley.

Kristen was staring at the side of the building.

"I don't want to know what it says," she said, looking at his face.

Ralph stood in front of her and held her face in her hands.

"Kristen, we have to," he said, and grabbed her right forearm with his left hand while turning up the wristband to read the message.

> *"What terrible luck. We are sorry at the loss of John. Still, the journey is not yet over. You must finish the tasks and come home. It is important that those remaining understand the value of each other."*

Kristen was looking at Ralph's face as he read the note. By the look of concern in his eyes, she knew it was as she suspected.

"They know, don't they?" she asked.

"Yes. They know." He thought about that for a moment. After all they had been through, there was not a doubt in his mind that Mr. Baldwin knew exactly what was going on at all times. Any attempt to avoid playing his game would end in disaster. That was not an option for him. Whatever hoops he had to jump through, he was determined to make it home. It was just like he was ten all over again and the class bully made him give up his sandwich every day for a month as a 'penalty' for stepping in the bully's path. He had made it through that, and he would make it through this.

"What are we going to do?" Kristen asked.

"It's not like we have a choice. Obey them or die. I think it's pretty clear, don't you?" Ralph's voice was irritated. "I'm sorry. Look. We have to do what he says. We *have* to, no more ifs, ands or buts. Let's follow the instructions and get home. This is no longer an adventure, it is our life – and I, for one, will do whatever is necessary to make it back alive."

Chapter 16

Sarah woke up to total darkness. Her mind inventoried what she knew and what her senses could interpret. She had a blindfold on, and her hands and feet were tied together. It felt like some kind of thin rope. She lay on her side with her head against a mat of some sort. The mat was hard, so likely she was on the ground. There were voices outside, at least three distinct ones. The only good thing was that she no longer had a gag over her mouth but that also meant that she was probably far out of earshot of anyone that could help her. The air hung like a heavy blanket, almost suffocating, which meant it was probably daylight, though she could not see any light. She was probably in an enclosure of some sort, because she felt absolutely no movement of air. Her neck was stiff, her mind a little foggy and her mouth stale. Last night she had eaten some food given to her by the man. It had to have been drugged by some sort of strong medication or narcotic. Sarah took a moment to contemplate whether they had molested her in anyway, she tentatively allowed herself to feel for signs that her clothing had been removed, or for soreness, and finally let out an unconscious breath upon the determination that they had not.

Last night, after Kristen and Ralph had left, she was initially angry. That quickly had dissipated when she realized that the emotion would not benefit her at all. She told herself that, if there were any chance of escape, she would need full control of her mind. The fear that she felt deep inside her would have to be pushed aside. As a child, she had learned that her thoughts controlled her emotions. Good thoughts meant good feelings, bad thoughts led to bad feelings and, even at a young age, she did not like having her actions dictated by her feelings. When she was thirteen, she had a fight with her mother. It was a common fight but, for the first time, Sarah had tried to fight back. Just remembering it made her sick to her stomach.

"I don't want to go to Karen's house," Sarah said.
"Listen. This isn't a negotiation. *We* are going," her mom said.
That's the problem Sarah thought. I don't want you to go.

"But, Mom! None of the other girls are coming with their mother!" her mom turned and put down the knife she was using to butter her sandwich.

"So, that's what this is about? You don't want me around?" Her mother's voice was calm and unemotional. Sarah had seen this ambivalence many times. She started to get warm and could feel the thumping of her heart. She wanted to hold firm.

"That's...not the point," she said, and cast her eyes toward the kitchen floor. "I just want to be with my friends sometimes."

"So you don't like having me around?" She could feel the heat of her mother's eyes on the top of her head.

"No. It's not like that. I just..."her mother interrupted her.

"That's fine. I don't want to be where I'm unwanted," her mother said.

Sarah stood there looking at the lines between the tiles and she wanted her mom to understand, but she knew that whatever she said would be taken the wrong way. Suddenly, from all the years of dealing with this, a surge of emotion hit her and, before she realized what she was saying, words started flowing out.

"You always do this. You turn it around and make it about you. It's not about you! It's about me. They're *my* friends and I don't want to be embarrassed. I don't need you around all the time. I am fine by myself! Why can't you just stop with all the guilt stuff!" Sarah was out of breath and she discovered, too late, that her mom's intense blue eyes were staring at her. Sarah was too scared to try and pull away, and they remained locked with hers. She watched as her mother's eyes narrowed and her brow furrowed.

"You don't need me? You're fine by yourself? OK. Let's see," her mom turned back toward her sandwich and Sarah found herself looking at her back.

For two days her mom refused to even look at her, let alone speak. By the third day, Sarah was desperate. She found her standing in the kitchen washing dishes. Sarah ran up from behind and threw her arms around her waist, pressing her head against her mother's back.

"I'm sorry, mom! Please talk to me! Don't hate me! I promise I'll never say anything like that again...please," Sarah sobbed. She waited, hoping to hear the water turn off and to feel her mom's hands on her arms or a gentle voice reassure her, but it never came. After a minute or so, Sarah released her grip, sat on the floor, and cried. Finally her mother turned around and looked down at her.

"I forgive you, Sarah. We'll just overlook this whole episode," she reached under Sarah's face and tipped it up with her wet palm while looking into her daughter's red eyes. "You are my favorite daughter. Just be good." At that, her mother turned back around and started washing the dishes again. Sarah felt on that day that she had lost something, but it was only as an adult that it even began occurring to her what. She had lost her right to determine her life on her terms. She was forever bound to be the perfect daughter, to complete every task so that her mother would be proud of her. And she vowed to never again lose control of her emotions. It only compromised your thought process, and it gave the other person power over you.

:

When she was fourteen, she had fallen in love for the first time. It was a boy at school that she knew she could never have, but she pined for him and dreamt about him every day. One day at school she was shocked to find him standing in front of her.

"Hi, Sarah, how's it going?" he asked.

"Umm…I'm…I'm just eating lunch." Sarah was carrying her lunch tray and thought it was the stupidest comment she could have made.

"I see that. You like the creamed corn?" He was taller than she was and she had to tilt her head back quite far to look at him.

"Wh-at?" She heard a group of her classmates start to laugh behind her.

"The corn? Do you eat it?"

"No… I mean, yes," she was more than puzzled and was getting very self-conscious.

"Say, I was wondering if you would like to go out some time?" he asked.

"Out?" Her eyes were wide open.

"Yeah. Out. Like to Henry's party this weekend."

"Uh. Yes, but my parents wouldn't let me go…"

"Your parents? Who cares – just sneak out."

"Oh no. I can't do that," she said, without thinking.

"Fine. Your loss."

She watched as he walked away. He went over to a group of his friends and held out his hand. His friend looked toward Sarah and scowled, then pulled out some money and gave it to they boy. Sarah watched it all happen.

"You were a bet," said a voice behind her.

"What?" Sarah turned around and saw a girl she barely new.

"Bet. You were a bet," the girl motioned over to the boy and his friend. "It's been obvious to everyone that you like him, so his friend made him a bet to invite you out on a date. The bet was that he wouldn't dare do it in front of everyone – he is, after all, one of the best looking guys in school and…" Sarah tuned her out and was starting to realize that dozens of eyes were watching her. She almost asked 'why' but she knew. She had been a late bloomer. Middle school had not been the kindest years of her life. Sarah lost her appetite, and threw her lunch out as she was leaving the auditorium. She swore she could feel all four hundred pairs of eyes burning her back as she walked out. Right then, she vowed to never let her emotions run out of control again. It would become her strength. Some people would call it being 'cold.' She called it survival.

:

Now, she found herself, years later, repeatedly on the verge of losing her poise. She was struggling with everything that had happened: the death of Matt, the tiger, and now her captivity. She could feel that her capacity for manipulating herself was being pushed to the limits. Still, she had no choice if she wanted to survive. As much as she would have liked to be able to depend on Andrew, Sarah and Ralph to save her, she could not afford to do that. She would have to escape. She would have to find a way.

"Hey!" Sarah said.

"Hey! I have to use the bathroom!"

She could hear some voices come closer to her, then and then felt the presence of someone. She thought about trying to kick him but would have probably missed. Instead she tried to sit up. Whoever it was helped her and then untied her blindfold. Even diffused, the light gave her an immediate headache. Sarah squinted to see who it was that had come. Their smell was not as objectionable as last night. When her eyes adjusted enough to see a few details, she was surprised to find a woman in front of her. She looked much like the men, only smaller, dressed in dungarees and an olive green shirt. She didn't smile.

"You have to toilet?" The woman asked. Sarah found herself thankful that the woman spoke some English, and she wondered whether it was a psychological move on the part of the soldiers. Then she decided that was giving them too much credit.

"Yes. Please," Sarah bowed her head to show submission. For once she was thankful to be short.

"You do not run. Important, you run. You..." the woman obviously struggled for the correct word, and finally just moved her hand in a cutting motion across her throat. Sarah understood perfectly. For now, she just wanted to see where she was and she nodded in reply.

Her feet were untied and she was led out of the tent. Sarah once again had to shield her eyes from the brightness of the sun, even though the jungle canopy was over them. She looked around and found that she was in a small clearing, about thirty feet in diameter. There was only one other tent and two men sitting around a small camp. They looked up at her briefly and then went back to some kind of game with small stones. Each of the men carried a rifle, as well as a sidearm. Sarah noticed that the woman did not carry a gun, but did have a knife on her belt.

"We go." With her hands still tied behind her back the woman led her about twenty feet into the growth, out of sight of the other guards. Sarah looked around as she walked but couldn't see anything at all. She had absolutely no idea what direction was east or west and she couldn't hear the sound of the river, which meant they had moved her, God knew where. The only solution she could think of was to try and get a weapon and force one of them to lead her out. The logical choice would be the woman who, at that moment, was shooing her off to do her business. Sarah stepped off a few feet and the woman reached for her knife. Sarah stopped and wiggled out of her pants, then squatted over the ground. She found it very difficult to go with the woman watching, and she eventually pretended that she was in a different place, until she felt her bladder finally release. She knew that asking for tissue was a waste of time, so she awkwardly pulled back on her pants and signaled that she was ready to leave. It was, then that she heard the beeping and the woman turned around to look at her. Sarah quickly covered her bracelet and pushed all the buttons. She had no idea what they did but the beeping stopped.

Receiving the message was like getting a phone call at 2:00 am. It was either really good news or bad, likely bad, but now that she knew it was there – she had to know why.

The woman had already turned back around and entered into the clearing, and Sarah followed her. The two men were playing their game and didn't even acknowledge them. Sarah took a seat on a log where the woman pointed, and her feet were promptly bound up again. The woman then moved behind her back and Sarah felt hands on her wrists. For some reason, the thought that the woman knew about her bracelet unsettled her, but then she felt her hands fall free and she pulled her arms to her front and massaged them. The woman came back into view with a bottle of water and handed it to her.

"Thank you," Sarah automatically expressed her appreciation, but she wondered again whether this was some form of elaborate psychological ruse to create the Stockholm syndrome, a common malady that formed a kind of weird friendship between a kidnapper and the captives. Even if this was true, perhaps Sarah could use it to her advantage. The woman didn't say anything in return, but did hand her a piece of fruit. Sarah smiled at her again and repeated the phrase. She wished she knew how to express it in Thai.

:

By the position of the sun Andrew knew it was sometime mid afternoon in Bangkok. The young man dropped him off at a dock in some sort of busy commercial area and he disembarked from the small boat and thanked him. He tried to communicate that he would return in one day, but gave up after several attempts and decided that he would just have to trust that Lew had conveyed the information correctly to both of them. On the trip down, Andrew had made some assumptions. If this was day three, which he believed it was, then it was Tuesday in Bangkok. That would mean that it was Monday afternoon on the West Coast of the US. At least his offices would be open. He had received the message on his wristband about John, which alluded to the group keeping the mysterious goals of Mr. Baldwin. He had to assume that something had happened to John.

That didn't bother him as much as not knowing how Ralph and Kristen would react to the event. He wouldn't blame them for panicking, but if indeed Matt, and now John, were dead, it could be disastrous for anyone to try and leave. The doubts that had most consumed his thoughts on the way down the river were about attempting to save Sarah. He knew the 'right' choice but, if he did this, they could still kill her despite his best intentions. Then his life would be ruined as well as hers. The thought aggravated him almost as much as it concerned him. He hated things out of his control.

It took him a few minutes to find someone who spoke English, and he was directed to a local bank. The sight of the familiar 'Cirrus' sign on the ATM almost made him smile. At least it was something he understood. Andrew walked through the doors and removed his small envelope. He had one more hundred dollar bill, and approached the first teller. She took it and without asking, did a quick calculation, then returned to him a little less than four thousand baht. Although Andrew knew what a baht was, he had never actually held one. It looked similar in color to Canadian money but had a man on the currency. He assumed this was the king, at least he thought he remembered that Thailand still had a royal family.

"Can you tell me..." Andrew could tell immediately that the teller didn't understand what he was saying so he just added, "Bank of America." The woman smiled and took out a piece of paper. She wrote down something on it and handed it back to him. It appeared to be an address.

"English?" he asked. She took back the paper and went over to a person at a desk. She wrote on the same note and the teller returned and gave it back to him. It said Bank of America - 313 Silom Road, Bangkok in Thai and English.

"Thank you!" Andrew said, and headed to the door. He stopped briefly to pick up a card with the address of the branch on it.

Andrew walked past a street vendor selling something hot, and he ordered a bowl. It was a cheap version of Pad Thai and he paid the vendor with his newly obtained money, then eagerly ate it with the provided chopsticks. It felt good to be back in control of this small part of his life. Several colorfully decorated motorcycles passed by with strange passenger contraptions attached. Andrew figured they must be some kind of taxi as he watched people flag them down and get on and off them. As soon as one stopped near him, he ran toward it and handed the man his paper, then without waiting, got in the back and sat down. The man took off so fast Andrew had to hold on to the rails to prevent himself from falling out. He soon found out that using the open air taxi had its advantages and pitfalls. The driver was able to weave expeditiously in and out of traffic, however Andrew was also regularly engulfed with exhaust fumes from passing vehicles.

Bangkok was a crazy octopus like city, and within a few minutes Andrew was terribly lost. He wondered if, by chance, the driver was another spy sent by Mr. Baldwin, but that was too ludicrous a notion, even for the omniscient self proclaimed Dream Maker, and Andrew settled back into the seat and watched the city with its millions of people pass by. About fifteen minutes later, the taxi pulled over to the side of the road, and Andrew looked up to see the familiar blue and red Bank of America sign. It wasn't America but it was as close as he was going to get today. Andrew got out and handed him a five hundred baht bill. The driver greedily took it and sped off. Andrew figured it must have been way too much but, at that point, he didn't care.

He walked through the glass doors into a large lobby with marble floors and walked up to the Bank of America banking center in the middle of the room, then waited for the agent whom was presently helping an older woman. She looked at him after the woman left and smiled. It made him wonder how bad he looked.

"Hello, Sir. May I be of assistance?" she asked. He let out an unconscious breath and put his hands on the counter.

"I need some help in arranging for a large bank transfer from the United States."

"Certainly, Sir, I will get someone to help you," she picked up a telephone and spoke to someone on the line. The only word he understood was 'American'. He hoped that was a good thing.

"Someone will be right with you," she said, and turned to help another woman.

Andrew waited for a few minutes before a well-dressed Thai gentlemen walked up and introduced himself.

"Hello. I'm Mr. Suda," he held out his hand to Andrew. His grip was firm and assured. "You are?"

"Oh. Sorry. Andrew Lee, I'm from Seattle, Washington, that's north of California," Andrew said.

"Very good, Mr. Lee. I'm familiar with Washington. The Huskies," the man referred to the University of Washington Sports teams and smiled.

"Yes. That's the one!" Andrew said, as he followed Mr. Suda to a private room. Mr. Suda showed him a chair and Andrew sat down. It occurred to him, as he felt the cool touch of the black leather, that he had not sat in a 'real' chair for days. It felt really good on his sore back.

"How can I be of assistance, Mr. Lee?"

"Please call me Andrew, I feel like my father when I'm called Mr. Lee."

The man smiled knowingly. "OK, Andrew, how can I be of assistance?"

"I need to arrange for a large transfer of funds from an account in the US."

Mr. Suda took out a piece of paper.

"Do you have your passport with you?" Mr. Suda asked.

"Uh. No. I've run into a few problems with my visit to your country and have no luggage or ID," Andrew said.

Mr. Suda stopped writing.

"This is a problem, Mr. Lee, sorry, Andrew... how much money are we talking about?" he asked.

"A million dollars," Andrew said. He expected more of a reaction than he received.

"That is a lot of money... Andrew, it will be difficult to arrange this without proper identification." Mr. Suda looked at him.

"Look. If I can call my office," Andrew looked at a clock, it was 3:00 p.m., "I can arrange for some kind of identification to be faxed to you."

"I'm sorry... Andrew, "Mr. Suda said. Andrew wished he would stop pausing before his saying his name, "we cannot accept facsimiles for such an amount of money."

"Mr. Suda, I anticipated that it might be necessary for some money on this trip and did arrange through your private banking division in the US to set up some special arrangements, perhaps we can contact that office?" Andrew asked. He really didn't want to waste a lot of time trying to negotiate with Mr. Suda.

"Well, we can try. Bank of America Asia is a different company than the US Company, however we do try and accommodate requests if at all possible. Do you have your contact information?"

Andrew gave him the telephone number by memory and Mr. Suda handed him the telephone after the operator picked up.

"Can I speak to Conella please?" Andrew asked. He fervently hoped he didn't get voice mail.

"Hello?" The familiar voice quieted his fears.

"Conella? It's Andrew Lee. How are you?" He felt the need to at least be cordial.

"I'm fine Andrew, how can I help you?"

"Actually, I'm in Thailand, sitting at your branch in Bangkok. I have had all my luggage and passport either taken or misplaced I don't know which. Anyway, a couple of weeks ago I had you set up a special account in case I needed emergency funds - you remember?"

"Of course. Let me bring that up," Andrew could hear her typing something. "There's ten thousand in that account presently. Do you need me to transfer those funds to you?" she asked.

"Kind of. I'm going to have my CFO, Frank Horowitz authorize a transfer of One Million dollars from our escrow funds into this account. Then I will need it wired over to Bangkok immediately – however, Mr. Suda here informs me that he cannot release the funds without proper identification and I do not have that at this time. I am hoping that the special codes that were sent up anticipating this kind of complication will be acceptable."

"Let me talk to Mr. Suda and see if I can offer him some assistance," Conella said. Andrew handed him the telephone and they spoke for some time, after which Mr. Suda hung up the telephone. It was 3:30 p.m.

"Mr. Lee, private banking is sending over some information that should help us arrange for this transfer, however, I sense that time is important in this matter. Perhaps you should contact your office and arrange for the funds to be transferred into your temporary account. If you tell me the number I will be happy to dial it for you," Mr. Suda said. Andrew had never been happier to be with the private banking unit. He made a mental note to send a bouquet to Conella. Andrew told him the number and was handed the handset.

"Goldie, this is Andrew, I need to speak to Frank, immediately please."

"Sure Andrew, he's in a meeting with the attorneys but I'll get him," she put him on hold and a minute later Frank was on the line.

"Andrew! So how's it going? Having fun?" he asked.

"Not exactly, Frank, there have been some unexpected complications," with Mr. Suda in the room he didn't feel like he could be too forthright. He was already worried about the bracelet and looked at it periodically. He hoped it didn't have a microphone on it.

"So, what's up?" Frank asked.

"I need some money, Frank. A million dollars."

"What?! We don't have that cash, and our lines of credit are already stretched thin because of the buyout. You know that. What's going on?"

"I can't get into the details, but it is imperative that I have the money wired to that temporary account at Bank of America – today! Even if it has to be manually deposited."

"But the only account that has that kind of money is the escrow account, if we don't get it back in time…" Frank dropped his voice.

"I know the consequences Frank. Believe me, this is a last resort. Whatever it takes get that money into that account in the next thirty minutes, *please* do it," Andrew said.

"I'll do what I can, but we need Denise to countersign on that kind of amount… hang on," Frank put him on hold for what seemed like an eternity. "OK. I found her. She was half way home already. Her kid has a cold. I'm going to meet her at the branch in fifteen minutes. Are you someplace I can call you back?"

"Yeah. Here's the number." Andrew took the card that Mr. Suda was handing him and read it off to Frank. "Thanks, Frank. I'll explain later."

"You make it sound like a life and death matter," Frank said.

If he only knew, Andrew thought, disregarding the comment.

"I'll talk to you in a few minutes," Andrew said, and gave the handset to Mr. Suda, who put it on the cradle.

Mr. Suda leaned back in his chair and folded his hands together.

"Mr. Lee, I am no clairvoyant but do you think the authorities should be informed of… something?"

Andrew looked up at him while controlling his breathing. "That is not necessary, Mr. Suda. This is just a simple business matter that has some time constraints on it," he said.

Mr. Suda didn't look like he believed him but dropped the subject.

"Can I get you something to drink? A coke? While we are waiting?"

"Yes. A Coke would be great," Andrew said. He had never enjoyed sodas but at that moment, in that city, he found it was exactly what he wanted.

Mr. Suda returned a minute later and gave him the reassuringly familiar can. Andrew opened it and took a large gulp, which resulted in a muted burp. He hoped that was not considered terribly bad manners in Thailand.

"Mr. Suda, assuming the funds are placed into my account and then wired first thing in the morning. Will I have the funds by tomorrow?"

"Not usually. It can take up to three days for international wires. Again, I understand you are very much in a hurry. Let's see if they deposit the funds, then we shall worry about the rest."

Thirty minutes later Mr. Suda answered the phone and handed it to Andrew.

"OK. It's done. Denise wanted to know why and I told her you had a deal that you were doing for a quick turn in Thailand. I think she went for it," Frank said. Andrew didn't really care as long as the funds were there.

"Thanks, Frank. I'll talk to you in a couple of days." Andrew hung up the phone before Frank could ask anything else.

Mr. Suda dialed another number and asked for Conella.

"This is Mr. Suda, can you verify the funds have been deposited?" Andrew held his breath until he heard him acknowledge the receipt, then he handed Andrew the handset.

"Conella?" Andrew asked.

"Yes. The funds were deposited and I'm arranging the wire," she said.

"Is there a way to get it expedited?" Andrew asked.

"I'm going to try. Also you will need to sign some paperwork tonight for verification. Let me speak to Mr. Suda and make sure we are all on the same page."

"Conella, you're a lifesaver," Andrew said. He meant every word.

Mr. Suda and Conella spoke for a few minutes, and then he left the room and returned with some paperwork for Andrew to fill out.

"Mr. Lee, come back in tomorrow morning and we'll see what we can do," Mr. Suda extended his hand and Andrew took it.

"Uh… just one more thing. Can I get a couple of hundred, I mean about ten thousand baht. I don't have any cash left," Andrew almost felt guilty asking for it.

"Not a problem," Mr. Suda filled out some more forms and Andrew signed them. By 4:10 he was back on the streets of Bangkok. He needed to find the jewelry store.

Chapter 17

Ralph and Kristen walked down the street of the small village for the third time that day. The sun was unbelievably hot and they were avoiding it by running from overhang to porch. They both watched in the distance as a man in a bamboo hat wheeled a cart of fruit in the same direction. A woman walked beside him, incessantly chattering in his ear. His shoulders were hunched over and his head was down. It looked as if he had stopped listening to her a long time ago. Ralph and Kristen followed them at a distance until the couple stopped at their stand. It was the same man and woman that they had all observed the first day.

"Did you notice that they have no children with them?" Ralph asked. Kristen looked around at the other people and he was right. Everyone else anywhere close to their age had children. The woman had disappeared inside the home where crying could be heard.

" I can't believe they left the kid home," Ralph said.

"She was obviously sick yesterday. Maybe that's the way they do it here... or perhaps there is someone looking after her," Kristen said.

Ralph wondered how she knew the child was a 'she' but dropped the subject. He took a gulp from the jug of water he was holding, and offered it to Kristen.

"What's it like having kids?" Kirsten asked.

Ralph was silent for a moment, then opened his mouth.

"I think I heard it best expressed: 'It is like having your heart on a leash," he mimicked, holding a leash on a dog. "It is both terrifying and exhilarating. You are constantly worried that you aren't capable of doing a good job, but every time one of them hugs you or smiles at you there is no greater feeling..." Ralph's voice drifted off and Kristen could tell he was in a better place. A loud noise from across the street broke the stupor.

The woman appeared again with the child and was berating her husband. The child was crying but its limbs were limp. Ralph and Kristen could see that it was emaciated.

"I wonder what's wrong with her?" Kristen asked.

Ralph remembered the first time that Devin had cried like that. It was terrifying to both him and his wife. They didn't know what to do. No matter what actions they took, there was no consoling the boy.

"Sometimes you just don't know what's wrong. It's extremely frustrating..." Ralph said.

"I wonder why they just don't take her to a doctor," Kristen asked.

Ralph thought the statement sounded like someone who was accustomed to health insurance or money.

"That's not an option for some people."

"What do you mean? If that was my kid I'd be on a boat or car or whatever to find out what was wrong," Kristen said.

Ralph looked at her. "What if you didn't have any money? No way to travel?"

It was as if a light turned on in her eyes. "Oh." She looked back at the couple.

"So, exactly what was the instruction about these two?" she asked.

Ralph tried to think back, "change his life so that he is something different than before...whatever the heck that means."

"Viewed different," Kristen said.

"What?"

"Change his life so that he is viewed different than before," she corrected him. He thought that, if she already knew what they were supposed to do, why did she bother asking?

"So what do you think it means?"

"I'm not sure. What things make a man viewed differently by his peers, his family?" Kristen wondered out loud.

"Money," Ralph said.

"Yes. We don't have any of that," she said.

"Wait a second. Why are you asking this? Are you seriously thinking of following Mr. Baldwin's instructions?"

Kristen looked at him.

"You have something else to do? Besides, maybe we can help him."

Ralph looked back at the man and considered their lives for the past three days. It certainly was not a priority for him to help this man. He just wanted to go home. He didn't care about the house, money, anything. He just wanted his family back. The thought made him cringe and he remembered last night.

"Art," she said, "that would make people view him differently."

"What? Turn him into Picasso or something?"

"No. Just teach him something. Help him be creative."

"I don't think that's practical…"

"Well, then what? Come on Ralph, think," Kristen turned and looked at him. He was repeatedly surprised to see her eyes at the same level as hers. She was a tall woman.

"OK. Fine. Turn him into a criminal," Ralph shrugged.

"That's not funny."

"Well, he would be viewed as different than before. I mean, that's all the instructions said." He was serious. "Besides, I think that would be a lot easier and faster."

Kristen ignored him.

"Education," she said.

"On what? That's a pretty broad subject," he said.

"I don't know. Look around you. These people obviously don't spend much time in school. We could teach him anything. Math. *English…*"

"In two, three days?!" Ralph said.

"How about this: Sports. We could teach him baseball or something. Certainly there's a ball and bat around her somewhere."

"And what use would he have for that? They look like they have to work twenty hours a day to survive. Who has time for a game here?"

"Look, the instruction said 'viewed differently'. It didn't say it had to be useful," Ralph said. If he was going to do this, it was to help him achieve the objective. He felt sorry for the guy but, in the grand scheme of things, there was just not a lot he could do for him and he had huge problems of his own.

"Cure his child," Kristen said.

"What? Are you Jesus?" Ralph said, but his mind was working.

Kristen ignored his comment. "What if it's something really easy. Let's go over there and see. Maybe it's like… I don't know, chicken pox." Ralph was surprised at her ignorance about children, but her comments had stirred something in his head.

"Why not. We've got nothing else to do." He stepped off the plank that he had been standing on and the touch of the sun nearly knocked him over. It was stifling. Kristen followed him over to the man. He looked up at them without a smile.

"Hello? My name is Kristen." She held out her hand toward him and he looked at it, then slowly grabbed it. His touch was rough and callused. It hurt Kristen's skin. Ralph just stood by and observed. He looked in the open door of the house and could see the mother trying to console the whimpering child.

"Can we see your baby?" Kristen asked. The man looked at her, puzzled, and Kristen mimed the rocking of a child. The man pointed inside the house and Kristen walked over to the open door.

"Hello?" She could see the woman holding the baby but there was no reply.

"Hello?" The woman looked up at her. The face was one filled with pain and anger.

"Can we come in?" Kristen asked, as she walked over the threshold.

"Kristen, maybe…" Ralph started, but stopped himself. The man had turned back toward the street to sell some fruit to a customer and Ralph tentatively followed Kristen into the home. The only light that entered the room was through the open windows and the shadows cast a gray pall over the room.

Kristen made her way up to the child and looked at it. It was thin and had sunken eyes. It looked like something from National Geographic. There were no visible sores. Ralph walked up beside her and greeted the woman, whose gaze had returned to her child, oblivious to the two strangers.

Ralph slowly reached out and touched the child's arm. Kristen was correct, it was a girl. There was no reaction, and Ralph softly pinched a bit of skin and then let it go. The skin failed to go back to normal.

"Dehydrated," he said.

Kristen looked at him. "Then let's give him some water," Kristen offered the jug to him.

"No. It's not that easy. She probably has diarrhea."

Kristen almost suggested Pepto-Bismol but, at the last second, she realized where she was.

"So, is it serious? Maybe she will get well?"

Both of them felt the mother look at them. Her eyes were wide, as if asking them a question. Ralph shook his head, and she quickly turned away and took the child with her to another room.

"Why did you do that?" Kristen asked.

"She was obviously looking for a miracle and we don't..." he paused and looked at Kristen.

"What?" she asked.

"I might have a cure. If it is dehydration..."

"Well, let's do it, then!" she said.

"We will need some items," he said, as they walked out of the house.

He led her back to the store where he picked up some salt and some sugar and took them to the counter. It was the same woman as that morning and he noticed, behind her, the idol they had traded for that morning. He pointed to it and then the two items. She waved them out the door.

"That was easy," Kristen said, "but I don't get what you are going to do with that." She pointed to the two bags.

"When you were talking to me about helping this guy I remembered that Lynn, that's my daughter, had really bad diarrhea a couple of years ago. She was so sick we thought something more serious was wrong, and took her to the hospital. The doctor prescribed this stuff, but we didn't have health insurance," Ralph paused so that Kristen would understand the implications of that, "so he wrote down a simple formula with salt and sugar. One teaspoonful of salt with eight teaspoonfuls of sugar in a quart of water, it tasted kind of nasty but it worked. Within days Lynn was back to normal." He looked at her after he was finished.

"But I have no idea how we are going to convey this information to that family," he said.

Kristen smiled. "I can do that. Let's go."

Chapter 18

The driver was weaving in and out of the heavy traffic like his ex-wife was chasing him for her alimony check, and Andrew hung on the ripped vinyl 'O God' handle, swinging like a chimpanzee. After nearly thirty minutes, the car came to a sudden stop. The driver extended his palm and, at the same time, pointed to a beige skyscraper. Learning from the previous experience Andrew took out two hundred Baht and gave it to the man, whose hand remained open. Andrew put another hundred in his palm with the same result, but this time he opened the door. The man smiled a toothy, yellow grin and put up one more finger. Andrew quickly calculated that it was about ten dollars and he thought he could live with that. He paid the man and got out of the car. It felt like he was in New York or Chicago. People were dressed in business attire and a few looked at him as he walked past. He pulled out the paper again and read the street sign. Charoenkrung Rd. He thought it was at least close to the correct spelling. The address indicated the skyscraper that the driver had pointed to and, upon looking closer, he realized that part of the address was actually a floor number, twenty-one.

Andrew walked into the building and took the elevator to the designated floor. When he got out it reminded him of the New York Jewelry district. The hallway was lined with bulletproof glass displaying incredibly gorgeous necklaces, bracelets and watches. He followed the address and found the store ThaiJem and immediately noticed the elaborate gold and emerald necklace displayed in the window. There was a special alarm collar attached to it. The gold was muted in color like it was made of 22 or 24kt unlike the bright 14 or 18kt most Americans would have been used to. It had a price tag of 43,000,000 Baht. In order to gain entrance to the store, which he could not see into, he would have to press the bell and be allowed in. He paused and thought about the possible outcome of this course of action. It could be a trap – though he could think of nothing to be gained by doing something to him. It could be an elaborate test. That thought almost pleased him because it would mean his whole life wouldn't go south. The Jewelry store could be a front for the guerrillas, but that didn't make a lot of sense because that would mean they owned everything in it – or maybe not. Most likely he decided it was just a store, or was in tacit cahoots with the rebels. Either way, he didn't see an immediate danger and pressed the button. A smartly dressed Thai man in a two piece suit and wide tie greeted him upon opening the door.

"Hello," Andrew said. The man glanced at him briefly, then stepped aside and allowed him to walk past. He never turned his back toward Andrew.

A woman stood at the nearest counter helping another customer try on rings and she glanced up at him as he walked by. It felt like he was in a fish bowl. He didn't know if the reaction he was getting was due to his color, his appearance, or both.

"Hello. How can I help you?" Another man appeared and stood behind the display case directly in front of Andrew.

"Hi. I'd like to see the necklace in the window," Andrew said, as confidently as he could.

"The ruby and platinum one?" the man asked.

"No. The gold and emerald one."

The comment caused a reaction that he couldn't have expected. The room got very quiet and the three visible assistants looked at each other. Andrew saw the man in front of him reach down below the counter. He gathered it was an alarm or something as, within seconds, he could hear movement from behind the mirrored wall in front of him. The only other customer was making her way to the door and Andrew decided that, if that door opened, he was going to follow her out. The room was highly air-conditioned but he could feel sweat dripping down the small of his back. It was almost ridiculous. A day ago he was feeling this way because of situations in a jungle surrounded by wild beasts and now he was nervous again in a big city encircled by even more dangerous predators. Man.

The doors in front of, and behind him, opened almost simultaneously and Andrew quickly turned around, just in time to see the door close on the back of the other customer.

"What do you want with the necklace?" The voice came from behind him and Andrew really didn't want to find out from whom. He willed the exit to reopen, to no avail. A woman clerk was looking at him, and he forced a closed lip smile, then turned around. A fourth and fifth man had appeared. The one not talking had his hand on a revolver harnessed under his shoulder. Andrew had no idea there were such large Thai men.

"Huh?" Andrew tried to buy some time for a reasonable answer.

"The necklace. You asked to see the necklace," the man said, with narrowed eyes.

Andrew took a gamble. He wiped the smile off his face and marched up to the man.

"What is this? I come in here looking to purchase something for my girlfriend and I get treated like this? Forget it. I'm leaving," he threw his hands in the air and turned around again but no one was moving except him.

"How did you plan to pay for this item?" the voice behind him asked.

"I'm just shopping today. I was going to return tomorrow, but you obviously are not interested in my business. Just open the door and I'll leave," Andrew half turned back toward the man.

"Mr…..?"

"Mr. Lee," Andrew said.

"Mr. Lee. I apologize for the behavior however, last week, someone attempted to steal that necklace you have just asked to see. He also was an American and also looked…disheveled."

Andrew thought it was probably a kind term, considering how he must look. He turned back toward the man.

"I have no weapons. I'm with no one, so obviously I'm not here to rob you." Andrew said. He was as curious as he was upset. "What happened to this man?"

"He is in jail. A Thai jail. Not a good place to be."

"Did he say why he was trying to steal it?"

"He said his wife had been kidnapped by rebels and was demanding a ransom…of this necklace. He did not have the money to buy it." The man waived toward the window.

Andrew didn't want to ask, but was compelled to.

"What happened to his wife?"

The man said something to the guard who disappeared for a moment, then returned with a paper. The man put it on the display case and Andrew walked over. It was in Thai, however the picture was unmistakable. It was of a blonde, Caucasian woman about thirty years old, with khaki shorts and a ripped shirt, her body was covered in mud and there was a huge gash across her neck. The woman looked like Sarah and Andrew felt acid rising in the back of his throat. He turned the newspaper over and looked at the man. His hands were shaking and he held onto the counter top.

"That's terrible," he said.

"Yes. But you see our concern."

At least the incident clarified that these people were not involved with the rebels, however it didn't make him feel any better.

"I need that necklace," Andrew said.

The man looked at him and Andrew held his gaze.

"I understand that, however we cannot just give it to you."

"How much?"

The man took out a calculator.

"One point one million dollars US," he said.

"I don't have that much," Andrew said. He couldn't believe he was about to negotiate over someone's life.

"I can give you $750,000 US," Andrew said.

The man shook his head.

"We are sympathetic, however it is too expensive a piece. There is nothing like it. The crown princess wore it last month at an official state dinner," the man said. At least Andrew knew where the rebels must have seen it or at least a picture of it.

"What is the least you can accept?" Andrew asked.

"One minute." The man turned around and disappeared for several minutes. The guard remained with his hand open next to his weapon. Andrew looked at the other sales people and wondered if they all spoke English.

"One million US," the man had returned with a pad of paper.

"$875,000," Andrew offered. He wasn't sure of the etiquette in negotiating in Thailand but he was not going to treat this like a taxi cab ride.

"$950,000," the man said, "I cannot go any lower. We are not the owners of the piece and that price does not include a commission to us. Given the bad luck the necklace has brought to us, we will be willing to sell it without one."

"Done," Andrew said.

"How would you like to arrange payment?" the man asked.

"Can you meet me with the necklace at the Bank of America Plaza?" Andrew asked. The man looked suspicious. "You may confirm that the funds are available prior to coming," Andrew added, hoping that the offer was acceptable, because he certainly didn't want to travel across town in a taxi with that much money.

"I think we can do that. We will need several hours notice to arrange the delivery. Please contact me at this number when you are ready to proceed." The man handed Andrew a card.

"I am very sorry about this," the man added. Not as sorry as I, Andrew thought.

"I appreciate your help," Andrew said. "May I leave now?" He pointed to the door and the man reached down and pressed a buzzer. Neither of them said a word as he left.

Andrew made his way downstairs, took a taxi back to the Bank, went inside and signed the papers that Mr. Suda had left for him in the lobby. Then he walked around the neighborhood until he found a familiar name: Holiday Inn. The green and gold lobby was somehow comforting to him, and he walked up to the counter.

"I would like a room please," he said.

"Certainly, sir," Andrew had to remind himself that he was in a foreign land. It seemed everyone spoke English.

"May I see your passport, please?" the man asked. Andrew was so tired and stressed out he had forgotten this small problem.

"Uh. I don't have it...I lost it. I need to go to the consulate tomorrow," he said, "is there something you can do? I have been working with my bank here in Bangkok," Andrew dug in his pockets till he found Mr. Suda's card and handed it to the clerk.

"Just one moment, please," The clerk left, and another man appeared a couple of minutes later.

"Mr?"

"Mr. Lee... Andrew Lee."

"Mr. Lee, we called Mr. Suda and he has explained your situation."

Andrew wondered just how much he had told him. "We would be happy to extend this courtesy. Mr. Anant will be happy to assist you. If you have any other questions please feel free to inquire."

Andrew couldn't remember anything over the last few days that had actually gone smoothly, and he slowly let out a breath of relief as the clerk typed in the information and handed him a room key. Andrew was able to provide a company credit card number by memory and asked him if there was a clothing store nearby that he could charge to his room. The clerk directed him down the lobby where Andrew found a tourist shop. It was good enough.

He went up to his room with his new clean shirt and shorts. The room was small, but comfortable, and smelled like lemon scented air freshener. He found it reassuring. After a long shower he laid down on the bed and feel asleep. The picture of the dead woman in the newspaper haunted his dreams. It was a terrible night.

:

Sarah couldn't determine it exactly but by her calculations it either the second or third day of her captivity, Tuesday or Wednesday. It drove her crazy trying to figure it out and she finally gave up.

The woman was still guarding her and Sarah gave absolutely no indication that she was anything but a compliant captive. The two other guards would come and go throughout the day and mostly they let her alone. She was fed with her feet tied together and the rest of the time her hands were also bound in front of her. At least they no longer blindfolded or gagged her. Every opportunity she got, she would bow her head and thank the woman. Still, there was no acknowledgement that she was anything but a prisoner.

The day was muggy and hot, and the insects relentless but Sarah kept herself busy planning a strategy. As the day finally started cooling off, the two men returned from their daily hunt along with their bloody catch. It looked like a miniature deer of some sort. They lit the fire and then disappeared as the woman took over the preparation. Sarah sat on the ground with her back against the now familiar log, watching her as she handled her knife adeptly, first gutting the prey and then hanging it up to skin it. The woman was always careful never to have her back to Sarah. If she did the same as last night, in a few minutes the woman would disappear to wash off her hands in some nearby water source and then return and put the meal on a crudely made rotisserie. Sarah waited until she had gone out of sight and then lay on the ground as if she had passed out. She concentrated on the sounds of the forest, listening for the telltale noises of her returning captor. Her knees were folded up and her head was in the dirt. Within a few minutes the woman returned and Sarah could hear her going back to her preparation, and then silence.

She figured that the woman finally had looked at her. The noises of the boot soles coming toward her reminded her of playing hide and seek – only this time she was in plain view, but the anticipation was still excruciating. The woman stopped directly above her and prodded her with a foot. Sarah lolled her head to one side and opened her mouth, she could feel an insect crawling across her forehead but she forced herself to ignore the tickling sensation.

Sarah had counted on the woman not calling for help, she had anticipated that it would be a sign of weakness and was sure, in this rag tag army, a woman couldn't afford to appear weak. She listened as the woman quickly walked away and then returned and poured water over Sarah's face, but she refused to react. The woman roughly grabbed her and pushed her into a seated position. Sarah hung her head like a rag doll until she felt hands push her head back and water poured down her throat. The cough was a reflex action but she used it to roll her eyes back in her head and fall backwards, which caught her captor off balance. The woman struggled to hold her up and Sarah made some gurgling noises and tried to use her hands in a feeble attempt to hold herself upright, but intentionally failed.

The woman was still facing her, but had bent over Sarah to reach behind her back in order to release Sarah's hands. In that awkward position Sarah finally had her at a distinct disadvantage and, with her arms now released, she wrapped them around the woman's legs and pulled violently toward her at the knees. The move propelled her captor backward into the air and she fell to the ground landing on the flat of her back with a thud. Sarah hoped the air was knocked out of her and she rocketed forward, pushing herself parallel to her shocked captor. In one motion, she grabbed the knife out of her belt, then held it against the woman's exposed neck. She could hear the gasps as the woman struggled to fill her lungs with air, and Sarah whispered in her face: "Shssh!"

Sarah looked into the woman's eyes and saw nothing but a hollow stare. There was no emotion. With the woman still attempting to gain a full breath, Sarah rolled to one side and pushed her over onto her stomach, then held her there with the knife point jabbing at the small of the woman's back. Sarah took her free hand and forced first one arm, then the other behind the soldier's back, emphasizing the movement by pressing the knife firmly. The woman reacted by arching her back and letting out a grunt. Sarah reached behind her and grabbed the leather tie that previously had bound her own arms and wound it around the woman's wrists. Standing above and behind her, she pulled backward on her arms and the woman got onto her knees, then stood up. Sarah pushed the knife into her back and followed her, grabbing the canteen of water on her way out of the camp. In the distance she could hear the jabbering of the other two guards and felt her captive turn toward the sounds. The woman said something to her, but she couldn't understand it and she prompted her to keep moving out of the camp into the brush.

Within a few hundred feet Sarah had the déjà vu feeling of being totally lost and the woman provided no direction.

"Home! Go home!" She whispered in her ear. The woman turned around and gazed at her again, the foliage falling around her shoulders.

"No," she said. Sarah was a few feet away and held the knife in her right hand. She didn't know whether she could really use it if she was forced to, and she acknowledged that it gave the soldier a distinct edge if she was pushed too far. But for now, the guard didn't know that.

"Yes!" Sarah narrowed her eyes and lifted the knife but received no reaction.

"I not....I..." the woman shrugged her shoulders and looked toward the ground.

"What? You not take me?" Sarah found this whole language barrier beyond frustrating. Besides, she didn't know whether it was play-acting or not.

"No home." The woman turned her head around in a semi circle and nodded her head every ten degrees or so, then shrugged her shoulders again.

Sarah couldn't mentally accept the gesture.

"You don't know where home is?!" she asked.

"No home," the woman repeated. Both of them reacted to the gunshot and loud shouting that rang out from behind them. Sarah looked at the woman and, for the first time, saw fear.

"They kill me," the woman said.

"You mean they will kill *me*," Sarah said, pointing to herself.

The woman shook her head slowly.

"No. They kill me," Sarah was suddenly mortified. The thought that she had threatened to harm this woman hadn't really meant much to her because she did not intend on doing so. But realizing that, if they went back they would kill her, made her sick and she looked at the woman for clarification, but her head remained down.

"We go," Sarah said, and pointed in a direction. From the setting sun it seemed to be south. She wished Ralph had been there, despite what had happened the day before. Still, she walked forward and the woman obediently led the way. Behind them they could hear the heavy footsteps and the sounds of hacking as the other two guards searched for them. Sarah noticed that the woman walked carefully so as to not break limbs and that she stepped on solid surfaces so as to not leave prints. Sarah mimicked the actions.

In a matter of thirty minutes or so she found herself uncharacteristically discouraged as she realized that, unless God gave her a vision, they would not find a way out of the jungle and she heavily doubted that he was going to do so. Her clothing was completely sopped in sweat, her shoes caked in mud, her legs cut and bleeding from the underbrush. Her lungs were burning, along with her arms, from holding onto the knife and branches that constantly swung in front of her face, but the woman kept walking, never looking back, and Sarah followed. She understood that, for the woman, there was no point in giving up, because the alternative was lethal, so they kept moving forward. She stared at the woman's back while she considered the ramifications of just letting the woman go, waiting until the other two guards caught up. Perhaps by some miracle the woman would find her way out of the forest. Sarah let out a breath and ran up behind her, grabbing her arms. The woman didn't react, or even turn around, and Sarah untied her hands and let her go.

The girl had not even walked ten feet when the crack broke the heavy still air and Sarah watched as the splotch of red slowly grew to the size of a grapefruit on the back of her worn shirt. The woman stopped in her tracks and, without uttering a sound, slowly knelt down, then fell onto her side. Her eyes, which remained open, were partially blocked by a small fern that fell over her face. Sarah found herself transfixed on the appalling scene in front of her. She was too stunned to scream or move, even though she heard the forest come alive behind her and felt the rough hands grab her by her arms and force her to the ground.

"Sorry," she whispered to her one-time captor as she stared at the woman. She heard the anger in the men's voices behind her as if through a concrete tunnel, and then felt the blunt force on the back of her head. As the blackness overtook her consciousness she found herself wondering what the dead woman's name was, and whether she had a family somewhere whom would miss her.

:

Kristen and Ralph returned to the couple's home and found the man still sitting at his booth. It didn't look like he had sold anything since they had left, and she wondered how he could possibly make enough money to support a family.

Ralph walked up to him and put the sugar and salt on the table. The man looked up at him with a puzzled look and Kristen nudged him aside.

"Here, let me," she said.

Kristen had seen a pencil and cardboard in the house and, while the man watched, she pointed to the open door and went in and retrieved them. She could hear the child still fussing in the back of the house. On the brown cardboard she drew eight small containers and a face beside them with a child smiling. Below it, she drew one container along with another face of a child sticking out his tongue and squinting his eyes. On the third line she drew a container of water about ten inches high, with a chopstick stirring it and arrows from the nine containers into the water. Next she sketched a sick child and drew an arrow from the water to its mouth. At this the man looked up at her and his face softened. He pointed to the back of the house, and then to the two bags in front of him and the cardboard instructions. Kristen and Ralph nodded an encouraging yes, and both of them smiled. The man continued to watch them, and Kristen opened the first bag and stuck her finger in the white granules, touching the tip to her mouth. It was sugar, and she smiled and pointed to the happy child on the cardboard. The man imitated her and also smiled. Next she did the same with the salt, grimaced, and stuck out her tongue. The man again followed, and the look on his face indicated he understood. He grabbed both bags as if they were gold and carried them inside, only pausing for a moment to turn back to Ralph and Kristen and bow. It was the humblest thanks either of them had ever experienced. They only hoped the cure would work.

Chapter 19

Andrew awoke famished. He couldn't remember the last time he had eaten. The clock beside him read 7:00 a.m. and, as he hopped out of his nice clean bed, he felt guilty that he had enjoyed such a restful nights sleep while Kristen, Sarah and Ralph had slept God knew where. Bangkok was already bustling, and the sounds of the city echoed up the hotel's glass windows. He walked over, looked down at the metropolis below, and saw a Tony Roma's sign in the distance. It made him wish that he were home.

After eating a wonderful and very western breakfast, he checked out of the hotel a little after 8:00 a.m. and walked to the Bank of America building, which was about six blocks away. Mr. Suda was waiting for him.

"Good morning, Mr. Suda," Andrew wasn't sure to bow or shake hands, so he did both.

"Good morning, Mr. Lee. I have good news for you. The funds are already here. To be honest, I have never seen an international transfer appear so quickly." Andrew made another mental note to send Conella something when and if he ever made it home.

"How would you like to accept the funds?"

"Actually, I need to make a telephone call first. I want to have something delivered in exchange for the payment."

Mr. Suda looked at him quizzically and Andrew clarified the statement.

"I am *purchasing* an item that will be delivered. A small, valuable article."

"Certainly. I understand. Would you like some privacy or should I dial the number for you?"

"If I could have some privacy, I would appreciate it." Mr. Suda got up and left the room after giving him instructions on how to dial the telephone number.

Andrew picked up the handset and typed in the number before realizing that he had not asked for a name the day before.

The person said something that sounded like crab or krup, so Andrew just said 'hello' and immediately the person switched to English.

"Hello. This is Andrew Lee. I need to speak to a man about the emerald necklace."

"A moment please," a woman said.

"Hello, Mr. Lee, this is Mr. Boon Mee. We spoke yesterday."

"Mr. Mee? Or is it Boon Mee?" Andrew didn't really want to waste time with names, but he also didn't want to offend the guy.

"Mr. Boon Mee."

"Oh. Sorry, Mr. Boon Mee. I am at the Bank of America corporate office on Silom road. If you will bring the article, we can do the exchange here."

"Mr. Lee, we can arrange that. Can you please provide me with a telephone number that I can return your call in a few minutes?"

"Uh. Sure, one second," Andrew dug out the card and read him the number and extension.

"And whose extension is this?"

"Mr. Suda, he is a..." Andrew realized he didn't know what his job description was, "a personal banker." He hoped that was good enough.

"I'll call you back in a few minutes, Mr. Lee." Mr. Boon Mee, hung up, and Andrew dashed out of the room looking for Mr. Suda. He figured Mr. Boon Mee was just verifying that everything was kosher.

Mr. Suda was standing outside another office a few feet away and walked up to Andrew.

"Is everything arranged, Mr. Lee?" he asked.

"They are going to call you back in a few minutes. I'm sure it's for verification," Andrew said.

"Not a problem." Mr. Suda walked back into his office and sat down in his leather chair facing Andrew.

"I sincerely hope this goes well for you Mr. Lee."

"So do I," Andrew said. He had no doubt that, by now, Mr. Suda fully understood the real story of what was going on, and found himself wondering how often it happened. He was almost tempted to ask him when the phone rang and Mr. Suda picked it up. He had a conversation in Thai for a few moments, then handed the handset to Andrew.

"Yes?"

"Mr. Lee, it seems that everything is in order. We will meet you in Mr. Suda's office in two to three hours. Please stay there until we arrive."

"I understand, Mr. Boon Mee." Andrew handed back the phone to Mr. Suda.

"He said a couple of hours..."

"Yes. Can I help you with anything else while we are waiting?" Mr Suda asked.

Andrew thought about the question for a moment.

"How often does this happen?" Andrew gestured between the two of them and was a little surprised at the non-reaction of Mr. Suda.

"Thankfully, not too often. I have only seen it once or twice and it usually happens only near the Cambodian or northern borders. I'm very sorry..."

Andrew actually thought that he really was.

"Some people have chosen to involve the police," Mr. Suda said.

Andrew looked at him and waited.

"However, I understand the reluctance to do so."

"What would you do?" Andrew asked.

Mr. Suda looked over at a photograph on his file cabinet. It had a picture of two children and what he presumed was his wife.

"I hope I never have to make that decision, however, I think if I had the money I would do as you are. The police are much better these days, still... problems exist." The comment made Andrew feel a little reassured at his decision. Andrew put his left hand over the black wristband and held it tightly.

"Have you ever heard of a Mr. Baldwin?" The question came out of Andrew's mouth before he realized it.

Mr. Suda looked at him suspiciously.

"Mr. Baldwin? Why do you ask? Do you think he has something to do with..." Mr. Suda allowed his voice to drop off.

"I don't know," Andrew was concerned about the reaction, but wasn't sure how to proceed. "He brought me here to Thailand."

Mr. Suda shook his head and did not immediately reply. Instead he started typing on his computer.

"How much money should we have ready for Mr. Boon Mee?" he asked.

Andrew was surprised at the change in conversation but went along with it.

"$950,000."

"US dollars, correct?"

"Yes."

Mr. Suda had turned his computer screen toward Andrew and he was able to read a note on it.

"If you'll give me a moment, I'll arrange for the funds to be ready," Mr. Suda said, and started doing some paperwork.

Andrew read what was on the screen. *'He is very well known in Bangkok. It is said that he is involved in many different activities and is very well protected by his connections. He plays 'games' in the jungle. The local stories say that he hunts men for pleasure.'*

Andrew shivered at the confirmation of what he had feared. The whole nightmare was unbelievable. He had ventured into this 'game' looking for fifteen minutes of fame and was instead living what seemed like an eternity in hell.

"I'm going to go outside and wait in the reception area," he said, as he got up and walked out the door. He needed some air.

:

Two hours later Mr. Boon Mee, and three guards, showed up with a locked briefcase. After confirming that everything was correct, Andrew made the exchange and asked Mr. Suda for the most secure way to travel back to the floating city. He was thankful that Mr. Suda himself volunteered to take him and, by 1:00 p.m., he was back at the river, the briefcase wrapped in a large shopping bag that Mr. Suda had given him. He thanked him profusely, took his necklace, and walked along the foot walk until he saw the young boy. He was eating a bowl of noodles.

"We go?" he asked.

Andrew nodded, and gingerly got into the glorified canoe. As the bustle of Bangkok disappeared in the wake of the boat, Andrew gripped the suitcase tightly. For the first time in many years, he prayed to a God that he wasn't sure cared. In all honesty he didn't know whether the strength that he asked for was for Sarah's sake, or to give himself the fortitude to forfeit the life he had built over the last fifteen years — and all in exchange for a person he hardly knew. Either way, the piece of jewelry that he carried in his arms didn't seem to have much worth anymore.

:

Sarah opened her eyes and saw nothing but blackness. Her head was throbbing and she felt a crusty film caked on the side of her face. Her mouth tasted like it had been stuffed with cotton. She could feel the heat of her own breath as it reflected off of the gag, which was securely inserted between her lips like a horse bit. The sounds of a fire crackled, and the air was cool, so either a few hours had passed or an entire day. It really didn't matter anymore, she thought. There was nothing left for her to do. Her left shoulder was asleep, so she attempted to rock herself to her other side but stopped when the men's voices hushed. The last thing she wanted was for them to realize she was awake. At least, while the woman was around, she didn't feel a terrible danger of being attacked. The woman... Sarah felt terrible about her, but also feared for herself, for she was now all but certain that the men would do whatever they wanted to her and, despite her reluctance to admit it, there was nothing she could do to prevent them. The only question would be whether she allowed them to take her mind along with her body. She was starting to question whether she should even attempt to stay alive. The reasons for doing so were being decimated by the hour.

Sarah strained to hear any noise that would indicate the men had gone, but the only thing that changed in those few moments of silence was the touch of a cool breeze against her chin. She knew what that meant. Someone had opened the tent and was coming in.

:

Andrew saw the small village from about a half mile away and had terribly mixed feelings. He wondered if he would find himself alone, or if Ralph, Kristen and John had stayed. He wouldn't have blamed them if they had left. Still, it would be have been nice to see Kristen's smile in a sea of unfamiliarity.

The suitcase had made its way between his legs to the bottom of the boat, where he touched it periodically with his feet to reassure himself that it was still there. He wasn't into symbolism, but as far as they went, it was as large as they could come. The boy motored his way right onto the beach and jumped into the water to steady the canoe so that Andrew could disembark. He gave the boy five hundred Baht, and the boy grinned from ear to ear. Andrew waived goodbye and carried his precious cargo back into the town. It was getting late and he really missed the Holiday Inn.

He walked into the village and, from habit, looked for the man with the bamboo hat. He didn't see him, only a vacant stand. Andrew stopped by and saw Mr. Lew for a few minutes, then continued up the street to the house of Nan. It didn't look like anyone was there, but he knocked anyway, then opened the door and went in and up the stairs, hoping to hear some familiar voices talking, but there were none.

Andrew opened his door first and saw the room left exactly has he had departed two days before. The note was gone but everything else was the same. He went across the hall and checked on Kristen's room. It, too, looked the same. Finally, he checked on John's room. He didn't like the guy, but he had to acknowledge to himself that it still would have been nice to see him. No one was there and he found himself walking back to Kristen's room and laying on the bed with the suitcase on his chest.

He hated being alone.

Chapter 20

"Patience, Mr. Pandit, patience," Mr. Baldwin said, as he lay on his fish net hammock overlooking the Bang Tao Beach on the Phuket Peninsula.

"I am running out of patience, Mr. Baldwin. I'm not sure you understand the pressure of the situation. My considerable investment in the BMSAT Company is at risk, let alone my yet unappreciated rewards. If this tension continues I will lose my entire fortune. I cannot allow this to happen," Mr. Pandit said. He was hot, dressed in his western suit and irritated at Mr. Baldwin's nonchalance.

Mr. Baldwin let out a heavy sigh and sat upright facing him.

"I fully understand that your six billion baht investment with the Burmese government is in peril. And as you know, it is in my best interests to alleviate the situation as well. Still, it will take time for my plan to work."

"And what exactly is your plan? You haven't shared anything with me." Mr. Pandit stood up and faced him. The small brown skinned man did not intimidate Mr. Baldwin.

Mr. Baldwin took a deliberate sip from his freshly made ice cold guava juice. He had not offered any refreshments to Mr. Pandit.

"This is a political matter, Mr. Pandit. You should know by now that sometimes it is best to be able to truthfully deny events, should they prove to become public. All that you need to know is that I will succeed in embarrassing the Royal family. It is the best solution to aid our common interests. The King must be given suitable encouragement to back off from his current policy. You know my reputation, Mr. Pandit, and it certainly speaks to my ability to select the right persons for the job at hand."

Mr. Pandit glowered at him for a moment and then transformed into the politician that he was.

"Perhaps you can just let me know how much time we are talking about?"

"Only a week or so. Not much time at all," Mr. Baldwin said. A pretty native Thai woman appeared at the deck door and Mr. Baldwin turned to Mr. Pandit.

"It's time for my massage. Please excuse me. I will contact you when it is required." Mr. Baldwin left the porch and followed the girl to the massage table. He didn't even bother waiting for Mr. Pandit to leave. As the masseuse climbed up on the table and started walking on his bare back, Mr. Baldwin wondered if Andrew had arrived back at the village yet. He was quite impressed with his resourcefulness. Although a lot of money was at stake, over one hundred and fifty million dollars of Mr. Pandit's alone, not counting all the illicit trade, he was immensely enjoying observing the 'participants' as they jumped through his hoops. The matter of embarrassing the King was just icing on the cake.

:

"Andrew! Wake up!" Andrew was in that polarizing place between sleep and consciousness when one knew they were dreaming but couldn't snap out of it.

"Andrew!" Kristen grabbed his arm and shook it. Andrew was holding onto a case of some sort.

"What?" Andrew blinked his eyes rapidly and found Kristen's face a few inches away. It made him jump.

"God Kristen! You scared me half to death," Andrew sat up rubbed his eyes and ran a hand through his black hair.

"You look better than I feel," Ralph said.

"Hi, Ralph. Yeah. Well I don't feel that great."

"I'm happy to see both of you though." Andrew smiled at both of them and Kristen sat beside him and gave him a hug.

"OK. OK…." Andrew said.

"What's in the case?" Kristen said.

Andrew's face got very solemn as he unwrapped the bag and showed them.

"Oh," Kristen said. She wanted to reach out and touch it but it would have been too weird.

"Where's John?" Andrew asked.

Ralph and Kristen looked at each other.

"What happened?" Andrew asked, as he shut the case and laid it on the bed next to him.

"I think he's dead," Kristen said.

"You *think*? What does that mean?" Andrew asked.

"Look. We… I mean, he said he was going to leave after you disappeared. Said he saw a policeman or something and was going to

150

go home. We found him a couple of days ago, badly beaten up, surrounded by locals."

"So is he dead or not?" Andrew asked.

"Uh. I guess so. I think so. He *looked* it," Ralph said.

Andrew contemplated it a moment.

"And you obviously feel that it happened because he was trying to leave?"

"Do you think there is another logical explanation? I mean, we haven't had any problems for the last two days here. People avoid us like the plague," Ralph said. Andrew looked at Kristen, her fingers gripping her legs.

"Kristen?" he asked.

"I don't know what to think. Ralph says that if we don't obey the instructions we are all going to be killed…"

Andrew thought about telling them what Mr. Suda had said, and then decided it would only fuel the fear.

"I suppose it is the only logical conclusion." He looked down at the bracelet.

"Any messages since I left?" he asked.

"Yeah. A pseudo warning about John and that we needed to complete the tasks," Ralph said. "Any idea what Mr. Baldwin is up to? It would certainly help to understand his motivation."

"I wish," Andrew said, "either he is just some sick bastard enjoying our misery, or he is after something. Sooner or later I guess we'll find out."

"So now what?" Ralph asked.

"We try and save Sarah," Andrew said.

Both Ralph and Kristen wanted to know how he managed to get the necklace and the million-dollar price, but it seemed a bit vulgar to ask.

"So. Who's going?" Andrew asked. It was a forgone conclusion that it was either he or Ralph and they looked at each other.

"I guess, I'll do it," Ralph said. He really didn't want to, but he didn't feel that there was a choice.

"Fine. What were the instructions?" Andrew asked.

"Just to take a walk and they would find us." Ralph stood up and waited for someone to say something but no one did so he reached over and pressed the clasps to lock the case. Andrew stopped him.

"What are you doing?" he asked.

"What do you mean? I'm taking the ransom," Ralph said. The word made the reality of the situation sink in and Ralph took his hand off the case.

"No. If you do that – there is no reason for them to release Sarah alive. We need an exchange point," Andrew said.

"What do you mean?" Kristen asked. The whole discussion reminded her of the unpleasant decision she had made.

"I mean a place where we can make sure we get Sarah in exchange for the necklace," Andrew said. He added in his mind, 'or where we can get Sarah and keep the necklace'.

"So what do you want me to do?" Ralph asked.

Andrew reopened the case removed the necklace and replaced it with a piece of paper, then locked the case and turned the combination.

Ralph and Kristen looked at him.

"Instructions on where and when to meet," Andrew said. "Take the case and give it to them, then get the hell out of there." He handed him the now empty case.

Ralph took it and considered what he was about to do. If the soldiers found an empty case he might be the recipient of their wrath. Andrew saw the hesitation and looked at him sternly.

"What? You can't do *that*?" Andrew knew he was embarrassing him, but he was getting irritated at Ralph's reluctance to take on risks.

"No. Yes. I mean. I'll do it." Ralph looked at Kristen and then walked out the door. When he was out of earshot Andrew turned to Kristen.

"So, what happened while I was gone?" Kristen had no idea where to start.

:

Sarah felt the movement of the air on her face right before she smelled the smoke. In a manner of moments she could hear heavy panting and rough hands on her face as the blindfold was pulled down. She quickly looked around to see if there was anyone else visible but the man was alone and he knelt down at her side and touched her hair. Sarah froze and looked through him. He mumbled something and ran his hand over her lips, her neck, then across her breasts. She forced herself to think of something calming. Another place and time, another life.

She was nineteen and in college. It was springtime in Toronto and the thought of University life should have been more thrilling than it was. She looked around at the stately buildings and all the men and women involved in discussions, flirting. It felt as if she were watching some movie, 'The College Years'. A girl bumped into her, knocking a book from off the top of the stack.

"Sorry! I'm such a klutz. You new here?"

"Uh. Yeah. Sarah," she said.

"Brenda. Hi! Nice to meet you. Where are you staying?"

"Campus D."

"Really? What room?"

The conversation revealed that they were neighbors and soon to be best friends. Sarah recalled the first double date they went on. Two cute guys from their drama class. Sarah was sure that the guys had joined the group just for the girls. Brenda didn't care. The evening went just fine until Jay and Brenda started necking in the front seat and Riley, Sarah's date, attempted to imitate a 'made for TV' petting move. Somehow Sarah's knee ended up in his groin and the double date ground to a halt.

The thought made Sarah reflexively jerk her knees up. The soldier saw the move a little too late and her knees hit him in the stomach as he tried to roll away. Sarah knew the consequences would be immediate, and harsh, but she just couldn't lie there and do nothing. The soldier cursed her under his breath and used his left knee to pin her legs against the ground and then slowly climbed on top of her using his weight to hold her down. She lay with her hips flat against the ground but with her torso twisted due to her hands that were still tied behind her and she stared at him as if she were trying to bore holes in his face. He just smiled with a mouthful of filthy teeth. Sarah tried to wrench herself away but soon grew exhausted and was gasping for air through the tight gag. As he started unbuttoning her shirt she relaxed in order to recuperate the last vestiges of her sapped energy. His hands moved toward her shorts and she tightened her teeth, closed her eyes and clenched her abdomen muscles propelling her torso up towards his face. She felt her head meet something slightly softer than his skull and hoped it was his nose or cheek. The contact made a terrible crack, like someone had broken a dry twig, and she heard the 'ugh' as the blackness again overtook her. At least if she died, she had caused him some pain.

:

It was twilight when Ralph entered the forest. He started whistling some nameless tune and walked forward down the overgrown path that he and Sarah had taken two days earlier. He listened intently for the noises that would indicate that someone was approaching, but all he heard were the sounds of the forest that he had grown so accustomed to. He thought about yelling 'hello' but couldn't get himself to do it, so he continued walking deeper into the jungle. By the time he realized that there was someone following him it was too late. He felt the burlap bag pulled over his head and the smell of mold permeated his nose. He heard a piercing scream and every muscle in his body froze until he realized that it had come from his own lips. The men laughed and pushed him forward, tripping him, and he crumpled to the ground. He could hear the men pounding on the brief case and he prayed that it didn't open. The sounds and voices seemed to fade slowly away and Ralph lay still on the ground until he was absolutely sure that he was alone, then he pulled the rice bag off of his head and looked around. There was no one left. Ralph got up and ran back to the village, only pausing long enough to slow his breath down before going back into the House of Nan.

"You look like you saw a ghost," Andrew said, looking up from the floor as he entered the room. Andrew had been contemplating what kind of life he would have if he ever made it home, and Ralph had disturbed his thoughts.

"They...they took it," Ralph considered telling him how it had happened but decided that he didn't need to know.

"Then we wait," Andrew said. Kristen was already asleep on the bed beside him. Ralph looked at her and felt the same old guilt. He wondered if she had told Andrew what had happened.

"Go to bed." Ralph took it as more than a suggestion and left the room. He was happy to be alone anyway. Before he shut off the light, he took out the picture of his family and kissed each of his children goodnight.

By the time Ralph awoke the next morning, Andrew and Kristen were already dressed and eating.

"Did you get some sleep?" Kristen asked.

"As much as could be expected." Ralph walked over to the food without looking at Andrew. He again wondered if he knew what had happened between him and Kristen.

"We need to get moving in a little over an hour," Andrew said, without looking at him.

"Where are we going?"

"Back to the river. There is a bridge about a mile downstream. That is where we will make the exchange. Make sure you bring everything that you want to keep with you when we leave. I don't think we'll be coming back," Andrew said.

Ralph really wanted to know where they were going but it didn't seem that Andrew was in the best of moods. He hoped it wasn't due to him.

The temperature was already rising by the time they left the House of Nan and walked through town for the final time. The crowd that had gathered was moving like a cup of mealworms in front of the home of the man with the bamboo. It made Andrew stop.

"What's going on there?" he asked.

Kristen and Ralph looked at each other.

"Umm. I'm not sure but we did help the guy yesterday... I should say Ralph helped him," Kristen said, looking at Ralph.

"We had nothing else to do so we figured we would try to help the guy. His child was dehydrated, we think..." Ralph said, but Andrew was already walking toward the crowd which continued to grow. They followed him. The twenty or so people parted when they realized the Americans had shown up and Andrew walked all the way up to the house entrance with Ralph and Kristen behind. The woman was sitting in a chair about ten feet inside the house with her child in her lap, facing the crowd. Her husband immediately saw Ralph and Kristen and ushered them in. He was gesturing wildly and making all kinds of sounds that they could not understand.

"He says it is a miracle." They all turned around and Andrew immediately recognized Mr. Lew.

"What is a miracle?" Andrew asked.

"The salt and sugar mixture Ralph gave him," Kristen said. Andrew looked puzzled.

"It was just something I learned with my daughter. I think the Africans call it 'the drink that saves lives'. Looks like it worked," Ralph said.

The man in the bamboo hat walked up to Mr. Lew and talked to him.

"He says thank you very much. You have given him reason to live," Mr. Lew said.

"Don't…." Ralph was interrupted by Andrew's hand.

"Tell him he is welcome and we hope he shares his knowledge with others in need," Andrew said. Mr. Lew translated.

"He promises to do so and wishes you his ancestors protection and blessing," Mr. Lew pointed to the little temple hanging on the wall.

"Tell him…oh, never mind. Tell him we must go," Andrew said.

"We hope his child brings him much happiness," Kristen added as they walked back through the crowd and into the burning sun.

"What was that about?" Ralph asked, obviously a little irritated.

"Sorry, I didn't mean to be rude. The man says it has changed his life, which is what we were supposed to do –" Andrew started.

"I know that." Ralph interrupted him.

"Yes. But it may come in useful, so I didn't want to give away too much information. It might be good for them to think of us as miracle workers at this point. Who knows what will happen in a few hours," Andrew added.

:

It took the better part of the next sixty minutes to follow the river downstream. The water was muddy, and moving fast, and the men were already returning from the morning's fishing.

"Maybe they know something we don't," Ralph said.

"Yeah. Like the river is going to overflow its banks. You can see the watermark is already covered. There must have been a storm up north," Andrew replied.

"Andrew, what are we going to do exactly? I mean, what if they start shooting or something?" Kristen asked.

"I don't know, Kristen. Let's just hope they don't." Andrew touched his hand to his pocket and felt the reassuring weight of necklace through the fabric.

"What if..." Kristen hesitated long enough for both of the men to look at her, "what if they did something to her?"

To Andrew it seemed as if she was feeling guilty about something.

"I would expect it." Andrew said, with a clenched jaw.

The conversation ended until they arrived at the bridge. They stood at the end and looked at the rickety construction. It was made of wood, about two hundred feet long, and three feet wide. There was a single rope running along the north side of it and sporadic splintered planks across its length. The bridge was supported by timbers that were placed every twenty feet or so, and sunk into the murky water. Hopefully into something solid, Andrew thought. In the middle, there was a make shift turnstile about twenty feet across. Currently it was open to allow boat traffic to pass through, like Andrew had done the day before. Today, before crossing, he stopped to pick up a long tree branch, and then walked over to the entrance and put a tentative foot on it.

"We need to get to the other side," he said, as he grasped the rope and cautiously started walking. Kristen followed him with Ralph bringing up the rear. As each of them walked on the gangplank it would sway in an off balance rhythm and every ten feet or so they would halt to allow it slow down. At about a hundred feet in, right before the turnstile Andrew stopped and pushed the tree branch into the water. The top of the flow was less than a foot below him and he attempted to take a measurement but the end of the stick never hit bottom so he let it go and watched it drift under the planks as the current took it downstream. It went faster than he had anticipated. They used a long pole that was mounted to the bridge in order to grab the trestle and pull it into place, then Ralph held onto one side as Andrew and Kristen crossed. He followed as Andrew gripped the other end. They released it and it swung back open.

Kirsten's arms were aching from gripping the rope so tightly. By the time they reached the far side she sat down on the first dead tree trunk she could find and rubbed her arms while Andrew and Ralph looked back across the water.

"Now what?" Ralph asked.

"We wait." Andrew squatted on the mud bank and tried to picture the exchange in his mind. After a few minutes he turned back to Ralph, who had walked over to Kristen.

"Can I have your belt, please?" he asked. Ralph dug it out of his bag and handed it to him, then watched as Andrew attached his belt to it and wrapped it around his right hand.

"What are you doing?" Ralph asked.

"I have no idea. In case someone goes swimming...and hang on to this." Andrew took out the necklace and put it in Ralph's hand, then looked at him.

"I'm going to go and wait on the bridge. When they bring Sarah out I will signal you to show it, if necessary, then bring it out to me. Any questions?"

"No," Ralph said.

"Be prepared for anything," Andrew said, as he took off back toward the bridge. Ralph had no idea what that meant, and he looked at Kristen. She shrugged her shoulders.

Andrew waited on the bridge in the sun on the near side of the trestle. There was no shade, and he was about to return for some water when he saw movement in the trees on the opposite side of the river. He anxiously waited as several soldiers appeared in rag tag clothing. One of them took a step on the bridge and lit a cigarette, not seeming to be in a hurry for anything. Andrew could feel the tightness in his chest, the humid air invading his lungs with every breath, and he consciously told himself to relax. The sweat in his right hand made the wound up belts feel like he was holding onto a snake. Finally, after ten or so men had appeared, he saw a glimpse of blonde hair and Sarah was shoved into view. She stumbled forward and fell into the mud, her hands tied behind her. The men laughed the sounds of their voices echoing over the surface of the water. Andrew's inclination was to run over to her and he had to remind himself to be patient. Losing his poise would not help her.

Sarah managed to get back on her feet and looked over to where Andrew stood. She had a gag in her mouth and her despondent posture made his heart hurt. He tried in vain to make eye contact in order to give her reassurance, but a guard spun her around so that all he could see was her back. Even from his distance he could see that her clothing was torn and covered in dirt or blood.

A particular soldier started barking orders again, and the men stopped their laughing and talking. Andrew watched as the man walked out across the planks until he stood on the other side of the turnstile, twenty feet away. He took a long drag on his cigarette and exhaled slowly into the air while he looked at Andrew.

"You give me gold!" he yelled.

Andrew shook his head and pointed toward Ralph. The man narrowed his eyes and took another puff, then threw the butt into the water.

"You want woman. You give me gold!" He turned his head slightly and yelled something to the men. One of them turned Sarah around to face Andrew, then took out a gun and held it up to her head. She refused to react and stared straight ahead.

"No," Andrew said, as calmly as he could.

"Ralph! Show it to him," Andrew yelled. He could tell by the reaction on the soldier's face that Ralph had done it. The man barked something back to his men and several of them pulled out their rifles and pointed them across the river.

"Ralph! Get Kristen out of sight!" Andrew yelled behind him. He should have thought of it sooner. The tension in the air was rising faster than the temperature.

"You bring her here," Andrew pointed to the bridge, "then I give you the gold!" He tried to draw the soldier's attention back to him, and he emphasized the sentence with his hand.

The man tilted his head slightly as if he was considering doing something rash and Andrew could feel a very unsettling feeling in his gut. He needed to do something.

"You bring the woman. I bring the gold!" he pointed back to Ralph, then yelled: "Ralph get on the bridge and walk ten feet!" He could feel the rope move and knew that Ralph was now standing somewhere behind him. He hoped he wouldn't do anything sudden.

The soldier smiled and gave a verbal command, which his men immediately followed. Sarah was brought out about ten feet on the other side. Two guards accompanied her. The process was repeated several times until only the trestle separated all the parties. Andrew reached behind him and held out his palm for the necklace, which Ralph gave him with shaking hands. They could both see Sarah clearly. It seemed as if she had tears in her eyes.

"What do you want me to do?" Ralph whispered behind him.

159

"Nothing. Wait," Andrew said.

The leader barked out another order. Two other guards, who were carrying something heavy, started making their way out on the bridge. When they met up with Sarah one of them took out some rope and tied whatever it was to her right leg. The man smiled at Andrew.

"You give me gold. Woman go river." To make his point he acted as if he was throwing something into the water. Andrew understood perfectly. The laughter of the men accentuated the point.

Andrew pointed to the long gaff and the soldier used it to pull the trestle into place, allowing Andrew to walk out a few feet. He then turned his head and spoke to Ralph.

"Take this and hold onto the bridge." Andrew handed him the coiled up belts without looking, and felt the span stabilize as soon as Ralph grabbed it. Andrew proceeded until he was a few feet away from the man. The necklace was grasped in his right hand and he watched the man's eyes follow as he lifted it over the water. The man didn't even flinch as he spoke to his subordinates behind him. One of them pushed Sarah forward until she was directly behind the leader. The rope that was attached to her leg and extended back to the object remained on the fixed part of the bridge. It took all of Andrew's effort not to look at her.

"No one get hurt. Give me gold," the soldier held out his hand. Andrew knew that, sooner or later, he would have to take a leap of faith. If the man wanted him dead he could shoot him at will after he got the necklace – no matter when the exchange took place. Andrew took a step forward and held out the million dollar piece of jewelry to the soldier. The man opened his hand and Andrew laid it in his palm while firmly grasping it in a handshake. The move surprised the man but he didn't let go, and stepped aside to allow Sarah to walk past him. When she was within Andrew's reach he let go of the man's hand and grabbed Sarah with both arms.

Neither of them was prepared for what happened next. Andrew heard Ralph yell and turned toward him, shielding Sarah with his body. The first thing that crossed his mind was that someone was aiming a gun at her. Suddenly he heard her scream and she was wrenched out of his arms, her face frozen in shock as she was dragged backwards, into the swirling water. Andrew looked up at the soldiers who were all running off the bridge and immediately noticed that the heavy object was no longer where it had been. He looked down and reflexively jumped into the river at the last place he had seen Sarah.

"Can you see her?" he yelled at Ralph who was looking on in horror.

"No. No! But she was there." Andrew didn't bother to look at where he was pointing and dived down into the depths. The current was stronger than he expected,and he fought it with all his strength, his arms flailing in front of him as he haphazardly tried to touch anything connected with her. After what seemed like an eternity of seconds, he felt something soft and grabbed at it. It was an arm. He followed it to Sarah's head and could feel her panic, but he was out of air and he tore himself away, breaking to the surface and gasping for air.

Andrew pushed off from the nearest wood piling and dove back down. He found Sarah's arm and cradled her face, trying to give her some kind of reassurance. She was holding on to him so hard that it hurt, and he had to pry her hands off so that he could cover her mouth with his.

THINK, SARAH!

It was as if she heard his thoughts when she relaxed her lips under his touch. He sealed his mouth over hers and blew into her a breath of air, but some water seeped in and she began to cough. In a panic he again rushed to the surface, took a deep breath and repeated the procedure. This time she took the air eagerly before he dived further down and tried to untie the rope. It was too tangled.

DAMMIT!

He surfaced again and yelled at Ralph.

"Get in here!"

Ralph obediently jumped in the water, but held onto the bridge, bracing himself against a piling.

"The belt!" Andrew grabbed one end of it and dived back down to Sarah, who rapaciously kissed him to accept more air. He took the end of the belt placed it in her hand and closed it, then cinched the opposite end around his leg and resurfaced. At least she could feel the contact.

"The knife! I need the knife!" Kristen had already started running out when she had seen Ralph dive in. She was about fifty feet away, and Andrew dived back down to breath into Sarah. By the next time he surfaced, Ralph had the knife in his hand. Andrew snatched it from him and dove down again, this time bypassing her mouth and the air that she was expecting. He could feel her confusion but he pulled himself upside down along her body toward the bottom until he felt the taunt rope, which held her. He used the blade to carve at it until it finally released, then dropped the blade, grabbed hold of her, and propelled to the surface. They broke through the top of the water, both gulping for air like fish on dry land. Andrew held onto her as she coughed up water and gasped for breath. Though the heat was almost unbearable, he could feel her shivering in his arms as the current carried them downstream.

:

At the same time that Sarah and Andrew were floating down the river with Ralph and Kristen running along the bank, news of the miraculous cure of child from the village had reached Bangkok and Mr. Baldwin was meeting in his home with a Thai man with an English accent. They were sitting on his veranda in shorts, sipping on Pineapple juice, watching tourists play in the turquoise blue water.

"How did you know what they would do?" the man asked. The satellite phone rested beside him.

"I had no idea. But it didn't really matter," Mr. Baldwin was very pleased with himself.

"I don't understand."

"You see, it really would have made no difference whether they turned him into a criminal, killed him, or whatever. We just needed an excuse to get the news media involved," Mr. Baldwin said.

"Why not just call them in the first place – why all the games?"

Mr. Baldwin smiled and thought to himself that he *liked* games, but that was not all.

"Better for it to be stumbled upon. People resist being told something, but let them think of the idea themselves and it becomes much more powerful."

The man seemed to accept the thought and took a sip of juice.

"How long should I wait?"

"Call your contact tomorrow, as if the news had made it's way down the river to you. Your contact ought to like it. The capital is always complaining that only Bangkok gets news coverage, and mostly bad news at that..." Mr. Baldwin moved his hand across the sky like he was writing a headline.

"Miracle in Quan Lukc," he said. "If your man is as good as you say, it won't take long for him to discover the real story that we want to come out."

They both smiled. Miracle in Quan Lukc. Or 'Illegitimate son of King banished to Quan Lukc'. The second headline was the one he really wanted to read.

"In a day or so, make sure someone up north realizes the irony that Americans were responsible for healing and discovering the King's illegitimate grandson, and with such a simple cure. As our King is quite vocal about his rural health care initiative, questions should be raised about his competence...and desire...Of course, we will do this in Burma where they are happy to criticize the King. That should help our friend in office here," Mr. Baldwin said.

"And what about the necklace?" the man asked.

"That event has not yet run its course. But we will talk tomorrow."

The man got up from his chair and bowed to Mr. Baldwin, who barely acknowledged it. He was already thinking about what needed to happen next.

:

Several hundred yards downstream a boat rescued Andrew and Sarah delivering them to the bank of the river where Ralph and Kristen panted for air from their run. Kristen managed to walk up to Sarah as she waded ashore, and hugged her. She did it as much for herself as Sarah. The guilt was killing her.

"Thank god you're..."Ralph struggled for the right word, "...here." He looked down toward the ground. Andrew walked up beside Sarah and helped her to a shady spot, then kneeled in front of her. Neither of them spoke as he held her face in his hands and slowly examined her from head to toe. She looked beat up, and had a bad bruise on her head, but there did not seem to be any permanent damage, at least visibly.

"How do you feel?" he gazed at her eyes, attempting see beyond her normal façade.

Her lips started quivering and she rolled the bottom one into her mouth trying to stop the tears, but they were already welling up. Andrew gathered her in his arms right before she broke down.

"It's over. It's over," he said. Ralph and Kristen left them alone and wandered off down the riverbank. They both wondered if Sarah would tell him how it had been determined that she had become the ransom victim instead of either of them.

It took several minutes, but Sarah calmed herself down and sat across from Andrew with her hands in her lap.

"Thank you." She looked at his eyes and allowed her normal protective shell to fall away.

"You would have done the same," he said. The comment made her contemplate how unselfish would she have been.

"I hope so. If I could have."

They sat in silence for a minute.

"Did they hurt you?" Andrew asked. She knew what he meant.

"No. I thought they were going to…" It made her remember the woman that had been killed.

"I… I tried to escape. I didn't think anyone was going to help me." Her eyes filled with tears again but she blinked them away. She wanted to ask about the money, but it just didn't feel right, so she tenderly looked at him again and mouthed the words 'Thank you.' Andrew smiled and bent over and kissed her forehead. She looked at him as he stood up and turned toward the river.

A few hours ago she had thought that she was going to be killed, or worse. She had woken up that morning, outside, with a terrible headache. The soldier that had attempted to rape her sat a few feet away with a bandaged nose, scowling at her. They didn't give her anything to eat before they started marching. The trek had taken hours, and she had not taken a single break. When she had finally heard the sounds of the river she panicked. The pain in her chest got so intense she thought she was going to faint. Drowning was her worse fear; the thought of suffocation was paralyzing. She thought that her mind had played a trick on her when she caught a glimpse of Andrew as she was shoved forward into the banks of the river. When she looked up and saw him, actually standing on the bridge, it was like every nerve let go of their endorphins and she felt an illogical giddiness. It was almost as if her mind had forgotten everything she had been through. When the man put the gun to her head, it meant nothing at all. She stared straight ahead and concentrated on what it would be like to be free again.

The anticipation of the walk on the gangplank, then watching the exchange, all took place like she was merely an observer, watching the spectacle unfold. But when she had felt Andrew pull her toward him, and his arms holding her, the emotions had rushed up so fast that she started to cry—only to be ripped from him backwards toward the water. She had watched the shock on his face as she flew through the air, torn apart by the appalling weight dragging her downward, her eyes burning as she refused to close them in the muddy water. She had kicked with all her force trying to return to the surface but was relentlessly pulled under, until the sky became only a faded light. Then, like a dark angel from heaven, the shadow of Andrew appeared above her. When he had pressed his lips to hers the first time she had panicked but, upon feeling the calmness of his hands on her face, she realized what he was attempting to do. Soon the unreasoning panic was replaced by a logical fear… Fear of running out of air in between the gifts of breath that Andrew brought her. The whole event had not lasted more than a minute or so but, in that short period of time, buried alive beneath the swirling water, Sarah trusted that someone beside herself would save her. Her heart had told her that whatever it took he would make sure that she survived. And she had.

Sarah gazed at his back as Andrew knelt down and threw a small pebble into the river. One day she would find the words to show her appreciation for the incredible gift that he had given back to her.

Ralph and Kristen saw that Sarah had composed herself and returned. Sarah smiled at them. There was no need to be angry.

After the group had rested a while longer, they drank some water and started walking south to Bangkok. Andrew estimated there was a town a couple of miles downstream, and he still had some baht with him. At least they could get a good meal, a place to clean up, and get some sleep. Sarah walked in silence beside him, and Ralph and Kristen followed. By the time they reached the village it was late afternoon. Andrew managed to find a place to stay and they purchased some food from a street vendor. After taking showers everyone fell asleep on the two beds in the room.

The next morning everyone except Sarah awoke early. Ralph and Kristen left the room and Andrew shook her gently. She awoke with a start, and Andrew could see the fear in her eyes.

"You're OK," he said. Immediately, she relaxed and lay back on the bed facing the ceiling.

"I wish it was all just a nightmare," she said.

"It was. But it's over."

Sarah sat up and looked around.

"Where are Ralph and Kristen?"

"I think they're downstairs."

Sarah thought about telling him what had happened in the camp with Ralph and Kristen. It was tempting to share her frustration but she recognized it also would not be helpful. She got up and stretched.

"Ouch!" she grimaced at a shooting pain in her left side. She lifted up her shirt and found a large bruise, as if someone had kicked her there. Andrew touched the swelling and she reflexively flinched.

"Sorry."

"It's OK. I'll be fine," she said. He allowed his fingers to remain a little longer than necessary, then pulled away.

"You want to clean up before we get some food?" he asked.

"Yes. Just give me a few minutes." Sarah went into the small bathroom, looked at her bruised face in the mirror, and sighed. It would be a few days before she looked better.

Andrew was waiting in the hall when she came out, and they walked downstairs where Kristen and Ralph sat drinking some kind of juice.

"Find anyplace to eat?" Andrew asked.

"There's a place next door. We were just waiting for you two. Good morning, Sarah," Ralph said.

"Morning." Kristen gave her a hug.

"I'm famished," she said. They all walked out the door and into the restaurant next door. Kristen led the group and stopped, immediately inside the threshold.

"What? I though you were dead?" Her mouth was agape and she was pointing to a badly bruised, Caucasian man at a table.

"Yeah, me too," John said, as he got up from his seat. "Thought you guys *left* me for dead. You know, I heard you two standing above me on the street. I just couldn't talk. It was like I was paralyzed or something."

Andrew found the whole thing hard to believe. He was more than suspicious. As if on cue, his wristband started beeping. He ignored it, but Ralph and Sarah stared at his wrist.

"How did you get here?" he asked John.

"This – dude," John handed him an envelope. "Open it. Some of it is written to you guys. Just got it this morning." John sat back down and leaned in his seat. Andrew took the envelope and sat opposite him.

"What happened to you back in that town?" Andrew asked. He wasn't about to give John time to think.

"After you guys left me, someone came and dragged me off to the shade. A couple of hours later I could stand up, and I high tailed it out of town. A kid gave me a ride in a boat to Bangkok. I think I fell asleep. Next thing I know, I'm back here." John pointed to the envelope. "One of those was by my bed and it basically said to stay put. I may be a little stubborn, but I know when to take a hint. I've been here a couple of days. So what happened to you all? I see Sarah is back with us," he smiled at her, "glad to see you're OK. You've got the most beautiful eyes."

The comment ticked Andrew off and he tore open the envelope. The three others stood behind him to read it.

Chapter 21

Dear friends,

If you are reading this, then you have been reunited with John Matthews. It is good that he is feeling better. You have all performed marvelously on your tasks and I look forward to your continued success. It is good to have Sarah back with the group! You have one more task in Thailand: Go to the Wat Benchamabopit, a temple in Bangkok. Cross the red bridge (Sapan Thouy) and go behind the monks quarters until you see a group of four buildings (Sala Si Somdet). Inside this building you will find many pictures of King Rama V. You are to remove any one of the pictures and bring it to the address below after dark. (Don't worry! We will return the picture!). If you complete the task, your passports will be given to you as a reward.

Keep your eyes on the Prize!

Andrew finished reading and looked at John.

"Do you know what this says?" he asked.

"No, but it looked mighty crowded over there so..." John extended his hand and took it from Andrew.

"It raises more questions that it answers," Ralph said.

"And he wants us to steal." Sarah said. They all waited until John had finished and looked up.

"This seems like the best opportunity to get out of this country. Let's just do this and go home," Ralph said, resigned.

"Look. I'm not relishing it but if it gets me home....I'm in," John said. Everyone was silent and looked at him.

"What? You think I have something to do with this nutcase? Take a good look at me, I've been trashed, I have this stupid thing on my wrist, no money and no way home." He threw up his arms and was silent.

"John, I'm sorry. We are all a bit edgy," Sarah said.

"Yeah. It's OK. So how did you get away from... you know..." he asked.

Sarah looked at Andrew.

"He paid the ransom."

"Damn," John said.

"OK. Let's eat something. Maybe this will make more sense on a full stomach," Andrew said. He doubted his own words as soon as he heard them. The group sat down at the table and ordered by pointing to the dishes at the other tables.

"So are we going to do this or not?" Ralph asked, after they had eaten.

"Do we have a choice?" Andrew asked.

"I realize that probably none of us are Buddhist here but what about the violation of religious beliefs? I mean they obviously revere this king-monk as a demigod or something…" Kristen said.

"Um. Does this have anything to do with what we are talking about?" John asked, confused.

Sarah understood that Kristen was already feeling guilty about a lot of things.

"Who cares? Good lord – he says they have plenty of these pictures – they aren't going to miss one. It'll be like stealing a cross from the Catholic church," Ralph said.

"Would you do that?" Kristen asked.

"No. My wife's Catholic, she'd kill me," Ralph said, then quickly added, "but they certainly wouldn't miss one cross."

"That's not the point. *They* believe it is sacred. It just seems wrong. No one else here believes in a God?"

"Kristen, that's not really the question. I don't see that we have any other choice. I mean we know what he's capable of and we have no way out of the Country let alone getting back in the US. Without our passports were jammed," Andrew said

"I know…I just don't think it's right," she mumbled.

"Amen there," Sarah said, trying to give her support.

I'll do it." All of them were shocked at Kristen's offer.

"Where did that come from?" Ralph asked.

Kristen shrugged her shoulders.

"I've done so many things already – what's the difference?" It was like watching an already drunken alcoholic reach for one more shot of scotch but no one said anything.

"Besides, I haven't been worth anything to this group. It's time I did something," she said.

"Are you sure?" Andrew asked.

"Yes. Besides a woman will draw less attention than a man will. She can carry a purse or bag and… Sarah has been through enough." No one argued with the statement.

"OK. Let's get to Bangkok. The quicker we do this the sooner we go home." Unless this is some sort of trap or lie Andrew thought.

"How far is it?" John asked. His feet were really swollen.

"About fifty miles or so but I saw a ferry yesterday. I believe it was here," Andrew said, as he paid for the meal.

It was more like a homemade dock than a ferry terminal but after some confusing conversation and an hour wait the group boarded a very old fifty foot boat with a wooden canopy and headed down the river. The vessel was packed, making the odors from the animals and pungent foods almost unbearable. Kristen finally resorted to breathing through a piece of cloth while Sarah gazed out over the water in deep thought. Andrew walked up beside her.

"You OK?" he asked.

With him standing so near, what she wanted to do was lay her head against him but she fought the urge and looked at her hands.

"I'm OK. Glad to be free, sad to be trapped in this hell. All I wanted was to finish my schooling…what a stupid mistake that was…Hey but I am alive!"

"Well if you're stupid, we all are. At least that means you have company," Andrew said.

Sarah wasn't really listening, she was contemplating her feelings toward him. It was a confusing subject to her right now. She didn't know whether her feelings were one of obligation or attraction. Either way, now was neither the place nor time. Besides, he had a girlfriend she reminded herself.

"I'm going to take a walk," she said. He took it as meaning alone and he watched her go up to the bow where John joined her. Andrew stayed where he was. He didn't know whether she was making a point or just needed some time and didn't want to push her.

"So, you like boats?" John asked her.

"I guess. It's not like this is a cruise or anything," Sarah replied.

"The water is my thing. Love the ocean. There's nothing like the sound of crashing waves and feeling that power under your board…"

Sarah turned to him.

"I thought you were a rock climber?"

"Oh Yeah! That's right, but I love to surf too," John nodded his head like a turtle.

"You have family?" she asked.

"Yup. Two sisters and a brother, I'm the second oldest. Everyone else is hitched."

"And where do you live again?"

"I'm kind of floating around right now. Spent some time with my sister in Cal. She lives near Yosemite then went to Hawaii – the big island. You know, rolling stones and all that…"

Sarah looked back over John's shoulder and saw Andrew in the same place she had left him. Am I making a point here? What am I doing she wondered. God, she hated acting like a girl.

"So, sounds like something bad happened to you back there. You think maybe you ate something?" she asked.

"Maybe. It was kind of like an out of body experience. I mean, man, I was like floating about myself looking down. Really gnarly. But look, nothing like you went through. I'm really sorry about that. We were really worried," he said.

"Thank you. I'm OK. I can't believe Andrew did what he did…"

"Man, he must really like you or something…" he said.

Something that he had said did not set quite right with Sarah. It finally occurred to her and she turned to him.

"Did you know I had been kidnapped?" she asked, while facing him.

"Uh. Yeah. I heard Ralph or Kristen talking about it. Must have been really… intense." The reply was either a really fast recovery or the truth. Sarah couldn't tell.

"Well, hey. I've had enough sun. I think I'm going to head back and catch some shade," he said, as he turned and walked away. Sarah looked back toward Andrew but he too was gone.

They reached Bangkok in the late afternoon and found a youth hostel where they could stay for the night and obtain directions. After a light dinner they all headed to bed early. Andrew had seen an Internet kiosk in the main lobby and snuck down in the middle of the night to do some research and send a couple of emails. He was surprised when he returned to the shared room to hear John and Sarah talking. As he laid on the bed with the neon lights of the city reflecting into the room he had the most sickening feeling. It was completely foreign to him and he had to think hard about what it was. On one hand it was like a stone in his gut and on the other it was almost anger. When he finally figured it out, the thought was as unsettling as the emotion. For the first time in his life it occurred to him that he was jealous. It stole his sleep for the entire night.

"Did you read the papers?" Mr. Baldwin asked. He held the awkward handset up to his left ear.

"Yes, I did. Well done," Mr. Pandit said, "and what about the … jewelry, "he added.

"It should break today, tomorrow at the latest. By the end of the weekend he will have enough embarrassment to back away from the Americans and their offer for help," Mr. Baldwin said.

"And if he doesn't?" Mr. Pandit asked.

"Don't worry. He will," Mr. Baldwin hit the end button on the encrypted satellite phone.

The English version of the Bangkok Post, with the article about a man in Quan Lukc, who was said to be the Kings illegitimate son, was up on his computer screen. The claim had so far, been met with silence by the Imperial House. Mr. Baldwin knew that more questions would surely unlock the mystery as he had done many years ago. The news would undoubtedly distract and embarrass the King but it would not be enough to change policy. That, he was certain would come within a couple of days.

The Wat Benchamabopit Dusitwanaram or The Marble Temple was located in the heart of Bangkok. Andrew had learned that it was considered a royal temple with a history dating back well over a hundred years. A Thai King, Rama V had become a monk and lived as well as died there. From what he had read Royalty frequently visited it. Andrew purchased a canvas bag and then took a taxi with Kristen to the compound.

"Are you sure you can do this?" They stood outside the temple gates. Kristen looked pale.

"Yes. I can do it. I'll be fine," the trembling in her voice gave her away.

"Look. I'll do it. You can wait here," Andrew attempted to take the bag but she put it behind her back.

"No. I'll do it. Really, then maybe we can all go home..."

"Breathe. Deep breaths," Andrew said, as he watched her enter the gates.

The South entrance opened into a courtyard and Kristen walked slowly through it observing the grounds. She continued around the temple with its white walls and golden doors into another courtyard where dozens of full-sized Buddha statues in bronze and other colors were displayed in cloisters forming a perfect quadrangle. The floor was covered in white marble and she could feel the slickness under her sandals. Every so often bald headed monks in orange garb would walk by in pairs and it would make her heart speed up as if they knew what she was planning. None of them even looked at her.

She followed a couple of other tourists into a medium sized hall where a group of monks gathered together under a large Buddha. It looked like an ordination of some kind and she quietly walked behind the ceremony without anyone noticing. The hall opened into a small canal, which was filled with fish and turtles. The smell reminded her of the swamplands in Florida.

On the far side of the canal was a small shelter where she sat down in the shade. Surrounding the ornate gazebo were gardens full of flowers and it made Kristen miss Portland. Some of her favorite times were spent in the Washington Rose Garden and she loved flowers of all kinds. She concentrated on steady breathing until she could feel some of the tension in her shoulders release, then stood up and proceeded to the small red bridge that Mr. Baldwin had described. She paused for a moment at the crest to watch the Koi fish swim underneath her. It helped calm her nerves.

The first building near to the bridge had some large drums and a series of shields that were hung under the elaborate gables. Kristen wandered over to them attempting to look like a tourist and thumped one. To her horror and the obvious displeasure of a passing monk, the sound echoed off the nearby building. She quickly withdrew her hand continuing on her way until she found a group of four beautiful two-story buildings. She picked one and went through the golden doorway into a chamber with walls covered in gold and bronze paint and decorative fabrics. Murals and pictures of what had to be King Rama stared down on her as she softly shuffled past several tourists and a monk. She was happy that there were no obstructions to the art or religious artifacts. It also made her feel guilty because they obviously didn't think anyone would take anything from them. The perspiration from the heat and her nerves were drenching her clothing. That, along with her rumbling of her stomach made her certain that someone would come by and haul her off, figuring that she was up to something. In the background she could here the chanting of voices mixed with the rumbling of drums. Fragrant exotic incense filled the air and it made her both slightly nauseated as well as providing her a heightened consciousness. It was as if she could feel every wisp of air, hear every insect, smell every aromatic cinder that was burning and she wondered if it was the feeling that the monks experienced when they meditated.

Despite the misgivings that screamed from the back of her mind she walked up to the smallest of pictures that she could find and reached out to touch it with one finger, quickly withdrawing it. The picture softly rocked against the wall indicating it was merely hanging on a nail or picture hanger. Kristen looked toward the door as she reached out with one hand to attempt to lift the portrait off of the hook but hesitated when the sound of a foot slapped the marble right outside of the door and two monks walked in. She turned away exhaling strongly through her nose, her heart hammering in her chest so hard it hurt. Her skin crawled as two men walked directly behind, her mind consumed with the thought that she could feel their hands reaching out to grab her shoulders. She was about to turn and run when the men's voices started to fade and they walked out the other side of the room.

Kristen squinted her eyes closed to relieve the strain and tried to move the canvas bag to her other hand only to find that her fingers had been gripping the handle so severely that her hand was locked around the handle. Looking down she could see the veins on the back of her hand bulging out and she consciously told one finger, then the next to let go. They creaked as if they were old door hinges but finally gave way and she moved the bag to her other hand. No one had yet appeared in the room and she flexed her fingers to make another attempt. This time she looked at the picture straight in the eyes and grabbed it without allowing herself to think about what she was doing. The next thing she remembered was she was walking out the door, across the bridge and over the marble courtyard. About two thirds of they way over it she heard voices and running feet behind her. She didn't dare look back and took off running like she hadn't done since high school track, with the bag crashing against her legs with every stride. She followed the corridor to the South gate and didn't stop until she turned the corner and nearly ran over Andrew.

He had a look of shock on his face.

"Everything OK?" he asked.

"I don't know. Let's get out of here," she said, finally looking behind her at no one. Still, her mind was screaming to get as far away as she could but Andrew was standing in the same place as if waiting for an explanation.

"*Please!*" she said.

"Alright. Let's go." He took off in a light jog and she followed him. A couple of blocks later he hailed a cab and they sat in the back seat. She was clutching the bag and he took it away from her.

"What happened in there?" he asked.

Kristen looked out the window grasping her hands on her lap.

"Nothing. That place gave me the creeps."

The taxi dropped them off at the hostel and Ralph, John and Sarah were in the lobby reading some old US newspapers that someone had left. They all looked up when Andrew and Kristen entered. Andrew was carrying the bag and Kristen looked exhausted. She sat down on one of the cloth chairs and let out a long breath. Sarah handed her a bottle of water and Kristen hungrily drank it.

"Done?" John asked.

"Done," Andrew replied.

"Now what?"

"We wait until tonight, then go to the address and get our stuff. Hopefully we are home by tomorrow," Andrew said. No one even mentioned trying to get their rewards from Mr. Baldwin. Even if it were for real it would be like accepting blood money.

At a little after 8:00pm, the group crammed into a taxi and stopped at a large native looking home with a locked gate out front. Andrew directed the taxi driver to continue a few more blocks and then they got out.

It was a mostly residential neighborhood and not many people were on the streets.

"Perhaps we should break up into two groups? Just in case something happens?" Andrew asked.

"He's probably got someone watching us right now, but fine. Who wants to go?" Ralph asked.

"You and I. Let's have John wait with the girls," Andrew didn't mean for it to come out the way it sounded but he didn't bother correcting it.

"Good by me. Shall we?" John said, to Kristen and Sarah, "There is a café over there. Can we have some cash?"

"If we are not back in an hour...do something. Go to the American Consulate. You'll have to take your chances with these things," Andrew moved the black band on his arm.

Andrew handed him a couple of hundred Baht and he and Ralph walked the two blocks back to the home. When they arrived Andrew pressed the intercom bell. A buzzer went off and Ralph pushed the Iron Gate open. Andrew followed him.

It was a large painted black door with an old brass knocker in the middle. Andrew reached out to use it but the door swung open and a man in a colorful skirt bowed to them. The home smelled of Jasmine.

"Sawat-dee kraap."

"Hello. We are looking for Mr. Baldwin," Andrew said.

"I'm sorry but he is not here," another Thai man appeared in the hallway.

"Come in. I'm Tauk. I believe I have something for you," he said.

Ralph followed Andrew into the house where the man motioned for them to sit but Andrew remained standing and the man looked puzzled.

"Here." Ralph handed him the bag. He looked inside of it, smiled, then picked up a manila envelope from the table and handed it to Andrew who was closest to him.

"I believe that is what you wanted," the man said.

Andrew tore open the end and saw five comforting blue passports.

"You should read this as well," the man handed him a computer print out of a newspaper.

Andrew froze when he saw the picture of the Wat Benchamabopit. Ralph noticed the look on his face and moved beside him to read the paper. It was an article obviously from that day about a theft at the temple. It said that the theft came at an embarrassing time because the King was due to visit the Monks on the weekend. What was of greater concern to Andrew was the mention of five American's that were wanted for questioning.

"There are pictures of you on the next page," the man said. Andrew turned over the print out but it was blank.

"Sorry. I did not print it. You can see it on the Internet or I'm sure it will be in the newspaper tomorrow," the man added. Andrew couldn't tell if he was ignorant or just regaling in their trouble.

"I need to speak with Mr. Baldwin. NOW!" Andrew said.

"I'm sorry but Mr. Baldwin is not here. I am merely the messenger," the man said. Andrew looked around at the house. It had the feel of an office not a home. The whole place was probably just for show.

"Ralph. Let's get out of here."

Mr. Baldwin received the phone call shortly after they had left the rented house in Bangkok. He had just finished enjoying a lobster dinner and was reading the afternoon edition of the Phuket paper. The lead story was about an anonymous gift of a million-dollar necklace to the crown princess. There was even a picture of her wearing it. By tomorrow the news reporter should have tracked down Mr. Boon Mee at ThaiJem and would have learned that an American purchased the necklace. That was very important information and he wanted to make sure that it was presented correctly. By tomorrow the theft of King Rama's portrait would be attributed to more Americans (albeit one semi-Canadian) and his plan would be complete. The miserable Mr. Pandit would not lose his investment in the BMSAT Satellite company and he would gain a measure of protection for his own endeavors. Everyone ended up happy – except the King.

Andrew and Ralph met the group in the café and showed them the article.

"It's worse. There are evidently pictures," he said.

"Of who?" John asked.

"All of us."

"Was he there?" Sarah asked.

"No. Just some lackey," Andrew said.

"So, now what?" Kristen asked, "We have our passports and we still can't leave." She was visibly shaking and Sarah put her arm around her.

"What if we just turn ourselves into the police?" Sarah asked.

"IF Mr. Baldwin doesn't have us killed first, we go to prison for stealing," Andrew said, "and I might add that Thai prisons are nothing like America. They are very bad places."

"For how long?" Kristen asked.

"Five years...maybe longer...who knows," Andrew said, referring back to the research he had done on the internet.

"That's not an option. Let's just forget about the police right now," Ralph said.

"How about the American Consulate? You mentioned them earlier," Sarah asked.

"Again, if we are not killed before, then they would still probably turn us over to the local authorities. I mean, in the end we did it," Andrew said.

"I did it," Kristen said, softly.

"Look. We're not leaving you behind and besides we all were accomplices. We need another alternative," Andrew said, "first of all we need to get out of the public before someone sees the pictures."

"If he wants us turned into the police he can just track us with these...so what's the point?" Kristen said.

Andrew looked at John and wanted to ask him to leave but felt he couldn't.

"I'll be right back. Everyone wait here," he said, as he walked out the door and down the block. He found a phone booth and pulled out the business card from his wallet, then dialed a number. He was relieved to hear a man answer.

"Mr. Suda. It's Andrew," he hesitated to say more. Mr. Suda paused a moment before answering.

"Hello Andrew. I assume you are aware what is on the news?" he asked.

"I haven't seen anything but I can guess...I need help. It's not what it looks like." Andrew hoped it wasn't at least.

"I'm not sure if I can help you. What do you need?"

"I need a place to stay...someplace downtown, where there are lots of buildings and concrete," Andrew said. Mr. Suda paused again.

"Hold on please," Mr. Suda said. He came back on the line a couple of minutes later.

"There is a place called the Garden Orchid hotel. It is downtown. Room 962 will be left open *only* for tonight. You must leave by 8:00 am before the maids come. I cannot say what condition the room is in however you should be safe for the night." Mr. Suda gave him the address.

"Thank you, thank you so much," Andrew said.

"I sincerely hope your ordeal will be over soon....did you help your friend?" Mr. Suda asked.

"Yes. Thank you again. Your help is appreciated more than you can possibly know."

"Good night Andrew. Try and call me tomorrow. I will see if there is something else that I can do. May your God protect you."

Andrew hung up the phone doubting whether either Mr. Suda's god or his cared.

When he returned to the lobby the group had obediently stayed in their seats.

"Let's go," Andrew said. He had Sarah ask the front desk clerk for directions to the street but not the address of the hotel. He was certain that sooner or later the clerk would watch the news and if that happened tonight he didn't want him knowing where they went.

The hotel was about two miles away and the group walked in the rain. Andrew and Kristen were in the lead with Ralph, Sarah and John behind them.

"Listen. What you did back there was incredible. I don't know quite what to say," Andrew said.

"I don't feel like I did anything that I can be proud for. Especially since it looks like it was for a lie anyway. I mean we went from a bad situation to a much worse one." Andrew had no answer to that and he continued in silence. Behind him John was talking very animatedly.

"OK. So let's say we actually make it through the night. And due to some miracle or another, that lunatic, Mr. B., doesn't send the police to our door – " Andrew cut him off and turned around.

"Look. I don't have a better solution than to make it through the night. If you have some worthwhile idea, we're listening. If not – quit complaining." It was the closest Kristen had ever seen to him being angry.

179

"I'm not complaining. There is just no way we are getting out of this country…unless we give up someone…" John said.

"You're suggesting that we turn in Kristen?" Sarah asked.

"No. I don't know, I mean what choice do we have? Either all of us or one what do you want to do – go to jail for something you didn't do?"

"We are not going to give up anyone. It is not a choice. If that is the way you feel, then you need to go on your own. Do what you need to do," Andrew said, glad that he had not given anyone the exact address of where they were going to.

John looked at him and stopped walking. The rain had drenched all of them and water was dripping down his face.

"Do you have a way to prevent us from being tracked by these things?" John pulled at his wristband. Andrew considered his question for a moment, wondering how much he should tell him.

"Maybe," he said. The group looked at him.

"How?" John asked.

"Look. I don't know if it will work or not. These things seem to be both a GPS and some kind of communicator. That means there are several ways of tracking us with them. I may be able to slow down the process that's all."

"So you can't guarantee that he won't find us?" John asked.

"No. In fact I would venture to say that he would find us. The question is if that can be delayed…"

"Delayed until what? Armageddon?" John asked.

"Until we can find out what is really going on," Andrew said, but he had no idea how he would do that – yet.

"Fine. Let's go," John said. Andrew didn't move. He didn't trust him.

"I think we need to vote and see if you go or stay," Andrew said, "maybe you're working for him. I know I'm not convinced." Andrew looked at the other three but no one reacted.

"Is it just me who has doubts?" Andrew asked. Sarah wanted to speak but felt a great pressure not to. If she agreed and then something happened because of it, she didn't want to have that on her conscience.

"Alright. I guess John comes with us," Andrew said, "Let's go. I don't think even my underwear is dry anymore."

Chapter 22

Mr. Baldwin hung up the telephone for the third time in the last hour. Mr. Pandit was either getting very nervous or was up to something. Either way, he had a bad feeling. The news media had already found the American link to ThaiJem and, much to Mr. Pandit's pleasure, the story would hit the headlines in the morning. As for the stolen picture, Mr. Pandit had insisted on having it picked up that evening from the house in Bangkok and Mr. Baldwin could not figure out why that was so important.

"Henry!" the Thai manservant appeared out of nowhere. Henry was not his name but Mr. Baldwin had never learned to pronounce it properly and 'Henry' stuck.

"Yes, sir?"

"We have a change of plans. We are going to Bangkok this evening. Please arrange for a room at the Four Seasons. Put the room under your name and pay cash," Mr. Baldwin said.

"Do you perhaps mean the Mandarin Oriental?" Henry asked.

"No. Not this time, Henry. The Four Seasons. Make sure you pack the equipment," Mr. Baldwin pointed to the steel briefcase that was open on the coffee table. He needed to keep track of his guests.

An hour later Henry opened the back door to Mr. Baldwin's 500SEL and drove him to the airport. By midnight they were in a suite at the Four Seasons Bangkok, booked under Henry's very common Thai name.

:

Andrew insisted on blindfolding John the last three blocks to the hotel. To his chagrin Sarah led him by the arm like a guide for the blind as they passed by the hotel's main entrance and went in through a side door. They were all happy to find that the floors were covered in carpet. The stairway was set off to the side of the lobby and Ralph held the door for the girls and John. Once in the stairwell they removed his blindfold and walked up to the ninth floor. Andrew insisted that they all stay on the landing until he had confirmed the room's location.

Room 962 was at the end of the hallway and he tried the door. It had old fashion keyed lock that released when he pushed it down and the door swung open. It was an interior room overlooking the atrium on the inside of the hotel. That was the good news. The bad was that it had obviously been already 'used' for the night. Andrew ripped off the sheets and stuffed them into the closet, then went back to the stairwell where the four were making quite a puddle on the concrete landing.

"OK. It's not the Ritz, but it is shelter....and put back on his blindfold."

John gave him a look, then closed his eyes and bent over for Sarah who slipped the folded up tee shirt over his eyes and guided him down the hall where Andrew had pointed. Kristen followed them and Andrew turned to Ralph.

"You trust him?" he asked.

"No. Not one bit."

"Then why didn't you say something?"

Ralph shrugged and Andrew looked at him disgusted.

"What's with everyone anyway. It's like you've all given up." He followed him into the room and shut the door.

"We'll isn't this pleasant," John said, noting the unmade bed, "looks like someone has been sleeping in our bed." No one reacted to his comment and he walked over to the mini bar and opened it.

"Let's not do that..." Andrew started, then figured what difference did it make in the grand scheme of things. John opened up an Orange Fanta, took a gulp, then burped.

"Sorry," he said.

"Andrew. Isn't he going to be able to just track us with these?" Kristen asked, looking at her black band.

"Possibly, but I don't think it's him we have to worry about tonight. Besides all the concrete and steel is going to hinder the GPS signal... at least if he is using a GPS signal in these things." Even John stopped drinking to listen. "As I understand it, GPS has a hard time in Metropolitan areas because it relies on line of sight to several satellites simultaneously. In fact one of the largest satellite consortiums is based here in South East Asia. A company called BMSAT... anyway, as long as we are not near an outside window we should be OK. That doesn't mean he can't still track us because these things also have some kind of communicator in them, that along with some sophisticated hardware he could still use to do a triangulation and figure out our approximate locations."

"So is it safe to stay here all night?" Kristen asked, she had a towel wrapped around her wet hair and Andrew couldn't help but smile at her.

"What?" she asked.

"Nothing. Seeing you like that just reminded me of something…" Her mind flashed back to a year ago in her loft and she smiled. Everyone else looked lost.

"Sorry," Andrew turned his attention back to the group and sat on the bed, "to finish what I was saying. I don't think its Mr. Baldwin we need to worry about tonight. It's the police. On the other hand I really don't know."

"It's not like we have any other choices," Sarah said.

"Dandy. So who gets the bed?" John asked.

Andrew and Ralph looked at each other, then him.

"The women," they said, simultaneously.

"Look. That's not necessary. I'll sleep on the floor," Sarah offered.

"No. Makes things too complicated. Lets just do guys on the floor, girls in the bed," Andrew said. No one else objected and Kristen went into the bathroom. They could hear her turn on the hair dryer and Sarah joined her. A minute later the shower turned on.

"Any idea why he is doing all this to us? It's like slow torture. Give us something then hit us over the head. I feel like a baby Norwegian seal who's constantly being offered a herring from a man with a wooden club," Ralph asked.

"No. But I think in order to get out of this mess we are going to have to figure that question out," Andrew said, as he was observing John who had stretched out on the floor in the middle of the hallway, blocking the door. He had two decorative pillows propped under his head. He was either totally disinterested or tired.

"So do you even know where to start?"

"I have some ideas but not until tomorrow," Andrew said.

"So tomorrow shall take thought for the things of itself. Sufficient unto the day is the evil thereof," Ralph muttered.

"Amen," John said, from the floor, "can we go to bed now?"

Andrew took a pillow from the closet and lay down on the floor, knees bent, staring at the ceiling, his mind going full speed. He could hear Kristen and Sarah's voices behind the closed door and within a few minutes the heavy breathing of the other two men. The bathroom door opened and he watched as Sarah looked briefly at John, then toward him. He signaled to her that the others were asleep and she gazed down at him with her blue eyes and smiled. His eyes went to her forehead and she reflectively touched there. The bruise on her face was still healing. Kristen followed her and they quietly crawled into bed.

Andrew tossed and turned most of the night trying to make sense of everything that was happening to them and had come to one of two conclusions. Mr. Baldwin was either just a very psychotic masochist or he was up to something much larger than they could see. Sarah's kidnapping, the necklace, and the theft of the picture in the temple seemed related. They all had links to the Royal family. However, he couldn't figure out the man in Quan Lukc. There seemed to be no connection but he was certain that there was. The more he thought about it the more he was sure that Mr. Baldwin was trying to manipulate a much greater plan than just the ruination of their four lives. And he was more convinced than ever that John was not what he seemed.

:

Around 4:00 a.m. he finally fell asleep and remained so until Kristen inadvertently kicked him. He woke up with a start and looked at the clock. It was 7:00 a.m. and he laid back down, feeling exhausted. Kristen mouthed 'sorry' and crawled back into bed. Andrew reclined back to the floor but soon realized that something had been amiss when he had looked at the clock. He propped himself up on his elbows and stared toward the door where John had been the night before. He was missing. Andrew sat up alarmed and grabbed Kristen's foot under the cover, she looked up at him.

"Where is John?" he whispered.

"Uh... he said he was going to get some food and come right back," she looked concerned.

"How long ago?" Andrew asked.

Kristen closed her eyes for a second, "Uh... I guess ten minutes or so, I woke him up accidentally when I got up for the bathroom."

All the talking had disturbed Sarah and she sat up in the bed. Her blonde hair was wrapped around her face and she gently untangled it.

"What's up?" she said, groggily.

"I don't know," Kristen said.

"John's gone," Andrew said.

"Why?" Sarah asked, her mind starting to focus.

"I have no idea but I don't think it's good," Andrew said.

"He said he was just getting some food," Kristen answered.

"Maybe so," Andrew said.

"I think we should get up," Sarah hopped out of bed and into the bathroom.

"Ralph!" Andrew repeated it.

"Huh?" Ralph mumbled.

"Get up!" Andrew was on his feet nudging Ralph with his bare foot.

"What?" Ralph opened his eyes and stretched his neck before sitting up.

"We should get going," Andrew said.

"OK."

"John's gone," Kristen offered. She did it because she felt responsible.

"Where?"

"We don't know, but I don't think we can wait around to find out," Andrew said.

Someone turned on the TV as they each used the bathroom. Andrew stopped and watched it as a picture of a wealthy middle aged woman was shown wearing an unmistakable piece of jewelry. He really wished he understood what the newscaster was saying. The next story was even more frightening, and everyone watched transfixed as pictures of the Wat Benchamabopit were shown, along with the four of them. The only word they could read was 'Americans' on the bottom of the page.

"We have to go," Andrew said, to no one's surprise, but they stood there, transfixed, until the story changed.

"OK. Let's get out of here," Andrew repeated as he headed toward the door and grabbed the handle.

"Andrew!" Kristen exclaimed and pointed back to the television. He walked back over as if about to see pictures of a gruesome accident. A camera followed a familiar man with his child and wife. The child looked happy and healthy.

"It's the guy with the bamboo hat," Kristen said, what everyone already knew, "and his daughter is doing better, Ralph!"

Ralph ignored the statement.

"What in the world is he doing on the news?" Ralph asked no one in particular.

"Look, I haven't the foggiest. but everything we've done has ended up ... on TV, I would say that it not good for us. Let alone that everyone in Bangkok has now seen our faces," Andrew said.

"What does it mean Andrew?" Kristen asked, looking even more concerned than normal.

"I wish I could tell you, but I'm as lost as you are right now. Let's get out of here before someone comes. We can worry about that later," Andrew said. He really needed to call Mr. Suda and find out what was going on.

"I don't think it's a good idea that we all stay together. We will only attract more attention," Sarah said.

"Agreed. We need to split up," Andrew said.

"And do what? Go where? I mean, I don't know what to do?" There was more than a hint of panic in Kristen's voice.

"Kristen, we're just buying time, that's all. Give me some time to try and figure out what is going on," Andrew said.

"We can go together, Kristen," Sarah said, as she grabbed her hand. The relief on Kristen's face was immediately noticeable.

"Where are we going to meet up and when?" she asked.

"There is a Holiday Inn about a mile from here, " Andrew wrote down the address for everyone. "Meet there at 8:00 pm tonight. There is a small sitting room off the main lobby."

"I don't have much cash left, but take this, "Andrew handed a hundred Baht to Sarah but she declined.

"It's OK. I can take care of us. Give it to Ralph."

"Ralph?" Andrew handed him the money. Ralph took it tentatively.

"You understand?" Andrew asked. He looked almost as apprehensive as Kristen did.

"I just don't understand the point. They're going to catch us, why not just stay here?" he asked.

"OK. I know they might catch us, but while we are still free we, I, need to try and understand what is happening. Perhaps there is something we are missing that will help us. While we are on that subject, stick close to buildings – the taller the better, underground is the best, keep moving. Don't stay in one place too long and, *if* you get a message on the bands, move *immediately*. He may be able to use it to find your location. Go to where there are other tourists… hotels, shopping malls, whatever. Got it?"

"Got it. Let's go Kristen," Sarah stood up and, as she exited the door, she paused to look back at Andrew.

"Be careful," she said.

"What if we get caught by the police?" Andrew heard Kristen ask Sarah as they walked toward the stairwell. He turned back to Ralph.

"Are you going to be OK?" Andrew asked.

"Yeah."

"Tell me, Ralph, what did they boy scouts teach you about survival training and your attitude?"

Ralph looked up at them. "If you believe you are going to die, you will."

"There you go." Andrew said, "8:00 p.m. at the Holiday Inn." He left Ralph standing in alone in the room.

:

"I see you found it easily," Mr. Baldwin said.

John looked around at the meeting room at the bottom of the Four Seasons. It reminded him of waiting in line back in San Francisco when he had interviewed for this nightmare of an adventure.

"So. Here I am, just as you requested. I've baby-sat them and they are at a hotel," he said. "Now, when you show me what I want, I will give you the name," John said.

"I've arranged for your money and your ticket," Mr. Baldwin said, as he handed him an envelope. John took it and checked the flight time.

"Tell me, Mr. Matthews, how are you planning on getting on that flight without getting caught?" John looked at him with a blank stare.

"The name, Mr. Matthews?"

"Garden Orchid Hotel," he answered.

"What about this?" John pointed to his wristband. Mr. Baldwin smiled and typed in something on his laptop computer. John heard a click and tugged on the band. It came off in his hand and he tossed it on the floor.

"So why didn't you just use your whiz bang gear there to find them yourself?"

"Doesn't work too well in the city. I lost track of them yesterday afternoon, at least temporarily."

Andrew was right John thought.

"Nice doing business with you, Mr. Matthews. Have a good life." Mr. Baldwin stood up and excused him as he would a servant.

John turned around and walked out the door. At least he had his passport, an airline ticket, and twenty thousand dollars in his pocket. He wouldn't be going home empty handed like the rest of the fools.

:

As soon as he had left, Mr. Baldwin made a call on his satellite phone.

A voice answered and he said: "Garden Orchid Hotel." Then he hung up, went back up to his room, and waited. About thirty minutes later the telephone rang.

"Where are you?" Mr. Pandit asked.

"Why do you ask, Mr. Pandit?"

"They were not there. Gone. Someone had given them a room without registering. Now what?...we should talk in person," Mr. Pandit said.

Mr. Baldwin did not like the tone.

"Not right now. I'm very busy. Look. Don't worry about them. I'll make sure they are caught."

"*Today*, Mr. Baldwin. *Today*,"

"Yes. Today, Mr. Pandit, you'll have them today." Mr. Baldwin ended the call. It was becoming more and more obvious to him that Mr. Pandit thought he would no longer be needed when the Americans were caught.

My trained monkey is trying to become independent, he thought to himself. This would definitely make things more interesting.

189

Mr. Baldwin opened his metal briefcase and tried to get a lock on any of his four remaining guests. Although he couldn't get a present location on them, the computer showed brief contacts that indicated, over the past hour, they had split up. Two were traveling together and the other two were separate. They had all remained downtown. It had to be Andrew directing them.

"What are you up to, Mr. Lee?" he said to the keyboard as he opened a software program and typed in a message.

:

Ralph was standing in a very touristy shopping mall. He had purchased a cheap hat and sat with his head down looking at an old USA today from several weeks ago. He was reading an article about the 2004 Olympic games in Athens when his wristband went off. It startled him so much that he ripped the page that he was holding onto. He told himself to calm down and then slowly turned his arm to read the message.

> *"We must talk. I can help you. Your family depends on it. Four Seasons hotel, Emerald meeting room. One hour."*

Ralph stared at the message for several seconds, then off into the distance as he tried to evaluate the meaning of the cryptic note. He found himself inadvertently looking directly at a police officer that appeared to be more than casually interested in him, and he felt his heart skip a beat as he hurried to his feet, his newspaper in hand, and walked the opposite direction. The heat on the back of his neck was nearly unbearable, but he forced himself to walk steadily on the marble floor and, within seconds, was lost in the maze of people.

He told himself there was no way that he should follow the instructions. In fact, until he had received the message, he had every intention on keeping moving until the group was supposed to meet that night. Sttill, the words 'your family depends on it' kept resounding in his mind until finally he gave up and asked someone where the hotel was. Ralph found himself walking inexplicably into a trap. All he could hear in his head was the warning. With everything he had already done, he couldn't stand the thought of causing even more harm to his family.

At the door to the Emerald room Ralph paused one last time to consider what he was about to do. His mind told him to run, but he reached for the handle and walked in. Mr. Baldwin was sitting behind a table on the far side of the room. He remained seated, but looked at him and smiled. Ralph clenched his teeth and proceeded forward until he was looking down at the man that had ruined his life, and nearly had killed him several times over.

"Thank you for coming, Mr. Gabriel. You've lost a little weight," Mr. Baldwin said. "Have a seat."

Ralph gazed down toward the chair and wanted to refuse but, again, felt compelled to obey, as if he was being remotely controlled. His stomach was doing flips and he could feel beads of sweat forming above his top lip, but he took the seat.

"What do you mean 'your family depends on it'?" Ralph asked, barely moving his jaw.

"My, Mr. Gabriel, you act as if you are very angry. Are you?"

Ralph felt his face flush.

"Of course I'm angry! Look what you've done to me!" Ralph had his hands extended at his sides.

"I haven't done anything to you, Mr. Gabriel. All this was your choice. As was this..." Mr. Baldwin pushed a manila envelope toward him, and he stared at it.

"What is it?" Ralph asked, his eyes transfixed on the table.

"Open it," Mr. Baldwin said.

Ralph told his right arm to get the envelope but it refused to obey. Given the results of all Mr. Baldwin's prior messages it was almost a Pavlov response.

"Go ahead. Open it," Mr. Baldwin urged.

Ralph swallowed and watched his extended arm slowly move toward the table. When it finally touched the envelope a burst of acid came up from his stomach and he burped. To his embarrassment, Mr. Baldwin laughed. He could taste the acrid flavor in his mouth as he unfolded the flap and reached inside. His fingers touched several thick papers and he grasped them with his index and middle fingers, withdrawing them from the sheath. The moment the first edge appeared he knew they were pictures and his mind fervently went over the past few days hunting for possibilities of what they had recorded. There was only one event that propelled itself forward into his consciousness and, as the first picture came into view, his heart sank.

Kristen appeared first, then himself, on the bed at the House of Nan. The angle of the shot suggested that it was taken from the ceiling. There was no mistaking his face in the next photo as he and Kristen kissed. Ralph put the pictures back on the table and pushed himself away, staring at them as if the small amount of distance would make it all go away.

"What do you want?" Ralph asked, without looking up.

"As I said, I need your help."

"What do you want me to do?"

"I need to know where the group is."

"I don't know," Ralph said, while looking at the ground. It was the truth.

"Well, that's too bad because these pictures were on their way to your wife and family and it took quite some effort to stop them. I thought that we could help each other here. I guess I was mistaken. Thank you for coming anyway, Mr. Gabriel."

Ralph could hear Mr. Baldwin get up from his chair but he remained seated.

"Do you have something you would like to say, Mr. Gabriel?"

Ralph knew in his heart that he would have to tell Melanie what had happened in the Jungle, but he was horrified that she would learn like this, without being given the chance to try and explain *how* and *why* it had occurred. She would leave him and take the children. He was certain of that, and he couldn't imagine a life without his family. It was no life.

"What do you want with the others?" Ralph asked, as Mr. Baldwin sat down. They both knew who was about to give in.

"I need to finish off what we started. Don't worry, they won't be harmed," Mr. Baldwin said.

Ralph looked at him. "And what have you started?"

"Ralph, look, we are in a bit of a time crunch here. Just tell me where they are."

Ralph forced himself to focus.

"What do I get from this betrayal?" The words stung as he said them.

"Well, let's see… I won't send those. You have my word. And I'll guarantee passage back to the US. The rest is up to you," Mr. Baldwin said. "That is, if you choose to go back to Caymans to claim your reward."

"How do I know you'll do this?"

"Have I lied to you before?"

Ralph thought the answer was obvious.

"Think about it. I have always done what I said I would do. You have your passports, don't you? There may have been unforeseen consequences but you can trust me," Mr. Baldwin said.

"No. I don't think I can. I want something else," Ralph said.

"OK." Mr. Baldwin leaned back in his chair. "What?"

Ralph thought for a moment, but didn't know what to ask for.

"Remove this," he pointed to his wristband, "and I want…" Ralph thought to ask for money but it seemed so graceless. "I want you to tell me why you did this to us."

Mr. Baldwin seemed genuinely surprised at the question.

"Very interesting request, Mr. Gabriel. First things first: your wristband." Mr. Baldwin opened up the laptop in front of him and typed for a few moments. Ralph heard a click and he tugged on the black metal. It fell away from his hand. He thought that must have been how a slave felt when he was given his freedom.

"Now we must trust each other. I will have no guarantee you will tell me the truth about where to find the group, and you will have to trust me that I will not send the pictures. Quid pro quo, Mr. Gabriel. As to your request, make no mistake that the game is for real. If you performed as was requested you would receive your house, however, as to my motivations, I can only say that the tasks you have done have immensely helped me with some business." Mr. Baldwin stood up again.

"Now it is your turn, Mr. Gabriel. The location."

"8:00 p.m. at the Bangkok Holiday Inn," Ralph said.

"Good. That's settled, then. Here, take this with you." Mr. Baldwin pushed a small cell phone across the table. Ralph let it sit there.

"Look, I'm not that stupid. If I carry that you can find me," he said.

Mr. Baldwin smiled. "I suppose that's true, but I really don't see why I would want to. On the other hand, you may want to reach me. Just push redial… "

"No. I'm not interested in your help. It's like trying to cut a bargain with the devil. You always lose." Ralph wanted a stronger reaction than he got.

"Alright. Well, look: keep a low profile for the next couple of days. It'll be best for everyone. You'll need this," Mr. Baldwin pulled another envelope from his pocket and slid it to Ralph.

"Take it. Don't be a complete fool. It's money," Mr. Baldwin saw Ralph's eyes harden and he quickly added, "It's not a lot of money, just some baht so you can stay someplace, out of sight."

Ralph fingered the envelope. "Why?"

"We may still need each other," Mr. Baldwin said, as he stood up from the table and left Ralph sitting there. Taking the cash made him feel even more like Judas but, again, he found himself without a choice, so he took the money out of the envelope, kicked the wristband across the room, and walked out. As he left through the front door and made a right turn he felt sickened, and stopped to lean against the building until the naseua passed.

Chapter 23

4:00 p.m. - Several hours earlier

Andrew stood at a telephone booth, waiting for Mr. Suda to pick up. After several minutes, he came on the line.

"Hello?"

"Mr. Suda, this is – "

Mr. Suda cut him off. "Yes. I recognize your voice. Have you seen the news today?"

"Uh, a little. Couldn't really understand anything though. I was hoping you could tell me what is going on."

"It is a very strange series of events. The necklace that you purchased resurfaced as an anonymous gift to the Princess, who unwisely wore it in public, much to the King's embarrassment."

"I'm not sure I see –"

Mr. Suda interrupted him.

"Can you make it safely to the bank?"

"Yes. I think so. Is it open today?"

"Certain parts are. I think there is someone that you should talk to. Perhaps you can be of help to each other."

"When?" Andrew asked.

"About two hours, but you can come early if necessary… please be discreet," Mr. Suda said. "Ring me at my office from the lobby."

"Of course," Andrew hung up the phone. He had a pair of dark sunglasses on, a week's worth of facial hair and a newly acquired backpack. As far as tourists went, he blended in perfectly, and made his way on foot to the bank.

It was nearing 4:00 p.m. by the time he reached the front doors. The lobby was vacant, except for a few guards who paid no attention to him. Andrew picked up a lobby phone and dialed Mr. Suda's extension.

"Hello?"

"It's me," Andrew said.

"Yes. Please go to the executive elevator. Press floor thirty-eight, but do not get off on that floor. The doors will close and it will continue up to the next floor. You will be met by someone." Mr. Suda hung up the phone and Andrew followed his instructions. The executive lift was behind the west bank of public elevators and was operated by a key. He was momentarily puzzled until the door opened. Andrew entered, and pressed the top floor, thirty-eight. Just as Mr. Suda said, the lift stopped. Andrew peeked out for a moment before the doors shut and saw no one there. A moment later it reopened and three men, in Western style suits, greeted him. They put out their hands to stop him while he was still inside, and carefully frisked him before letting him out and guiding him down the hallway. Andrew could hear the sound of a helicopter above him. He figured he must be on the top floor.

He had expected to see Mr. Suda standing in the room that he was invited into. Instead, a dignified man in Native dress met him. The man looked vaguely familiar and another similarly dressed man accompanied him.

"Mr. Lee?" the second man asked.

"Yes. Who are you?"

"You may call me John." Andrew smiled at the name. He didn't look like a 'John' to him.

Neither man extended a hand, and Andrew kept his distance. He was very aware of the guards, who still stood behind him. The second man noticed his discomfort, said something in Thai, and they left, shutting the door behind them.

The man in charge spoke in Thai to the man that Andrew assumed was his interpreter. John bowed in response.

"Would you like something to drink? A coke?"

"No thank you," Andrew said.

"Do you know why you are here?"

"No. I have no idea."

"Do you know who this is?"

Andrew looked again at his boss, and it finally occurred to him where he had seen his face. It was all over the money in his pocket.

"Yes. I know who he is." Andrew was shocked and concerned. It meant that they were embroiled in something much bigger than he had guessed.

"Thank you for coming, Mr. Lee." The King spoke in English, which surprised him. Andrew didn't know whether to bow or just stand there, so he just stood his place, as far from the windows as possible.

"I'm not sure I understand what is happening," Andrew said.

"It must be very confusing," the King said. "However, if I may first ask some questions…"

"Of course," Andrew said. The interpreter had sat down and was taking notes.

"May I ask how you came to be in my country?" Andrew noted the possessive pronoun, and it made him squirm.

"To be honest, I am not sure. Myself and three, no, four others were dropped off in the middle of the jungle to the north of Bangkok. We were supposedly on a television show from the US, but it turned out to be something much different."

"Can you explain how you came to meet the man you helped in Quan Lukc?"

"We were told to find him." Andrew wondered if he should mention something about the now dead Matt Garrison, but decided that it was probably not the appropriate time. "I really didn't have anything to do with saving his son. That was due to two of the others… my friends."

"I see… and how about the necklace? How did you come to purchase that?"

"Several days ago one of the women was kidnapped by soldiers–"

Upon hearing that, the King interrupted him.

"Do you know where this was?"

"Due west of Quan Lukc."

"How many were there?"

"I'm not sure – twenty or thirty."

"Can you describe them?"

"Worn army fatigues… black bandana's…" Andrew said. The King spoke to the interpreter, who immediately left the room.

"And the necklace?" the King continued.

"I was told to go to ThaiJem in Bangkok…. Mr. Boon Mee, I think." The King narrowed his eyes upon hearing the name.

"Where did you get the money?"

"I had it wired from my business in the United States." Andrew thought about asking to get it back, but stopped himself.

"Where did the exchange happen?" the King asked, as his interpreter reentered the room and sat back down.

"About two miles South of Quan Lukc. There is a bridge…"

"What can you tell me about the Temple from yesterday?"

"It was another task that we were told to do."

"And you willingly rob temples and pay ransoms?"

"No! Not at all. We were blackmailed... one of the first men that were with us was killed for disobeying," Andrew said. The King pointed at his wristband.

"And that is how he finds you?"

"Yes. And he communicates."

"Does he know where you are now?"

"I don't know. I think the buildings prevent him from using the signals."

The King looked concerned and spoke again to his aide. He got up and opened the door calling to one of the guards, who brought in a small black electronic box.

"And what is this man's name?"

"Mr. Baldwin," Andrew said. The King didn't react.

"No one else? Anyone from this country?"

"No. I'm sorry. I do not know of anyone else... other than a servant of Mr. Baldwin's."

"His name?"

"Tuk, Tack...something like that, I think."

The King turned his attention to his aide and conversed with him for a few minutes, then turned back toward Andrew.

"Mr. Lee, these events have, and seemingly will, cause me significant political costs. It seems that my enemies in the government would like to prevent me from fighting the drugs and other trades that mar Southeast Asia. They may just well succeed by using you and your friends."

"I'm very sorry..." Andrew couldn't think of what to call him. "I don't know what to say. We didn't realize what was going on, and we were under threat of our lives. We thought it was a fantasy, not reality. Perhaps an explanation to the public..."

"Mr. Lee, political power is perception, not reality. If something is perceived by the people, then, to them, it becomes real. What most of these unfortunate events portray is that Americans are, as a whole, unfeeling and unconcerned with the world. If I accept your President's help, even for my good cause, it appears that I am merely a pawn of your country, a country with only its own interests at heart, and that is unacceptable for any ruler. It gives my enemies the ability to smear my name and thus damages my political goodwill. It is a difficult fact in politics that even minute shifts in perception can cause a large loss of face, especially here in Asia. Because of what has happened, and may yet occur, I will likely be forced to change my position, at least temporarily. That, unfortunately, will hurt my people in the present. However, I must think of the future."

"I don't know what to say," Andrew said. He wanted to ask more questions, but was getting the distinct feeling that the interview was coming to an end as the King moved toward the exit.

"I do not blame you, Mr. Lee, nor, I'm afraid, can I help you at this time. My enemies are very powerful and very discreet. If I were you, I would be very careful. In time, this will all become old news and things will go back to the way they were." The aide opened the door and the King started to leave.

"I apologize for asking, but we are wanted by the police. Is there anything we can do?"

The king stopped to have a discussion with his aide.

"It is very difficult. All I can recommend is that you try and stay hidden for awhile until we can try and stop whomever is behind this. If you do get taken into custody, be cooperative and request your American Consulate Liaison immediately. My enemies remain a chameleon to me. Perhaps, soon, they will change their colors and I will be able to see them clearly. Then, perhaps, I can help you."

Chapter 24

Andrew left the King and boarded the elevator. It stopped on the eighteenth floor and he was quite surprised to find Mr. Suda standing there. He didn't attempt to get on.

"How…." Andrew started.

"The money you used to pay ThaiJem was traced to me," Mr. Suda said as the doors closed. "Be careful, Mr. Lee."

Andrew continued on to the ground floor and walked out of the building. He had several hours before the group was to reassemble, so he found a large Internet café and lost himself among the cybernauts doing research and reading the news. He didn't find anything terribly useful and left shortly after 7:00, walking through the mostly deserted streets as it started to drizzle. He again found himself in the Holiday Inn, barely three days after he had left it the first time. Sarah and Kristen were in the sitting room when he entered. Kristen, who was pacing behind the sofa, saw him first and ran up to give him a hug. Sarah stood behind her and smiled at him.

"Where's Ralph?" he asked.

"I don't know. We haven't seen him yet," Sarah said.

Andrew sat on the opposite couch with Kristen beside him and Sarah across.

"So what did you do to preoccupy yourselves?"

"Got these," Kristen pointed to her hat, "and these." She pulled out some sunglasses.

"Any problems?" he asked.

"No. How about you?"

"Not really. I did get some answers though, kind of."

Both the girls grew very attentive.

"I wish Ralph was here," Andrew looked around. "I hope he is OK. Anyway, it seems that our whole past seven days have been to do with embarrassing the King of Thailand: the necklace that was paid for ransom, the man in Quan Lukc, who is supposed to be the Kings illegitimate son, and the theft of the picture. Someone is trying to get him to do something, and we are just the pawns."

"But why us? What does Mr. Baldwin have to do with it?" Sarah asked.

"I'm not sure. The man I spoke to seemed to think it is politically motivated to change a national policy. Mr. Baldwin must have some personal motivation but I don't know what." Andrew looked up at the clock on the wall. It read 8:00 and he was getting worried.

"Do you think he got caught?" Kristen asked, looking around.

"If he did, we probably shouldn't stay here. I'll be right back." Andrew got up and left the room for a moment.

:

Ralph watched the hotel front door from about a hundred yards away. He hadn't eaten anything since that morning, and his stomach was grumbling constantly. It was 8:00 p.m., and nothing yet had happened. His mind was a confluence of disconcerted thoughts. He wanted to run over and warn them, but he knew that it was too late and so he just stood there, disgusted at his compromise with Kristen, disgusted with the pain that he was causing his family, disgusted at his lack of courage.

A few minutes later he watched as a half dozen unmarked cars silently surrounded the building and uniformed men covered the entrances. Ralph moved back into the shadows and rested the back of his head against the glass as he tried to see what was happening through the reflections in the storefront windows.

As the drizzle turned to rain pouring over the sidewalks and into the gutters of the city, Ralph was eerily reminded of a story that his mother had read to him as a child a long time ago. It was the account of Jesus standing in the Garden of Gethsemane, patiently awaiting his betrayer. Ralph unconsciously inserted his hand in his pocket and withdrew the money that Mr. Baldwin had given him. He lifted it above his eyes until the glow from the streetlights reflected off the fibers of the bills. Under the strange luminescence of the rain soaked windowpanes, it had the horrifying sheen of silver.

:

Andrew saw the car as it quickly came to a halt blocking the front door. Four uniformed men jumped out, and he quickly ran back to the girls.

"It's a trap!" he yelled. Kristen immediately froze, her eyes wide with fear. Sarah grabbed her by the shoulders and yanked her up to her feet.

"Kristen!"

"Come on!" Andrew waved to Sarah and ran to the back corridor, which went into the garage. He opened the door and waited as the girls passed through. They could hear the commotion in the main lobby and the sound of leather soled shoes as they ran across the marble foyer.

"Down!" he said.

Andrew followed them down three floors and then out into the garage.

"Now what?" Sarah asked.

"I don't know…" he looked around at the garage full of cars and wished he knew how to hot-wire one, but he didn't. "I'll take suggestions…"

"I don't want to go to prison…" Sarah was struggling to keep Kristen upright on her feet.

"Kristen. Snap out of it. We need you here!" Sarah said.

"Try some of the doors," Andrew said, as he ran to several metal doors and yanked on them. Sarah did likewise.

"I've got one!" she said, after a few seconds. It was an electrical room and Andrew ran to it. They both looked back at Kristen who was seated on the concrete floor, holding herself and shivering.

"Kristen! Come on!" Andrew started out after her and froze as the door behind Kristen opened up and two policemen with guns drawn yelled at him. Kristen crumpled to the ground as Andrew and Sarah raised their hands. One of the men spoke into a radio but neither moved. They waited in silence for what seemed to be ten minutes, until several more men arrived through the stairwell as well as a police van. A woman pulled Kristen up from the ground and handcuffed her as she sobbed. Sarah stood stoically still as she was cuffed and taken away. Andrew felt his hands being pulled down and forced behind his back as a man in a suit approached him.

"I'm an American. I want the American Consulate," he said. The man smiled.

"Yes. We will inform the American Consulate *tomorrow*," he said. "We will take good care of you."

202

Andrew was put into a car separate from the women. As they were driven out of the garage he swore he saw Ralph hiding in a doorway.

"What have you done Ralph?" he said, under his breath.

:

By the time they arrived at the police station a large crowd had gathered, including what appeared to be several news reporters. Andrew had a feeling they were about to be put on exhibition. Sarah and Kristen were taken through the crowd first. The police hardly attempted to prevent anyone from touching them, and Kristen was crying. He couldn't tell if it was the police or the crowd that scared her. At the top of the stairs, an impromptu podium had been assembled, and the girls were held there while Andrew was removed and ceremoniously walked up the steps. Even in the dark, Andrew could see what had to be several hundred people staring at him. As soon as he had joined the girls on the landing a well-dressed man walked out of the building and stood at the lectern. The crowd hushed, and he made a very passionate speech that seemed to inflame the people, who started chanting something about Americans. Andrew tried to move closer to Sarah and Kristen, whom had huddled together.

"It'll be OK," he said, unconvincingly.

Sarah gazed at him with a solemn look.

"Don't give up Sarah, don't," he repeated as she was dragged through the doors.

The man finished his speech and walked down to the street where a black limousine drove him away.

"You are in mighty big trouble," the same officer that had talked to him in the garage said. Andrew remained silent. He was taken to a holding cell where he was locked in.

"Where are the women?" he asked, several times, but no one would answer him.

:

Sarah and Kristen hung on to each other as the policewoman roughly dragged them through the front of the station. They were taken to a back interrogation room and locked in. There was only one chair, and Sarah guided Kristen over to it.

"Kristen? Kristen. Look at me." Sarah bent down to look her in the eyes.

"Look. Nothing is going to happen… at least tonight. Be strong. If you show weakness they will come after you like a pack of wolves," Sarah tried in vain to see some recognition in Kristen's eyes.

"Kristen. Look at me. Think of things you love. Art, Music, God." Kristen finally looked up at her.

"OK. I'll try," she said, just as a man opened the door and walked in.

"Get up!" he said, and Kristen jumped to her feet. He walked over and took the chair while lighting a cigarette. Smoke immediately filled the room.

"Tell me. What are you doing in Thailand?" the man asked.

:

Ralph was lying on his bed flipping channels. There wasn't a single one that he could understand, but the pictures spoke for themselves. He watched as Sarah, Kristen, and then Andrew were dragged up the steps. He listened as the well dressed man made some kind of impassioned statement to the crowd and could only guess as to the content. The only word that was readily understandable was 'American' and it didn't sound like it was complement. Ralph opened another travel size whisky and drank straight from the bottle. What he desperately wanted to do was call his wife and children, but he had no idea what he would tell them. 'Your father is a Judas. A liar. A thief. An adulterer.' It didn't sound any better the more he heard the words in his head. The money that Mr. Baldwin had given him burned in his pocket and he withdrew the small wad and threw it on the floor. A small piece of white paper separated from the bills and floated through the air landing on the side of the bed. He picked it up and read it.

'In case you want to reach me.'

There was a phone number below the note. Ralph dropped the scrap and cursed at it. Why in hell would he want to contact that Lucifer?

:

Mr. Baldwin made the call shortly after the first news conference.

"As I said. I delivered them," he said.

"You delivered *three* of them," Mr. Pandit said. "Where is the fourth?"

"I don't know. Why don't you ask them? It doesn't really matter. You have your scandal. The job is complete. I would like your assurances as to our agreement," Mr. Baldwin said.

"Our agreement, Mr. Baldwin, was for *all* of them to be delivered to me, not *some* of them. As you have failed, there are no assurances. Goodbye, Mr. Baldwin," Mr. Pandit ended the call.

"You little bastard!" Mr. Baldwin said, a little too loudly. Henry appeared a moment later.

"Do you require something, sir?" he asked.

"No, nothing, Henry. Thank you."

Mr. Baldwin sat in his suite and looked out over the city of Bangkok. It was a beautiful city at night, a city that catered to the most sublime and fiendish delights, and he knew of most of them, as well as the identities of the men that regularly partook.

"Mr. Pandit, our business is not yet concluded," he said, to the city skyline.

Chapter 25

"I want them released!" Ralph said. It was 1:00 am and he had partaken of most of the mini bar.

"Ah, Mr. Gabriel, it is a bit late for this discussion," Mr. Baldwin turned on the light beside his bed and sat up.

"I don't care. I want them released. You can send the pictures if you want... I don't care."

"I see. Well, I think you will see things as differently in the morning, however, there is something you can do for them tonight."

There was silence on the line as Ralph tried to figure out what he meant.

"What do you want?" Ralph finally asked.

"Something that will help both of us. Did you see that man on the news that spoke to the crowd?"

"Yes. Of course."

"That man is the one pushing both of us to make these difficult decisions, and I fear that he will do much worse to your three companions if allowed to."

Ralph's mind was clearing up slowly. "I'm listening," he said.

"That man has a weakness that we can... make work for both of us, but it needs to be done tonight, Saturday night."

"So why don't you do it yourself?"

"Tell you what, Mr. Gabriel, come to the Hotel, same room, and we will discuss it... say, in thirty minutes?" Mr. Baldwin asked.

"Fine." Ralph hung up the phone and stumbled out of bed. He cleaned up as best he could in the bathroom, then went downstairs and caught a cab to the Four Seasons. When he arrived at the Emerald Meeting room, Mr. Baldwin was not present but his aide was.

"Good evening, Mr. Gabriel. I was asked to deliver this to you." He handed Ralph a canvas case with something heavy inside of it, then left the room. Ralph sat down at the table and opened the package. Inside was a camera that looked like a cross between a camcorder and an old 35mm. There was a note inside the bag.

"Mr. Gabriel, this is a very special video camera that will take infrared pictures. Assuming you still wish to help your friends, take a taxi to the Nana Entertainment Plaza (also known as the NEP). It will likely be closed by the time you get there. Locate the Angel disco and go across the street to the alley. There is a door with a marker on it that looks like a dragon. At the opposite end of the alley, there are always a large stack of wooden crates. This would be a good place to be inconspicuous. The man you want will come out of that door in about an hour. Capture him on film and it will help your friends immensely. After you are done, give the bag to the concierge at the front desk. He will know what to do with it."

Ralph sat at the table pondering this newest request. He couldn't think of a reason why Mr. Baldwin would go through all this trouble only to catch him again. If he wanted to do that, he would be in custody right now. On the other hand if he was caught filming this man doing something illegal, then that might put him in serious danger, but he really didn't care. His conscience was bothering him so much he desperately needed a reason to feel better about himself. He got up from the chair and went to the payphone and dialed the number again.

"How do I know that you aren't just creating some elaborate rouse again?" Ralph asked.

"Ah, Mr. Gabriel. Look at the bottom of the camera," Mr. Baldwin said. Ralph pulled it back out of the bag and turned it upside down. There was a small plaque permanently affixed to the metal. It read 'Baldwin Enterprises, USA' and had an etching that looked like four birds in a circle.

"Do you see it?"

"Yes," Ralph said.

"Then ask yourself if I would send you out to get caught with something with my name on it?" He paused for effect. "Now, Mr. Gabriel, you have less than an hour to get across town and take those pictures." He hung up the phone.

Ralph easily found a taxi and sat in the back watching the city of Bangkok pass by. It was nearly 2:00 a.m. and people were milling around the streets under the innumerable neon signs. He played with the camera for a few minutes making sure that it worked, and then tried to enjoy the ride but found himself consumed by his own thoughts. After about twenty minutes, the driver snapped him out of it by breaking hard under at a brightly-lit canopy.

"Nana," he said.

Ralph paid him two hundred baht and got out from the back of the cab into the drizzle. A pretty Thai woman, dressed very provocatively, approached him and grabbed his arm. It was the last thing on Ralph's mind and he smiled politely, then walked around the block until he saw the Angel Disco. It was closed but, just as Mr. Baldwin had indicated, there was an alley across the street and Ralph avoided several cars, then made his way into the dimly lighted lane. It smelled like every other back alley in any city he had ever visited and he breathed through his mouth to prevent the gags from coming. About a hundred feet in he saw a door illuminated by a single overhead incandescent bulb. It had a worn dragon design on it, but no words or numbers. Ralph quickly passed by it to the stack of wooden crates that Mr. Baldwin had mentioned. They were about fifty feet away, in clear sight of the door, and Ralph jostled them until he had formed a small but unobstructed view of the dragon entrance. He waited in silence.

About fifteen minutes later a dark Mercedes with heavily tinted windows drove up and stopped in front of the door. Ralph had the camera out and started filming the car. The driver got out, went over to the door and knocked lightly on the metal frame with his gloved hands. It opened slightly and he turned around to make sure the alley was clear, then stepped back and allowed a man that Ralph immediately recognized to come out of the building. The driver walked over to the back door of the car and reached out to open it when something made a noise in Ralph's direction. Both he and the Man stopped in their tracks. The Man hurried inside the car while the driver took something out of the inside of his jacket and started walking toward Ralph. With every step, Ralph could feel his chest getting tighter and tighter and he knew that we would be forced to do something. The thought crossed his mind whether Mr. Baldwin had set him up, but it didn't make sense. With the man now less than ten feet away Ralph was crouching on his haunches peering through the wooden slats. The camera was still running and he could feel the soft vibration in his right hand.

The driver started moving the wood crates with his free hand and, with a rush of adrenaline, Ralph stood up and shoved the crates toward the man as hard as he could. The driver yelled and tried unsuccessfully to step aside, then crashed backward to the ground covered in empty wooden cases. Ralph kicked and shoved his way out toward the opposite end of the alley and ran as hard as he could, the puddles of water shooting up his legs as he barreled toward the street. He heard the driver screaming at him, but then another voice barked an order and the shouting stopped.

As Ralph turned the corner he could hear the Mercedes start up and head in the opposite direction. Ralph kept running until his lungs burned and his head hurt. He finally stopped in front of a closed clothing store and looked around. His head was soaking wet and the water made it difficult to see. There was no doubt that he was very lost but, on the good side, he was still breathing and he staggered off in a semi-jog for several more blocks. As he hailed a passing taxi it occurred to him that he had lost the camera bag in the alley. The cab didn't even slow down, so he stuffed the camera inside his shirt and kept walking. A few minutes later a taxi did stop and Ralph got in the rear and stared nervously out the back window for the first several miles, expecting to see the dark Mercedes appear at any moment. It never did. He finally settled back into the seat and cradled the camera in his lap until they arrived at the Four Seasons.

He got to the Hotel just after 3:00 a.m., still sopping wet, and walked through the plush lobby. The front desk clerk looked at him, but Ralph ignored the gaze and continued until he reached the bank of pay phones where he dialed Mr. Baldwin.

"Hello?" Mr. Baldwin sounded very tired.

"I have it. We need to speak."

"Mr. Gabriel, it is very late and, as you undoubtedly know, I am in bed –" Ralph cut him off.

"And I have been nearly *killed* taking these pictures. We need to talk."

"Fine, Mr. Gabriel. Give me fifteen minutes. The normal room," Mr. Baldwin hung up the phone.

Ralph walked up the stairs to the Emerald meeting room and sat outside the front door. There was no one else that he could see on the entire floor. Someone had left an unopened soda can on a catering table and Ralph opened it and took a swallow, then looked at the can.

209

It was an exotic flavor similar to grapefruit. It made him wish for a normal grape soda.

Mr. Baldwin arrived a few minutes later carrying a briefcase and wearing a gold set of silk pajamas. He looked quite haggard, and sat down beside him on the bench.

"May I see it?"

Ralph handed him the video recorder and Mr. Baldwin pressed a couple of buttons. Ralph watched the small screen as it adjusted to the darkness and the black Mercedes pulled up. After a few minutes Mr. Baldwin looked up. He was obviously pleased.

"Nice work, Mr. Gabriel."

"Who is he?"

"You mean this man?" Mr. Gabriel pointed at the LCD at the man coming out of the door.

"No, the Easter Bunny! Of course that man."

"Oh. He is the Prime Minister," Mr. Baldwin looked at Ralph, waiting for the response.

"Prime Minister of what?"

"Thailand," Mr. Baldwin said, and smiled.

"This man is the Prime Minister of Thailand?"

"Yes. That is what I just said."

"And what was he doing there?"

"Now that is the interesting part. You see that dragon that you so nicely captured on the film?" Mr. Baldwin pointed to the door of the building that the Prime Minister had come out of. "That dragon is the symbol of the Changmi. They are a group of… what you would call Chinese Triads." He paused and waited for Ralph to look up.

"And?"

"In Thailand they run child prostitution."

Ralph's eyes lit up. "You mean the Prime Minister is a ped… pedo,"

"Pedophile. Yes that is what you would call him in the US. Of course, his predilection for young girls is not commonly known."

"But I thought that was illegal?"

"Illegal, yes. Unobtainable, no. Anything can be had for a price in Thailand," Mr. Baldwin said, with another smile.

"So, then. Let's use it. Get Andrew, Sarah and Kristen out of jail and let us go home. We've been through enough," Ralph said.

"Hmm. That would be easier that it sounds. Timing is everything Mr. Gabriel. All in time."

"The point is, Mr. Baldwin, "Ralph said, sarcastically, "we don't *have* time. But you know that. Let's use it now."

"Mr. Gabriel. Blackmail is like caviar. There is a time and a place. If you serve it out of place it only reminds people of decadence. If you serve it at the wrong time it cannot be fully appreciated, say when you are ravenously hungry. But serve it at the correct place and time and there is nothing quite so special. Patience, Mr. Gabriel, your work will be well worth it. Trust me."

"That is a problem, Mr. Baldwin, because I do not trust you. How do I know you will use it for their benefit and not just your own?" Ralph asked.

"Ah. Now you are thinking like Mr. Lee. I tell you what... Give me a day to use this properly. I will make you a copy," Mr. Baldwin opened the briefcase and inserted the memory card into a small device and pressed a couple of buttons, then ejected the card and gave it to Ralph.

"May I?" Ralph put his hand out and Mr. Baldwin handed him the camera.

"Of course," Mr. Baldwin said.

Ralph verified the card, then put it in his pocket.

"Until Monday, 10:00 a.m., Mr. Gabriel. I would appreciate a call before you do anything. I'm going to bed. I hope you can find your way out." Mr. Baldwin got up and left Ralph wondering what room Mr. Baldwin was staying in, and if that information could somehow be used.

Chapter 26

"I asked what you are doing in Thailand?" Sarah looked at Kristen who was trying to bury her face in her blouse to escape the smoke.

"Could you put that out?" Sarah asked. The man looked at his cigarette for a moment, then back at Sarah. His back was to the mirror that Sarah assumed was one way glass.

"We were supposed to be on a TV adventure series, but something went wrong," she finally said. The man smiled and put out his cigarette.

"What do you mean it went wrong?"

Sarah considered the question and had no idea where to even start.

"Look. What it comes down to is that we were taken here against our will. Just let us go back to the US and we'll forget this ever happened."

"I'm afraid I can't do that." The man got up and walked over to Kristen who was still trying to avoid the remnants of the smoke. "You are very beautiful," he said to her as he ran his fingers through her hair.

"Stop it! We don't want any trouble. Just contact the American Consulate and we can work this all out. We have nothing to hide," Sarah said.

The man stopped touching Kristen and walked over to her.

"Where is your companion?" he asked.

"You mean Andrew? I don't know. *You* have him somewhere. How should I know?" She was getting irritated and she reminded herself to keep calm.

"Not Mr. Lee. The *other* gentlemen that was with you." The policeman showed her a picture from the newspaper and pointed to Ralph, "him," he said.

"I... I'm not sure," she said, wondering why he was asking her the question. She had assumed Ralph had already been caught and had given them up.

"And what are those?" He pointed to the wristbands.

Sarah looked at him, puzzled again. Either he was just playing with them or Mr. Baldwin had nothing to do with their current predicament.

"We don't know. We can't get them off." Sarah tugged at hers to demonstrate. The man came over and picked up her arm to inspect it, then left the room. A few minutes later he came back with a large set of bolt cutters.

"Put your hand on the table." Sarah did as she was asked. If he was going to cut it off she was happy with that. The bigger question was her assumption that Mr. Baldwin had arranged to make them fugitives and to get caught. If it wasn't him, then whom? With a loud snap the wristband fell away.

"Yours as well," he said, to Kristen. She obediently put her arm on the table and supported it with her other hand. After he had removed them both, he picked them up and left the room again.

"Why did he do that?" Kristen asked, when they were alone.

"I don't know, Kristen. I'm trying to figure that out. I think we all assumed that Mr. Baldwin was behind the arrest but, if he wasn't, I don't know what that means."

"I'm worried about Ralph," Kristen said.

Sarah had her doubts as to whether he was innocent in the previous day's activities. They could hear some muffled yelling coming from somewhere in the building.

"What do you think they are going to do to us?" Kristen asked.

"Let's just hope they get in contact with the Embassy."

"Do you think they will let us go?" Kristen asked, with a very worried face.

Sarah didn't know what to say.

"I'm sure it will all work out. Let's not panic just yet." She hoped Kristen believed the words because, at the moment, panic seemed to be a reasonable option.

:

Andrew was thrown into the next room where he was chained to a chair and left alone. He could see through the one way privacy glass and observed the girls being questioned. He watched with great concern when the man approached them with the large cutters. Andrew yelled to try and get his attention as he lifted the large steel blades to Sarah's arm, but then calmed down after he understood what the man was doing. A minute after the officer had left the girls, he entered Andrew's room.

"What do you think so far?" the man asked, as he walked behind Andrew with the large tool.

"She's telling you the truth. We don't know why we are here …" Andrew paused, expecting to feel the cold metal against his wrists but, to his disappointment, the man did not attempt to cut off the wristband.

"So, you are telling me that you know nothing about the theft of King Ramas picture?" Andrew couldn't answer that without implicating him or the girls, so he remained silent.

"Ah. I see. So you *do* know something about the theft."

Andrew wanted to object to the statement but he was unsure of the consequences to a reply.

"Do you realize that theft of a religious object alone is considered very serious. However the object that you are accused of stealing is both religious and Imperial. Combined, it could be construed, in our written law, that corporal punishment would be in order."

Andrew looked up at him to see if he understood correctly.

"You mean you would kill someone for stealing a picture?"

"Actually, the King has recently forbidden capital punishment. I said *corporal.*"

All Andrew could picture was his second grade teacher wielding her wooden paddle. How bad could that be?

The man continued. "In fact, our Prime Minister, Mr. Pandit, you saw him a few minutes ago when you arrived, is expressing his opinion that we make an example of you. It seems our tourist police are not as respected as they should be. You Americans think you own the world and can do whatever you want."

"What exactly do you want from me? An admission? That's not going to happen. First I want to speak to the Embassy and then we can discuss *our* statement." Andrew hoped that he accepted his word as representative of them all.

"It seems you are all in agreement that you want an Embassy representative, however, the Embassy is reluctant to get involved with guilty parties. And there are many witnesses that will testify to seeing you and the women at the temple."

Andrew mentally acknowledged it was a possibility.

"Where is Mr. Gabriel?" the man asked.

The question surprised Andrew and the man noticed it.

"Ah. You don't know. You have assumed, as did the women, that Mr. Gabriel turned you in. Interesting."

"The answer is, I don't know where he is," Andrew said.

The man walked behind Andrew and stood where he could not be seen. Without warning Andrew felt a blow to his head, it strained his neck and for a second he blacked out.

"Mr. Lee! Do I have your attention now? This is no game. We want to know who stole the picture and where it is!" The man's mouth was inches away from Andrew's right ear, and he winced with every word.

"I... I don't know where the picture is. We..." Andrew stopped himself and gathered his thoughts. "We don't know."

Andrew felt the man grab hold of the back of his chair and he braced himself for something. Suddenly he was looking at the light fixture in the middle of the ceiling, falling backward. He hit the floor with a thud, his hands caught beneath the chair. The pain from his pinned wrists shot up his arms into his shoulders and radiated through his neck and upper back. The chair rolled over to its side and he tried to catch his breath. His mind momentarily was disconcerted and he leaned his head against the cool concrete floor to try and regain his thoughts.

The man stood over him and lit a cigarette, allowing the match to fall through the air and land on Andrews's chest. He felt the heat of the burning ember before it went out.

"Mr. Lee. Do you have some answers for me?" The man jostled him firmly in the ribs with the tips of his boots.

"If I knew where the picture was I would tell you. But I don't. That's the truth," Andrew managed to stammer.

"Who took it, Mr. Lee? Which one of you? Or should I say, which one of the women?" Andrew attempted to open his eyes, but the ceiling fixture blinded him, and he turned away. He heard the whoosh of air before he felt the blow to his diaphragm. The kick knocked the air out of lungs and he wheezed for breath.

"I'll be back in a moment, Mr. Lee," the man said, as he left the room. Andrew heard his voice again within moments as he continued the interrogation next door.

"We require some answers. And you need to see something," the man said. A few moments later Andrew heard his door open and Sarah and Kristen gasped. He opened his eyes toward the sound and saw all three of them looking at him.

"Andrew!" Kristen exclaimed and attempted to move toward him. The man prevented her, and she started to cry.

"We are going to do this the easy way or the more difficult way. It is your choice. I need to know where the picture is and who took it. Mr. Lee has indicated it was one of you but I need to have a confession. It would be much better for all of you." Andrew opened his mouth to deny the allegation, but he decided it was useless. If Sarah and Kristen believed him, so be it.

The man removed the two women and left Andrew alone. He had finally gotten his breath back, but the incessant throbbing in his head and side was making it hard to concentrate.

"So, if neither of you are ready to talk I'll be forced to take one of you at a time into the other room until you are more cooperative. At least Mr. Lee will have company in his suffering!" he said.

"What do you want? Money? I have some money," Sarah said.

"Is that an offer for a bribe? That is a serious offense, Ms..." he pulled out a paper from his shirt pocket, "Connell," he said.

Sarah glared at him. The man sighed.

"Well, I guess we shall have to do this the hard way. Come, Ms. Connell, we require some private time." The man walked over to Sarah and grabbed her by the arm. Kristen had a panicked look in her face. She couldn't believe she was about to again cause Sarah pain. Sarah saw her look and spoke to her sternly.

"Keep quiet, Kristen. Don't say anything. Sooner or later the Consulate will find us." At the comment, the man laughed.

"Maybe. If they know where to look," he said.

Kristen had had enough. She was shaking and the tears were freely falling down her cheeks.

"It was me. I did it. Leave her alone." Kristen looked at the floor and slowly backed away from the man who had released Sarah and was walking toward her. He stopped and looked toward the ceiling.

"Good. That's settled. The video tape of your confession should be very helpful." Sarah immediately looked up and saw the camera. The red light was on. The officer left the room and shut the door.

"Kristen. What have you done?" Sarah asked, as she stood facing her. Kristen's head was leaning back against the wall her eyes closed.

In the next room Andrew was lying still on the floor but he had heard every word and wondered what this would mean to the much grander scheme that they were embroiled in. Certainly the confession was meant to add to the King's shame. But he didn't quite understand why. As far as the three of them, he could only hope that whatever was going on, it would be over soon.

:

Mr. Baldwin watched the confession on the news and had mixed feelings. He was happy that his overall plan had been so successful and, at the same time, irritated that the Prime Minister had gotten exactly what he had wanted. The question remained, what would Mr. Pandit do now?

"Henry!" he exclaimed. His aide quickly appeared.

"We need to change hotels and please have the King Air made ready at Bang Phra Airfield," Mr. Baldwin said.

"Yes sir. Where would you like to move to?"

"The Peninsula, please, under your name. Thank you, Henry."

After Henry left, Mr. Baldwin made another phone call, then started packing up his gear. He didn't know whether Mr. Pandit would be bold enough to try and come after him but, until his next strategy was ready, he was going to be cautious. If it were not for a few loose ends he would have already left for the United States. Perhaps, he thought, in a few more days.

Chapter 27

Andrew had again blacked out and failed to wake up until his chair was lifted upright and dragged toward the table. His feet were still cuffed to the legs of the chair, but his hands were released. There was a glass of water in front of him and he grabbed hold of it and took a couple of gulps. The pain in his side had subsided into soreness, and he tentatively stretched his torso to see if something was broken. It didn't feel like it.

"Mr. Lee." It was a different interrogator this time. Andrew looked up.

"Mr. Lee, are you with me?"

"Uh. Yes." Andrew reluctantly opened his eyes to find a well dressed Thai man in a suit.

"Who are you? You already got what you wanted. Now what?" Andrew asked.

"Mr. Lee, I apologize for your treatment. It is not our policy to beat our... suspects."

"You can knock off the good cop-bad cop routine. What do you want?"

"Mr. Lee, are you aware of the serious situation you are in?"

"I think I have gathered that at this point. Thanks for your concern," Andrew thought the comment might have been a little too sarcastic, and braced himself for a response.

"The Prime Minister has said that an example should be made of your friend, Ms. Conrad, I believe."

"That was mentioned to me already." Andrew looked past the man into the next room, but the women were gone. It made him worry.

"The reason why I am mentioning this is that if you are given the opportunity to... leave here..." the comment got Andrew's attention and he looked at the man's eyes, "...it would be good to make haste of the opportunity."

Andrew noticed the watch on the man's wrist. It was a TAG. His clothing was pressed and modern. He didn't look like any policeman he had seen so far.

"Who are you?" he asked.

"I'm afraid I cannot answer that question. However, I was told to give you this and tell you that I am a friend." The man pushed over a five hundred baht bill. Andrew looked at the purple bill and the King's picture, then back at the man.

"Are you releasing me?" he asked.

"No. I cannot do that at this time. The Prime Minister is on his way here right now." The man looked at his watch. "He will undoubtedly take advantage of the situation for more publicity. After he is done with you, we will see what can be done. Remember, if you are given the opportunity, you must do it immediately. There is no going back. Our mutual friend will be able to do nothing else to help you." The man walked over to the door, then returned and, much to Andrew's consternation, replaced the handcuffs and picked up the glass of water. He put the bill, along with some other money, in Andrew's waistband.

"I am sorry for your… bruises. It is unfortunate. We have much to work on in our country," the man said, before he left.

Andrew was left alone for several hours until the original officer came in. He gave Andrew a strange look.

"How did you…" he started.

It occurred to Andrew that he had last been seen lying on the ground.

"Never mind. We have an appointment." The officer opened the door, and two other guards came in to remove his restraints. Andrew took the opportunity to rub his wrists.

"Follow me," the man said.

Andrew's muscles were tight and ached from the beating. His joints felt like rusted hinges. It took a concentrated effort in order to stand and he walked stiffly between the two guards as they departed the room. About fifty feet down the corridor, he was directed into a large chamber and onto a platform. There were several hundred empty seats facing him. Sarah and Kristen were already seated and chained to their chairs. They could hear voices outside the doors on the opposite side of the room. Kristen's eyes were red and puffy from crying. Sarah looked exhausted.

"Sit down and stay seated," the head guard said, and then left the room.

"Are you OK?" Andrew asked.

"We just want this to be over with," Sarah said.

"Did they…" Sarah looked at the two remaining guards, then back at Andrew, "do anything else to you?"

"No. I think I blacked out."

"I'm sorry," she said.

"Actually, I don't feel as bad as I should. Maybe it's adrenaline."

"Do you know what they are going to do with us?" Kristen asked. Andrew slowly shook his head.

"Where did they take you?" he asked.

"Some kind of doctor examined Kristen, but I was just told to watch. Then they put us in a cell and we fell asleep," Sarah said.

"Any idea what time it is?"

"I think early Sunday morning," Sarah said.

They were interrupted by a posse of men preceding the Prime Minister. He spoke to an aide, who walked over to Andrew and the girls.

"This is the Prime Minister of Thailand, Mr. Pandit," the interpreter said. Kristen raised her eyebrows and looked at Andrew, then back at the man.

"He has asked me to inform you that he is holding a press conference in five minutes. You are instructed to not say anything at all. If you do, the guards have been instructed to discipline you accordingly." The threat made Kristen shudder, and she scooted toward Sarah until their legs were touching.

"Do you understand?" the interpreter asked.

They all nodded assent.

The Prime Minister announced something to his aides and they hurried to the back of the room and opened the doors. A flood of reporters came in with flashes going. When the crowd had calmed down, Mr. Pandit took the lectern and spoke for about ten minutes. Andrew desperately wanted to know what he was saying and, at the same time, he was looking through the audience to see if any Americans were present. He didn't see any.

Mr. Pandit answered questions for another five minutes, then headed off the stage, ignoring barrage of inquires from the audience.

"What do you have to say for yourselves?" A voice yelled out in English, and the crowd immediately quieted down. Mr. Pandit stopped and turned around, looking at Andrew and Sarah. They both clenched their mouths closed. Mr. Pandit smiled and said something to the audience in Thai. The crowd erupted in laughter, and Andrew,

Sarah and Kristen were led back into the police station. Their cuffs were removed and they were taken into a holding cell and told to stand against the far wall. After ten minutes the Prime Minister, along with an interpreter, entered the room and spoke to them.

"You are to be given a choice. All three of you can go to trial for the stealing and disposing of a sacred artifact, or Ms. Conrad may accept punishment for all three of you." Mr. Pandit stared at them when no one answered.

"The Prime Minister says that you will be punished. The only question is who, and the severity of the discipline. You must answer." Sarah felt as if her mother was making her choose between a swatch and a rubber slipper for her spanking, only she wasn't sure of the penalties.

"I think we will go to trial and take our chances," Sarah said.

"Ms. Connell. You could choose that option, but be very clear that our courts are not like America's. We do not allow criminals to get off on … technicalities. If you go to trial, you *will* be convicted."

"What is the… what penalty is given for stealing?" Kristen stammered.

"If you were to choose prison, five years for each of you," the interpreter said. Kristen grabbed her arms and hugged herself.

"No-o. That's not right. We were forced to do it," she said. The man ignored her comment.

"And what if it is just me?" Kristen looked at the man, pleading with her eyes.

"If you agreed to the penalty, then you will all be allowed to leave immediately."

"But what is the penalty?" Andrew asked.

The interpreter discussed something with Mr. Pandit, who was obviously adamant about whatever he was saying. The Prime Minister turned toward Kristen and used his fingers to put a cuff around a wrist.

"You will lose your hands," the interpreter said. The Prime minister interjected something and the interpreter repeated, "Yes, you will lose your hands."

"WHAT?" Andrew asked, "That's not – possible!"

"Actually, it is. It is your choice. All of you go to prison or Ms. Conrad will lose her hands."

"But that is cruel! It's wrong!"

221

"Some may consider it so but, since it is your choice, or rather Ms. Conrad's choice, it is acceptable to our judicial system. I believe you have something similar with your child molesters in the United States. Did not one of them just choose castration to avoid a long jail sentence?"

Sarah thought that she did remember a case like that.

"You can't just cut someone's hands off. That's barbaric!" Andrew exclaimed.

"Quite right, Mr. Lee. We don't cut them off. We are much more progressive. We use a toxin to paralyze the nerves. It is just as effective and, as you noted, much more humane."

Andrew opened his mouth to protest again but the Prime Minister had his hand up.

"We will leave you to discuss it. You have ten minutes," the interpreter said. He and Mr. Pandit closed the door behind them.

Kristen and crumpled to the floor and was sobbing uncontrolled. Sarah bent down to hug her but didn't know what to say.

It took several minutes for Sarah to calm her down. When the tears had dried Andrew sat down in front of them both.

"Kristen, you don't have to do this. I…" he looked up at Sarah and she nodded, "*we* cannot ask this of you…" he ran out of words.

"But… we can't stay here for five years!" She gazed at Andrew first. "I can't do that to you but I don't know how to… to allow them to take my hands." Kristen held out her palms in front of her as if trying to imagine what life would be like without them.

"Maybe, someone will help us," Sarah said, looking at Andrew. His face showed no conviction in the idea.

"Who, Sarah? I mean I did take the picture." Sarah looked up at the camera in the ceiling but it was too late to start trying to hide the truth.

"The guy said the same thing that Andrew did yesterday: five years. I just can't do that to us…" Kristen's voice drifted off and the group sat in silence for a few minutes.

"Kristen. I don't know what to say. I'm sorry you are faced with this," Andrew said, as he painfully got up on his feet and stared at the one way glass. He wondered if they were watching them right now, taking pleasure from their misery. He couldn't get himself to encourage Kristen to take the offer of prison—not only for his sake, but Sarah's as well. The things he had read about the Thai prisons made the loss of one's hands almost seem a reasonable exchange. Then again, he was not an artist who depended on their hands for their sense of self-worth and pride.

Sarah leaned her head on Kristen's shoulder and grasped her hands in hers. She, too, was unable to guide Kristen to take the prison option. Her emotions told her that they should not give in to this blackmail. But her mind reasoned the logical thing to do was to have one person pay the price instead of all three. Deep inside, she questioned her motives and whether Kristen's choice during the kidnapping was swaying her judgment, but she couldn't see that far inside herself, or didn't want to.

Mr. Pandit entered the room with another guard and sat in a chair facing them.

"What is your choice?" he asked, looking at Andrew first. Andrew looked at the ground.

"Ms. Connell?"

"You are a sick bastard!" Sarah said. The reaction was swift and violent as the guard quickly moved over to her and hit her across the face with a closed hand. Sarah yelped in pain and crumpled to the ground. Andrew threw himself over her to protect her from further blows but the guard had already backed off at Mr. Pandit's command.

"Well, now that we have that out of the way... Ms. Conrad, it seems that the decision is yours alone."

To Andrew and Sarah's amazement, Kristen stood up and faced the shorter man.

"What assurance do I have that if I consent to this brutal punishment that you will keep your word?" she asked.

"A judge of the Criminal court has already consented to the punishment in exchange for commuting the five year sentence. Here is the consent order. I took the liberty of having it translated for you," Mr. Pandit handed her an official looking document. Sarah stood up and read it along with Kristen. It looked real but she had no way of knowing for sure.

"You agree to also sign it and have that document faxed to my office, if Miss Conrad agrees to your terms?" Andrew asked.

"Why not, you can even mail it to someone if you choose," Mr. Pandit said.

"Ms. Conrad. Your decision?" he asked, again.

"I accept," she said.

Mr. Pandit handed her a pen, Kristen grasped it in her trembling left hand, bent over the table, and signed her name to the paper. She wondered if it would be the last thing she would ever do with her hands and the thought made her start to shudder again. Sarah came up behind her and put an arm around her waist. The Prime Minister came up beside them and signed the document without even touching it.

"Take me to a fax machine," Andrew said.

Mr. Pandit barked an order at the guard, who escorted Andrew out of the room.

"That was a wise choice, Ms. Conrad," the Prime Minister said.

Neither Sarah nor Kristen bothered answering or looking at him.

A few minutes later Andrew returned with an envelope and handed it to Kristen. She grabbed it and felt the smooth paper for a moment, then gave it to Sarah who folded it and placed it in her front pocket.

"The doctor will be in momentarily," Mr. Pandit said.

"What? You mean right now? Here? That's not sanitary," Sarah exclaimed.

"Ms. Connell, this is not an invasive procedure. It is a simple matter of two very well placed shots. The sooner this is done, the sooner you will go free," he said.

"Fine. Just get it over with," Kristen said.

"Can we have our passports back now?" Andrew asked.

Mr. Pandit said something to the guard, who opened the door and spoke to someone. A man appeared with a manila envelope and handed it to the Prime Minister. He pulled out the three passports and put them on the table under his hand.

"When it is done," he said.

Kristen and Sarah were huddled in a corner, whispering something, and Andrew stood with his back to the glass window staring into the air when the knock broke the silence. Kristen jumped into the air and turned around to face the door. Sarah was holding on to her left arm. The doctor that had checked Kristen last night was allowed in the room and set up a small array of items, including a rubber tourniquet and three needles. Two chairs were brought into the room and placed at the table.

"Have a seat Ms. Conrad," Mr. Pandit said, indicating the one closest to him. Sarah helped her walk over and Kristen sat down facing the doctor who was talking to her in Thai.

"Put your arms on the table, face up," Mr. Pandit translated.

Kristen's arms felt like lead weights at her side. Her mouth was pasty and her heart hammered in her chest. Almost everything that she was proud of was about to change. As she managed to lift her right hand to the table the doctor grabbed it and flipped it up so that her palm was facing the ceiling. Mr. Pandit seized her left arm and placed it beside her right. Kristen looked down at the underside of her arms, which were tanned despite their protected location. Her arms were long and thin and narrowed at her wrist. She could see the faint blue veins as they traveled down its length and spread out to her fingers. The deep life lines on her palm were slick with moisture, her index finger on her left hand still bore a scar from a branch she had broken accidentally in the jungle a few days before. Her left hand bore no jewelry but her right hand had a silver band on her ring finger. She could feel the warm metal as she looked at it.

The doctor swabbed her arms from her wrist to the back of the thumb, then picked up one of the needles and Kristen reacted by yanking her arms back to her lap. The doctor sounded like he cursed, then pointed to Mr. Pandit.

"He says that if you move during the injection, you could lose the use of your entire arm or it even may kill you. I advise that you keep still. Let's try it again," Mr. Pandit said.

Kristen tried in vain to lift up her hands and she looked up pleading at Sarah. Sarah softly first took her right, then her left arm and placed them on the table. Kristen fixed her eyes on Sarah's as the doctor swabbed her hands again and picked up the needle. With tears welling up in both their eyes Sarah cupped her hands around Kristen's face and maintained eye contact as the doctor injected the toxin first into the flesh between the back of her thumb and index finger, and then into the opposite side of the area, below the thumb, in her palm. Kristen felt the prick of the needle and closed her eyes. As the tears flowed down her cheeks she could feel the numbness start in her thumb and then creep slowly through each finger as if she were slowly dipping her hand in warm water.

As the toxins gradually radiated through her muscles it killed the nerves in her hands and along with it her hopes and dreams of attending Juilliard in New York, Art school in France, or even holding the hand of someone she loved.

Oddly when the doctor grabbed her left hand it was almost reassuring. The sense of his touch meant that there was still hope, and she found herself praying fervently to the God that she had come to believe, through the appreciation of nature, must have loved mankind at some time.

The yell came simultaneous with the opening of the door. Two men dressed in gray military uniforms rushed in the rooms and pointed semi-automatic weapons at everyone. Kristen yanked her left arm away from the doctor and turned around in time to see Mr. Pandit's guard falling to the floor after being hit across the face with the butt of a rifle. Mr. Pandit stood up and looked intensely at the men, who both wore masks and vehemently said something to the two men, who ignored him.

The first man rushed over to the table and grabbed Kristen. Sarah hung on and they were rushed toward the door. Andrew, who wasn't sure exactly what was happening until that moment, ran over to the table, grabbed the passports, and followed the women. He could hear the first man and Mr. Pandit having words, then some loud thumps and silence. He hoped that it had hurt.

The two men escorted them down the corridor back to the room where the press conference had taken place, once inside. One of them pointed to the back door and spoke.

"Go!"

Sarah grabbed Kristen by her good arm and ran down the aisle.

The man gave Andrew an envelope and smiled.

"For you," he said, in broken English.

"Thank you. Thank you," Andrew said, as he ran out the door into the sunshine. Sarah was twenty or so feet in front of him and ran hard in order to catch up while directing them across the busy street into a shopping area. Once they were several blocks away, they stopped in a shaded entry and caught their breath.

"Who was that?!" Sarah asked.

"I'm not sure. I think… I hope it was a friend, and not another game," Andrew said, as he ripped open the envelope.

"What is it?" Sarah asked.

"It's a train schedule," he said.

"For what?" she asked.

"I think it is telling us to take this train…" he looked at the paper.

"Where?"

"It stops… Singapore. It ends up in Singapore," he said, as he looked at the girls. Kristen looked like she was in shock.

"Any idea what time it is?" he asked. Sarah stepped out of the hallway and stopped someone, pointing to their time. She came back a second later.

"10:30," she said.

"It doesn't leave until 2:45, if I'm reading this correctly," he said.

"Can we trust it?" she asked.

"I honestly don't know. I was told that someone might try to help us, but this could just as well be another trap. It's not really like we have a lot of choices. The airports are no-brainers, so that leaves car, bus or train. Car is too expensive and I have no idea how to even get one…so bus or train. Evidently, we are being told train is best. I don't really care, as long as we are out of this country."

Sarah shrugged her shoulders and held onto Kristen.

"Then let's do it," she said.

"OK. Let's get some food, and then we can take a taxi." Andrew pulled out the wad of bills and Sarah looked at him.

"A guy came in and gave me this sometime this morning. I don't know who he was, but I think he was a friend," Andrew considered telling her about the King but it didn't seem wise at that time.

"He's the one who mentioned about the 'help'?"

"Kind of… he didn't really say it exactly, but I got the idea an opportunity would happen," he said.

"Why would he do that?" Sarah's brain was working fast.

"He evidently does not like Mr. Pandit. Actually, I think his boss is one of the PM's targets. So can you get some food? I think a woman would be better, and I'll wait with Kristen," Andrew said to end the conversation.

"Sure. Give me a few minutes," she said.

Chapter 28

Ralph had turned the television on first thing Sunday morning but there was nothing about Andrew, Sarah or Kristen so he took a shower and headed out to buy some food. The streets were missing a lot of vendors that had clogged the streets on the previous days. He had to walk several blocks until he found something with noodles and some kind of green vegetable that looked edible. On the way back to his room he passed a small grocer, and absently walked up and down the aisles trying in vain to occupy his mind so that his conscience would stop beating him. He a finally gave up, purchased a few snacks and magazines, and went back to his room where the television remained on. With the entire day to wait, he attempted to eat the noodles using the disposable chopsticks. It was the best diversion he had yet found, and it took him the better part of the next hour to manage to eat the meal. Afterward, he tried to clean up the splatter with a towel, and then leaned back on a pillow and started flipping channels. He saw the news flash as it interrupted a scheduled program.

There was a picture of the police station with the Prime Minister in front of the building making a statement. Only this time, he didn't look so good. His head was bandaged, his clothing crumpled and he sounded really mad. The television picture split into two and on the right appeared the picture of Andrew, Sarah and Kristen with what looked like a reward being offered. After the Prime Minister stopped talking, the story continued with a reporter inside the police station interviewing what appeared to the a ranking police officer. He was acting out what Ralph assumed was the escape. It looked pretty vicious.

Ralph picked up the telephone and dialed Mr. Baldwin, who answered on the second ring without saying a word.

"Hello?" Ralph asked.

"Ah, Mr. Gabriel. You realize that these phone calls can be picked up electronically? I hope you are calling on a public phone…"

"Uh. I'll call you back," Ralph said, hanging up, his heart rate already increasing. He didn't know whether to pack up and leave or stay. He decided that, since the news hadn't shown his picture, it was probably safe to stay, but he left the hotel and walked a couple of blocks to a pay phone booth and dialed the number again. He had no idea how much to put in, and so he just added several coins until he got a dial tone.

"It's me again," Ralph said.

"I can hear that. You must think before you act, Mr. Gabriel. A small slip up can be very costly in these high stakes games," Mr. Baldwin said.

"Uh...OK. So, you used it?" Ralph asked. Mr. Baldwin thought a moment about the fortuitous turn of events and decided that what Ralph didn't know wasn't important to tell him.

"I did say that I would do what I could, and now your friends seem to be out. I hope they make the best of their freedom," he said.

"Was the news offering a reward for their capture?" Ralph asked.

"Yes. Quite a lot of money, actually, one hundred thousand baht. It seems the... man... got beat up in the escape," Mr. Baldwin chuckled, "serves him right. But he is very angry and is saying that your friends are armed and dangerous. Let's hope he doesn't find them. I have a feeling a bad accident would occur if he did. Can we speak a minute about your plans?"

"You told me to lay low for awhile. That's what I'm doing."

"One minute, I have another phone call," Mr. Baldwin put him on hold for a few minutes.

"There is a problem, Mr. Gabriel. One of my informants has just told me that there has been a bounty placed on your friend's head, an unofficial one, of course, but it is for substantially more money than is being reported on the news."

"Uh... I guess that the... guy is taking this pretty personal..." Ralph said.

"I don't think you quite understand, Mr. Gabriel. The offer has been made for their capture 'dead or alive'. And, by the sound of it, 'dead' would be preferable. This presents some problems for me as well."

Ralph tried to think about what Mr. Baldwin was telling him, but found his mind was panicking and there were no coherent solutions presenting themselves.

"Mr. Gabriel?" Mr. Baldwin asked.

"Uh. Yes. What do I do?" Ralph asked. The words made him sick as soon as he said them. He was asking this man what to do. It seemed like a perverse and desperate action.

"I don't know… yet," Mr. Baldwin said. "Call me back in ten minutes." He hung up before Ralph could respond.

Ralph told himself to remember who he was dealing with; that nothing he said could be trusted, but he had no other options. He put some coins into the phone, dialed zero, and heard the line click several times before a voice picked up.

"English please. Emergency!" Ralph said, before he was put on hold again.

"Hello? May I be of assistance?" A woman's voice asked.

"I need the American Consulate phone number please."

"Yes sir….053 252629."

Ralph repeated the number to her.

"Yes that is correct, sir," she said. Ralph hung up the phone repeating the number out loud as he deposited some more coins. He waited impatiently as the phone rang.

"You have called the Chiang Mai American Consulate outside of our normal operating hours…" Ralph pressed zero for an operator, but was disconnected. He swore at the phone putting in more coins and listening to the entire message. There was an option for 'emergencies' and he pressed it. The voice said to leave a message and someone would call him as soon as possible.

"Dammit!!" he said, as he slammed the handset down. He dialed the operator again and was connected to someone who spoke English.

"Please help me. I need an emergency number for the American Consulate in Bangkok," he said.

"One moment please," a female voice said. He thought it sounded like the same woman.

"I do show a number for emergencies. 662 205-4000." Ralph frantically looked around for something to write with, but there was nothing available. He repeated the number as he hung up the phone and reached into his pocket for more change, only to find he was out. In frustration. he slammed his open palm against the concrete wall and immediately regretted the decision.

"Ouch!" he yelled.

"Hey? You OK?" A man with a French accent stopped and asked him.

"I need some coins for a phone call. It is very important!" Ralph exclaimed.

"No problem," the man said, as he put a few coins in Ralph's hand.

"Thank you," Ralph said, not even waiting for the reply. He deposited a couple of coins, then realized he had forgotten the number and had to start the whole process over again. When he finally was successful, and the phone was ringing, he closed his eyes and muttered 'please, please, please'. A male voice answered.

"What is the nature of your call?" he asked.

"It is an emergency. I am an American citizen. I am here, in Bangkok, with some friends and we are in trouble. I think someone wants to kill us." Ralph knew it sounded over the top, but he hoped the man would take him seriously.

"Are you safe right now?" the man asked.

"Yes, but my friends may not be," Ralph said.

"And where are they?"

"I... I don't know," he said.

The man paused.

"Mr...?"

"Mr. Gabriel. Ralph Gabriel."

"Mr. Gabriel. Why are you and your friends in danger?"

Ralph had no idea where to even start to answer the question. He decided the incident at the temple was the most relevant information.

"The temple. The missing picture, have you heard about that?" Ralph asked.

"Of course. It is all over the news. I hope you are not somehow involved in that, Mr. Gabriel," the man said.

"Well, kind of. We were forced to take the picture. I mean, one of my friends was... did."

"So your friends are the ones wanted by the police right now?"

"Yes, and I have reason to believe there is a price on their heads," Ralph said.

"That wouldn't surprise me. They embarrassed some very powerful people. Why didn't you contact us yesterday?" the man asked.

"I… well, my friends… I don't know. I think maybe they couldn't." Ralph stammered. "I wasn't with them," he finally got out.

"Ah. Yes. You are the missing American," the man said.

"I guess so."

"Mr. Gabriel, I don't know quite what to say. If you find your friends they can come to the American Embassy and we will see what we can do. If your friends get arrested, I would strongly suggest that they ask for the American liaison. Is there anything else I can help you with at this time?" he asked.

"I guess not… I guess I need to find them first," Ralph said.

"That would be the first priority. Yes."

"Thank you," Ralph said, and hung up. That was fairly worthless, he thought. He picked up the handset and dialed Mr. Baldwin again.

"Let me ask you something," Ralph started.

"Yes, Mr. Gabriel, go ahead," Mr. Baldwin said.

"Why do you care whether we live or not? Wouldn't it be better for us to just disappear in some godforsaken prison…" he asked.

"I realize you might not believe this, but that was not the intent of this adventure, and besides, all of your families back home undoubtedly know my name, and all your disappearances would present some significant problems to me in the US. No. It would be better that you go back home to your lives," Mr. Baldwin said.

The comment made Ralph irritated.

"What lives? You've destroyed them!" he said.

"Better a live dog than a dead lion," Mr. Baldwin said.

"What?"

"Never mind. Shall we get to the matter at hand, Mr. Gabriel? You wanted to know how you might help your friends. Is that correct?"

He didn't wait for an answer.

"First of all, you must find them. When you do, hopefully today, you must get them to the Bang Phra Airport. B-A-N-G P-H-R-A. Got it? It is just south of Bangkok."

"Uh. Yes," Ralph really wanted a writing utensil. He tried to remember it by a mnemonic. 'Bang! Frat!' he hoped it would work.

"My plane will be there. It will take you out of the country."

"Where?" Ralph asked.

"I'm not sure at this point. The important thing is to get out of Thailand," Mr. Baldwin said.

"That still leaves the problem of where to find them," Ralph said.

"Ah. Yes, I believe I have located at least Mr. Lee. Seems they are at the Hua lamphong Station…"

"Hula what?" Ralph asked.

"Tell you what – just ask for the Train station. The taxi driver should know where that is… if not, keep asking them until you find someone that does. I'm assuming that they are trying to leave the country and there is a train that leaves in forty-five minutes headed to Malaysia. I suggest you get moving, Mr. Gabriel."

"Uh. OK. Hula what again?"

"Hua lamphong," Mr. Baldwin sighed, "and what was the name of the airport Mr. Gabriel?"

"Bang Fat?"

"Bang PhRA," Mr. Baldwin said, and hung up.

:

Hua lamphong looked like an outdoor version of Grand Central station in New York. They had bandaged Kristen's right hand in a scarf from a street vendor, and slung it around her shoulder. Sarah walked beside her, with Andrew in front, until they entered the main terminal. Andrew found himself wishing it were a weekday, as the crowds were relatively thin and he felt conspicuous. He arranged to meet the girls a few minutes before departure and told them to stay out of sight as much as possible. He watched as they entered the women's restroom, and then waited in line for train 35 departing Bangkok at 2:45, purchasing two first class sleeper tickets for privacy and a single second class non air-conditioned sleeper ticket in order to save the money. He figured the third person could just crash on the floor. It came to a little over five thousand baht. It was almost all the cash that he had left. With several hours to kill he found an inconspicuous wooden bench off of the main platform and people watched as he munched on the bag of cashews that Sarah had bought.

He must have drifted off to sleep shortly after, because he awoke with a start at the sound of a train blowing its whistle.

The clock on the platform showed 2:30 and Andrew looked around cautiously to see if there was any activity that he should have been aware of. A blonde couple walked passed him, glancing his way, and Andrew attempted to turn the opposite direction, but the man walked up anyway.

"I'm sorry. I know it's none of my business but I think there is someone looking for you," he said.

"Uh. Why do you think so?" Andrew asked. The blonde woman had moved off to the side. She looked nervous.

"When we were out front a couple of guys were showing a picture that I would swear was you without the beard and mustache," he said.

"How long ago?" Andrew asked, both thankful for the stranger's help, as well as very concerned.

"Just a few minutes. You might want to be careful. They didn't look like police but, in this country, you could disappear and not be seen for a long time. Be safe," the man said, as his girlfriend or wife took a hold of his arm. They quickly walked away.

Andrew stood up from the bench and looked tentatively toward the platform where train 35 was boarding. There was quite a line in the queue, and he walked the fifty yards slowly as he tried to observe if there were any suspicious movements, but he didn't see any and he took his place in line. The steward was checking tickets and it occurred to Andrew that Sarah's and Kristen's were still in his pocket. With only two people left in front of him, he was about to step out of the line when Sarah came up and grabbed his arm. She smelled like something sweet and exotic, and he looked at the flowers, which were in her hair, then glanced over at Kristen who was very pale and staring straight ahead.

"Is she OK?" he asked.

"Yes. I think so… Very tired. I hope there is someplace to lay down," Sarah said.

"I got a cabin," Andrew said, as he handed the agent the stubs. They were directed to the third car where they easily found their numbered cabin and let themselves in. It was small and had two seats that looked as if they converted into bunks. Andrew adjusted the air conditioning as Sarah helped Kristen lay down on one of the benches. He sat down on the opposite side and Sarah joined him.

"Any problems?" he asked.

"No. Not really. We stayed out of sight," Sarah said, "You?"

"No." There was no point in alarming her.

The train started moving and they found themselves in the sun looking at the now familiar buildings of Bangkok. The train picked up speed and Andrew felt a great relief. In less than twenty-four hours they should be safely out of the country.

If nothing went wrong.

Ralph arrived at the train station frustrated and ten minutes late. He walked through every platform, but there was no sign of Andrew, Sarah or Kristen, so he sat on a bench and stared at the group of Japanese tourists that were taking pictures of the ticket booth.

"Now what," he mumbled to himself.

:

Mr. Baldwin received the call from Mr. Pandit shortly after he had hung up from Ralph.

"Mr. Baldwin, you will pay for this," Mr. Pandit said.

"First of all, Mr. Pandit, what am I to pay for? Secondly, you seem to forget that I am not one of your local lackeys. If you threaten me, Mr. Prime Minister, you had better be able to carry it through."

Mr. Baldwin could hear the seething anger of Mr. Pandit's voice as he attempted to speak calmly.

"Do not underestimate me, Mr. Baldwin. If you cross me… it will be costly."

"Mr. Pandit, first of all, what is it I supposedly have done?"

The Prime Minister slowly let out a breath before speaking.

"You know what you have done. They have escaped. Rather, they have been allowed to escape from the police station…"

"Ah, yes. That is what you are referring to. May I remind you that there are others who would benefit from their escape or rather your… mishap. By the way – it looks like that is a nasty bump on your head," Mr. Baldwin said, attempting to elicit a rise.

"This is no laughing matter, and they did not do this on their own. It was a national that helped them – and blindsided me," Mr. Pandit said.

Mr. Baldwin pondered the information for a minute. Could the King have been behind this? It was all very interesting.

"Well, I am sorry to disappoint you, however, I repeat that I did not have anything to do with it… although I do admit the thought crossed my mind. Besides, if I wanted them released, I would have had you do it," Mr. Baldwin waited for the inevitable reply.

"What are you talking about? I wouldn't have let them go! And you think that you could have ordered me to do so? Are you on your own opium?"

"Mr. Pandit," Mr. Baldwin spoke very deliberately, "are you in your office?"

"Of course. I wasn't going to stay in the pig hole."

"I want you to open a web page," Mr. Baldwin said.

"Wh… I don't have time for this, Mr. Baldwin. Games are for children," Mr. Pandit replied.

"*Life* is a game, Mr. Pandit., and you only get to play it once. Open the web page." Mr. Baldwin read him an address and could hear the Prime Minister typing on the other end of the phone, then silence.

"When… this does not mean anything." Mr. Pandit was looking at a picture of a door with a dragon on it.

"You must use your imagination, Mr. Pandit," Mr. Baldwin said. "It was what came *next* that many people would find interesting."

"You're bluffing, Mr. Baldwin. Besides, may I remind you that you are still in Thailand? It would be very unwise …"

"True. I guess we have a stalemate then. Shall we stop with the threats?" Mr. Baldwin said. There was a pause before Mr. Pandit continued.

"If you did not have them released, then the person that did knows what is going on. It is time to make sure that the trails are wiped clean."

"Be careful, Prime Minister, you could cause more attention than the perceived threat… or is this just a matter of revenge? Let us not forget that the overall operation was successful. It would seem prudent to walk away from the table with the gains intact. If the cards are dealt one more time, who knows what surprises may await?" Mr. Baldwin said. He knew that the proud Prime Minister wanted revenge on the Americans who shamed him, but Mr. Baldwin did not relish the attention it would draw to them both.

"I'll consider your request, Mr. Baldwin," Mr. Pandit said, ending the call.

Mr. Baldwin considered sending him another, more incriminating, picture but decided that was showing more than was necessary at the moment. It was like playing cards, best if your opponent knew only as much as you allowed him.

"Henry!"

His aide appeared momentarily.

"Is the King Air ready?"

"Yes sir. The pilot is standing by. Shall I pack?"

"No. Not yet, tell him to wait."

The telephone interrupted him, and he signaled Henry to leave.

"Hello?"

"I missed them," Ralph said.

"That's unfortunate, Mr. Gabriel. I believe things are heating up. Hold on a moment."

Mr. Baldwin typed into his brief case and saw an intermittent signal with Mr. Lee's wristband.

"They appear to be heading south. I would assume you might be able to catch them at Nakon Pathom, the next station. Or you could just let them try and make Malaysia. It's your choice," Mr. Baldwin said.

Ralph hung up the telephone and, with a pencil that he took from the woman in the ticket booth, he wrote down the name of the next town from the reader board. He ran out of the station and flagged down taxi, gave the driver the piece of paper along with two hundred Baht, and added a gesture that he hoped would be understood as 'step on it', then got in the back. The driver took off zig zagging in and out of the traffic with Ralph in the back trying to hang onto the door handle to keep himself from sliding across the seat. He made a mental decision that, if he could not catch up with them at the next station, he would have to let them take their own chances. This game of espionage was way beyond his comfort level.

:

Kristen was laid out on the bench, either asleep or pretending to be, as Sarah and Andrew looked on, concerned. The rhythmic ticking of the tracks along with the air conditioning was as good as a sleeping pill and they soon joined her, each of them leaning against the opposite ends of their shared bench, their feet barely touching in the center.

It was only the blaring of the whistle and the squealing of the brakes that finally awoke Andrew, and he quietly exited the cabin to see if he could figure out where they were. The air from the non air-conditioned corridor hit his lungs, and he stopped for a second to allow his body to adjust. His shoulders were stiff and he ached all over, so he attempted to stretch some kinks out as he walked down the car. The train was just entering the station, and Andrew put his cheek against the window in order to see where they were. He soon forgot about looking for the name as he noticed a line of what had to be government officers of some sort awaiting the train. His heart rate immediately started increasing, and he turned around and ran back to the compartment.

"We have to go! Wake up!" he said, urgently.

Sarah looked at him puzzled.

"We have to go!" He walked over to Kristen and grabbed her shoulder. She awoke with a panic and it made him feel guilty, so he paused for a second and held her face in his hands.

"Kristen. Look at me. I'm sorry, but we have to go. They are waiting for us." He looked in her eyes for a glimpse that she understood him.

"OK?" he asked. Sarah took over for him and helped Kristen to her feet, hastily arranging the sling. The train was coming to a stop as they exited the cabin and turned away from the station to the next car. They hopped off the airway between the cars, and ran into the brush covered field that was opposite the tracks. When he thought they were far enough away, he signaled them to stop and they looked back at the train where they had just been so comfortable. There were men in and around the cars, shouting and talking to each other on radios. Andrew was positive that it was them they were looking for. He signaled for the girls to remain stationary, and they sat there in the harsh sun for over thirty minutes until it appeared that all the men had left, then they got up and carefully walked parallel to the tracks till they found what appeared to be a protected corridor.

Andrew signaled to the girls that he was crossing, and for them to wait. He took a deep breath, hunched down, and ran the fifty feet or so to the tracks, jumped across them, and kept going. At first he thought that the snapping sound he was hearing was being caused by rocks that he was inadvertently kicking, but then he heard Sarah yell at him, and he turned around to look at her.

The bullet passed by his head so close that he could hear the rush of the wind. His body reacted reflexively, and he spun around to land on the ground. The violent action sent a shot of pain through his side from his previous injuries, and he looked back at Sarah, who was standing in the brush waving at him to move. He didn't know where to go, so he got up and ran frantically toward her. Kristen started screaming and running in the opposite direction, Sarah looked back at her, and then at Andrew, who yelled at her to get going. The brush tore at their exposed arms and ankles. The uneven ground made it difficult to run at any speed, and the sounds of the men behind them pushed them to keep moving.

Sarah caught up to Kristen who was trying in vain to protect her right arm. She grabbed her firmly by one side as Andrew moved up on the other. In front of them, about a hundred yards or so, was the river bank which was littered with people selling items. Andrew headed in that direction, hoping to get lost amongst the throngs of shoppers and tourists. Someone behind them shouted something, and it seemed as if they were right at their backs, but a quick glance did not reveal anyone. The brush had given way to short trees and shrubs, and offered a little shelter as the three panted onward, their legs getting thick with exhaustion. The gunfire had died down, Andrew figured, because of the proximity of the floating market, and they took the last twenty yards to slow down and enter the crowds without making a ruckus.

There was an indoor open market adjacent to the floating one, and Andrew led the girls into it, looking for the exits and a place to hide. In the far corner he saw what looked like some kind of professional office, and they made their way over to it, constantly looking behind them. There were enough tourists out that Andrew hoped it would at least buy them some time from the police, or whoever was chasing them. The office was tucked away into a corner of the market with the door facing away from the crowds and down a short hallway. Whatever it was, the business was closed, but the door looked flimsy so, with Sarah and Kristen blocking his back, Andrew grasped the knob and firmly shoved his weight against it. He was relieved when it gave under the pressure and he hurried in, followed by the women, making sure to secure the door behind them. Once inside they moved down a short corridor and opened a door at the far end where they found a desk and a couple of chairs on a floor of bamboo mats. Without a word they all sat down, and closed their eyes as they took a mental inventory of their bodies. Remarkably, other than some cuts and bruises, no one had gotten seriously hurt.

Through the thin walls of their protective hiding place, they could hear numerous voices a few inches away as people walked by the shops and haggled with the keepers.

"Who were they?" Sarah whispered.

"I have no idea. They weren't wearing uniforms that I could see," Andrew said.

"Why would they try and kill us? I mean, out in the open. They had chance enough when we were in custody," she asked.

"The only thing I can think of is that we've really pissed off the Prime Minister. Other than that, I don't know," Andrew said.

Kristen, who was obviously beyond exhausted, looked at Andrew.

"Can your friend help us?" Her eyes looked desperate for hope.

"I don't know. Maybe if I could call them," he looked around the office but saw no telephone. "He said that he would only be able to give limited help, if any. We might be on our own."

"What are we going to do?" she asked.

Andrew thought about it for a while. They were almost out of money. If they weren't before, the trains were definitely being watched now, and he had no idea of where they were.

"I don't know, Kristen. I'm sorry. I don't even know where to start at this point. I suppose we should at least wait awhile before trying anything. Why don't you try to get some rest?"

Sarah pulled Kristen down to her lap and petted her hair. Andrew looked at her, then at Sarah. She shook her head. There was nothing else to do.

:

Ralph reached the station almost simultaneously with the five unmarked cars. He waived the taxi driver forward, who was more than happy to oblige. It seemed that no one in the country trusted anyone that even looked close to being affiliated with the government. As they drove past the terminal Ralph heard the gun shots and strained to see out the window. In the distance, he saw three people running through the brush and men following them. As several of the men ran passed the taxi, which was stuck at a light, Ralph pushed himself into the back and turned away from the window. By the time he looked back out, the three people had disappeared. It made him even feel more guilty, and he prayed that they had escaped. Ralph stopped the driver about a half-mile up the road and waited inside a shop for fifteen minutes, then walked until he found a pay phone booth.

"I need to know where they are now," he said, without so much as a greeting.

"One minute," Mr. Baldwin put him on hold, then came back on. "They're in the open, or at least not in a modern structure... somewhere near the river. It looks as if Mr. Lee has stopped."

"Which direction from the station?" Ralph asked.

"Southeast, less than 1000 meters," Mr. Baldwin said, then added, "Sorry, a little over half a mile."

Ralph hung up the phone and saw a single large open-air structure in the distance on his right, next to the river. It was the only possible hiding place within the prescribed area, so he walked to the entrance of the large building and looked around. He had no idea where to even start. The police, or whoever was looking for his friends, were disappearing through the far end of the structure, and Ralph took a tentative step inside. When he saw no evidence of anyone suspicious, he started methodically searching. If Mr. Baldwin was correct, and they were no longer moving, they could have been caught. However, the men appeared to be actively hunting, so that most likely meant that they were still hiding somewhere.

Most of the traffic was moving against him, and Ralph felt like he was a fish swimming through a sea of human bodies. Every few feet he would stop and peer into the individual stalls to see if there was any place to hide but, after nearly an hour, he couldn't see any possibilities. He looked around for a telephone, but only saw a single wooden structure and headed over to it. There was no booth on the outside, so he tried the entrance door with the intention to try and pay someone to use their telephone. The door opened easily and Ralph walked in.

"Hello? Is anyone here?" There was no reply and he walked down the dimly lit hallway to the first door knocking and then trying the knob. No one was in the vacant room, and there was no telephone. Ralph continued on down each door with the same result. There was one final door and he looked in. There was a desk and two chairs, and he stuck his head in further to see if there was a telephone. In the corner of his eye he saw an object flying toward him and started turning towards it when the thing hit him over the top of his head, and he crumpled to the floor. He thought he heard someone say his name before he blacked out.

"Ralph!" Sarah said, simultaneous with the blow from the heavy book that Andrew had in his hand. It was a little late, and the book hit with a dull thud that Ralph duplicated when he hit the bamboo floor.

"What the hell is he doing here?" Andrew said. Kristen, who was standing behind him, moved over to Ralph and kneeled down.

"Is he going to be OK?" she asked.

"Compared to what we've been through, I'd say his headache is a decent exchange," Andrew said.

"But how did he find us?" Sarah asked. Andrew held up his wrist and Sarah nodded.

"So that means that he either became a whiz kid overnight or that he is working with Mr. Baldwin," she said.

"That would be my guess," Andrew said.

"I can't believe he would do that," Kristen said, as she shook him with her left hand. Andrew left the office for a moment and returned shortly with a mostly empty bottle of water.

"Should we tie him up before we use that?" Sarah asked, as she looked around. There was nothing there.

"Here, hang on to the book and stand behind him," Andrew handed her the book and Sarah felt a little ridiculous as she held it above Ralph's head. Andrew emptied the water on Ralph's face and he blinked his eyes.

"What?..." his eyes got big when he saw the book above him and he shielded his eyes with his arms.

"Ralph. What are you doing here?" Andrew said. The comment drew Ralph's attention to Andrew, who was standing at his feet. He was still cowering under his hands but managed to open his mouth.

"I... I came to help you," he stammered.

"Don't you think you've been quite enough help?" Andrew said.

"Andrew, let him speak. We don't know what happened." They were all surprised at the strength in Kristen's voice, but it had its desired affect as Andrew stopped talking.

"I'm sorry. He made me do it... I'm sorry," Ralph said.

"He made you do what, Ralph?" Sarah lowered the book and stepped around to face him. Kristen helped Ralph up to a seated position. He was rubbing his head with his hands and let out a long sigh.

"Mr. Baldwin. He told me..." Ralph's voice drifted off as it occurred to him that he was about to reveal something that neither Sarah nor Andrew knew about. He turned to look at Kristen but saw no indication that she understood either. "He blackmailed me. He said he would... hurt my family unless I told him where to find you. I'm very sorry, I panicked... I'm sorry." Ralph hung his head and Kristen backed away.

When Ralph felt her leave he looked at her and knew something was wrong.

"What did they do to you?" He looked at all three of the others.

"They beat up Andrew and tortured Kristen," Sarah said. At hearing the news Ralph looked horrified.

"Ralph – they took away her hand," Sarah pointed to Kristen's right hand as it sat motionless on her lap, "and it would have gotten much worse if someone hadn't interfered and saved us."

Ralph suddenly looked back up. "That was me, I mean, Mr. Baldwin, he... I mean, I got something on the Prime Minister and he used it to free you."

"What?" Andrew asked. "That doesn't make any sense. Why would he first use you to throw us in prison, then use you to let us out? No. It was someone else. I know who it was."

"No! Really. I know it seems confusing but Mr. Baldwin and the Prime Minister had a falling out after you were captured and he told me to go to this place and take pictures of the Prime Minister leaving a private club. You know, one of those places that... offers children." Sarah looked at him and cringed.

"I'm sorry, but I got the pictures, the film and delivered it to Mr. Baldwin in exchange for helping you." Ralph dug into his pocket and removed a memory card. "I even have a copy of the film. I made him give me it in case he was trying to pull something on me."

"Look, Ralph. You can believe whatever you want but the person who let us escape wasn't Mr. Baldwin. This is just some elaborate gimmick of his to use you. Whatever. It doesn't really matter anyway. The problem is, what do we do now?" Andrew asked.

Ralph pointed to Andrew's wrist.

"Don't you see? If he wanted those guys to catch you he would have just told them you were here. That's how I found you," he said.

Sarah looked at Andrew and could see he was considering the thought.

"Fine. Let's say he doesn't want us caught any longer. That the Prime Minister is… what…going rogue? Why? Why would he change his mind?"

Ralph was getting excited.

"I know this! I asked him. He said that, after you escaped, the Prime Minister took out a ….a… -"

"Hit?" Sarah offered.

"Yes. A hit. He said the word on the street was there was a very large reward for all of you, dead or alive. Preferably dead was his comment," Ralph said.

"That still doesn't explain why he changed his mind. It would seem to benefit him if we just disappeared," Andrew said.

"But you don't understand. He told me that if anything bad happened to any of us it would raise questions in the US because all our friends and family know that we were on this adventure, and that Mr. Baldwin was involved, or at least could be tied to us. He insisted that his intention in having us here in the first place was only for some political reason – he didn't want us to get killed," Ralph ran out of breath and stopped, his eyes looking at Andrew, hoping for a modicum of sympathy.

"So, what did he tell you to do when you found us?" Sarah asked. Andrew remained silent.

"He told me to take you to the Bang... oh damn!… what was the name of the airport? Bang Fit… Bang Frat. That was it Bang Frat airfield. That he had a plane there waiting for us," Ralph said.

Sarah looked over at Andrew.

"What do we have to lose? We have no money. These guys are out to kill us," she said.

"Mr. Baldwin could be out to kill us. Just in his own masochistic way," Andrew offered.

"I believe him," Ralph said, "I think he is worried for his own safety as well."

Andrew started to say something sarcastic but stopped himself.

"Well. Let's vote on it," Andrew said, "All in favor?"

He kept his hands at his sides.

"It looks like we are going to Bang Frat or whatever it actually is," Andrew said. "I strongly suggest we wait until dark."

Chapter 29

At twilight, the group managed to catch a bus back to Bangkok, because they couldn't find anyone who could direct them to the Bang Frat airport and Ralph insisted that Mr. Baldwin said that it was near Bangkok.

Ralph got out off of the bus and volunteered to get directions.

"Sarah, how about going with him?" Andrew asked. "I'll stay with Kristen." He pointed to a hole in the wall café across the street.

"Come on, Ralph, let's go," she said.

Andrew and Kristen made sure there was no television set in the place, and then accepted a table. They ordered four meals by the pictures hanging on the walls and hoped the actual food looked better than the depiction. Ten minutes later, Ralph and Sarah returned.

"Well, he was partially correct. It was Bang something. Bang Phra to be exact. It is a small private airfield south of where we just came from."

Ralph was noticeably uncomfortable at the comment.

"I'm sorry. I could have sworn…" he said.

"Forget it. Let's eat something and get out of here. You do have directions?" Andrew asked.

"Yes. They said we could take the bus –"

"How about a taxi?" Kristen interjected.

"I think it would probably be safer to take a bus close to the airfield and then walk… less chance of someone remembering four Americans heading to an airport," Andrew said.

Kristen went back to eating and, a few minutes later, they headed out to find the bus station.

The Ekkamai Bus Station in Bangkok was much more confusing than the train station. It took Ralph, who was assigned to buy the tickets because he wasn't as wanted by the police, almost thirty minutes to figure out the right bus to take. He finally figured out that they could board the bus to Pattaya and get off in Bang Phra.

The bus was packed, and Ralph and Andrew stood as the girls sat beside them. Andrew wondered how many people actually watched the news, because no one seemed to give them a second glance. Ninety minutes later the driver stopped at a Seven-Eleven store and announced something that sounded close to Bang Phra and they got off.

Ralph went into the store and was amused to find that, instead of smelling hot dogs, his nose was inundated with unfamiliar exotic aromas. He wondered if the US home office had any idea what their stores looked like a world away. Ralph took out a napkin on which Kristen had managed to draw an airstrip along with a pretty good looking plane and showed it to the cashier, who immediately shook his head and pointed up the street, then followed Ralph out the door.

He kept saying, 'Tuk, Tuk'.

"Taxi. But where are we going to get one?" Andrew asked. He got the man's attention and held his hands up. The clerk looked around, then smiled and locked the front door to the store. He pointed to a rusted out old Toyota, then gave hand signals for one hundred baht. Andrew vigorously shook his head yes and, a minute later, they were barreling up the dirt road.

The Bang Phra airport was a very small field and it looked like it was closed, though some of the hanger lights remained on. The largest plane was a King Air and Ralph saw what looked like an emblem on the fuselage, so he led the group closer.

"This is it," he said.

"How do you know?" Andrew asked.

"The emblem. The four birds. It was engraved on the camera he gave me."

Andrew walked around the airplane and stood with everyone else, facing the front of the aircraft. It was a very nice King Air 200, a fast and comfortable plane.

They were interrupted by a man's voice that came from behind them out of the shadows.

"May I help you with something?" he asked.

Sarah grabbed Kristen when she yelped, and all four of them turned around to find an American, about forty-five or so, with brown hair and a five o'clock shadow.

"We were told to meet a plane here…" Ralph said.

"Who's plane?" the man asked.

Ralph looked at Andrew.

"Baldwin," he said.

"Good answer. You're looking at her. I'm Keith," he shook hands, then stepped back.

"I was told to take you out of the country," Keith said.

"When can we leave?" Andrew asked.

"Right now. I've been waiting all day," Keith said, as he walked over to the air step door and let it down.

"Ladies first," he said, stepping to the side after flipping on a small guide light. Sarah climbed up first, and then helped Kristen in.

"It's so small…" Kristen said.

"I've been in a lot smaller, it'll be fine, " Sarah said, taking a seat opposite Kristen. There were only two vacant seats left in the rear and Andrew headed up to the co-pilot's seat. Ralph sat in the rear, facing the front next to Sarah.

"OK… Everyone keep your seatbelts firmly fastened at all times. If you start to feel sick, you can find bags in the backs or sides of the airplane." Keith pulled up the air step and locked the doors, then headed up to the cockpit.

"How far are we going?" Sarah asked.

"A couple of hours or less. Should be a decent flight," Keith said.

"Where are we going to?" Andrew asked. He didn't really care as long as he was out of Thailand.

"I think Rangoon would be the easiest. It's also the closest place where you should be able to catch a flight in the morning to wherever you want to go," Keith said, as he put on his headset and started going down his checklist.

The whine of the turbines started up and Keith waited for the receivers to pick up the Satellites, then turned the plane toward the end of the runway and started taxing. Andrew was watching what Keith was doing carefully, but he didn't say anything.

"Everyone strapped in and ready?" Keith asked, after finishing his run up. No one responded. "I'll take that as a yes. Hang on," he said, as he held the brakes until the throttles were full forward, then let go. The aircraft started moving, slowly at first, but quickly gaining momentum until they were all pressed back in their seats. Andrew watched, as the jungle in front of him grew larger and larger in the windshield. At ninety knots Keith pulled back on the yoke and the King Air seamlessly took to the air. He pulled up the landing gear and flaps, then continued to climb on an assigned 340 degree heading until they reached twenty five thousand feet, where he finally released the yoke to the auto pilot, and just monitored all the systems.

In the distance the passengers could see the lights of Bangkok slowly disappear. It was like watching the credits roll on a terribly bad movie, a mixture of relief and happiness.

Kristen, Sarah, and Ralph closed their eyes as if they were wishing away the last ten days of their lives. Soon they were all lost in their own thoughts, except for Andrew, who was paying rapt attention to the settings on the aircraft and on Keith.

"How long have you worked for Mr. Baldwin?" he asked, into the boom mic on his headset.

"Couple of years. Mostly hang around here in Asia. Never had passengers other than him before," Keith said.

"So what do you do when he's not around?" Andrew asked. A voice said something in English on the frequency and Keith held up his right hand to Andrew. After he replied to the instructions he turned to back toward Andrew.

"Sorry. The controller was just a little curious about our night flight. Not a problem. What were you saying?"

"Just... what do you do when your boss isn't around?" Andrew asked.

"He's got some businesses around here so a lot of the time I'm picking up or dropping off things. Not a big deal. Sometimes I just play around. He'll call me when he wants...which reminds me..." Keith punched in a number to the Global Star Satellite phone mounted on the panel, and Andrew heard the phone ring.

"Hello?"

"Mr. B. I'm in the air with the packages. Any instructions?"

"Good. No. Make sure they are delivered safely to the commercial terminal, then go to the prearranged meeting point," Mr. Baldwin said. Andrew didn't know whether to believe him or not but, whatever the case, the moving map display was indicating that in less than ninety minutes they would be out of Thailand. It was all that mattered to him at this point.

"Will do." Keith hit the end button.

"Cool equipment huh? Just had that installed last annual," Keith said.

"Yeah. Very nice. So what's he like?" Andrew asked. The man had obviously not been told to keep quiet.

"Mr. B? He's cool. Seems like he has some mission in life or something. Always asking me if I want to do more," Keith said. Andrew was tempted to warn him off.

"You hungry?" he asked.

"Sure," Andrew said. Keith reached behind him and pulled out a very tiny cooler.

"Snickers bars, from the US. They just don't taste the same here." He handed one to Andrew, who looked back at Ralph before opening it. His eyes were closed. Andrew gently ripped open the package and took a slow bite, allowing his teeth and lips to feel the soft chocolate, caramel and peanuts. It was like eating a piece of heaven.

"Thanks. Man, I've missed good old fashion American junk food," Andrew said.

Keith laughed. "I know what you mean. So, how long have you been in Thailand?"

"I think nine, ten days."

"Have a good time?" Keith asked. The question was so inappropriate that Andrew was convinced that Keith had no idea what was going on.

"Not really. Glad to be leaving. By the way, will we need a Visa or anything in Rangoon? And where is Rangoon anyway?"

"Myanmar. Burma. And no, I think Mr. B probably has everything set up. They're used to seeing this plane all the time. Should be a breeze," Keith said. Andrew thought, Yeah. Probably like a small tropical storm or something.

Andrew picked up the small cooler.

"Never seen anything like this…"

"Oh. Yeah. He's thinking of importing those things. I think they're great," Keith said. Andrew flipped it over in his hands and saw the emblem with the four birds on it.

"What's this about anyway?" Andrew pointed to the design.

"Interesting story, that one. Hang on a second," Keith acknowledged instructions that he received from the controller by inputting some numbers into the Nav/Comm. The Airplane started a slow left turn. Keith took the cooler from Andrew and traced his finger over the picture.

"A while ago Mr. B, was engaged in some kind of business with an American Indian tribe, I think in New Mexico. I don't even think the tribe exists any more. Anyway, he runs into this Shaman or holy man – whatever they are called. Anyway, he starts talking to this guy and the conversation turns to dreams. Seems like Mr. B is into dreams. Heavy. So he tells this guy that he has this reoccurring dream about these four crows, which are talking and walking around until they come to form a circle. See that in the emblem?" Keith gave Andrew back the bag and Andrew could see the four crows in a circle, facing one another, their beaks in different positions.

"So, the holy guy tells him that crows are unlucky omens. Means despair and grief or something like that. Four crows together are really bad, but the clincher was the circle that they form." Keith looked over to Andrew and grinned. "You following me?" he asked.

"Yes. Go ahead," Andrew said. Keith was obviously enjoying the story.

"The circle supposedly meant a… what do you call it… a forum, discussion, like a judge and jury kind of thing. Seems the crows get together to make decisions about peoples lives. Like, remember those three Greek Fates….what were their names?" Keith turned around and started digging through some papers. He pulled out a handwritten note.

"Here. I actually looked this up. Bizarre." He held the note up and read it.

"The Moirai. Clotho, Lachesis, and Atropos, and they give mortals their share of good and evil. Read this part." Keith pointed to the next paragraph.

> *'The three goddesses who supervised the spinning of human fate evolved into a more concrete concept. The Fates came to be identified as three older females who handled the threads of human life. One of these threads was placed to every person, and each goddess took her turn in manipulating this thread. Clotho selected the thread, Lachesis measured it, and Atropos cut this thread to signify the end of a person's existence.'*

"OK. So, the holy man says that the dream of the four crows is essentially telling Mr. B that he has the power to control people's lives, for good or bad."

Andrew looked very concerned and the smile vanished from Keith's face. He took back the paper and stuffed it into his shirt pocket.

"Hey. It's just dream stuff. Don't be telling Mr. B about any of this. I just thought is was... interesting. We OK?" Keith looked worried.

"Yeah, Keith. Don't worry about it. Sorry, my mind is really preoccupied right now," Andrew said.

"No problem. Why don't you take a nap? I'll wake you when we get to Rangoon," he said.

Andrew closed his eyes and leaned against the airplane. Four Crows. It almost explained Mr. Baldwin's twisted game. If he believed he could control people's fate, he would see no problem in ruining people's lives. He might even think it was altruistic, in some weird way. It was just one more reason why religion was a hindrance in mankind's collective side. All those warped beliefs gave people the excuses they needed in order to act out their repressed complexes.

Andrew tried to forget the conversation and concentrate on formulating a plan for when he finally returned home. His planned merger was going to be in ruins, and he needed to make some decisions as how to handle that bad scene. Really, there wasn't a lot he could do about it, and that was probably the hardest thing to accept.

"Hey."

"Hey. Time to get up." Andrew heard the words but it took a second to sink in. When he opened his eyes Keith was looking at him.

"Look," he pointed to a large lit runway in front of him, "Rangoon."

Andrew peered out the windshield and felt a huge wave of relief come over him. For the first time in a week and a half he felt back in control.

"You might want to get the others up," Keith said.

Andrew loosened his seatbelt and turned around toward the others. They were all asleep and he gently pushed Kristen's right arm until she awoke. She looked at him.

"We're here," he loudly said.

She responded by reaching out with a foot and touching Sarah, who woke up immediately and looked questioningly at Kristen. Sarah reached over to Ralph and grabbed his arm.

The pilot performed a flawless landing and, on touchdown, reversed the engines. The plane slowly came to a crawl and they rolled out to the end of the runway, pausing on the taxiway before receiving further instructions. Keith read them back several times looking puzzled and scratching his head.

"Everything OK?" Andrews concern was already rising.

"I'm sure it's fine. Must be because we are coming so late," Keith looked at his watch. "It's nearly 11:00."

Keith taxied the King Air past the main commercial terminal and paused for a moment in front of a dark building. Andrew could hear him having a discussion with the tower as to whether he could turn off the engines. He was instructed not to do so. After a few minutes three open-air jeeps pulled out with men in military uniforms.

"Uh oh," Keith said.

"What? What's going on?" Andrew asked, trying not to raise his voice too high.

"I... I don't know. These are not the normal customs people," he said.

The lead jeep signaled for Keith to follow them and the two other vehicles took a flank position on either side.

Keith slowly followed them and, at the same time, dialed in a number on the satellite phone.

"Mr. B?"

"Yes?"

"We have a problem. We're being escorted right now by the military," he said.

"Where?"

"I have no idea," Keith said. Andrew could tell that he was getting nervous.

"Can you get out of there?" Mr. Baldwin asked.

Keith looked around. The vehicles formed a tight triangle around the plane.

"No. I don't think so," he said.

"Do they know who's on board?" Mr. Baldwin asked.

"Uh. No. We haven't been allowed to stop taxiing."

"Keith, I don't know what to say other than, if you get a chance, get out of there. I think someone may assume that I am on that plane. I'll see what I can do. Call me back when you can."

"*If* I can," Keith muttered under his breath, then looked around. The main runway was off to their right, and Andrew knew what he was thinking but there was no way without running over one or more of the jeeps, which the plane would not survive.

The jeeps came to a stop far away from any other buildings. The officer signaled for Keith to stop the engines, which he did. With the engines off, Andrew could hear the excited chatter of the others behind him. They were talking about what they were going to do when they got back home.

"There is a problem," Andrew said. The group immediately shut up and looked toward the cockpit. Keith got out of his seat.

"Everyone stay calm. Don't do anything to draw attention. Don't attempt to get out of the aircraft unless instructed to do so. Have your passports ready." Keith unlocked the door and lowered the steps. The officer stood below him with his hand on his revolver. There were two other soldiers with their rifles pointed toward the ground and their fingers on the triggers. It was not a encouraging sight.

"Mr. Baldwin?" the man asked.

"No. Mr. Baldwin is not on the airplane," Keith said. The officer immediately gave him a nasty look.

"Mr. Baldwin is not with you?" he asked.

"No. I just have passengers with me. Americans," Keith said.

"Stay there," the man said, and held his hand out like a stop sign. He walked off while talking into a radio but left the two armed guards behind.

When he returned he was obviously irritated.

"Passports," he said, "You, get down." He pointed to Keith who was visibly shaken.

The officer took the passports and thumbed through each one, then climbed into the cabin to see everyone. Andrew turned around to look toward him and the man's flashlight caught him full in the face. He squinted, but remained in the pose so that the man could verify the passport photo. When the man was finished, he put the passports into his pocket and climbed back down the stairs, then again spoke into his radio.

Sarah and Ralph watched as he talked to the pilot, then escorted him about fifty yards away and made him sit on the tarmac. The pilot was obviously trying to explain something to the man, but it was not going well and, after about five minutes, Keith was left alone facing into the darkness. The officer had yet another conversation on the radio, then walked back toward Keith, stopping behind him. Keith started to turn around but the man prevented him. As Sarah and Ralph watched in horror, the man took out his gun and pointed it at the back of Keith's head. The pop was so soft that it didn't seem possible that they had just heard a gunshot but they watched as Keith slumped forward to the asphalt, his hands splayed at his sides. The man hovered over him, extended his arm and fired another shot, then turned away. Sarah covered her mouth with her hand to stop herself from screaming and Ralph leaned back and closed his eyes. Kristen, who had not been watching, stared at Sarah after the shot went off and could tell that something terrible had happened by the look on her face. Andrew reached back to grab her arm for reassurance and could feel that she was already shivering.

When Ralph opened his eyes the killer was approaching the still open door. The man was smiling.

Chapter 30

"What are up to, Mr. Prime Minister? It is very late on a Sunday to be working." Mr. Baldwin had called him on his private line.

"Mr. Baldwin, I'm not sure what you are referring to. I've been quite busy."

"We need to speak. In person," Mr. Baldwin said.

"That's fine with me. You want to come to my office?"

"I'll be there in an hour." Mr. Baldwin gathered up several items and placed them in his leather briefcase, then called Henry.

"Henry, could you please finish packing and meet me at the house. I should be there in a couple of hours. Are the arrangements finished for Kuala Lumpur?"

"Yes sir. Marquis has a jet expecting our arrival this evening," Henry said. "I have not yet given them a final destination."

"Just tell them the West Coast of America, any city of their choice."

"Yes sir." Henry left and Mr. Baldwin finished some emails on his laptop and left the hotel. He knew that Mr. Pandit would expect him to arrive in his car, so he took a taxi instead and arrived at the Government House just before midnight. The Villa Norasingh was situated on a large piece of land surrounded by ornate lawns and a painted high iron fence. Mr. Baldwin was dropped off by the taxi and allowed to enter the compound by the guardhouse. It was quite a lengthy walk, and he was sweating by the time he made it to the building. The rear entrance door was open and the greeting desk was unmanned. His leather soles tapped on the polished yellow marble steps as he walked up to the second floor and down the deserted hallway. Mr. Pandit had his office door open waiting for him, along with an aide who patted Mr. Baldwin down and ran an electronic scan of his person and case.

"Mr. Baldwin, you are full of surprises. I could have sent a car for you if you had told me you were without one," Mr. Pandit said.

"I appreciate the offer, Mr. Prime Minister, however, it was a perfect evening for a walk." The conversation was like two lions circling a prey, with each move carefully orchestrated.

"Have a seat." Mr. Pandit moved behind his desk and took a seat. His hands were no longer visible. Mr. Baldwin remained standing.

"It seems my airplane had some trouble in Yangon." Mr. Baldwin used the local name intentionally.

"Oh really? What happened?" Mr. Pandit asked.

"Come now, Mr. Prime Minister, enough of this dancing. You were expecting me to be on that plane. But, as you see, I am not," he said.

"That is quiet evident, Mr. Baldwin. However, you are here," Mr. Pandit kept his right hand below the desk but offered his left in an encompassing motion.

Mr. Baldwin sighed. "Look, I have no desire for these theatrics. We had an agreement. I would arrange for the Americans to embarrass the King. I have succeeded in doing that. From what I am seeing on the news, this strategy is working. He is backing away from the American President's offer for foreign aid. So I have done exactly what we set out to. I want you to keep your agreement."

"Except that there were several problems. And I don't like problems," Mr. Pandit replied, as he touched the bandage on his head.

"I see. Well, neither do I. Perhaps we should conclude our dealings, since you are unsatisfied with our arrangements," Mr. Baldwin said.

"I agree." Mr. Pandit sat with his jaw firm, and leaning slightly back in his chair.

"However. I do not want to be looking over my shoulder," Mr. Baldwin said, as he reached into this briefcase. He saw the flicker of fear in Mr. Pandit's eyes as he was doing so, and found himself enjoying the reaction, but only pulled out a picture and put it on the desk. Mr. Pandit looked down at it and tried not to give a response. It was very difficult.

"What do you plan to do with that?" Mr. Pandit asked.

"Absolutely nothing... Unless." Mr. Baldwin waited, forcing him to ask.

"Unless what, Mr. Baldwin?" Mr. Pandit was more than irritated, and it showed.

"Let's just say that the picture, and more like it, are primed at a web site off shore. If I do not manually input a code to stop them, by tomorrow, they will automatically be forwarded to the major news agencies—local and international."

"I understand," Mr. Pandit said.

"Good. I thought you would. Mr. Prime Minister, I regret having to make my point in such a vulgar way, however, I did not want there to be any misconceptions. I understand that you are unhappy with our prior agreement, although I think that it was masterfully accomplished. Anyway, I am willing to negotiate my payment for what I have done," Mr. Baldwin said.

"And what would that be?" Mr. Pandit asked.

"I want 5% of BM SAT. I'm willing to forgo the other 5% that we agreed upon."

"Agreed… If the trade agreements keep the borders open long enough for it to go public. If it does not, then you get nothing."

"Fine. A year is not that long," Mr. Baldwin said.

"I'm glad we could reach an arrangement, Mr. Prime Minister. You may keep the photo for your personal collection." Mr. Baldwin turned around and paused at the door.

"Oh, and one more thing, leave the Americans alone. They do not know anything and it would only focus undue attention on both of us if something permanently damaging happened to them," Mr. Baldwin added before he walked out the door.

The guard that was standing outside looked in questioningly at Mr. Pandit, but the PM waived him off. Mr. Baldwin smiled at the man as he left. Outside the building, he called Henry with the change of plans. He told him to come and get him outside the Government House.

Mr. Pandit tried to reach his contact in Burma several times but failed to get through. There was nothing more he could do about the Americans tonight, so he sent an email and then went home. If they died at the hands of the notoriously abusive Burmese army he could always profess innocence.

:

"Get out!" the officer said. Ralph looked at him, terrified. Sarah grabbed his arm and held on, as if somehow she could prevent the man from taking him.

"Get out! All of you!" Sarah unconsciously let go. The clarification made things much worse. She watched Ralph slowly step down to the tarmac, then followed him down the steps. Andrew came next, and he helped Kristen, her right arm hanging lifelessly at her side.

The air was cool and would have been refreshing under different circumstances. As it was, it made them feel exposed and unprotected.

"Who is in charge?" the officer asked. Andrew quickly looked at the women, then turned to face the man.

"I am," he said.

"You are?"

"Mr. Lee."

"Mr. Lee, this aircraft was reported as having illegal drugs aboard. We take that very seriously here," the man said. Andrew wanted to ask him, if that was the case, why hadn't they searched the plane, but he realized that it was just an excuse. He didn't want to give him any more reason to escalate the incident.

"We are just passengers, sir. It is not our aircraft."

Someone interrupted them on the radio, and the officer backed away for a moment, then barked something to the other jeeps, which left, squealing their tires. The two remaining guards were given instructions, then the officer hopped in the jeep and tore off. One of the soldiers came toward Ralph, who attempted to move backwards away from him and his gun.

"*I'm* in charge," Andrew said, to the man, drawing his attention. He was no more than twenty-five with a very dark pock marked complexion, and much shorter than Andrew. The man signaled with his rifle for Andrew to move toward Keith's direction and Andrew could feel his heart speed up.

"What do you want?" he asked. There was no response.

"Money? Dollars?" Andrew tried. They were now about thirty feet away and he could see the dark liquid pooling around Keith's torso.

"Baldwin," the man said, in a thick accent.

"I am NOT Mr. Baldwin. He is NOT here." Andrew turned his head attempting to make the point ,but was just shoved forward. He could hear Kristen crying behind him. His mind was cluttered with thoughts: money, running his business, Kristen and Sarah, all became a clouded collage as Keith's inert body lay in front of him.

"Down!" the man said. Andrew slowly got on his knees – his hands still in the air. The beating of his heart felt like someone was pounding on a bass drum, the echo's resonating through every nerve in his body. With everything that had happened, and that they had overcome, he couldn't believe it was going to end with a bullet in the back of the head while kneeling on the ground in some god forsaken country that he didn't even know the real name of. Andrew tried to picture the scene unfolding behind him. The man wrapping his hand in the rifle strap, then lifting up the weapon and pointing it at him. If he could gauge the timing just right, a quick spin to his left might catch the soldier off guard. He would have only one chance.

Sarah was panicking back at the plane. Each step Andrew took away from her it was like watching herself being caught and led off by the kidnappers, not knowing what was going to happen and fearing the worst. The second soldier stood fifteen feet away, his weapon aimed in her direction, looking as if all he wanted was a reason to pull the trigger. When Andrew got to his knees Kristen lost control and started crying. Ralph, who was standing beside her, looked at the soldier, then slowly stepped sideways until he could put an arm around her shoulders. As Andrew's guard lifted up his rifle, Sarah could no longer think of herself. If Andrew died after what he had done for her…

"NO!" she screamed and ran toward him. Andrew heard her voice echoing through the silence and perceived the reaction of his guard. He twisted his body around just in time to see the guard lower his rifle and take aim. The second guard was in the line of fire, and his eyes opened wide as he realized what was happening. He jumped out of the way as the crack of his partners gun rose above all the other sounds, reverberating through the air in slow motion. The bullet missed Sarah by about three feet, glancing off of the tarmac, spitting pieces of asphalt. She attempted to raise her arms to guard her face and turned briefly away. Andrew saw his opportunity and rushed the guard from his crouched position, but the soldier saw the movement to his right and reacted by hammering the butt of the rifle into Andrew stomach. The air rushed out of his lungs and he crumpled to the ground gasping. Sarah screamed again, but the soldier had stepped away from both of them with his rifle aimed at Sarah. Andrew was writhing on the ground, gasping.

"Stop!" the man said. The second guard was back on his feet and looking very nervous. His weapon was shaking as he leveled it at Ralph and Kristen.

"No!" The second soldier shook his head, and Ralph held his hands up. Everyone stopped moving and looked at each other.

"Sarah, get... out... of... here!" Andrew said softly, as he managed to get to his knees.

"I can't let him do this!" Sarah exclaimed.

"Jus... back off... you're... going to... get hurt," Andrew wheezed. He felt very lightheaded.

Sarah turned away from him and looked at the guard.

"I can offer you something," she held his gaze and slowly walked toward him as unthreatening as she could.

"No. Sarah. Don't!" Andrew managed to get the words out, but he ran out of air and hung his head to keep from fainting.

Sarah kept walking until she was a few feet away from the guard, who was ravenously watching her approach him. She could see the look in his eyes, and it made her feel soiled, but there was no doubt she had his attention. Andrew was not going to die if she had any chance of stopping it. He had already proved that he would do the same for her.

Sarah held his gaze and deliberately unbuttoned her shirt, allowing it to hang open exposing her sternum and stomach. She felt the wind as it evaporated the sweat on her belly and it caused goose bumps.

"Not here," Sarah pointed to a building about a hundred feet away. She reiterated the motion by pointing to herself, at the guard, then the building. The other soldier, still standing at the plane, yelled something to his partner but received a curt reply. The man had already made up his mind, and he lowered his gun at Sarah motioning for her to lead. She closed her eyes for a second to gather up strength, then walked in front of him toward the structure.

The already poor lighting got worse as they walked and, in the darkness, Sarah hoped that Andrew could figure out something to do with the other guard. Perhaps at least three of them could walk away from this hell relatively unscathed. Either way, it bought precious time. She found herself resisting thinking about what she was about to do. She knew that, if she allowed herself to think, she would not be able to go through with it, and this was one time she couldn't afford to be rational.

There was a door on the side of the building that was unlocked, and the soldier went in, pulled a chain to illuminate the single overhead light, then followed her into a small vacant office. There was a metal desk sitting askew on the fragmented linoleum floor and she turned around and leaned against it with her back. The soldier looked at her warily, then grabbed her arm and spun her around and pushed her down so that she was lying face down on the desk, her feet on the floor. He held her there with his hand pressed into her back as he placed his rifle on the floor and shoved it a few feet away with his boot.

Sarah closed her eyes and tried to relax by taking steady breaths but when his callused hands reached under her shirt to fondle her, she instinctively tensed up. He reacted by harshly grabbing her hair and pulling her head back, bending her neck until it hurt. She forced herself to calm down and reached behind her head to gently remove his fingers from her hair, then submissively laid back on the cold metal. He pressed his body into her back, and she could feel his arousal as he began to run his hands up and down her body. She felt him hungrily reach around to the front of her shorts and unbutton, then unzip and tug her pants to the floor.

Sarah struggled out of them in order to keep her legs unrestricted, all the while trying to concentrate on the job at hand, her goal of saving Andrew, but her concentration began to splinter. Between the hammering of her heart and the sound of the man's ragged breath from behind her, she could feel the deep down panic, rising. The man's touch, and his body movements, were getting demanding, and she felt him remove his belt and pull down his pants while keeping his body pressed to hers. When she had first decided on her course of action, she had fully intended on seeing it through to its distasteful end, but suddenly, there was an opportunity. The man was so excited that he had grabbed her panties and was attempting to pull them aside. She felt the tumescence of his member against her skin for the briefest second and, at that moment, she flung herself backwards from the desk, propelling her body with the force of her legs into his body and kept moving until she heard him slam against the floor.

Sarah contorted to her right where she had heard the rifle fall, saw it in the shadows, and grabbed it, thankful that her father had taken her target shooting when she was a teenager. She turned back toward the man who was scrambling to get to his feet, his trousers tangled around his legs, and pointed the rifle steadily at him. He stopped moving and stared at her menacingly, reaching down to slowly pull his pants up, buttoning them at the top, and then taking a step toward her.

"Stop!" she said firmly, panting for breath. He paused for a second, then took another step as she was backing up.

"Stop!" she said, again raising her voice above the sound of her own heart reverberating in her head. When he was only a few feet away she saw his hand move from his side toward the gun and, without thinking, she pulled the trigger. The sound was deafening in the closed room. She saw look of shock upon the man's face as he looked down and saw the hole in his chest, then fell backwards, holding the wound with his hand. The scene would remain permanently engraved in her memory for the rest of her life. Sarah dropped the rifle to the floor and backed away from it like it was a live serpent, her eyes wide with the knowledge that she had just taken a human life.

:

The soldier that had remained with Andrew, Kristen and Ralph heard the shot and nervously looked over at the building before taking a few steps toward it, then stopped. He glanced back at the prisoners with a confused expression.

"No…" Kristen said, under her breath, looking in the direction of the gunfire. She was sitting on the asphalt, along with Ralph, staring into the darkness and hoping for some movement or indication of what had happened.

The guard started jogging, and then running toward the source of the gunfire. Andrew stood in the soldier's path where, before the shot had occurred, he had been in a stare-down with the man. As he passed, Andrew quickly followed him, trying his best to match his cadence. The man was intent on his destination and didn't seem to hear Andrew. In less than twenty feet Andrew had caught up to him and vaulted into the air grabbing the man by the shoulders and forcing him to the ground. He hit the pavement with a sickening thud and was flattened by Andrew's full body weight. The rifle struck the ground, bounced, then came to a rest several yards away but Andrew didn't want to release his hold on the man, so he ignored it and instead reached for the man's arms, pinning them behind his back. The man feebly struggled for a moment, but quit as soon has he felt his arms harshly pulled upward.

"Ralph!" Andrew yelled.

"Coming!" was the reply. Ralph arrived a few seconds later and picked up the gun. They both looked toward the building but no one had come out.

"Get up!" Andrew forced the man to his feet with Ralph in clear sight. He had the rifle lowered at the guard's chest.

"Go," Andrew said, in his ear. He was holding his arms firmly, and shoved him forward. If necessary, he had no qualms about using the man as a human shield. Ralph walked parallel to them but kept a safe distance. They were intent on looking for any signs of life from the building, but all that could be seen was the dim glow from a light. As they approached the door Andrew held the man in front of him and yelled into the room.

"Sarah!"

"Sarah!" he repeated, but there was no answer. Ralph stood to his left, out of sight, holding the weapon on the man.

"Come out! Or we will kill your soldier!" Andrew yelled into the room as his prisoner squirmed.

"Stop it!" he hissed, and emphasized it with a yank on the man's arm. He stopped moving again and said something incomprehensible.

"Please…" Andrew heard the soft voice coming from the next room, and shoved the soldier forward, hard.

"Keep an eye on him!" Andrew said to Ralph, who had already stepped forward into the space, keeping the rifle aimed. Andrew ran through the next door, expecting the worse. The body that was lying on the floor, staring at the ceiling with vacant eyes, was not Sarah and he didn't know whether to be relieved or horrified at the scene. He quickly turned to survey the rest of the room and found Sarah sitting in a corner as far away as she could get, her knees pulled up to her chest and her arms wrapped around them. She was nearly naked and shivering uncontrollably.

"Is she OK?" Ralph yelled from the adjacent room.

"I think so," Andrew replied, as he rushed over and wrapped his arms around her.

"I… I didn't have a choice… I killed him, Andrew… I killed him," she mumbled in his ear.

"OK, Sarah. OK. Let's get out of here." He pulled back and held her in his gaze. He had never thought he would again see that kind of fear in those blue eyes. It pained his heart.

"I'm going to get your clothing," he said. He maintained his gaze with her, but carefully stepped back towards the body and picked up her shorts.

"Sarah. Can you stand?" he asked, as he returned to her.

He cupped his hands under her elbows and, while holding on, lifted her to her feet, then knelt down with her shorts on the floor.

"Can you step into them?" he asked. Without saying a word, she lifted each leg and he was able to pull the khakis on. Then, starting at the bottom, he buttoned up her shirt while she held onto his arms.

"Andrew? Are you coming?" Ralph asked, nervously.

"Yes. We're coming." Andrew shielded the killing scene with his body and walked Sarah out of the room. The second soldier had a menacing scowl on his face and was facing Ralph.

"Sarah, are you OK?" he asked. She just nodded as Andrew took her out of the building into the night air.

"What do I do with him?" Ralph asked. Andrew was tempted to tell him to shoot, but he considered Sarah's mental state and decided she wouldn't handle that well.

"We have to do something or he'll run. We need some time," Andrew said.

"Can you stand?" he asked Sarah softly. She was leaning against the concrete block wall.

"Yes. I'll be OK," she said. Andrew bent down to kiss her forehead.

"That was really stupid and really brave. Thank you," he said, and smiled. She tried to reciprocate but only half succeeded.

"You're welcome. We're even," she managed.

"I'll be right back. Stay put," he said, caressing her cheek.

Andrew went back in the room and joined Ralph, then walked back to the deceased soldier and removed his belt and shoelaces. He returned to the second soldier and showed him the items. The man took his off and threw them on the floor at Andrews's feet.

"Get down," Andrew pointed to the floor, and the soldier obediently obeyed while spitting and cursing.

"You're the Boy Scout," he said to Ralph. "Remember any of those fancy knots?" Ralph handed the rifle to Andrew, then bent over the man and hog-tied him.

"Not bad. Stuff something into his mouth too," Andrew said. Ralph looked around but didn't see anything.

"You know what, never mind," Andrew walked over and lifted the butt of his rifle over the man's head and hammered him with it. He looked over to the door to see if Sarah had heard the blow, but she remained out of sight.

"Let's go," he said to Ralph, and headed out the door.

Sarah was looking much better and was standing in the shadows, looking at the plane.

"Now what. We're trapped here. They'll be back soon," she said.

"We have to leave," Ralph said. "Maybe there's a car somewhere."

"I've got a better idea: let's fly," Andrew said, and started walking toward Kristen, who could be seen looking out of the rear seat of the plane. When she saw Sarah she jumped down and ran toward her.

"And who are we going to get to fly it?" Ralph asked, as they passed Keith.

"I'm going to," Andrew said. Ralph got noticeably silent.

"I'm a pilot, Ralph. I haven't flown a King Air, but I watched Keith carefully and I know I can do it," he said. Kristen had caught up with them and enwrapped Sarah in almost a two-armed embrace.

"I'm so glad you're safe. When I heard that shot, I thought..." Kristen stopped herself.

"I'm glad you're safe," she said, as they walked back to the airplane.

"Now what?" she asked.

"Andrew says he's flying the plane," Ralph said.

"He can. He flies all the time. Can we get home?" she asked.

"No. It's too far but, if we can take off, we can get out of Burma," he said.

"To where?" Ralph asked.

"Not Thailand. Let's worry about that after we get in the air," Andrew said. "Ralph, do you want to be up front with me?"

Ralph paused to look at Kristen.

"Actually, if you don't mind, Kristen and I have something we need to talk about," he answered.

"OK. I guess we can do all three in the back. I don't know the weight and balance on these planes, but it probably won't make a difference," Andrew said. He boarded the plane and took the left front seat.

"Ralph can you get the door?" he asked.

"I'll sit up front, if you want," Sarah said. Andrew turned around and smiled at her.

"I'd like that," he said.

Sarah joined him up front and was followed by Kristen and Ralph.

After Ralph closed the door with some difficulty, Andrew turned toward them.

"Seatbelts on – tight. Look, I'm not exactly sure on how the procedures work here. But I'm not planning on listening to them anyway. It appears the airport is closed, which is actually better. I'm going to start this thing, taxi really fast, and get in the air whether or not they agree. Just hold on and be prepared for anything. Everyone ready?" Andrew said.

He put on his headset, then helped Sarah with hers. He found Keith's red flashlight, turned it on, and started down the checklist that Keith had used. As he lit the igniters and pushed up the fuel condition lever he hoped no one was in earshot. The turbine slowly came to life as he watched the gas indicator stabilize. He turned off the starter and igniter, then started the procedure on the other engine.

"Let me know if you see anyone," he said to Kristen as he worked. She was already actively looking around.

"Nothing…" he was happy to hear it.

With both engines solidly in the green, he released the brakes and turned the plane toward the nearest ramp intersection, pushing the throttles forward. The plane lurched forward and he attempted to steer the aircraft with the foot pedals as he looked for the straightest course to the runway. There were no voices on the frequency and the moving map display was charting their progress on the ground, so he accelerated to about 40 knots and headed down Bravo taxiway.

"Someone's coming!" Sarah said. He looked at where she was pointing. There was a small convoy of jeeps on the far end of the airport accelerating fast. Andrew pushed the throttles farther but he already knew that there was no making the runway.

"Hold ON!" he yelled to everyone as he turned the plane in the opposite direction, down the taxiway, and pushed the throttles full forward. The engines roared to life and he fought the torque with his feet firmly planted on the pedals.

"What are you doing?" Sarah said, her hands gripping the sides of her seat.

"We can't make the runway. I'm taking off now..." Andrew replied, as he was rapidly scanning the gauges. As the plane neared ninety knots on the narrow taxiway he pulled back slightly on the yoke and the nose lifted off the ground for a moment, then sunk back to the ground.

"Dammit!" Andrew yelled at the plane. Sarah's neck was craned toward the back where the jeeps were trying to keep up with the rocketing King Air.

At one hundred knots Andrew tried again and was relieved as the heavy plane smoothly took to the air and rapidly climbed out of the airport. Andrew withdrew the gear and flaps and set the climb rate.

"Whew," he said. His whole body was so tense that he had to mentally tell himself to relax the muscles in his left arm so that he could remove it from the yoke.

"Nice job," Sarah said. "You sure you can fly this thing?"

Andrew laughed.

"That was the hard part. This is easy."

He set the heading and hit the Autopilot button, Sarah looked on nervously as the guidance system took over and continued on the course Andrew had set.

"Where are we going?" she asked.

"I'm trying to figure that out," he said, as he pressed some buttons on the Shadin monitoring system. "It says we have about 1200 nautical miles of fuel at cruise." He checked some lists that he brought up on the GPS. "Looks like we can make Malaysia or Singapore – but either is going to be close,"

"How close?" she asked, nervous again.

"Depends on the winds," he said.

"Should we be talking to someone?" she asked.

"Probably, but I don't really want to until we get out of Burma," Andrew said.

Sarah looked below them and saw the lights of Rangoon.

"If I never see another city in Asia it will be too soon," she said.

"Amen," he said.

Chapter 31

"Kristen. I need to explain what happened in Bangkok," Ralph said. The plane had just leveled off and he could finally hear inside the cabin. He knew it wasn't the best timing, but Andrew and Sarah were busy up front, and he didn't know the next time he would get the chance.

"It doesn't matter, Ralph. We've all made some really bad decisions," she said, her right hand on her lap.

"It does to me, Kristen. Just please hear me out." She nodded.

"He had pictures," Ralph said. She looked at him, puzzled.

"Pictures in Quan Lukc… the bedroom," he explained. Her eyes got wide.

"Oh," she said.

"And he said he was going to send them to Melanie."

"Oh."

"I know I need to tell her –"

"Why?" Kristen interrupted him, suddenly concerned.

"Because my family means everything to me. If I don't tell her, I won't be able to ever look her in the face again," he said.

"If you tell her you may never have the opportunity to look her in the face again," Kristen said.

"I know. But I can't handle…."

"The guilt?" Kristen asked. "So, if you were going to tell her anyway what did it matter that she get the pictures?"

"Because I need to be the one to tell her. If she just got the pictures I know it would be over," Ralph said.

"I'm not sure it really matters, Ralph, but whatever. It was still a very costly betrayal… for me," she said. Ralph was mortified and he showed it. The tears welled in his eyes and he tentatively put a hand on her arm, then pulled it away.

"I know you want forgiveness, Ralph, but I don't know what you want me to say. It was your choice to do or not." The edginess in her voice was unmistakable.

"For my family," he said, softly.

"I realize that. Still, your decisions have affected me – and I'm speaking about more than what happened in Bangkok, but also in

Quan Lukc… both with and without Mr. Baldwin's interference," she said.

They sat in silence, Kristen with her eyes closed, leaning her head against the seat while Ralph stared at the floor. He saw her limp hand out of the corner of his eye and felt the hot exhale of his breath upon his own as he tried to think of something that he could say. Finally he gave up.

"So now what?" he asked.

"You mean assuming we actually get back home alive?" Kristen asked. "We go back to our homes and try to figure out what to do with what's left of our lives."

Ralph turned toward her with his hands gripping his legs.

"I don't have a life left," he said.

"Exactly," Kristen replied, as she massaged her unfeeling right hand. It felt like a warm piece of meat.

"Exactly." She turned away and looked out the window at the black night sky. The airplane was level and she could see lights dotting the land. There were people down there in their homes… people sleeping, eating, playing, laughing. She wondered if she would ever again find a place that felt like home. A place without reminders, a place without fear.

"See this here?" Andrew was pointing to a corner of the moving map display "This shows our ETA and speed." He pressed a couple of buttons and put a frequency into the Comm.

"Sarah?" She hadn't replied and he turned toward her. In the darkened cabin he could see that she had turned toward the window and he laid his hand on her shoulder. She didn't respond.

"Sarah? Are you alright?" She lifted her palms up and covered her face. He could feel the tremble run through her body.

"It's OK, Sarah…" he left his hand where it was and felt her take several deep breaths. When she finally turned, she faced forward and not towards him.

"I hate crying. It's a sign of weakness." Her voice pleaded to be contradicted.

"Or a sign that you are human," he said.

He felt her take another breath and, as she exhaled, the mic picked up the noise.

"You know, it is OK to be human. Imperfection and all…" he said.

271

"I…" she stopped.

"What?" he asked.

"Nothing. It doesn't matter," she said, staring at the screen. "What were you pointing to?"

"Sarah. Look at me," he said. He watched as she blinked away the last vestiges of tears and turned to face him. The red lights from the panel cast a pale shadow over her features.

"Why do you do that?" he asked.

"Do what?"

"Divert attention when someone gets to close to you?" he asked.

She was silent for a moment and looked out towards the night.

"I don't know… I suppose I don't want people to learn too much about me."

"Because?" he asked.

"Because I'm afraid they won't…" she stopped herself and pursed her lips.

"Because you're afraid they won't like the real person inside?" he asked.

"Yes."

"So you do all these things. Set goals, meet people's expectations so that they will love you?" he asked.

"I… don't know…"

"Have you every let anyone see *you*?" he asked. She hesitated before replying.

"I… I've tried. My mom… but I don't want to go there. We are all who we decide to be."

Andrew sensed the vulnerability and wasn't sure if it was due to the old bad memories or the recent ones.

"Sarah, do you want to talk about what happened back there?"

"I… it was… bad. Terrible, I don't want to think about it, please…"

"OK. Alright. No one here is going to say anything…" he said.

He removed his hand from her shoulder and started speaking to someone on the frequency.

"Well, he's not a happy camper…" he said, to the voice.

When Sarah felt Andrew's hand withdraw from her shoulder she was startled at the feeling of isolation that the loss of his touch elicited. It was as if she was alone in the tent with the soldier again, watching herself slowly die. With the last vestiges of her strength, she pulled the blackness into a tight ball and held it in her chest. It caused her to start shivering.

"Sarah?" she heard the voice through the mental haze but couldn't respond.

"Sarah?" Andrew put his hand back on her shoulder and she immediately felt the blackness lift. She wanted to ask him not to leave her alone, but her mouth would not form the words. As if he already knew what she needed, he moved his fingers down the length of her arm and grabbed hold of her hand, holding it just firm enough to be reassuring. She felt the nervousness slowly leaving her body and released a silent sigh until she was finally able to relax her hand. Andrew kept his on top of hers as it rested on her leg.

She took a couple of deep breaths before speaking again.

"I'm sorry. It seems that I've been only thinking about myself. And I know that you have had your share of… heartaches." It didn't seem like the appropriate word, but it was the only one that came to mind. "I am very grateful for what you did for me. I'm lousy at showing my appreciation, but I really do appreciate it. God that sounds so… sterile," she said. He laughed.

"It's alright. I know what you mean," he said.

"Do you always allow your… your aid victims so much honor?"

"Is that what you think you are? An aid victim?"

"I guess so… you rescued me. I needed help," she said.

"And you are not used to that feeling?"

"No. I'm not. I find it very disconcerting."

"So is that why you … stopped the soldier from shooting me?"

Sarah bit her bottom lip and thought about the question before answering.

"I think, in part. If I had done nothing, I don't think I could have lived with myself," she said.

"Well, I'm glad you did. I mean, I'm not glad you… you know… but I'm thankful for being alive," he said.

"Sheesh, this feels like a bad TV talk show," he said, and they both laughed.

"What are you going to do when we get back home?" he asked, as he turned a knob and the plane started a slow roll to the right.

"Are we going to make it home?" she asked.

"I certainly didn't come all this way *not* to," he said.

"Well, let's see. I think with all the crimes I've committed I can pretty much rule out law school -"

Andrew interrupted her.

"But no one is going to know… I guess I can't say that for sure…"

"Either way, I know," she said. " So anyway, I think the answer is 'I have absolutely no idea.'"

"And how does that make you feel?"

"Like there must be someone else saying these things. I've always had a plan. Goals. I knew what I wanted to be," she said.

"For you or for someone else?"

"I don't know," she said.

"Might be worth figuring out," Andrew replied.

"I'm starting to think that is probably a good idea – "

Andrew and Sarah were interrupted by what sounded like a ring in the headsets. It took a second before Andrew remembered the Satellite phone. He pressed the 'talk' button.

"Hello?" he answered.

"Keith?" Andrew recognized the voice.

"No. This is Andrew. What do you want, Mr. Baldwin?"

"Uh. Oh. I just assumed… where is my pilot?"

"I'm afraid I don't have good news there. He was shot back in Rangoon. Seems that you are not welcome there anymore," Andrew said.

"I'm sorry to hear that… and yes, I've figured out that my welcome in Burma has run its course. May I ask who is flying the airplane?" It took a second for Andrew to figure out that he was still wearing the bracelet.

"That would be me. What do you want, Mr. Baldwin?" he asked.

"You?! Oh…" Mr. Baldwin seemed to digest the information, then added, "I wanted to know where Keith was taking the plane… so where are you going, Mr. Lee?"

"You know I just don't think I want to answer that question, Mr. Baldwin, I have to go…"

"Wait. Please!"

"Look, Mr. Baldwin, we've had plenty enough of your sick games. I don't see a reason to continue this conversation."

"Mr. Lee, if you will just allow me a moment. You see, your lives, your decisions – they were all guided by fate. This was your destiny."

"That's a bunch of crap, Mr. Baldwin. We make our own destiny. You tried to manipulate our lives and we have no intention on continuing the theatre. Goodbye –"

"Just one more thing, Mr. Lee. It appears that you are heading to Malaysia or Singapore. I would much prefer Malaysia. Besides, you may find it very inhospitable, considering you are in my plane."

"Why?" Andrew asked.

"Let's just say Singapore and I have had some disagreements in the past, and they know that plane," he replied.

"Well, I guess you will find out in a couple of hours. Either way, consider it fate, Mr. Baldwin. It's all fate." Andrew pressed the end button.

"Sorry, Sarah. I forgot what we were talking about?" Sarah turned toward him and smiled.

"I think we should deliver Mr. Baldwin's plane to Singapore," she said, mischievously.

"My thoughts exactly," he said.

"So I wonder who he pissed off," Andrew wondered out loud.

"Has to be the Prime Minister, Mr. Pandit," she said.

"I think so. That means that the Prime Minister and Mr. Baldwin were up to something…" The thought hit him suddenly and he couldn't believe that he had just figured it out. He dug in his pocket, pulled out a rumpled business card, and dialed a number on the telephone. The voice was groggy when it was answered.

"Saw wa–" Andrew cut him off.

"Mr. Suda?"

"Oh, Mr. Lee. Where are you?" Mr. Suda suddenly sounded awake.

"We are headed… out of the country, Mr. Suda." Andrew hated to be vague with him but it definitely seemed prudent.

"I understand. That is good news. Can I help you with something?"

"Actually, I think I may be able to help our… mutual friend."

"I see. And what would you like me to convey… if I can reach him?" he asked.

"Tell him that we believe that Mr. Baldwin, and the man who tried to get us thrown into prison, are behind the... publicity. Do you understand?"

"I think so, Mr. Lee. Do you mean the powerful person who was encouraging your arrest was working with Mr. Baldwin?"

"Yes."

"Are you certain?"

"Yes. I am. There must be a connection between the men and something they mutually wanted although, at this time, they no longer seem to be working together. There is some additional information I need to get to you later. However, please express our thanks to our friend and convey this call." Andrew hung up and closed his eyes. Mr. Pandit must have hired Mr. Baldwin to embarrass the King. It had something to do with the Burmese border, or some related business, but he didn't know what. Whatever the case, he was sure that the King's own Prime Minister was the one trying to shame him.

He put his hand back on top of Sarah's, and she held it lightly. Strange, he thought, a moment of tenderness in a week of terror.

Chapter 32

The King was driven to the house of Mr. Pandit at around 1:00 a.m. The house lights were still on and one of the King's aides knocked on the door. Mr. Pandit personally opened the door dressed in a native robe. Somehow he didn't seem too surprised.

"Your Majesty. It is an... unexpected privilege."

The king entered the premises without asking, and Mr. Pandit bowed his head as he passed. He had just finished eating dinner, and the smell of coconut chicken was still hanging in the air. The King walked into his study and gestured for Mr. Pandit to follow. He then closed the doors for privacy. Mr. Pandit walked around the desk and sat down, but the King remained standing and the Prime Minister quickly got back up to his feet.

"What can I do for you, your majesty? It must be of some importance for you to come here at this hour."

"Mr. Prime Minister, what do you know about a man named Mr. Baldwin, an American?" the King asked, throwing a phone log book on the desk.

"Nothing. Should I?" the Prime Minister said without hesitating, but his body temperature increased several degrees and he loosened his robe without thinking.

"Then how do you explain these telephone calls between your office and a telephone owned by Baldwin enterprises?" the King asked.

"I do not know the answer to that, your majesty, but I will find out in the morning. May I ask what this is in regards to? My office communicates with America, as well as many other countries, on a regular basis, and it would be helpful to know the context..." Mr. Pandit said.

"So, your criticism of my efforts to gain American aid in order to fight the illegal trade coming across our borders would have nothing to do with Baldwin Enterprises?"

"As I said, your majesty, I will look into this matter first thing in the morning. My stand on accepting foreign handouts is clearly noted in my political record, and I do not see the connection that you are..." Mr. Pandit carefully picked out the next word, "*implying* here."

"Mr. Prime Minister, there is no need for these games. I know you oppose the acceptance of foreign aid. And you know that I have actively solicited it in order to stop the traffic of women and drugs across our borders. The question is why do you so vocally oppose my efforts? I do not think it is a coincidence that, in the last three days, I have been personally embarrassed by innuendo and speculation from many seemingly disparate events."

"I am aware of your present difficulties, your majesty, but you know as well as I they are only temporary as these things go. I'm sure, in time, this will pass," Mr. Pandit said, smoothly.

"As I am as well, Mr. Prime Minister, however, as you undoubtedly heard today, I have had to decline the American President's offer for the sake of political considerations. I am sure that you are fully aware of this."

"Yes. Those events are quite unfortunate. But again, I am not sure what you are asking of me, your majesty? Would you like me to see if I can perhaps help with the media? I'm sure I could do something, if you so asked," Mr. Pandit was obviously feeling in control of the matter.

"No, Mr. Prime Minister, you have done quite enough," the King said, as he turned around and went to open the study door.

"Tell me, Mr. Pandit, you wouldn't know anything about BMSAT preparing to go public, would you? Because I'm sure you are very clear that the now held up bill that was in front of Parliament would have made that unlawful - investing in Burmese State Owned companies. After all, you have been so vocal about opposing that reform legislation as it has passed through the hearings." The King paused and looked back at Mr. Pandit, who said nothing.

"No. I'm sure you don't know anything about that," the King said, as he opened the door and walked out.

:

"Singapore Approach, this is King Air N5555, twenty miles to your north, inbound with Lima," Andrew said.

"*N5555, Singapore Approach, we have been advised that the aircraft you are flying was taken from Burma without permission. Advise your attentions,*" the controller said.

Andrew was not surprised at the request given the flack he had been getting by the Center controllers, but he was determined to land.

"Singapore Approach, N5555. I understand, however we are declaring a fuel emergency and must land immediately."

"*N5555, stand by,*" approach said. Andrew waited for nearly a minute while the controller handled other aircraft.

"*N5555. Advise the number and nationality of your passengers.*"

"Four. All United States citizens," Andrew said.

"*N5555, and I don't suppose you have a customs appointment?*"

"No sir. We do not have one," Andrew said, intentionally leaving out the other part that he just remembered – they also had no passports. Those were back in Rangoon in the dead soldier's pocket.

"*N5555, and can I presume you are either Mr. Lee or Mr. Gabriel?*" the controller asked.

"Well I guess they found the passports," Andrew said, under his breath.

"N5555, I would be Mr. Lee," he said.

"*N5555, Contact tower 128.875, information Mike is current,*"

"Switching to tower N5555," Andrew paused a moment to listen to the weather information on Comm number two.

"Singapore tower this is N5555, minimum fuel, request immediate landing," Andrew said. He held his breath waiting for the response.

"*N5555, Singapore tower, you are cleared to land 05L, wind is 040 at 21 knots.*"

With the airport coming up fast, Andrew pulled back the throttle to five hundred pounds of torque, lowered the landing gear, and put in ten degrees of flaps. The landing gear horn sounded loudly, and Sarah jumped in her seat. He took a moment to reach over and squeeze her hand, then stabilized the approach.

The King Air caught the ground effect and floated a little down the runway before Andrew forced her to the ground with a hard thud. He didn't know if Sarah was more relieved to be on the ground or he was.

"*N5555, turn left taxiway Delta, contact ground 127.4 off the runway. Hold short for further instructions.*" Andrew repeated the command and used the brakes to stop the plane off of the runway.

"Ground, this is N5555, I assume we need to go to customs," Andrew said.

"Actually N5555. Hold short right there. They are going to come to you." Andrew and Sarah looked up and saw numerous flashing lights as several vehicles barreled toward them. They both prayed that this would go better than the last stop.

Andrew turned to Ralph and Kristen, who were anxiously awaiting information.

"They're sending Customs to meet us. I don't suppose anyone has their passport still?" Andrew asked.

Kristen and Ralph shook their heads with their eyes wide open.

"Hey, listen, don't worry. This is a big airport with friendly ties to the US," Andrew hoped the statement was accurate. "I'm sure we will be fine." As he finished the sentence he looked out the window at the men pouring out of the military van. At least three of them stood in front of the air step door with semi-automatic rifles drawn and pointed at the plane.

"Oh. Crap," Andrew said.

:

"Henry?"

"Yes. Mr. Baldwin," Henry had been seated in the rear of the Marquis jet, reading a local newspaper. He had no idea when they would be returning to Thailand, and he was feeling homesick already.

"Can you please ask the pilot if he can find about anything about my King Air, N5555."

"Yes. Mr. Baldwin," Henry disappeared through the pilot door and was gone for five minutes or so.

"I'm afraid it is not good news, sir. It seems Mr. Lee arrived in Singapore about an hour ago, and the government has impounded your Aircraft on an outstanding warrant. I'm very sorry, sir," Henry said.

Mr. Baldwin leaned back in his leather seat and took a drink from the square bottle of Fuji water.

"Touche,' Mr. Lee, Touche'," he said, as he looked out the window to the vanishing lights of Southeast Asia.

"Goodbye, mistress. Until our paths cross again." Mr. Baldwin touched his lips to his palm and blew a kiss out the window, then laid back and closed his eyes. It would be a long flight home.

:

Andrew came off the plane first with his hands extended in the air. A man in a blue uniform came up to greet him.

"Mr. Lee?"

"Yes," Andrew replied, relieved to not be thrown to the ground and handcuffed, though the guns were still pointed at him. But that had happened so many times lately it seemed almost routine.

"May I ask the purpose of your visit to Singapore?" the man politely asked.

"Trying to get out of Burma. Really, that's it," Andrew said. The man almost broke a smile but then quickly straightened up his face.

"Ah. We often get that response here," the man deadpanned.

"And you do not have your passports?" Andrew shook his head.

"Any identification whatsoever?" the man asked.

"No. I'm sorry, the soldiers took our passports in Rangoon. We barely escaped with our lives," Andrew said.

"And whose airplane is this?"

"I'm not sure. I think an American's named Mr. Baldwin," Andrew said.

"Hmmm, our records seem to indicate that as well. In fact, the plane is on our watch list," the man said. Andrew shrugged his shoulders.

The man signaled for the other three to get out of the plane and they obeyed him, reluctantly. It was cool out and the air was stimulating, but they moved slowly. He saw the hesitation and spoke to all of them.

"You will all be treated well here, however, there is some paperwork that will need to be filled out. I don't suppose you have any money for tickets back to the US?"

"No…" Andrew said,

"Uh. Actually yes," Ralph said, as he headed back into the plane and then looked back at the official for permission.

"Go," the man said. Ralph disappeared for a moment and pulled out a wad of bills.

"Yes. We can purchase our tickets," he said, excitedly.

"Good. That should expedite matters. There is a Singapore Airlines flight leaving this morning to Vancouver. We would very much like you to be on that flight," the man said.

"So would we," Sarah said.

"Please get into the… would you prefer the jeep or the van?" the man asked.

Andrew looked at the group and knew that they would prefer to not feel trapped.

"The jeep," he said.

As the driver drove them to the terminal, Andrew whispered to Ralph.

"Where in hell did you get that from?"

"Kristen found it. She was bored and started pulling at panels in the back of the aircraft and found a stash of money. I like the idea of using Mr. Baldwin's money," Ralph said.

"Yeah. So do I."

When they reached the immigration office the man, who had been following in another vehicle, approached Andrew.

"Mr. Lee, may I presume you have no objection to us seizing the airplane? Seems it has an outstanding warrant on it," the officer said.

"None at all. Knock yourselves out," Andrew said.

"I thought you would say that," the man said, as he barked orders to the guards who took off toward the plane. Andrew looked at him as he walked off and wondered why he was being so overtly helpful and polite. Perhaps the King? He didn't know.

The paperwork was nothing more than each of them filling out a form, then they were escorted to the Singapore Airlines booth where they purchased tickets to Vancouver. The guards stayed with them until the flight took off six hours later. They boarded the airplane and took their seats, dirty, exhausted and, for the first time in ten days – happy.

There were lots of empty seats so they all spread out. As the in-flight meal of steak, carrots and potatoes was served, they were laughing and joking. Ralph thought he was in heaven. That was at least until the turbulence started, then he thought he might still be in hell.

It was an awful flight.

Twenty long hours later they arrived in Vancouver, British Columbia. It was still the same day but a different world, and they were cold, watching the pouring rain from the waiting area. Once again they were delayed in immigration but, through some miracle, they were assigned another officer who helped them fill out the proper forms before they were escorted by private car to the American side of the Peace Arch crossing. As they arrived at the border the sun broke out and the movement of the cars stalled. After listening to some of their story the driver kindly let them get out and stretch their legs.

They sat on a bench facing a vast stretch of green grass.

"Look over there," Sarah said.

"What?" Andrew asked.

"There. Do you see them?" she asked.

"Yes."

"Ralph, Kristen – that remind you of anything?" Sarah asked.

"Creepy. Baldwin. His emblem of the four crows," Ralph said.

They all sat in silence as the four crows moved deliberately towards them. When they were about fifteen feet off, the driver honked his horn.

"We've got to go! The line is moving!" he yelled. The four got up from their seats and glanced at the car.

Andrew and Sarah looked one last time at the four ebony colored birds with their inquisitive faces. It almost appeared that the crows were somehow disappointed at their departure and Sarah stopped and said something under her breath to the one with the polished beak, then she turned toward Andrew and grabbed his hand.

"There's no such thing as fate," Andrew mumbled under his breath as he glanced one final time at the birds.

"Just go home," he said. Sarah looked at him, puzzled for a moment, unsure if he was talking to the four crows or her.

On the way back to the car, Sarah watched the moist blades of grass bend under her sandals, sprinkling her feet with dew as she lost herself in thought.

Home. It was the last place she wanted to go.

Chapter 33

Three months later.

Sarah saw him first, walking towards her from across the park. He was wearing silver rimmed glasses and dressed in a black leather coat with a cream white shirt with jeans. The sun was behind him and it reminded her of a scene from Bad Boys. She smiled as he got close enough to make eye contact.

"Hi," she said.

"Hi Sarah. It's great to see you. I'm glad you came." Andrew stopped a few feet away and they stood awkwardly for a moment before he grabbed her in a hug. She closed her eyes and unconsciously let out a breath. In the cool air she could feel his warmth and could have stayed there longer if he had held on.

"Hi, Andrew," she looked up at him, gazing into his eyes, "I'm sorry it took so long."

"It's OK. We all had a lot of junk to work through." He looped his arm in hers and started walking over to the base of the tower.

"So how is Kristen?" Sarah asked.

"Struggling."

"How is her hand?"

"Doctors said that they injected her with some Neurotoxin from a frog. The nerves are in paralysis. I guess there is a chance for recovery, with therapy, but no change as of yet," Andrew said. They stopped at a park bench and sat down facing the lawns.

"What is she doing?"

"I think still painting, still angry. She has kind of tried to just forget about the whole thing – like it never happened. Anytime I bring up something even minutely related she changes the subject. Last week I was trying to tell her about the Prime Minister but she acted like she didn't know what I was talking about. It's been a little strained between us... I mean our friendship."

"I'm sorry. I wish I could forget too but that just isn't realistic." Sarah threw a peanut from her pocket to a pigeon that was cooing in front of them.

"So, what did happen to the dear old Prime Minister?"

"Oh? I assumed you would have heard. He was impeached or whatever it is called. Seems the King found out that he was secretly invested in a satellite company based in Burma, which is against Thai law. I guess Mr. Pandit was planning on making a killing when the company went public."

"So that was what it was all about?" Sarah asked, "Money?"

"Yup. Think so. You see, the King was going to accept some foreign aid from the United States in order to shut down the Burmese-Thai border. There was a bill that the King was promoting to officially make it illegal to do business in Burma and that would also have accepted the US foreign aid to help in stopping the underground activity from Burma. The Prime Minister didn't want that to happen as he was, or had, invested over a hundred million dollars in the company. Anyway, and I'm only guessing at this part, he embarrassed the King, using us, through Mr. Baldwin in order to try and get him to back off of the bill by straining the relationship between Thailand and the US. The king didn't want to look like a pawn of the US government and, by having Americans involved in a series of humiliating incidents, it made it politically unwise for him to push the issue at the time. It did work, for a while, but some pictures of Mr. Pandit surfaced. Seems Ralph was right, he liked young girls. *Very* young girls. Anyway, they impeached him. Parliament has now passed the bill and the government seized his stake in BMSAT."

"Well I guess that makes me feel a little better. Nothing about Mr. Baldwin huh?" she asked.

"Not a thing. Can't even locate him. I've tried, though I have no idea what I would do if I found him. It's all in the past now... probably better to leave it there."

"So what do you think he got from the deal?" she asked.

"Money, but I also think he was just some manipulative, wealthy bastard who enjoyed seeing if he could play with peoples' lives. Remember, he loved the whole idea that he was a master over Fate, the four crows and all."

"So how have you been? Are you still doing your food business?"

"Uh. No. Not exactly. I ran into some snags when I returned home. Pretty much lost everything," Andrew said.

"Oh. I'm sorry. I..." she looked at him with a solemn face, "was that due to what you did for me?" she asked. Andrew thought about the question for a moment.

"No. It was just something that happened. No big deal. I'll survive, just do something else," he said.

"Like?"

"Well for one, I'm doing a lot of flying for Angel Flight, you know, the charity that helps out people in need, a lot of children with serious illnesses. I think we had a discussion about doing something more than making money," he smiled at her.

"Hmmm. I believe we did. I was wrong about some of my assumptions about you, and I admit that," she said, "in the end, no one has ever come through for me like you did." Sarah's voice was very soft and he felt impelled to rest his hand on her arm.

"And you for me," he said, "it went both ways."

Sarah looked up at him, her eyes just slightly moist.

"Why?" she asked.

"Why what?"

"Why... did you save me?"

Andrew looked at her, puzzled.

"Because you were worth it. And I don't mean you were worth the money. I mean that you were worth saving because you have so much to offer; so many great qualities," he said

Sarah tried to laugh, but it came out very self-conscious.

"Like what? I certainly have not contributed anything to anyone lately," she said.

Andrew looked at her and saw the pain hiding beneath the surface.

"Perhaps. But you can and you will. I believe in you," he said.

Sarah felt awkward and said the first thing she could think of.

"So what ever happened to Ralph?" she asked.

"Actually, I haven't spoken to him in about a month. He was separated from his wife, I think her name was... Melanie. He sounded pretty devastated."

"Why? What happened?" Sarah asked.

"I really don't know. I'm just guessing, but I think something transpired between him and Kristen in Thailand..."

"Wow. I had no idea. Probably because I was so consumed... with everything going on," she said.

"So is he going to be OK?"

"I hope so. He sounded determined to be back with his family. That was… is, his life," he said.

"There could be worse things to have in your life," Sarah said.

"Agreed."

A couple walked by arm in arm and they watched until they had passed.

"So what about you?" Andrew asked.

"Oh. I'm OK. Just been wandering a little. No big deal," she said.

"That's not what I meant. How are you doing here?" Andrew pointed at his own heart.

"Oh… I'm fine, really. I can handle it."

"And you have tried to do that without getting help?" he asked.

"What… like a shrink or something? No. I couldn't do that, aren't they all quacks anyway?" she asked, tentatively.

"No. I've been seeing one," he said.

"Oh… I'm sorry, I didn't mean… perhaps I…"

"It's OK ,Sarah. She's been helping me deal with everything."

"Like what? I mean, if you don't mind telling me?"

"Like the loss of my business, what I always thought was important to me – accomplishments. I still haven't figured everything out, but I'm a work in progress!" Andrew laughed, then quickly became more solemn as he felt her continued unease.

"Is there anything I can do… " he said, as he looked into her blue eyes and lost himself for a moment, "anything?"

:

Sarah thought about everything that had happened in her life over the past three months. Her goals, that had once filled her with purpose, now held no significance. She struggled making even the most mundane decisions. It was all very unfamiliar ground to her as she had never been one accustomed to drifting without direction. She had removed her family and friends from her life. In looking back, she realized the reason that she had done so was that she didn't feel safe around them, or anyone, for that matter. It wasn't a new feeling but it was much stronger after what had befallen her in Thailand. Sarah looked at Andrew.

"I…" she couldn't get herself to finish what she wanted so badly to say.

Andrew leaned back in the chair and gazed out over the park, the sun's rays dancing through the barren branches of the tree that attempted to shelter them. He took off his scarf and wrapped it around her neck, then, without looking down, laid his hand on top of hers and enveloped it. Sarah waited as she tried to fight back an overwhelming need for affection but, with a final breath, she ignored the inner voice, which screamed at her to protect herself.

She had never felt as naked and exposed as when the words fell gently from her lips.

"Love me," she said.

Andrew heard the words and grasped her hand tighter. He didn't feel the need to respond, but instead looked at the city that surrounded them.

Paris.

It was a good place for a new start.

And there were no crows.

The End

Epilogue

Mr. Baldwin sat on his veranda watching the blue waves lap at the white beach. It was summer in Grand Cayman and he enjoyed watching the tourists with their happy smiles and oblivious bliss walk by his home on the north end of Seven Mile Beach. It was an elegant but much smaller home than the one he had rented out for Mr. Lee and that group of adventurers. The heavy aroma of Jamaican Rum wafted up to his face from the glass that he held in his hand, while the smell of Jerk Chicken drifted out of the kitchen door to where he was sitting. It was almost lunchtime.

"Mr. Baldwin?" Henry appeared dressed in a stark white cotton shirt and shorts.

"Yes Henry? It is a glorious day," Mr. Baldwin said.

"Would you enjoy to partake outside or inside today?"

"Hmmm. I think inside, in the dining room, so I can watch the beach," Mr. Baldwin said, as he got up from his chair, drink in hand, and followed Henry into the adjoining dining room. He sat down at the end of the table and waited for a few moments for Henry to return. There were a lot of sounds coming through the covers of the very large cage which acted as a room divider between the dining and living room.

Henry appeared a few moments later with a platter of food and set it down on the table in front of Mr. Baldwin, who reveled in the smell.

"Henry, could you please pull the curtain on the aviary? I think I would like their company for lunch."

"Certainly, sir." Henry walked over to the enclosure and pressed a small silver button until the curtain was fully retracted into the ceiling. The aviary covered the entire length of the wall, over fifteen feet long. It was nearly as wide and rose the full height of the two-story home.

On seeing Mr. Baldwin, the squawking increased until he finally threw over some scraps from his plate and the sounds immediately quieted down. As usual, the leader, whom he had named Andrew many years ago, was bold enough to stand at the very edge of the cage staring at him with his intense ebony eyes. Kristen, one of the females, ate the scraps, then went back to collecting dead leaves, rocks and a bracelet some unfortunate guest had lost when she had attempted to reach inside the cage. She was making a collage, of sorts, to adorn the branch, which she roosted on in the evenings. Sarah, the other female was diligently working on the lock to the cage door that Henry had already changed three times in the last week as she kept figuring them out. Mr. Baldwin was very impressed with her. The final crow was 'Ralph' and he was acting depressed, his head down skulking in a corner, away from the others.

Henry disturbed his thoughts.

"Mr. Baldwin? There is a gentleman at the door that requires a signature," Henry said.

"Oh? I'll be right there." Mr. Baldwin got up from his seat with a napkin full of scraps and put it on the floor outside of the cage, then headed towards the front door.

Ralph saw the scraps and hopped over to them, extending his neck through the wire mesh, but it was just out of reach. Kirsten quickly joined him, but with the same results.

"It's a game, Ralph, Kristen. He's just messing with you. Don't do it. Once he finds your weaknesses he'll make you pay. Mark my words. He'll make you pay," Andrew said.

Caveat

Although this story is based on certain current and historical figures and facts, it is fiction. Any resemblance to any actual person or event probably took place only in the mind of the author.